Impossibly
TONGUE-TIED

By Josie Brown

Impossibly Tongue-Tied
True Hollywood Lies

Don't miss the next book by your favorite author.
Sign up now for AuthorTracker by visiting
www.AuthorTracker.com.

Impossibly
TONGUE-TIED

Josie Brown

AVON
TRADE

An Imprint of HarperCollinsPublishers

This novel is a work of fiction. Any references to real people, events, establishments, organizations, or locales are intended only to give the fiction a sense of reality and authenticity, and are used fictitiously. All other names, characters and places, and all dialogue and incidents portrayed in this book are the product of the author's imagination.

IMPOSSIBLY TONGUE-TIED. Copyright © 2006 by Josie Brown. All rights reserved. Printed in the United States of America. No part of this book may be used or reproduced in any manner whatsoever without written permission except in the case of brief quotations embodied in critical articles and reviews. For information address HarperCollins Publishers Inc., 10 East 53rd Street, New York, NY 10022.

HarperCollins books may be purchased for educational, business, or sales promotional use. For information please write: Special Markets Department, HarperCollins Publishers Inc., 10 East 53rd Street, New York, NY 10022.

FIRST EDITION

Interior text designed by Elizabeth M. Glover, based on design by Diahann Sturge

Library of Congress Cataloging-in-Publication Data

Brown, Josie.
   Impossibly tongue-tied / by Josie Brown. — 1st ed.
      p. cm.
   ISBN-13: 978-0-06-081588-2
   ISBN-10: 0-06-081588-4
   1. Hollywood (Los Angeles, Calif.) — Fiction.   2. Cashiers — Fiction.
   3. Telephone sex — Fiction.   4. Actors — Fiction.   5. Married people — Fiction.
   6. Divorce — Fiction.   I. Title.

PS3602.R715I47 2006
813'.6 — dc22   2006010809

06 07 08 09 10   JTC/RRD   10 9 8 7 6 5 4 3 2 1

For Mario and Patricia,
with love and appreciation.

Los Angeles Superior Court

PETITION FOR DISSOLUTION OF MARRIAGE

PETITIONER: Nathan Harris Harte   March 10, 2---

RESPONDENT: Nina Sue Wilder Harte   **CASE #:** BD3730444

Dissolution of marriage is based on irreconcilable differences

PERIOD BETWEEN MARRIAGE AND SEPARATION: 6 years, 2 months

DECLARATION FOR MINOR CHILDREN:

CHILD'S NAME: Jake Harris Harte   **SEX:** Male   **AGE:** 4 Years, 3 mos.

Legal Custody of children to __TBD by courts__
Physical Custody of Children to __TBD by courts__
Spousal Support payable to __TBD by courts__

Petitioner confirmation as separate property assets and debts, the items listed below:
- '61 Corvette roadster
- Elvis Record Collection: *All Shook Up, Ultimate Gospel, GI Blues, Blue Hawaii, Elvis' Christmas Album, etc.*

I have read the restraining orders on the back of the summons, and I understand they apply to me when this petition is filed.

I understand under penalty of perjury that under the laws of the state of California that the foregoing is true and correct.

__NATHAN HARRIS HARTE__   *Nathan Harris Harte*
    Type or Print Name   **Signature of Petitioner**

HOWARD CROSS of Cross & Levinski   *Howard Cross*

Sadly, Another Hollywood Fairy Tale Ends...

Just when you were ready to believe that the Hollywood rags-to-riches storybook ending can in fact come true, another showbiz couple unties the knot.

Actor Nathan Harte, Hollywood's newest heartthrob, who is set to star in his very first feature film—Hugo Schmitt's upcoming release, *Forever and Again*—filed for divorce yesterday in Los Angeles Superior Court.

Harte, 24, and his wife, Nina Sue Wilder Harte, also 24, were high school sweethearts from the small town of Joyous, Missouri. They have one child, a four-year-old son, Jake.

The announcement has been issued through the actor's publicist, Fiona Truman. "The decision is mutual and amicable. The couple is recently separated. They hope that the press will respect their privacy during this difficult time."

Truman denied the rumors that the marital rift was caused by Harte's "very close and deepening friendship" with his *Forever and Again* costar, the Academy Award–nominated actress Katerina McPherson, whom Harte is now "rooming with until the trauma from his divorce is mitigated somewhat. You know, the institution of marriage is sacred to Mr. Harte, which is why he feels lucky to have found an understanding friend with whom he can share his pain."

Serenity's Scandal Sheet, 3/10

Two months earlier . . .

1

The Backstory

As in high school, in Hollywood's film industry there is a pecking order. It goes something like this:

A-list star.
Studio mogul.
Film producer with ready cash and a strong track record for
    winners.
A-list director.
Agent with an A-list roster.
Other agents.
Other (struggling) actors.
Other (anxious) studio suits.
Screenwriters (A-list, struggling, anxious, and otherwise).
Those who serve all of the above.
Those who dream of being any of the above.
And, finally, those who are spouses of any of the above.

It wasn't hard to guess where Nina Harte—cashier-slash-head concierge at Beverly Hills' favorite "epicurean emporium," the Tommaso's on Doheny—and her husband, Nathan—a.k.a. the Disneyland Main Street Parade's Donald Duck (during the second shift on Tuesdays, Thursdays, Saturdays, and alternating Sundays)—stood in that pecking order.

Unfortunately, this very same hierarchy existed in the carpool lane at Sage Oak Academy, where Jake, Nina and Nathan's precocious four-year-old, went to school with the coddled offspring of those on Hollywood's upper rungs.

In fact, those doting SOA parents (at least, those parents who actually showed up periodically to drop off their children, as opposed to having their nannies do it) never waited in the carpool line at all. Instead they were discreetly invited to pull into the "headmaster's parking lot" to join the man himself, Bradley K. Pickering, in his private library for a nice hot cup of oolong tea and a slice of organic fruit torte or chocolate raspberry cake from Topozio's while waiting for their precious progeny to be ushered forth.

It was the school's version of a VIP lounge.

Needless to say, au pairs—and for that matter, parents who were Disney parade characters, and their spouses—were not on that VIP list.

So Nina took her turn in the carpool lane with the au pairs. She could live with that . . .

For now.

Because both she and Nathan knew that his true destiny lay far beyond the cobblestoned Main Street of Disney's Magic Kingdom. The fact that he was only one voucher away from securing his SAG card was certainly proof of that. They hoped it was also evident in his acting reel, which was made up of several tasty snippets from his starring roles in the six USC and eight UCLA student films he'd done, along with a few choice scenes from those three low-budget indie films he'd been featured in (none of which, sadly, had ever received a distribution deal).

The truth of the matter was that Nathan stood, both figuratively and literally, head and shoulders above any of the other extras in the numerous feature movie crowd shots in which he'd appeared. But until others realized this too, Disney's Main Street and Tommaso's concierge desk would have to do for the Hartes—and immediately, for Nina was already late for her shift.

Unfortunately, while attempting to disentangle Jake, his carpool partner Plum Silver, and their respective backpacks from her very cluttered eleven-year-old Honda Civic, Nina was waylaid by Brad Pickering who, upon seeing her car pull up to the curb, excused himself from a Pilates-toned mommy who was upset with his decision to suspend her five-year-old daughter over a belly button piercing. (This concern was expressed via Pilates mom's agitated body language, since her decade-long regimen of Botox injections had obliterated any ability she might have once had to actually frown in discontent.)

Whenever possible, Nina dodged Mr. Pickering because it was so obvious that he resented that the Hartes were at Sage Oak in the first place. This was something Nina had instinctively understood since the first time she'd stepped into his office to inquire whether the school had scholarships for students living below Los Angeles County's qualification for low income, which was set at approximately $25,575 per year.

He had warily conceded that, yes, the school did have one such scholarship, and that had recently come available.

Whereas the Hartes' taxable earnings the year before certainly qualified them as "low income," it was Nina's proud proclamation that Nathan was an actor that raised Mr. Pickering's consternation. Not that entertainers weren't welcomed at Sage Oak per se—at least, not since the 1980s, when SOA's board of trustees had finally done away with its unspoken policy of banning the children of actors, producers, musicians, directors, and their ilk. To the surprise of Pickering and his board, that decision had paid off even more handsomely with renewed interest in the school from L.A.'s old moneyed families as well. For every Ireland, Ella Corrine, Coco, Lily-Rose, Fifi-Trixiebelle, Jake Paris, or Homer James Jigme who roamed SOA's stately hallowed halls, the institution picked up another Getty, Kennedy (or Shriver, Lawton, Smith, Schwarzenegger, or whatever), Morgan, Rockefeller, Davidson, Ahmanson, or Taper.

Like Nathan, several of the other thespian parents had also worked with the Disney organization at one time or another. However, none had donned a costume while doing so. In that way, Nathan was unique.

And somewhat less than desirable.

What had tipped things in the Hartes' favor was the letter of recommendation Nina had brought with her, from Herbert Fitzroy Cahill, the patriarch of the oldest and most revered alumni family within the school.

Cahill money was old money. *Truly* ancient.

Which was why Brad Pickering was stumped as to how, when, and why Herbert Cahill gave a damn about a cashier from Tommaso's.

And so every time he saw Nina, he sucked up—*big* time—and dropped a casual query about Mr. Cahill in the hopes that she'd let loose with those obsessively desired facts, because Pickering just *loved* having the goods on all SOA's board members. For that matter, he valued highly whatever he could find out about every SOA parent. It was his contention that you never knew when such tidbits might come in handy . . . especially when it came time to fill the coffers for the Headmaster's Annual Fund Drive.

"Ah, Mrs. Harte, how are we this morning?" Because that comely little backside of hers was toward him as she unbuckled her Jake and little Plum from their car seats, Pickering missed the involuntary grimace she gave at the sound of his voice.

But the ever-watchful Plum saw her wince. And between that and the endearment Pickering had proffered Jake's very pretty very sweet mummy, Plum was moved to sing the one love song she knew by heart, albeit with some appropriate improvisation: "Nina and Mr. Prick Ring, sitting in a tree, K-I-S-S-I-N-G—"

"Now, now Plum—" Pickering, flustered at the child's ditty (not to mention her innocent albeit embarrassing pronunciation of his surname) turned as red as a Rahart's Jumbo Red heirloom tomato in season. "I was just inquiring after Mrs. Harte's demeanor—"

"My mommy *ain't* meaner than the other mommies!" Jake cried out belligerently, a clear indication that the caste system practiced by SOA's chief administrator was less than subtle.

"Of *course* she isn't!" Pickering panicked. He was making a muddle of his reconnaissance mission. "No one thinks that at all, Jake. Least of all *me*. Why, I was saying to Mr. Herbert Cahill just the other day that your mother was—was one of the—*nicest* mothers of all the mothers in the school." He nodded knowingly.

Nina turned to face him. "So you talked to Mr. Cahill—about *me?*" Her smile was serene, but her eyes flashed dangerously.

Rarely are grown men as perceptive as little children, and Pickering was no exception to that rule. Plum leaned over to Jake and whispered in a voice loud enough for even the adults to hear: "Is your mommy going to spank Mr. Prick Ring?"

The way the headmaster's coloring went from bright red to deep violet reminded Nina of Tommaso's heirloom Cherokee Purples when they were a little too far gone.

"No, no, sweetheart, of course not!" Nina's laugh might have been all sunshine and sweetness, but her words pricked like tiny daggers. *"He'd probably like it too much."*

As Pickering blanched and the children ran inside, Nina strapped herself back into the front seat and waved good-bye. "I'll be sure to give your regards to Mr. Cahill when I speak to him next."

With that, she squealed away from the curb in a very un-SOA manner.

How *dare* she!

In the subtlest of ways, this—this *mere cashier* had taken the mighty headmaster down a notch!

Thank God any parent who counted was already inside the confines of Pickering's private library having tea, and not out there on the curb. And thank God Cahill hadn't been there to see any of it, either. Still, Cahill would hear about it. *Through*

Nina. And perhaps call the headmaster in front of the school's board—which the old man ruled with an iron fist—to ask *what in tarnation* was Pickering doing butting into his personal business!

With cheeks still flaming, he stared out after Nina Harte's ancient Civic as it headed toward West Sunset Boulevard, and, thankfully, out of his life . . . for now.

Some way, although he didn't know how yet, he'd put that impudent girl in her place.

Besides, he wondered, *how did she guess I'm a bottom?*

That snot-nosed Brad Pickering was an ass.

Nina knew it. And of course Herbert Cahill knew it, too, because phrases like "suck-up turd" and "sniveling coward" had cropped up periodically whenever Pickering was mentioned (as he invariably was) in their conversations.

Not that Herbert—or Herbie, as he liked Nina to call him—was the chatty type to begin with. Like most of her clients, he preferred that *she* do most of the talking.

About erections, nipples, orgasms—that is, anything and everything even *remotely* sexual in nature.

Of course, none of these conversations happened inside Tommaso's, although Herbie *did* come into the store every now and then. She knew this because he had a file in the store's VIP database. Once she had asked her shift manager, Tony—oops, make that *Tori,* now that the sex change operation was considered a success—to point Herbie out to her, discreetly of course, because it was always so *cool* when she was able to put the name with a face, and then put that face with the voice—

—*a true rarity indeed, if you were a phone sex operator.*

As, in this case, Nina was.

In that regard, Nina considered herself lucky in that her day job at the oh-so-tony Tommaso's and her nighttime gig as the sultry, seductive "O" actually had some client crossover now and then.

It was true that many of her male customers at Tommaso's greatly appreciated her opinion as to which root vegetables were healthier (not sunchokes, but Asian turnips), which wine had a more subtle flavor (not the French Pouilly-Fuisse, but the German Gewerztraminer) and which cheeses were the firmest (Double Glouster as opposed to Buttercase). Many of these same fine gentlemen also unknowingly spoke to her as O; they hung on her every word as to what turned her on the most about him (the gargantuan size of his member, or the staying power she insisted he had?), what she'd like him to do to her first on these little fantasy dates (that depended on whether he was a breast man or an admirer of well-toned backsides), and which vibrator she found the most pleasurable (the Hitachi Magic Wand; then again the Fukuoko 9000 had its charms . . .)

In Herbie's case, as a Los Angeles blue blood who had spent a lifetime doling out cold-blooded directives to minions who jumped and scurried at his beck and call, he needed O for ab-solution. To that end, they always started with a little role playing (invariably O was asked to take on the role of Herb's former German nanny, Fraulein Von Berens), followed by some truly wicked verbal humiliation. ("Shame on you! You are a *very, very* naughty boy! Perhaps it's time that you *lecken meine strumpfbänder, ja?*")

Then afterward, because he was such a gentleman, Herbie

would wrap up the call with a little polite chitchat: about current events, or baseball (he was a devoted Dodgers fan, so she was sure to be up on the latest scores and plays prior to his thrice-weekly calls—Mondays, Wednesdays, and Friday evenings at one-thirty promptly, thank you very much). The old sweetie always asked after Jake, too. Nina couldn't tell him enough how much she appreciated him putting in a good word for them, but he'd hear nothing of it. Pshaw, he'd say in that old-fashioned way of his, he'd been happy to help them get accepted into SOA, since, as he explained with a chuckle, "I look upon you as the naughty second cousin twice removed from the wrong side of the tracks who I was never allowed to have . . .").

And finally they'd gossip about people they knew in common . . . like that jellyfish Pickering . . .

Well, the next time she talked to Herbie, Nina would take the opportunity to let him know that Brad Pickering had *the gall* to ask her about their relationship! Of course, Herbie would then ruminate out loud on the many ways he could make Pickering's life miserable. Or he'd venture: "What would *you* suggest I say to that buffoon?"

That would allow Nina to point out that Pickering had *never once* invited her to join his private parent tea parties.

And in no time at all, the Hartes' place in the Sage Oak Academy's pecking order would be vastly improved.

To Nina, phone sex wasn't lurid—or, for that matter, erotic.
It was just a job.

Or at least that was the way she had put it to Nathan almost five years ago, when she first suggested that she try the business—even if it meant she'd have to quit their acting class for a while and put on hold her dream of making it in "the town" (which, for the record, meant anything and everything that is Hollywood).

At the time she was six months pregnant with Jake, and the cashiering gig at Tommaso's meant enduring excruciatingly painful leg spasms and swollen ankles from standing on her feet all day. She was already concerned about how long she could last at the store, which, being a non-unionized grocery, paid just above minimum wage, although the medical insurance that came with her job meant that she wouldn't have to deliver her baby in a ditch somewhere off Hollywood Way.

Besides, Nina was fed up with their roach-infested Koreatown studio, where the landlord thought nothing of raising the rent every year by at least fifty bucks. At that point she'd have given anything to move to a rent-controlled apartment, preferably on the west side of L.A., that had room for them and the baby, too.

They had come to L.A. from Joyous, Missouri, population 4,397 and shrinking. Both of them had starred in their high school production of *The Music Man*. As a three-varsity-letter jock who easily had the pick of the high school's luscious litter of budding teen drama queens, the charismatic Nathan was a shoo-in for Professor Harold Hill. Nina Sue Wilder—the smartest girl in school, as well as the sweetest and most certainly the most ambitious student that had ever walked the halls of Joyous High—nailed the role of Marian the Librarian with a sultry, heart-wrenching rendition of "Till There Was You."

Nathan had to hear it only once before deciding that he had to have her, too.

If she'd only let him.

But Nina did not plan on being just another notch on Nathan's very long belt. *Her* scheme was grander: *She wanted to be his wife.*

And his strongest ally. And the woman at his side when he got that opportunity to stroll the red carpet toward fame and fortune.

Certainly he'd sung and danced his way into her heart. And yet, despite his flirting, wooing, and begging, she stayed chaste.

That is, until opening night.

Backstage with Mr. Bing, the drama teacher (and the only uncloseted gay man in Joyous), Nina watched through the dusty folds of the gymnasium stage's burgundy velvet curtain as Nathan belted out "Gary, Indiana" with two less musically blessed cast members. She winced when the director clucked his tongue and proclaimed in that pronounced lisp of his: "Hot damn, what a waste! That kid is *definitely* L.A. material. But he's stuck in this hellhole for life. And that's too bad, 'cause the last thing this town needs is another ex-jock car salesman pining over his long-gone days of glory."

Granted, Mr. Bing was sweet on Nathan too, but anyone with two eyes in his head could see that he was right!

That very night, Nina readily encouraged Nathan to get entangled in her very librarianlike petticoats, her lithe limber legs, and her dreams of getting out of Joyous.

The day after graduation, with his Marian at his side, Nathan did what multitudes of other handsome, talented Harold Hills had done before him: He headed out of town.

Specifically, he headed for Hollywood—but by way of Las Vegas, because Nathan wanted to get married in the same place Elvis had married Priscilla: the Aladdin Hotel Wedding Chapel.

And at his side was where Nina stayed, too: cheering him on, scrounging for acting gigs, and taking care of the business of their personal lives.

The move had been tougher than they'd anticipated. Still, both were auditioning all the time. And while every now and then Nathan scored work as a non-union extra, or got a featured role in a pipe dream indie of some wannabe director, it didn't take Nina long to figure out that she wasn't "anatomically augmented" enough to be considered for the typical Hollywood ingénue roles. Too bad, but that was how it was going to stay. She refused to enter the Silicone Valley of the Dolls and inject her forehead and lips with alien life forms, or get a nose job just because hers was a *little* off-center (or cheek/chin/eye jobs, either, for that matter).

But what difference did that make? After all, *Nathan* loved her just the way she was. In fact, he worshipped her. *That* was all that mattered.

To tide them over until Nathan got his break, Nina got a real job—the one at Tommaso's—while Nathan wangled the part-time gig at Disney. And both of them got creative about ways to offset starvation. Besides bringing home the much-too-ripe fruit jettisoned from Tommaso's produce bins and some canned goods yanked off the shelves because it was too close to their expiration dates, the Hartes would sneak into the Best Western on Sunset Boulevard and snitch bagels, bananas, and coffee off the continental breakfast counter. Then at night they'd hit anyplace that doled out free all-you-can-eat hors d'oeuvres with the purchase of a single drink, like Q's on Wilshire, or the Acapulco on La Cienega.

Sure, life in Hollywood was a struggle. Still, *they loved it.*

They loved the 340 days of sunshine and the loonies on Venice Beach.

They loved the palm trees and bougainvilleas that seemed to flourish in even the grimiest neighborhoods.

They loved how that sulky girl standing behind them in line at the movie theater at the Grove could possibly be Mischa Barton and her boyfriend, or that the guy at the next table at the farmer's market could be Ted Danson.

Even the horrendous traffic, and the smog, and the hundred other Nathan and Nina look-alikes they were up against at each audition didn't discourage them because they knew they were living the life they were meant to live together.

Of course, they loved their lives even more so when they found out that Nina was pregnant.

Because that made them a family.

That's not to say that Nathan and Nina weren't scared witless at the thought of being parents. Of course they were! But now they were more determined than ever to make it in Los Angeles.

And not head back home to Joyous.

Ever.

With their tails between their legs, so that Nathan could take his rightful place as heir apparent in his daddy's auto mall, where he'd spend his days cajoling customers into the newest Explorer Sport Trac pickup.

Although Nathan understood and appreciated Nina's motives for bringing up the phone sex gig, he didn't jump for joy at this idea for creatively financing his career.

"Okay, okay," said Nathan. "Let's just say I can live with the thought of my wife chatting up other men so that they get hard-ons and beat off. Honestly though, babe, do you actually think you can make enough money to support all of us?"

"Who knows?" Nina answered matter-of-factly. "All I can tell you is that there's this chick in our acting class—you know, the homely one who's a little on the chunky side—who does it a few hours every couple of nights, and *she's* got a two-bedroom cottage in the Hollywood Hills that she owns out-right."

"Yeah, I know the one." Nathan winced at the thought. "Jeez, it's a good thing that she's making *some* kind of dough with that voice of hers, 'cause she ain't going to make it in this town on her looks."

As Nathan pummeled a charley horse out of her calf muscle—a symptom of standing at a cash register all day while four months pregnant—Nina gasped, "Look at it this way: It *would* keep me off my feet."

He still wasn't totally convinced, but he knew better than to argue with her once she had finally made up her mind to do something. Instead he sighed, then gave her calf a kiss.

"Heck, you've got a much more seductive voice than she has. Why, you'd have them eating out of your hand." He laughed. "I guess you can think of it as another kind of acting, right? Ha, if you were a method actress, think of what kind of sex life we'd have."

What's wrong with our sex life, she wanted to ask, *other than the fact that I'm pregnant, I work a forty-hour shift on my feet, I'm tired all the time, stressed out about money, and married to a guy who is way too handsome for his own good, and wants the rest of the world to know about it?*

Of course, she'd never say that out loud to Nathan.

Instead, she called the number of Homely Chick's "dispatcher," Mrs. McGillicutty. The tough old broad, who doled out the calls with a throaty purr, took care of the credit card ins and outs, and paid her PSOs—that dainty acronym for phone sex operators—a respectable one dollar per minute.

She immediately put Nina to work.

"O" was born that very night.

To some extent, O truly was Nina's alter ego: Most certainly, she was much more playful—okay, *naughtier* than Nina. And she took no guff from her phone clients. In fact, after a day on her feet at Tommaso's, Nina looked forward to O telling her nighttime clients what she'd like to do to them. In turn, the clients *loved* her take-no-prisoners approach to their libidos—which made Nina wonder how much more respect she might incur from her daytime clients if she talked to them in the same manner.

But it wasn't all dirty talk. Sometimes it was just listening.

To guys who were having problems with their wives. Or their girlfriends. Or both.

Or their jobs.

And most certainly, their sex lives.

O was their ultimate fantasy. But she was also their buddy, their sounding board, and the person to whom they confessed their deepest, darkest secrets.

And sometimes she was their conscience.

That was the part of the job she loved the most.

Unlike Nina, O was never too shy to set an ambivalent guy straight, or to chastise him for a dumb move, or to pat him on the back for doing the right thing. For that matter, she thought nothing of putting a rude asshole in his place, either. Where Nina was shy, O was fearless.

And that made it all worthwhile.

That, and of course the money, which was why O also put up with the plenty of creeps who asked her to do things that made her skin crawl. But hey, it paid the rent *and* a heck of a lot more, because O was *really* good at what she did. The thirty-four clients she had who were regulars, not to mention the hundred or so others who she chatted up during any given month, were certainly proof of that.

Mrs. McGillicutty put it this way: "Kid, you're a natural. Your voice is an audio version of Levitra to these johns."

Quite a compliment, eh?

Well, money speaks louder than words, particularly to a PSO: by the time Nina was in her fourth month, the money was rolling in—in fact, at three times what she was clearing after taxes at Tommaso's—which allowed her to take a four-month unpaid pregnancy leave of absence from the store when Jake was born without feeling the pinch.

Within eleven months of becoming a PSO, Nina was able to pay off all their credit card debt. By the time she'd celebrated her fourteenth month, they'd moved into a two-bedroom rent-controlled apartment (with a walk-in closet large enough for O to put in a second phone line and set up shop) on a sunny block in Santa Monica that was within walking distance to the beach.

And Nina and Nathan started their Hollywood Hills cottage fund. But because cottages anywhere off Sunset go for a million dollars *minimally*, Nina was prepared for the fact that O would still have to do a lot of "oooohing and aaaaahing" on the phone—at least until Nathan scored enough commercials, or a sitcom, or *something* to make it feasible for her to quit and concentrate on doing voice-over work. On a mike, she could be anyone. And she had the client list to prove it.

First things first, though. Nathan's career was priority number one.

Because two four-year-olds singing the SpongeBob Square-Pants song at the top of their lungs in the back seat of a Civic are louder than the chirp of a Motorola RAZR V3c cell phone, it wasn't until Nina was clocking in for her shift at Tommaso's that morning that she noticed she had two voice mail messages:

January 11; Message #1, 7:37 A.M.: *Hi, sweetheart, it's Nathan . . . Okay look, you went to bed so late last night after your shift, and then you left before I got up, so I didn't have a chance to tell you that—well, don't be too, too mad but . . . well, I think we should scrub our plans tonight with Jamie and Helene. Barry—you remember Barry, right? He's that jumpy dude they got to play Goofy when Kenny got promoted into Beauty and the Beast—well, yesterday Barry mentioned that he's got a bartending gig at some big-time Hollywood party, and he says they could use an extra pair of hands. Heck, hon, we can certainly use the money, right? And—well, you never know who might be there, ha-ha . . . I'm trying to be positive here. Can you call the gang and break the news to them, 'cause*

I'm running late. I've got to get in a half hour earlier today because they're posting a new lineup for the Main Street Parade, but before that, I need to hit the gym to work out, and then I'm going to check out this photographer some dude in a casting office told me about, you know, who does headshots for only fifty bucks . . . Hey, don't be too mad at me about tonight, okay? Because everything I do is for us, *babe . . . right? . . . Kiss the little guy for me . . . Um, hey, if you want to work another shift tonight—well, I won't mind. I'm probably not going to be home till real late anyway. You know how those parties are . . . They can go on till all hours. Love ya. Bye.*

Great. Just great. Nina groaned. Of course she was disappointed that she couldn't get all dressed up and go out and play with two of the few friends they had who were as young, as poor, and as hungry as they were to catch a break in this town: Jamie Braddock, a comedian trying to expand beyond the periodic stand-up gig to commercials and maybe even a sitcom; and Helene Conover, who, despite having a Harvard MBA, always scored commercials that called for tall, willowy, dumb blond bimbos. Both of them were in Nathan and Nina's acting class—well, Nathan's acting class, anyway. Nina had dropped out right after Jake was born. Staying home meant she could man O's phone line an extra night each week, and that meant more money for the Hollywood Hills house fund.

Now Nina would have to call Jamie and Helene and beg off. Of course, they would assume it was because the Hartes really couldn't afford to go with them to the Lodge, a celebrity hangout that catered to the town's hottest and hippest young stars and their entourages. And while that was definitely the case, it still hurt to have others think that.

Besides, it had taken Nina, what, three weeks to find a babysitter? And now the babysitter was going to be pissed off, so pissed that she'd probably ask to be paid anyway, since everyone who was going out tonight had already lined up sitters, and would just *kill* their husbands if they were bailed on.

Everyone but Nina, that is.

Because Nathan was right. They *did* need the money. And he certainly needed to take every opportunity presented to him to make as many connections as he could, if they were going to make it in L.A.

As she tied on her regulation Tommaso's apron, a plump tear rolled down her cheek. Looking around to see if anyone else was paying attention, she caught the heavily made-up eye of Tori, who looked at her hot pink Anne Klein bracelet watch (an indication that, yep, not only had she seen Nina bawling, but she'd also noted that Nina had come in eight minutes late), then clucked her tongue in disapproval.

"You know, doll, with all that bawling you do over that *man* of yours, it wouldn't hurt you to invest in some waterproof mascara. We're having a sale on it, you know. Max Factor 2000 Calorie Aqua Lash. Simply to *die* for . . . Better yet, you should *seriously* consider going in for a little eye work. It's never too early, *I* say. Tuck now, and you'll wrinkle less later. *Comprenez-vous?* "

Since becoming the shift manager—and, finally, all woman—Tori had also become a bit bitchy about the little things that mattered.

Like *sympathy for her fellow man.*

Or woman.

On the other hand, Tony, the big lug, always had a free shoulder to cry on.

"Thanks, I'll check it out . . . the mascara," Nina murmured. She then turned back to her locker, a not-so-subtle indication that she'd prefer to listen to her messages without her boss's unsolicited commentary.

Tori knew better than to push. After all, Nina was the best concierge the store had ever had, and she'd be almost impossible to replace. Not only did that steel-trap brain of hers never forget which Tommaso's preferred customers wanted their deliveries on what days, she also knew every one of the VIP customers' food fetishes, gastronomic cravings, and culinary idiosyncrasies by heart.

For example, Nina knew that a certain movie actress known for her couturier-slim physique had for years kept it that way by living on large quantities of a specific brand of organic baby food, despite the natural assumption that she bought cases of the stuff for her adopted Russian toddler; she also knew that a young actor who publicly eschewed eating "anything that walked the earth" while espousing the benefits of a vegan diet had a weekly standing order for Kobe steaks. Best of all, when Nina was bitched out by some blue-rinsed Beverly Hills relic because the delivery boy had dropped off the wrong gourmet cat food, she let it roll off her back—which was why Tori knew better than to ruffle Nina's feathers too much. Having made her point, she huffed out into the store to see if there wasn't some lowly stock boy she could harass instead, leaving Nina to stare in dread at her still-blinking cell phone.

The second message was probably lousy news too, like

maybe Jake's teacher had noticed that he was sniffling, and Nina should pick him up and take him home before he infected all the other precious children at SOA, which meant that Nina would have to ask Tori to let her go home—without pay, of course, because a four-year-old with a bad cold (or strep throat, or chicken pox, or an ear infection, or pink eye) doesn't understand that the store's policy called for only five sick days a year, which, in Nina's case, had already been used up—and it was only *the second week in January*, for god's sake.

She was just about to pretend the message light wasn't blinking, toss her cell phone back into her purse, and stuff the whole kit and caboodle into her locker when it hit her that the call might be from Nathan again, saying that he'd changed his mind about taking the gig because spending a rare night out on the town with her was just too important.

That was the only reason that Nina pushed the "1" digit on the phone, and heard the following:

> **Message #2, 7:44 A.M.:** *Um, darling Nina, this is Becca . . . You know, Plum's mummy. You drove off so fast that the au pair didn't have time to tell you—er, to ask—a favor . . . Her English is so bad anyway, so I'll just ask for her. You see, Ylva won't be able to pick up the children this afternoon . . . she's got to go in and talk to the immigration people. Again . . . My gawd, considering she's Swedish and not Mexican, you'd think this wouldn't happen as often as it does, now wouldn't you? Sometimes I think Gordon is right and we should just go with an illegal. What do you think? Ooops, so sorry! I keep forgetting that you tough it out without a staff . . . and you work, too! And such hard work . . . So noble . . . I really admire you.*

Really . . . *Most certainly, Ylva should be home just a* few *minutes after you . . . An hour, tops . . . Um, speaking of your little job at Tommaso's, before you leave the store, would you be a dear and scoop up some of that* fabulous *tuna sashimi they have in the deli, for Plum's dinner tonight? Gordon and I have reservations at Lucques, and I just won't have time to stop until then . . . Oh, and throw in some of that* delicious *roasted bell pepper coulis. You can just add it to my tab there . . . In fact, I'll just call in the rest of my order, and you can take the whole thing home with you, you're* such *a doll. Ylva will get it from you when she picks up Plum. If my baby girl is hungry when you get her home, remember: She's allowed* fresh fruit only. *We don't believe in unnatural sugars . . . I assume that you buy* only *organic, correct? Seems that, working at Tommaso's,* that *would be a given. Am I right? You know, I really* do *admire you! Ciao bella . . .*

What, was that bitch crazy? This was, like, the third time she'd pulled this au pair no-show stunt.

As if Nina were on Becca Silver's staff, too.

And as if Becca was doing Nina a favor to entrust her darling little Plum to Nina's care in the first place, when it was so obvious that Becca felt gypped over having to carpool with Sage Oak Academy's one and only "scholarship family" to begin with.

All because, unlike Nina, every other Sage Oak "mummy" between Pacific Palisades and Santa Monica was already wise to Becca's carpool abuses.

Or at least their au pairs were.

Nina had once made the mistake of bitching to Nathan

about Becca's treatment. "Well, what do you expect in a school where none of the kids have *real* names, anyway?" was his comeback.

From the viewpoint of someone who had grown up in Joyous—where every third girl was named Brittany, if not Ashley or Lauren—it was downright *un-American* that every female child in their son's class was named for a fruit-bearing tree. Nina could have easily explained this away by informing him that these "fruity names," as he called them, were in fact Hollywood's version of Ashley, Lauren, and Brittany: in other words, a trend that had started with Gwyneth's highly hormonal whim to name her daughter Apple. Immediately, Cherry, Peach, (not even Peaches, but just *one* Peach), Pear, Lemon, and in Becca's devilish little angel's case, Plum, had been snapped up with fervor.

Certainly a Guava should make an appearance any day now.

Why, one couple—he was a studio wonk, and she could have easily passed for Gwyneth's twin sister—had even named their son Kiwi so as not to miss out on the trend. (And because she wanted to keep looking like Gwynnie, they had stopped at one child.) When Nathan heard that, he insisted that their kid would be scarred for life; that perhaps it would even turn the boy into "a fag." It didn't matter that the fruit in question came from New Zealand, the very country that had produced his favorite—and very macho—film idol, Russell.

"Don't say that about the poor kid!" Nina scolded him. "Despite what you may have been taught back in Joyous, a person just doesn't 'become' gay. Besides, a tenth of the population is gay! And everyone's got at least one gay friend, right?"

"Well, if anything *could* turn a guy gay, a fruity name is right there at the top of the list," Nathan insisted. "What was that dude thinking, anyway? A father's got to give his son every advantage, right up front."

As Nathan said that, he glanced proudly at Jake: his mini-me, his clone, the heir to his throne. The two of them were headed down to the park, Jake's tiny glove and miniature bat in hand, for "Team Harte's" thrice-weekly catch-and-hit game. For Nina, one of Nathan's most endearing features was how he embraced fatherhood so unabashedly. Heck, he had never even hesitated to change a diaper when Jake was a baby! Like most proud daddies, he reveled in those things that made his son uniquely special, and had made it his mission to encourage Jake's natural athletic abilities, even going so far as to arrange his work schedule so that it would never interfere with this sacred father-son ritual.

And because Nina's all-encompassing love for Jake matched his own, Nathan knew better than to balk at her insistence that Jake attend Sage Oak. After all, she pointed out knowingly, at what other preschool could Jake learn his numbers, letters, and a smattering of Spanish (a great course for those kids with Mexican au pairs), *and* give Nathan the opportunity to ruminate over the pros and cons of soccer versus T-ball with Patrick Dempsey on Open House Night, or mention to proud mama Felicity Huffman that Jake might actually have a crush on her little Georgia Grace—and then ask either of them: "Oh by the way, is your show still casting for that offbeat guest role?"

Certainly not the Little Lambs Preschool back in Joyous.

Because *that* was in the middle of nowhere.

And they—Nathan, Nina, and Jake—belonged at the center of that universe.

In fact, if Nina had her way, Nathan—her sweetheart, her lover, her knight in shining armor—would soon *be* the center of that universe.

Which was why she'd work an extra shift tonight, without complaint.

Having Sam Godwin as an agent is like being blessed by an angel. I never felt luckier than on the day he tapped me on the shoulder and said, "Jenny, I'd be honored to make you a star." I was, like, "No, Sam, I'd be honored to be one of the stars you've made."

Jennifer L., in Variety

When Sam is here at Sundance, his instincts are like a Geiger counter: Any film he's excited about means that the director and the actors are made—that is, if they are smart enough to sign with Sam and then listen closely to what he says they have to do in order to make it in this business. Of course, they'll never regret that they did.

Robert R., in Hollywood Reporter

When you're a nobody and all of a sudden your indie flick gets some buzz, a dozen agents will descend on you like locusts, and then tell you how terrific they are and what they can do for you. Not Sam. He's too Zen for that. He sees his job as your samurai, the one who slaughters all the bad guys so that you can make the movies you want to make. And trust me: The dude wields one bad-ass sword.

Quentin T., in Interview

You want to know about Sam as an agent? Let me put it this way: Both Ben and I had the opportunity to sign with Sam, but because people in Hollywood see us as joined at the hip, we decided, "Okay, we'll sign with different agents. How bad could that be, right?" So we flipped a coin, and I got Sam. Need I say more?"

Matt D., in Entertainment Weekly

2

The Ultimatum

In Hollywood, everyone has a dirty little secret.

And Sam Godwin, the managing partner of ICA—Intellectual Creative Agency, one of the biggest talent firms in Hollywood—knew most of them.

For example, he knew that a certain blockbuster director had recently been arrested in Utah for rolling around a lumpy TraveLodge mattress with the comely, buck-toothed fifteen-year-old daughter of a polygamist. What do you do in that situation, hold your breath and pray that no overly zealous stringer with the *National Enquirer* or *Hollywood Exxxposé* is Googling the court dockets from the *Deseret Morning News*? Hell, no! It was Sam's way of thinking that you had to be proactive, not reactive, which was why he convinced his client to make a fairly substantial contribution to the fifteen-year-old's "college fund." Sure, it ticked off Mr. Cradle Robber to have to do it, but he anted up. Case dismissed. End of story.

And Sam was the only person on the planet who knew that a certain up-and-coming television actor whose starring role in his first action film had tested through the roof still slept at home with his mother. No, not just in the same house; but in *the same bed* with Mommy Dearest.

Every night.

Nope, there would be no way in which to resurrect Sonny's career if *that* little ditty got out.

And then there was that *veddy* aristocratic British actress who was at the top of every film director's must-have list—you know, the one who comes off as the long-lost daughter of Audrey Hepburn, all fire and ice elegance? Well, *her* little indiscretions, which took place in her mid-teens, could be found on the shelf of any video porn shop in Germany. But thanks to the fact that she took Sam up on his suggestion that she change her name *and* find herself a top-notch Swiss plastic surgeon for a nose job, cheekbone augmentation, and let's not forget the breast reduction, no one else needed to find out about this, either.

In Sam's mind, knowing these juicy little tidbits and telling the world about them—or telling anyone, for that matter—accomplished nothing. In fact, it defeated everything he stood for, because keeping secrets was Sam's stock-in-trade.

He was, after all, a Hollywood agent.

Which was why he made every client's business his own, and worked very hard to ensure that their business became no one else's.

It was this kind of sensitivity that had rocketed Sam out of the mailroom of one of the oldest, most revered agencies in Hollywood, and into a partnership at one of the young Turk agency boutiques, and why he enjoyed a client roster that read like a "Hollywood's Hottest" special issue of *Vanity Fair*.

Not all his clients were comfortable about spilling their guts to him—at least, not at *first*. But once they got used to the idea that they *deserved* a keeper for their naughty realms, actually they were relieved to share all those embarrassing little incidents—or as Sam put it to them, "life-shaping experiences"— with someone who didn't pass judgment. He encouraged them to think of him as their very own father confessor, but with none of the hassles that come with converting to some repressive dogma, like $200 red-string bracelets or other sentimental silliness. Whenever his clients found themselves perched on some emotional way-out-in-left-field limb, he was the guy who talked them down.

Afterward, they actually believed that they'd come through it okay. Best yet, without their adoring public any the wiser.

And *that* was all that mattered, he told them.

Of course, out of sheer desperation, they chose to believe him, because he was their agent, and it went without saying that he had only their best interests at heart.

Right?

This was why, at six-forty-five that morning, Sam was cooling his heels in a discreetly placed banquette within the Beverly Hills Hotel's renowned Polo Lounge, waiting to meet with Lucinda Hardaway, the wife and producing partner of his dearest friend and oldest client, the renowned director Hugo Schmitt. Lucinda was also the only child of and heir to the billions accumulated by the multimedia scion Archibald "Archie" Hardaway. In fact, it was Archie's millions that financed the small, edgy, intelligent films made by Hugo's production company, Flagrant Films, which were revered by edgy and intelligent cinephiles and lauded by reviewers the world over . . .

. . . yet rarely made back its investors' money, no less a decent profit.

In other words, *Archie* never saw even a dime back from his investment in Hugo's films. Did that bother him? Of course! But Archie had learned years ago to suck it up because he'd do anything to make his only child happy. And as long as Hugo made her happy, too, he'd keep writing off Hugo's losses.

Which was why Hugo was the envy of every DGA member.

Now, according to Lucinda, it seemed that Hugo had a secret, too—one that even Sam knew nothing about.

This he had to hear.

Lucinda's arrival was as surreptitious as possible, considering that she swept into the Polo Lounge swathed in floor-length psychedelic Pucci and three-inch-heeled sandals with a runway stride that would have done Kate Moss proud. Now in her mid-thirties, Lucinda used her humongous bank balance to help offset the inevitable Malibu matron's mid-life depression, the result of living in a town that feared aging almost as badly as the alternative. Then again, considering how it deified those who die young, maybe Hollywood felt that the alternative *was* better.

Sam rose to give her the requisite peck on the cheek, but she wore her D&G shades until after the waiter had taken their order. When she took them off, Sam saw the reason: Her eyes were so swollen from crying that one would have thought she'd just had plastic surgery.

Not good.

Before he could ask what was wrong, she opened her Hermès bag and pulled out an unlabeled CD. He couldn't help but notice that her hand was trembling as she handed it to him.

"Hugo is—*he's in love with another woman.*" She sighed tearfully.

Sam blinked once, slowly, before he shook his head in disbelief. "Look, Lucinda, if that were the case, *I* would know about it."

"Yes, I realize that." She stared at him, as if determining whether his statement was a denial or a cover-up. After what was an uncomfortably long silence, she must have decided that he was telling her the truth because she put her hand over his for just a moment before pulling it away.

"How did you find out?"

His question brought a sardonic smile to her lips. "Our accountants." Seeing his puzzled look, she added: "Seems he's been making the calls on the company charge card—"

Jeez, that was stupid, thought Sam.

"—and according to this recording, I guess he used my own personal card, too."

"Calls, huh? Long distance? So, she's based somewhere other than here in L.A.?"

"She's everywhere. She's a *phone sex operator.*"

Just when I thought Hugo couldn't be any stupider, he proves me wrong.

Sam put on his game face and said, "So, that's it? That's the punch line? Come on, Lucinda, phone sex isn't *real* sex. It's— it's a naughty little boy's temporary infatuation, that's all. Why, I'll bet he's never even met this woman."

"That doesn't matter," she retorted. "Sam, I'm telling you, Hugo is *obsessed* with her."

"How do you know this?"

"Because . . . because he's not using her simply to—to stimulate *our* sex life. Believe me, that wouldn't be so bad. I've gone down that path before with him, so I know that. And I know *him*."

Her eyes were getting damp again. Fumbling to put her sunglasses back on, she choked, "If you must know, for over a month now, he's been *abstaining*. Which means that he'd rather be with *her*. And it's only a matter of time before he is."

Just then the waiter came with their coffees and fruit plates. After he departed, Sam asked, "So, do your people have any idea who this woman might be?"

She shook her head. "I had a PI bug the phones, but her line is untraceable. On the recording, though, he calls her O."

"Hmmm." Sam wanted to laugh but then thought better of it. "Not too original, is it?"

"Oh, I don't know about that. I mean, if the bulk of your clientele is film industry types, they might get off on the classic cinematic reference."

"How do you know that's the case?"

"The PI told me that O's got a rep around the town, and specifically among you boys."

"Hey, don't look at *me*. Verbal masturbation isn't my cup of tea." He put his hand on hers and looked her straight in the eye. "Listen, Lucinda, you and Hugo are my closest, dearest friends. Hell, I introduced you two, remember? And I was the best man at your wedding. I think I can say that, next to you, I know Hugo better than anyone. And I'm betting that, for the long run anyway, this O person doesn't really mean anything to Hugo, either."

Lucinda shrugged sadly. "Before you put a C-note on that one, listen to it yourself. *Then* tell me what you think." She stood up to leave. "Believe me, Sam, I'd much rather it be you who takes care of this, as opposed to Daddy. Because his way to make the problem go away would mean the end of Hugo and me."

Don't I know it, thought Sam as he watched Lucinda walk away, her head held high.

Not only that, it would be the end of Hugo's career in Hollywood, period, because no studio would dare cross Archie by distributing Hugo's films. They couldn't afford *that*. Most certainly not for an art house auteur whose films' net income barely covered the catering costs for the parties thrown to fete any Academy Award nominations thrown his way. Hell, even the DVD rights didn't make it worthwhile.

Sam grabbed the check from the waiter and headed out the door.

One of the classiest features of the Ferrari F430 is its perfectly balanced four-speaker high-end Bose sound system, ideal for listening to the seductive purr of an experienced phone sex operator in the throes of a professionally simulated orgasm:

SHE: (*In a sultry voice that sounds just a bit sleepy*) Hi! *Ooooh* . . . hold on . . . I just want to . . . *stretch* . . . I just woke up . . . and (*giggles*) well, these satin sheets are making me *shiver* because I'm naked!

HE: (*Shyly, anxiously*) Yeah, hi, O, it's, uh, me.

SHE: (*With that husky laugh that he's come to know and love*) Omigod, *Wilbur!* Hi, sweetie! (*Then, pouting*) You naughty boy, it's been, what, two days now? I thought you didn't *want* me anymore! *Hmmm.* Maybe I shouldn't be so sweet to you . . .

HE: (*Ashamed, flattered, excited*) Please, O, don't be mad at me! It's been really busy here at . . . at work. I'm home now, and I really shouldn't be calling you! My wife might walk in any minute! But I had to hear your voice, too!

SHE: Poor Wilbur. You're always working . . . (*purring now*) . . . SO hard . . . So, tell me, lover, what can I do for you?

HE: (*Complete silence; then*) I think you know.

SHE: (*Sighing happily*) Yes, Wilbur. I know . . . I just *love* our little role playing . . . I'll bet you don't know which is my favorite of our little fantasies.

HE: (*Gulping*) Which—which one is it?

SHE: It's the one in which I'm standing at my big picture window, and the curtains are wide open. You know, I *never* draw the curtains because I just *love* the thought that someone who I don't know or see may be watching me—

HE: (*Breathing heavily*) Like . . . me.

SHE: (*Gives a sexy chuckle*) Yes, Wilbur, someone like you. Or maybe it *is* you, my peeping Wilbur. Wouldn't that be *SO hot?* I mean, there *you* are, in one of those big beautiful mansions at the top of Mulholland, looking down into the canyon where I live . . . you know, in one of those houses with *lots* of windows. I love being . . . *exposed.*

HE: I'm looking now. I can just imagine you're there, in that house below me . . .

SHE: That's right, Wilbur. You see me in the big window, right? There I am, in my tiny black silky see-through negligee. You remember it, right? It's the one *so* sheer that it looks as if I'm wearing nothing . . . *at all* . . .

HE: Yes. I know the one. It's my favorite . . . Go on . . .

SHE: (*Gasps*) Omigod! Can you guess what happened just now?

HE: Your straps . . . broke.

SHE: (*In a husky purr*) Yes, lover. *Just now.* Right as you whispered into my ear, the thin gossamer straps on my negligee snapped right off! Imagine that!

HE: (*Swallowing hard*) I wished I'd been there, O. I would have—I would have torn them off of you!

SHE: (*Giggles girlishly*) Don't I just know it, you brute! And I would have *loved* it . . . So, now here I am, with my breasts— well, you know how perky they are—

HE: (Breathing heavily) Yes! Yes, I—I remember—

SHE: And they're *so* cold! You can just imagine where I have goose bumps . . .

HE: (*Groaning*) Yes! Yes! I can just imagine!

SHE: My nipples are so . . . so taut right now . . . so hard . . . (*She moans*) When I caress them, they tremble at my touch!

HE: (*Whispering*) You're touching them? You're touching them now?

SHE: Yes . . . I'm gently stroking them to keep them warm—

HE: (*Breathing even more heavily*) Warm . . . warm . . .

SHE: But my gentle strokes are having the opposite effect. They're getting larger . . . and harder . . . How about you, Wilbur? Are you getting harder?

HE: Yes! Harder! Harder!

SHE: (*Seductively*) Aw, gee, that's too bad, Wilbur, because I just got a text message from my dispatcher. Seems that your credit card is topped out. Sorry, hon, gotta go—

HE: No! No! Please! I've got—I've got to *finish* here, and I— I *can't*—without you!

SHE: Well . . . um . . . let's see: Do you happen to have another card somewhere?

HE: No. Yes! Yes, I do. It's—but it's—(*now somewhat deflated*)—it's a company card—one my wife uses, too. I did use it once before, but . . . Hell, I could get in trouble if she finds out!

SHE: Gee, that's a shame, Wilbur. Really it is. Because I'm still *very hot* down there.

HE: How . . . how hot?

SHE: (*Stroking each word tauntingly*) Steaming hot. Throbbing hot. So hot that, if you were here, I'd scorch you alive, and . . . (*Pauses, then sweetly*) But, hey, Wilbur, I thoroughly understand if you can't use the card. Well, I gotta run—

HE: Wait! *Wait!* Don't hang up! . . . Just let me get it out of her purse . . . (*Rummaging*) Hold on. Let me see . . . Um, hey, you do take Discover, right?

SHE: You know how I love plastic, Wilbur. It doesn't matter what kind of plastic it is, either. All of it makes me—you know, *hot*. Hot like you, Wilbur. I can just imagine that you're hot right now: long, hot, hard, and *throbbing* . . . Um, what was that number again? Oh, and don't forget the expiration date.

HE: (*Relief and joy in every word*) Yeah, yeah, I got it right here! It's 5555—

(*SFX of tape cutting off . . .*)

This O woman was the vocal equivalent of Viagra.

Hell, thought Sam, no wonder Hugo's obsessed with her!

Which meant that Hugo was in *deep shit*. Up to his hairy armpits.

And, from the sound of it, Sam would need a bulldozer to yank him out. He knew he had no choice other than to read Hugo the riot act tonight, when he'd see the director at the after-party for his new film.

Sam was glad he'd opted to play the CD while he was still parked in the hotel's lot instead of doing so while on the road. Otherwise he might have found himself wrapped around one of the many palm trees that hugged Sunset Boulevard's blind curves. Still lost in thought, he pointed the Ferrari west, back toward the office—

—only to have to circle back around Will Rogers Park in order to head back east, in the direction of the Beverly Hills Tommaso's on Doheny.

He'd almost forgotten that he still had to make one more stop before heading into the office.

To pick up something called teff.

No, of course he didn't have the time to stop, but if he didn't, he wouldn't be able to live with himself, because skipping the teff meant enduring another weekend with the current love of his life, Chastity Valentine.

'Nuf said. Teff it was. *Then* he could gently break the news to Chastity that their relationship was over.

On the way to Tommaso's, he listened to the CD again . . . And again.

Ironically, the only messes Sam's $3,800 made-to-measure size 12 John Lobb loafers never seemed to avoid were those involving his love life—which, at this very moment, was getting *way* out of hand.

Since he was a winner in every other aspect of his life, it was *not* something that he was particularly proud of. But, hey, he took total blame for the predicament. The truth was that he was married to his job, 24/7, which was what was needed—no ifs, ands, or buts about it—to be a success in this town.

And because he'd yet to find a woman who was just as exciting to him as this client's problem or that star's account or his agency's bottom line, it was inevitable that whoever occupied his bed at any given point in time would eventually figure that out and then take off in a teary huff.

Say, eight or nine months, tops. Unless he gave them his "you're way too good for me" farewell speech first.

Right at that moment, Sam and Chastity's relationship was just at a week or so beyond month seven.

Right on time.

Granted, Chastity had the full package: a great job—she was a well-respected syndicated radio astrologist-slash-sex therapist—and she was a live wire, albeit somewhat off-center . . . And yeah, okay, she was *certainly* easy on the eye.

And she loved sex. In fact, he could honestly say that the woman was a *machine*. It must have been all that Bikram yoga she did, all twenty-six positions of it, every day, without fail. And it never failed that by the time she'd reach position three—the totally submissive *pada hastasana*—he was fully erect and raring to go. For the first six months or so, he thought he'd died and gone to heaven!

But then little things started to get under his skin. Like the realization that she certainly wasn't the brightest bulb on the runway. That was not to say that she was a dummy. It was just that the kinds of things she *did* know well—like sun signs and tarot cards and ancient pagan lore—bored Sam to no end. Not that every woman he dated had to have Natalie Portman-esque Harvard smarts, or even project Uma Thurman-esque worldly wisdom, but minimally she had to be savvy enough for him to take to Susan and Tim's and not be mortified when she went into some New Age riff . . . which Chastity had a tendency to do, and certainly a little more often than *he* cared to hear her do, particularly in public.

Sam knew that no one woman he dated would or should be perfect. Last night, however, in regard to Chastity, the writing was certainly on the wall: They had been at a charity event at Reiner's place. Sam had been chatting up an actress whom he really admired. The word was out on the street that she was looking for new representation, and hell, he just *knew* he could take her career in a whole other direction. That was when he caught Chastity glaring at them from across the room. Jeez, anyone in Hollywood could have told her that Sam *never* mixed business with pleasure. If Chastity didn't get *that* after seven plus months with him, then as far as he was concerned, she didn't get anything at all . . .

Which was why their union could now only be described as over. *Fini.* As dead as a Best Supporting Actress's career two years after she'd taken home her gold-plated doorstop.

That very minute Sam had decided he'd break up with her the next morning, convince her that they should cut their losses, no hard feelings. They could even stay "just friends."

Ha. *As if.*

The breakup would have happened just like that, too . . . if he hadn't awakened with an erection. And because he was cuddled up against Chastity's luscious backside, of course she *felt* it, too—

—and she went for it.

Needless to say, one thing led to another . . . and another . . . and another . . .

And so, after three highly aerobic orgasms, his plan to break up with her was sidelined . . .

. . . At least for another day. No *way* could he break up with her after they'd just had make-up sex. He wasn't *that* big of a bastard.

He sighed. Well, at least *one* of them had gotten out of bed with a smile.

That is, he assumed she was smiling. It was hard for him to be absolutely sure because Chastity—hot, sweaty, naked, and limbered up—had already slithered out from under the seven hundred-count Egyptian cotton Anichini bedsheets to begin her morning yoga regimen.

As Chastity moved from one state of bliss to another, he resolved himself to his fate: He'd have to reschedule the breakup for tomorrow morning. Hell, after the sexathon they'd just had, there wasn't even time for a shower, let alone a breakup. Besides, he had to meet Lucinda Hardaway at the Polo Lounge in—*Jeez!*—less than thirty minutes!

As for that golf game he had scheduled for tomorrow morning with Bill, Samuel, and Kevin, well, he could kiss *that* goodbye now, too, because Chastity would demand at least a full morning of tearful introspection before riding off into the sunset.

With his stomach growling, Sam crawled out of bed, zipped up his charcoal gray Z Zegna slacks over a day-old pair of Everlast 1910 boxer briefs, and silently made his way to the door, Piatelli long-sleeve knit polo shirt and John Lobbs in hand. He was almost home free, too, when Chastity (who had by then moved into position eight, the very, very come hither hey-I'm-all-yours-for-the-asking *dandayamana bibhaktapada paschimot-tanasana*) called out after him: "Hey, my chart says it's *dire* that I should stay put today, so on the way home, can you stop by the store and pick up something we *desperately* need?"

Turning back around, he shot her an exasperated look, but she didn't see it. She had already moved into the *trikanasana* position: one leg bent forward, the other stretched out behind her, and an arm reaching up to the sky, which made it difficult for her to do anything other than stare up at the ceiling.

Sensing his reluctance, however, she added in that babyish singsong voice that had come to grate on his nerves sometime around month five: "Pretty please? With sugar on top? It's just one *itsy-bitsy teeny-weeny* item. You can pick it up at the Beverly Hills Tommaso's, you know, near your office."

"Yeah, yeah, okay. What is it?"

"Teff."

"Huh?" He didn't recognize the word. "Teff? What . . . what the heck is that?"

And when, he wondered, *in the next eighteen hours will I have the time to pick it up?*

Certainly not before the breakfast with Lucinda. And after that, he'd be racing back to ICA's offices to take a meeting with Quentin, and he certainly wasn't prepped for that. Not that the meeting would need much prep, since meetings with QT were mostly one-way gabfests-of-fancy: *his* way. (*God love him, the dude is a genius and all, but boy does he have diarrhea of the mouth, and even allotting only two hours was expecting a friggin' miracle!*)

Of course, if *that* meeting started late, then the hottest female actress on his roster, Katerina McPherson, would be left cooling her Manolos in ICA's lobby, and boy would *she* be pissed, because Katerina never waited for *anyone*, not even Sam. And her meeting was to be followed by one with a couple of whiny television writers who were pitching a feature script that they wanted him to slip to Mr. Cradle Robber . . . then lunch at the Ivy with a couple of suits from Sony . . .

. . . And in between all that would be at least eighty phone calls to make, and fifty e-mails to return, and several dozen contracts to review; not to mention the meeting he had scheduled on the Fox lot that wasn't even starting until the early evening because it was with that kid from *Lost*, which meant they'd have to meet after the day's shooting had wrapped . . .

Needless to say, he would have to miss Hugo's premiere of *Very Bad Boys*, so there was *no way* he could miss the after-party . . .

For which I'm determined to go without you, Sam thought, as he looked back at his contorted girlfriend. Hell, I'm not even *mentioning* it to you at this point . . .

And because he felt guilty about that, too, he was resigned to picking up the goddamn teff.

Okay, now think . . . think . . . The Beverly Hills Hotel is on Sunset, and Tommaso's is a mile or so east on Doheny, so maybe if I stop right after seeing Lucinda, it would work. Besides, how long could it take to pick up the stupid teff? Ten, fifteen minutes, tops?

Then *can we break up?*

"Sure, okay . . . teff. I'll remember."

"Trust me," Chastity said seductively, before folding herself into the silly-boy-how-can-you-resist-jumping-my-bones-

this-very-second *dandayamana bibhaktapada janushirasana.*
"You'll just *love* what I do with it."

At that moment, he tried to remember one instance when
he'd *ever* trusted her . . . but none came to mind.

In fact, he couldn't remember a time he'd actually trusted
any woman.

And that was Sam's dirty little secret.

ICED PRINCESS

This just in, my scandalacious snowflakes: Hollywood's newly crowned Princess of the Cinema, the purrrfectly luscious Katerina McPherson, is out to prove that last year's Best Actress nomination was no fluke—even if she has to do so at the expense of lust and l'amour. In fact, several of her ladies-in-waiting have confirmed that she's kissed off a certain titled Teutonic trillionaire who is legendary for his generosity with geegaws both glittery and golden. The broken-hearted Baron von Bling has retired to his Bavarian castle to lick his wounds in peace. Yessirree, our precious Kat is quite the vamp—and has the treasure trove to prove it!

Serenity's Scandal Sheet, 1/11

3

The Angel

"Excuse me, do you have something called 'teff'?"

The girl working the concierge desk in Tommaso's glanced up reluctantly. Seeing her straight on like that, Sam suddenly realized that she had been crying, which made him doubly embarrassed for having asked for something that sounded so ridiculous in the first place.

Although she might have been as old as twenty-two, she was such a *waif* that he found it hard to call her a woman. This allusion held up even further because she was also short, what you'd call petite—particularly here in L.A., the land of the stringbean-lean Amazons who came from the world over, modeling portfolios in hand, with their dreams of wooing the Eyemo as successfully as they had the Leica. She also had a beauty mark on her cheek (a *real* one, not some temporary L.A. Fashion Week paste-on mole) and straight, short dark hair with bangs long enough to graze her large, tear-smudged, doe brown eyes.

Seeing that he felt so guilty for actually bothering her, she did something that only the best actresses in a town full of actresses had the skill to do: *completely transform herself.*

With just a smile.

As if she didn't have a worry in the world, and only his needs were front and center on her mind.

As if she'd never been crying at all.

The metamorphosis was instantaneous. It was phenomenal.

Most certainly it was totally disconcerting, considering that, just moments before, he'd watched two perfect tears roll, in parallel paths, down the girl's face and onto her crisply ironed baby blue regulation BH Tommaso apron.

And it was certainly too early in the morning to be smitten by waifs.

Dammit, if only Chastity had lived up to her name *just once.*

"Teff," the waif repeated, and within a nanosecond, added efficiently, "Aisle twelve."

Still mesmerized, he looked off in the direction in which she'd pointed. "You said aisle . . . what again?" The damn place was an epicurean labyrinth. But he wasn't some Beverly Hills trophy wife with time on his hands to peruse the shelves' inviting larder. He needed to get back to the *real* world, and fast.

And listen to QT blather on about something he wanted to do, in Mandarin.

Not the blather, the *project.*

"Twelve. Here, let me show you, Mr. Godwin."

Following her lead, he tried hard not to stare at her cute rounded behind, which was clad in Tommaso's snug-fitting regulation khaki jeans. She was certainly a knockout in a town of knockouts. So what was she doing *here?* She was too good to be standing behind a gourmet grocery store's cash register, in tears over some terrible slight.

More than likely it had to do with some boyfriend.

The bastard.

She stopped short so unexpectedly that he practically tripped over her—how he wished he had!—as she pointed to a wall of bins filled with bulk grains.

"How much would you like?" Waif tore a plastic bag from a roll. Then she took a dipper and scooped up some tiny purplish brown pellets out of some bin.

He looked down on what she was showing him.

He didn't get it. "Teff—is *this crap?*"

I can't believe that this is what Chastity is making such a big deal over. Damn, I do need to dump that girl . . .

Waif laughed. It was a sweet, husky chuckle that aroused him in a way he hadn't felt since, well, since the first time he'd seen Chastity contort herself into a *pada hastasana.*

Or since he'd heard O, on the CD.

True lust.

"It's Ethiopian. Very high in calcium. And phosphorus. In fact, 150 pellets weigh as much as a single grain of wheat. Talk about taking in your bulk at warp speed." She spoke reverently, like a docent at the Getty rhapsodizing over Boudon's bust of Marie-Sébastien-Charles-François Fontaine de Biré.

He, too, could have rhapsodized over a bust: hers, which was certainly healthy and somewhat perky—not that he wanted to stare at it, but that was necessary in order for him to read her shiny gold name tag:

Nina.

Muy apropiado.

She smiled up at him again, gloriously.

Is she flirting with me?

Alas, that fantasy was shelved, at least for a moment, when she queried, "A pound maybe?"

"*Huh?*" Suddenly he realized that she was asking him how much "bulk" he thought he needed. He could feel his ears getting hot.

Christ, she probably thinks I'm constipated or something! He groaned inwardly.

"Oh, um, *nah*! Not *that* much . . . say, um . . . a cup?" He gave a small laugh. "It's not even for me . . . . It's for, uh, a friend."

She nodded sympathetically (which he interpreted to mean, "They *all* say that"), scooped, weighed, and clipped his teff stash.

Just then, the thought hit him: *Damn, does Chastity plan on us rolling and smoking this shit?*

"Here you go, Mr. Godwin. Come on back with me and I'll ring you right up. I'm sure you've got better places to be."

She handed it to him and, for a brief moment, their hands touched.

He felt a hot pulse run up his spine. His heart was racing like a Harley going down Topanga Canyon at full throttle. Hell, in his world, he was surrounded by the most beautiful women on Earth—*even Katerina McPherson*—and he'd never had *this* kind of reaction before!

He wanted to say something to her—*anything*—but all he could do was mutter "Thanks—*Nina.*" Well, at least she'd see that he'd taken special note of her name, you know, that he was a friendly guy.

Suddenly it dawned on him that she, too, had called him by *his* name.

Twice.

And *he* wasn't wearing any name tag.

So, who was she? Had he met her at some club? Or at some party?

More than likely she'd tried and failed to get past his assistant, Riley McNaught, to beg Sam to rep her.

Maybe she was pissed off about that, and now she was stalking him.

Would a woman do something like that? Stalk an *agent* who had scorned her?

Sure, if she were desperate enough, he reasoned.

And in Hollywood, every woman was desperate about *something*.

He stared at the back of her head as they made their way to her desk. Not once did she glance back, but glided as serenely as a princess until she was safely behind her counter again, where she tapped two register keys and murmured, "That will be $12.54."

Jeez, for just a cup of this stuff? What, is it gold-plated?

Still, he handed over a twenty-dollar bill. When she handed back his change, he felt the same charge run through him as the first time they touched.

She must have felt something, too, because she moved her hand away from his—far away, in fact, putting it under the counter.

He couldn't stand it anymore. Even if she wasn't going to say anything, he had to.

"So, Nina, I've got to ask: Have we met somewhere?"

"No, not at all, Mr. Godwin."

He had a hard time hiding his relief, but she didn't seem to notice.

"Then—then how did you know who I was?"

She blushed a deep scarlet, but this time her eyes did not turn away. "Well, you see, I read a lot of industry trade magazines. *Hollywood Reporter. Variety.* And Defamer.com, you know, online—"

He winced at that.

"—and I've seen your picture many times. And I know you represent—well, just about *everyone* who's important—and, well . . . I was just wondering—"

Ha! There it was, he thought. She was looking for a break after all.

And, hell yeah, he was going to give it to her. (*Come to Papa, come to Papa . . .*)

"Sure, Nina." He gave her his patented Sam Godwin eat-you-up-with-a-spoon grin. "Heck, you were my angel just now. So name it. What can I do for *you?*"

"I was just wondering—" Her hand came out from underneath the counter. In it was a DVD and a head shot. He smiled knowingly, expectantly.

"—if you wouldn't mind taking a look at my husband's reel."

Her *husband's* reel.

"You—have a husband? But . . . just how old *are* you?"

Her smile faded just a bit. He wasn't sure, but he could have sworn that those big beautiful brown eyes had clouded up again, just for a second.

Yep, there it was: *desperation.*

But for once in Sam's life, watching the person he was dealing with become desperate—watching *Nina's* desperation—wasn't such great sport.

No, he couldn't stand the thought of her being hurt at all.

"Twenty-four . . ." Her voice trailed off, as if it were a death sentence.

In Hollywood, it practically was.

Her eyes sought his, as if seeking his approval for being over twenty-one.

Legal, as it were.

Hell yeah. *Thank God* Nina was legal.

Down, tiger. She's also married. Remember?

The whole thing was so bizarre: his falling hard for some little cashier; she being a mere baby—and a married babe at that!

He looked down at the DVD. Sure, he'd watch it.

Hey, how bad could it be?

He took it out of her hand and got stung again by the ice-cold heat of her touch.

It's already bad enough, guy. She has a husband, remember?

As he watched the relief flow back into her face, and that angelic smile grace her lips once more on his behalf, he was convinced that his initial instincts were right:

That whoever the bastard was, he didn't deserve her.

It wasn't until Sam was halfway down Sunset that he realized he'd left the teff on the counter.

* * *

"*Ooooh*, I want *you!*"

Sam looked up to find Katerina McPherson—the most recent victor of *GQ*'s "Every Man's Wet Dream" contest—standing in his doorway and salivating over what he was watching on his video monitor:

Nathan Harte's reel.

Because Uma was in town, Quentin had skedaddled on time, leaving Sam with a few minutes to peruse the tape prior to Katerina's traffic-stopping, fashionably late appearance in ICA's offices. Looking at her now, he understood very well that it wasn't just Katerina's long, tousled tendrils that flowed down to the small of her back almost to her well-toned, sky-high ass, or the long, come-hither lashes over those deep-set aquamarine eyes, or those exquisitely chiseled cheekbones that put a rocket in the average Joe's pocket. Nor was it just the way in which her 37CC breasts were miraculously cantilevered, like the headlights on a vintage Jeep CJ-6, over that diminutive waist of hers.

Nope, it was none of that.

It was, however, the look on her face right now, that very moment, that bespoke the hidden desire of any man who saw it and eagerly read its openly blatant meaning:

"*I could eat you up alive . . . and you'd love every moment of it.*"

What was making her lick her collagen-plumped lips at that very moment was the tall, blond, and incredibly handsome Nathan Harte—all six-foot-two inches of him: broad chest, washboard abs, dimpled chin, curly locks—caught in a close-up as he emoted soulfully on a poorly lit set to a fidgety Betacam.

Which made Sam think: Imagine how millions of women would react to him in a film made by a *real* director, with a *real* script, and with a *real* budget!

Obviously he'd read Katerina's mind. Hovering so close to him that he almost choked on her signature fragrance (*Forbidden, by Kat*, of course), Hollywood's current princess said the one thing she needed to say to make it clear to Sam that her newest obsession—Nathan—should be his as well:

"He'd be just *perfect* for my project with Hugo, don't you think?"

Why, of course he did, Sam assured her. It was almost as if she'd read *his* mind. However, it was still Hugo's final decision, remember? And already Hugo had put out feelers to Russell and George and Brad and Matt, all of whom were *chomping at the bit* to costar opposite her—

Kat pursed her lips into that patented petulant pout that had been described by *Esquire* as "an instant erector set for big boys" and murmured, "But Hugo *will* do this for me, right? I mean, for the sake of the movie . . ."

To infer helplessness (an endeavor truly worthy of an Oscar if the woman deemed the most ruthless in Hollywood could pull it off), Kat let a glossy, Shu Uemura–coated nail meander from the collar of Sam's shirt to a point just above his nipple. Stopping there, she licked her upper lip and added, "Just think of the fun we could all have on *that* set . . ."

"Katerina, I think it's only fair to warn you that Nathan Harte is happily married—"

Poking him hard with her talon, she laughed demurely. "Sam, you're such a *cute prude!* This is Hollywood, remember? Where marriage is an illusion."

She had a point there.

Turning back to the monitor, he suddenly felt sorry for Nina.

Even more so, he felt sorry for Nathan.

Still, he'd call the kid first thing in the morning to give him the good news: He was going to be represented by Sam Godwin, and he was going to star in Katerina McPherson's next movie.

Sam Godwin's stucco beach cottage sat kitty-corner on the Pacific Coast Highway, where it intersected Sea Lane Drive. Because this was the four-lane highway's closest point to Malibu beach, it afforded the cottage some highly coveted frontage on this dream-laden stretch of sand. A solid wood door, surrounded by a high stucco gate, hid the house itself from view.

It was just as Nina had always envisioned a Hollywood agent should live.

And now, if all went well, this particular Hollywood agent would be Nathan's . . .

. . . and maybe, every once in a while, they'd be invited over to watch the sunset and splash around in the tide.

With Nathan's agent, Sam Godwin, right there alongside them.

Heck, she reasoned. Then they *would* be living the California dream!

Considering Sam had agreed to see Nathan's DVD, Nina felt that the least she could do was make sure he got what he had come to Tommaso's for in the first place. So she had looked up Sam's home address in Tommaso's VIP database, and after her shift ended, she picked up Jake and Plum from Sage Oak, then headed out on Highway One, toward the Malibu colony until she found Sam's place.

The moment she pushed the cottage's security bell, a dog started barking from inside. The voice that answered, a bit breathy and certainly annoyed at the interruption, demanded that she walk through the courtyard to the front door.

It was too much to hope that Sam would be home to greet her. More likely he was commandeering what she imagined was a football-sized corner office on the top floor of the three-story Frank Gehry-designed ICA Tower on Wilshire Boulevard at Rodeo, chatting up one of the Toms, or maybe Denzel, or perhaps even Nicole. Still, any brownie points she could secure on Nathan's behalf was her goal, even if that meant dropping off Sam's teff with his housekeeper.

Or, in this case, a very pretty, very agile, and certainly very buff Danskin-clad girlfriend, and an overly friendly Labrador retriever.

"Down, Towser, down," grumbled the girlfriend, seemingly helpless in controlling the friendly pup. Nina patted him on the back, then gave him a command to heel. Immediately Towser went down on all fours with a look of adoration in his eyes.

"So, you're delivering the teff. *Hmmm*. Well, *that's* certainly . . . surprising." Cocking her head in consternation, Sam's girlfriend ignored Nina's offering. Instead she reached languorously behind herself to grasp an outstretched leg.

Quite frankly, the position reminded Nina of one she had learned in a free pole-dancing class that Nathan had insisted she take when he'd seen it offered by the gym down the block from their apartment.

Scrutinizing Nina, the human pretzel then asked pointedly, "Say, what sign are you?"

Nina blew the bangs out of her eyes. She suddenly realized that she had forgotten to push the child-lock button on the backseat windows of the car, and Jake had already wrestled Plum's favorite Diva Starz from her with the aim of tossing it out onto the Pacific Coast Highway and causing a three-car pile-up. "Taurus," she answered. As if *that* mattered. "It won't affect your plans for the teff, will it?"

Slinky blinked twice. Obviously, it did matter, because she said with all seriousness, "Maybe. That depends."

"On what?"

"On why he left it on the counter in the first place." She let her leg snake vertically up the wall. Giving Nina the once-over, she added: "Believe me, if Saturn weren't in retrograde, I *wouldn't* be worried. *At all.*"

"Stop me if I'm wrong, but the fact that you brought it up in the first place makes Saturn's orbit immaterial, doesn't it?"

That notion suddenly made Slinky uncomfortable. With a barely civil nod, she snatched the plastic bag of teff out of Nina's hand and shut the door.

By the time Nina reached the car, Plum's Diva Starz pop tartlet had already been flattened by southbound traffic. *Great*, thought Nina. That little problem could be easily rectified with a stop at the closest Toys "R" Us, but she knew that doing so meant being bombarded with cries of "Buy me! Buy me!" from both Plum—a child who had yet to learn the meaning of the word no—and Jake, who, when the situation merited it, could be the perfect mimic.

Considering the day she was having, Nina couldn't endure that.

Instead she endured Plum's high-pitched howls of mourning until the kids were shuttled inside the Hartes' third-story apartment.

It was only after Jake and Plum had loaded up on Cap'n Crunch—her son's usual after-school treat—and were jumping off his tiny, messy bedroom's walls by using his bed's very thin, very cheap Sleep Train mattress as a trampoline, that Nina realized she had forgotten Becca's grocery order. The afternoon's only saving grace was that Ylva showed up not just one hour later but two, giving Nina enough time to swing back by Tommaso's for the groceries, and for precious Plum to crash from her sugar high.

4

The After-Party

By the time Sam had arrived at the Chateau Marmont for the after-party celebrating Hugo's latest film, *Very Bad Boys*, the booze was flowing as freely as the hyperbole coming from the mouths of all in attendance. From what Sam could hear, everyone was in development (as opposed to Development Hell); So-and-So was just a *dream* to work with (not, as had been previously reported in Page Six or Ted Casablanca's "Awful Truth" column or Defamer.com, an unparalleled bitch/raving lunatic/burned-out druggie); and everyone agreed that Hugo's latest film was "another winner from a true artist with a unique idiosyncratic vision . . ."

"Who do these fuckheads think they're kidding?" Hugo growled as he waved Sam over to the barstool beside him, then downed another Dewar's on the rocks. "They wouldn't know a hit if it bit them on the ass. These clowns are all here for whatever poontang they can scrape up for later tonight, not for my movie. Besides, by Monday, when the box office numbers are in, they'll all be back to calling me a has-been."

Because the bar's lounge was small, the crowd had naturally flowed into the restaurant and out by the pool on the terrace, which was why Hugo always chose the Marmont for his after-parties in the first place: It was a great place to hide in plain sight while he drank away his angst, ogled the glamorous women hovering about, and most importantly, avoided his constantly hovering wife, Lucinda . . .

Particularly when he had a reason to avoid her.

That reason being his infatuation with a phantom.

O.

"You know, Hugo, this bar is your purgatory. You sit right there on that same stool after every premiere and whine that same tune." Sam signaled the bartender that he'd have the same as his soused host. "Face it. You love what you do, and your public loves *you.*" Taking the glass placed before him, Sam tipped it in honor of Hugo and gulped it down.

"What good is that, if . . ." Hugo's voice trailed off.

"If what?" asked Sam.

"If you can't share it with someone you really love?"

Oh, shit! thought Sam. *This infatuation is worse than I thought.*

Still, he wasn't ready to turn over that Ben Franklin to Lucinda without first putting up a good fight.

Sam signaled the bartender for another. Grabbing the glass offered, he motioned for the director to follow him out into the Marmont's less crowded terrace.

It was a smart maneuver. Out by the pool the crowd was thinner and definitely choicer: A coterie of starlets had set up camp by the outdoor bartender, who was making appletinis by the pitcher full. Still, there was less of a chance that anyone could overhear what Sam had to say to Hugo:

That he had to drop a certain husky-voiced siren, appropriately nicknamed O because apparently she was quite an operator. At least she most *certainly* had Hugo's number—to the tune of some three thousand dollars a month.

And, oh, by the way, Lucinda and her accountants weren't very happy about that at all, either, Sam informed his friend.

Hugo frowned. "Jeez, Lucinda . . . *knows*? I spent . . . *how much*? I . . . I guess I lost count."

Sam gave a low whistle. "Hell, Hugo, I think this O character is making almost as much off of you as *I* did last year. She must have quite some, um, *technique*."

"Yeah, I'll admit it she's got quite a turn with a phrase . . . and that voice of hers . . . it's . . . so . . . Jeez, Sam, I've never heard anyone like her!" He turned to face Sam, head held high. "But I don't care. It was worth every penny."

Sam put a cube of ice in his mouth and sucked on it. He wanted another drink, but the outdoor bartender was still grandstanding for his very giggly, very appreciative audience, and Sam didn't want to wait in line.

What was that dude mixing those drinks with anyway, Manolo Blahnik stilettos?

"Look, Hugo, I think you should own up to the fact that you're getting somewhat carried away with this 'hobby.' No big deal. Hell, every third guy in this town has some PSO on speed dial. But still, it's got to mean something to you that you're breaking Lucinda's heart—"

Tears welled up in Hugo's eyes. "Of course I . . . I never

meant to hurt her. *I love her*. It's just that . . . well—I can't give up O! I just *can't*!" Hugo's frantic whispers were turning some heads now.

Sam put a hand on Hugo's arm, to warn him to lower his voice. Hugo took a deep breath, but his still adamant tone was proof that Sam wasn't changing his mind. "You don't get it, Sam. It's . . . it's more than just the dirty talk. I mean sure, she allows me to . . . to fantasize. But also, she . . . she actually *listens* to me. She's the only woman who knows the *real* me—without *really knowing* me, Sam!"

"I don't get it."

"She doesn't know that . . . that I'm *Hugo Schmitt*." He whispered this, as if he were afraid that even saying it out loud would change that.

And change how O felt about him.

Sam laughed out loud. "For sure, *that* would make a difference. For one thing, her rates would go up."

Pained at Sam's reaction, Hugo muttered, "There's nothing funny about this! Hell, I thought that, at the very least, *you* would understand."

"Let me tell you what I do understand." It was Sam's turn to get serious. "I understand that Lucinda is on the war path. And I understand that if she tells Archie how much you've spent on this—this little 'addiction' of yours, he'll pull the plug on Flagrant Films. Hugo, if he's vindictive enough, we may be talking *jail time* here! The world as you know it will blow up in your face, all because some certainly-too-ugly-to-be-a-real-hooker chick has a voice that gives you a hard-on!"

He moved in close so that only Hugo would hear him, and there'd be no mistaking his point. "Hell, Hugo, you haven't even *humped* her! That ain't the Hugo Schmitt *I* know." He took another gulp of melting ice. "Hey, has it even occurred to you that instead of yapping O's ear off almost every night, you could just hire her as your 'assistant' and bang her legitimately?"

At least it would be legitimate by Hollywood standards.

"Sam, I'll be honest with you: I haven't banged *anyone* since I met her. Not even Lucinda. I guess I feel that would be . . . well, *unfaithful* . . . to O."

Sam choked on his ice cube. "Shit, man! No *wonder* Lucinda's pissed. You're—you're not just obsessed, *you're in love!* And it's not just with a piece of ass. It's with *a voice*—which is probably attached to a face that might make you scream if you woke up beside it! You're about to blow your meal ticket, Hugo! Not to mention, you're also losing the one woman who will ever love your sorry ass unconditionally. Hell, do you know how lucky you are? And need I remind you that *I* was the one who set you two up in the first place?"

No doubt about it, it was truly a match made in heaven: Hugo was a creative genius; Lucinda was a trust fund baby looking to be a muse to a creative genius; and Archie, grateful that she'd chosen a guy in the town who was admired despite the fact that his projects would never be blockbusters like the teen gross-out flicks and the end-of-the-world special effects extravaganzas Archie typically produced. However, Hugo's "artsy-fartsy pictures," as he called them, were always up for Academy Awards, which was why Archie was more than willing to finance his son-in-law.

As the cold, hard clarity of the situation hit him, Hugo's eyes suddenly got big.

"You're—you're right. I can't blow this!" He clutched Sam by the elbow of his Piatelli. "You—you've gotta *help* me, Sam! Before . . . before I chuck it all away!'

Sam had never seen his buddy this desperate—another reason for needing that damn Scotch. But still there was no break in the drink line. If anything, the all-female crowd around the bar had gotten even thicker.

Hell, thought Sam, you'd think that bartender was giving away Victoria's Secret V-string panties or something with each drink . . .

Shit, what a great promotion *that* would be! He'd mention it to Fiona, the publicist on Katerina and Hugo's upcoming project. Suddenly remembering his promise to Kat, Sam groaned out loud. If Lucinda and Archie pulled the plug on Hugo, that project would go in the crapper, too.

He'd have to move fast.

"Look, Hugo, I've got a new client who I think would be perfect for the Kat project."

"I've decided to go with Brad. I think they'll be a good fit."

"Trust me, this guy runs rings around Brad. He really knows how to make love to the camera."

"How green is he?"

"Well, that's the problem. He's . . . he's only done a couple of indies."

"Anything I've seen?"

"Probably not."

"What, are you jerking me off? Put some newbie opposite Kat? Hell, she'd eat him up alive."

It was on the tip of his tongue to say that yes, that was what she had in mind, but Sam thought better of it. "Dude, you've got to trust me on this one. I've got a good gut instinct about Nathan Harte."

"Well, at least his name sounds like a winner. If he doesn't do anything stupid like shorten it, so that it doesn't sound like a Hollywood nursery rhyme: Brad Pitt, Tom Cruise, Jude Law . . ." Hugo's sense of humor had returned somewhat. "Look, tell you what: I'll pass on Brad—for Nathan—if you save my ass on this . . . this *other* thing. Otherwise, the picture doesn't get made anyway, with *anyone*. Heck, Archie pulls out, and we can put Smarty Jones up there with Kat for that matter, right?"

Considering the horse's stud potential, she'd probably like that too much, thought Sam, although he didn't say it out loud.

"Don't worry, I'll take care of your little problem with Lucinda. But that means no more calls to this O person, Hugo."

"No, no, no, Sam, I can't do that!" Hugo started to hyperventilate. "I can keep it on the sly, believe me, I can! But I just can't go . . . *cold turkey*." His shoulders slumped as he leaned up against his friend, his agent, his protector.

As he patted Hugo sympathetically on the back, Sam noticed that the crowd around the bar had finally cleared a bit, affording him a glimpse of the Lothario behind the counter, and yep, certainly he could see why the ladies were flitting about.

In fact, the dude looked familiar . . .

Sam shrugged off the inclination to remember who/what/when/how, and focused on reading Hugo the riot act instead.

"You can't chance another call, Hugo! What Lucinda wants is golden, and that's all there is to it. Hell, go to a strip club every now and then. Or buy some Viagra and some Femprox and some sex toys, and take Lucinda to some island paradise! We're talking about your *career* here, guy."

Hugo got it. Sam knew this because Hugo slipped him a business card before stumbling back into the bar.

On it was written the letter O and a telephone number.

Sam would call her later that night.

Then Hugo's problem would be solved.

He stared back over at the bartender. Suddenly he realized where he'd seen that face before . . .

Just that afternoon, in his office, in fact.

It was Nathan Harte, the man of the hour.

And now here he was standing right there in front of Sam: shucking and jiving for tips from tipsy pop tarts.

Well, Mr. Harte, your luck is about to change.

"I know you." Sam swapped the Dewar's the bartender had left for him on the counter with a ten-dollar bill.

"Probably not. I don't swing that way." The kid—he was maybe a few years younger than Sam, what, maybe about twenty-four, twenty-five, right?—nodded appreciatively if apologetically as he scooped it up and put it in his breast pocket. To make sure he'd made his point with Sam, though, he shot a dazzling dimpled smile at a sitcom actress who had apparently taken up shop permanently on one side of the bar. She preened appreciatively and matched Sam's tip with a twenty-dollar bill—*and* her phone number on a slip of paper.

At the inference, Sam turned a subtle shade of red.

Smart-ass kid. What, do I look like a fag?

Right then and there, Sam made up his mind to never wear the Piatelli again.

Ignoring Nathan now, he turned his attentions to Ms. Sitcom. Handing her his business card, he went in for the kill. "Hi. Sabrina, isn't it? Thought I recognized you, but you probably don't remember me. I'm Sam Godwin, with ICA. You're with . . . let me see . . . William Morris, right?"

As her jaw dropped, her chest shot forward suggestively. Hell yeah, darn tootin' she remembered him! And she was flattered he remembered her (despite the fact he'd passed on rep'ing her, what, about a year ago, before she lucked out with that pilot? And, admittedly, the pilot's director, too). Yeah, unfortunately, she *was* still at William Morris, but you know how *that* is: They sit on their laurels, take you for granted, never take you to the next level, yada yada yada . . .

Sam glanced over at the kid to see if he was taking this all in: her deference to Sam, her fawning adoration of him, the way she was practically creaming her jeans at the thought of working with him . . .

Yeah, the kid got it all right. Sam could tell by the hungry look in Nathan Harte's heartbreakingly soulful eyes. A look that said, *I want in. I can play this game too.*

As the girl finally shimmied off to find her posse, Nathan stammered, "Gee, sorry, Mr. Godwin . . . I didn't *know* . . . I didn't mean anything by—"

Sam held out his hand to shake. "No hard feelings. A pretty boy like you must get that all the time, huh?"

"Yeah, I do get hit on a lot. Girls *and* guys. Don't mind the ladies"—he winked at two who were worshipping him from across the pool—"but it still bugs me when a guy does it. And every other guy in the town seems to be light in his loafers, know what I mean? But I keep it polite, 'cause you never know how big a player he may be."

Translation: *Mea culpa, mea culpa, mea culpa. Just tell me where to pucker up, and* I'm there . . . *figuratively if not literally* . . .

He shot Sam a contrite smile, all pearly white. "So, you mentioned you'd, uh, seen me somewhere?"

"Yes. In fact, I have your reel sitting on my desk now. It's quite impressive."

In shock and awe that anyone of Sam's caliber would actually say that to him, Nathan puffed up involuntarily.

Great ego reflexes, Sam thought. Good, 'cause he'll need them.

"In fact"—he pulled out another business card and handed it to the kid—"I'd like to represent you. That is, if you don't already have representation."

"No! I mean—"

The kid didn't know *what* he meant, only what his brain was trying to tell him: that one of Hollywood's most revered agents was asking him, Nathan Harte, if he wanted to be part of his star-filled roster!

"—not at this time . . . Jeez, if I did, why would I be standing *here?*" He pointed to his station behind the bar.

"Nathan, you'd be surprised how many actors have agents and are *still* standing there." He smiled knowingly. "But I'm going to make sure you'll do better than that. Just come by tomorrow . . . say, five-thirty? And we'll talk."

As he walked away, he could hear Nathan closing up his station. In the kid's mind, he was already out from behind that bar.

And in front of the cameras.

*   *   *

By the time Sam got home, Chastity had worked herself up into a very un-Zen-like lather.

Over Sam forgetting her teff.

And for *conveniently* forgetting to mention Hugo's party to her.

And for his obvious attraction to "some little clerk from Tommaso's."

He didn't know how she figured all that out, but certainly it opened the door for him to lay it on the line:

That he had felt that they were growing apart for a very long time now. That he cared deeply for her, and always appreciated how she gave 1000 percent of herself to every endeavor, *especially to him*. But in truth, he asked, was that fair to *her?* No, of course not, he answered for her, before she'd had a chance to open her mouth. Not if *he* couldn't give her 1000 percent of himself, too.

And that's just it: *He couldn't*. And she didn't deserve any less . . .

This exact spiel had always worked magic with previous girlfriends—and, ironically, with a few deadbeat clients too. He held his breath for her reaction.

He didn't have to wait long. Tearfully, she looked him in the eye, threw the bag of teff at him, and slammed the door behind her.

Before Sam could find a broom, Towser had lapped up all the tiny purple pellets that had spilled all over the kitchen floor.

Great! Just great, thought Sam. As if his day hadn't been bad enough, the teff ensured that the evening would end—*literally*—on a crappy note.

And he *still* had to read that O person the riot act.

He picked up the dog's leash and herded Towser out the door, just in the nick of time.

Nathan burst through the front door as if he were on fire. But before Nina could open her mouth to tell him the exciting news about having given Sam his reel, Nathan informed her that he'd just met with Sam Godwin of ICA *not even an hour ago.*

"See, hon? Mailing out all those DVDs finally paid off. He wants to represent me!"

Nathan picked her up and swung her around, dipped her into a kiss. "Wow, I can't believe he actually recognized me, you know, behind the bar and all . . . although *that* was sort of embarrassing."

It would have been more embarrassing if Sam had seen Nathan in his Disneyland costume, thought Nina, but she didn't say that. Instead she wrapped herself in his arms and laughed. "Don't be. All of this was meant to happen. Oh, Nathan, I'm *so* proud of you."

She didn't have the heart to tell him that the contact had initially been made by her.

What difference would that have made, anyway? Sam Godwin had seen Nathan's reel out of the goodness of his heart, not because of anything *she* had said or done.

Gosh, it was nice to finally meet someone in this town who didn't have an ulterior motive!

5

The Proposition

Sam's conversation with O did not go exactly the way he had hoped, and for the life of him, he couldn't figure out why not.

He'd had the foresight to tape it, and he was glad he had, for a couple of reasons. First off, it might come in handy legally. Second, he had to admit that, like Hugo, he found himself intrigued with O's sultry voice, even more so each time he played it to himself:

SAM: (*In a very businesslike, take-no-prisoners tone*) Hello. I'm talking to O, I presume?

O: (*With a soft, tinkling laugh*) I can be anyone you want, lover . . . You don't mind if I call you lover, do you? I don't think you mentioned *your* name.

SAM: (*Pauses to consider the consequence of the nickname "lover." Because he remembers that he's taping the conversation, he thinks better of this.*) My name is—is Sam. I'm calling about a friend of mine. You know him as . . . Wilbur.

O: Ahhhhh . . . *Love* Wilbur. He knows just what to say to a woman to . . . well, get her all *hot* . . . and bothered . . . I'll just bet you do, too, Sam.

SAM: Uh, what? What's that?

O: (*Softly, achingly*) I said I can imagine you know how to make a woman . . . *come*.

SAM: (*After a long pause*) To tell you the truth, O, I don't want to talk about me. I'd prefer to talk about you and Wilbur.

O: Right, gotcha. You want me to tell you what we talk about . . . You want to know what words make him hard . . . and long . . . and hot as he imagines me there, beside him . . . aching for him—

SAM: (*Somewhat desperately*) No! I mean—what I'm trying to say is that I don't want you to take his calls. *Ever.*

O: (*Sighing*) Sam, darling, you really don't have to be jealous. From what Wilbur tells me, there's enough of him to go around for the both of us—

SAM: You think that I—that I . . . ? Listen, *babe*, you've got it *all wrong!* Hugo—I mean *Wilbur* and I aren't *lovers.* We're *buds!* And that's *all.* Just two guys who *love* the ladies.

O: I get it, Sam. So, what you're telling me is that you want *me* all to yourself. Right?

SAM: Uh . . . *me?* Why would I . . . No, sorry, hon, I like my women in the flesh.

O: *Ohhhh* . . . Fleshy women, huh?

SAM: Heck, no, I'm not talking about *looks.* If you must know, I prefer women that actually have something to say. Looks—particularly in this town—are a dime a dozen.

O: (*Laughing heartily*) Or as John Donne put it, "Love built on beauty, soon as beauty, dies."

SAM: That's . . . truly moving. I would never have suspected that—well, you know—

O: What, that I'd have heard of John Donne?

SAM: Well, not that you'd *heard* of him, per se, but that you'd be quoting him . . . you know, *here* . . . But—but that's beside the point! Look, O, obviously I haven't made myself clear. I'm really not calling to talk about me . . . Or you, for that matter, but Wilbur. Specifically, I need you to . . . to leave Wilbur alone.

O: Sam, you're right. There is certainly something being lost in translation here. Like why you should even care about my relationship with Wilbur in the first place.

SAM: (*Now it is his turn to laugh . . . derisively*) Jeez, I wouldn't think you could call what the two of you share a "relationship" exactly. He's just playing out some sick fantasy. Heck, you two could meet face to face, and that might kill it then and there, right? In fact, here's a quote for *you*, O: "Love is the delightful interval between meeting a beautiful girl and discovering that she looks like a haddock." John Barrymore. And *that* dude knew a thing or two about beautiful women.

O: (*In a sultry murmur*) Touché, Sam, touché. Now, are you sure you're not talking about yourself there?

SAM: What do you mean?

O: Well, maybe it's you who's attracted only to a woman's looks, because it's certainly not Wilbur. I'm proof of that, right? I mean, Wilbur—just like you, 'cause you're such a *player* and all—is surrounded by beautiful women all day long . . . And yet, each night, he calls *me* . . . whom he's never seen, never even plans on meeting . . . just for the witty repartee, or *whatever*. Go figure. You know, Sam, if you were to ask me, I'd say that Wilbur's thoughts on that subject run akin to Baudeliere's: "There are as many kinds of beauty as there are habitual ways of seeking happiness." Don't you agree?

SAM: (*After a moment of thoughtful silence*) Touché to you, O . . . So where does that leave us? How do I keep you from taking his calls?

O: Last I looked, Sam, it's still a free country. As long as Wilbur hasn't lost my number, he can call it at any time, and there's nothing you can do about it.

SAM: I'll make a deal with you: I'll pay you *not* to take his call. How's that?

O: (*Laughing incredulously*) Oh yeah? . . . And how will you do *that*?

SAM: Anyway you'd like it. If you want, I'll pay you in cash. In fact, go ahead and double your rate. I'll even put you on a retainer, whatever.

O: (*After a moment*) I think you've got it all wrong.

SAM: Whattaya mean? I said you can name your price! Hey, this is a once-in-a-lifetime offer that will be withdrawn at the end of this call, so, if I were you, I'd jump at it.

O: No, lover, *you're not hearing me*: I want to know what's *really* at stake here. Because any deal we make has got to be worth something to *both* of us.

SAM: Jeez, woman, don't be greedy, or this doesn't work for *either* of us. And by the way, I got your number from Hu—from Wilbur, so trust me when I say he's in on this and wants to break off this . . . this little addiction as badly as I need—*want* him to.

O: Level with me, Sam: Why do you *really* care?

SAM: (*Pauses. Then, in a voice that lets her know that all cards are truly on the table*) Because he's my oldest and dearest friend. Because the life he's built for himself is about to go up in smoke. Because if he screws it up, he doesn't just screw it up for himself, but for a whole lot of people who count on him for their livelihood.

O: (*After another very long pause, so long that Sam thinks they've been disconnected*) Okay, Sam. Under one condition.

SAM: Name it.

O: You tell me his real name.

SAM: That's it? No retainer, no cash, no nothing?

O: That's it.

SAM: How do I know you won't blackmail him if I tell you?

O: I don't want a last name, just his first name. But *no lies.* That's how this works. And this is a once-in-a-lifetime offer that will be withdrawn at the end of this call, so, if I were you, I'd jump at it.

SAM: (*Laughing. Besides, what are the odds that she'd ever figure out who he really is?*) Okay, you sold me. It's . . . *Hugo.*

O: Well, that's . . . unusual. Almost as unusual as Wilbur.

SAM: So, we have a deal?

O: I always keep my word. But that won't necessarily solve your problem.

SAM: Uh . . . why? What do you mean?

O: So he doesn't call me. What makes you think he won't call someone else? There are a lot of us out there, you know.

SAM: Huh . . . Good point . . . I dunno, ya got me.

O: Can I make a suggestion? *Let him call.* I can put the charges on any card you want. Even yours. And because he's your client, too, you can always bill it back to him. You know, "photocopy" or "transcription charges," whatever will pass the Mr. Tax Man sniff test. Of course, you'll have to make it clear to him that my number is the *only* one he can call. Not that he'll mind, because I always make it worth his while . . .

SAM: (*Now wishing he hadn't recorded their conversation*) Hmm. Yeah. Okay, that might work.

O: You know, Sam, I can make it worth your while, too . . .

SAM: Sweetheart, you already have.

O: (*All husky musky nuance*) That's what I want to hear, lover, 'cause I aim to please. Oh, and by the way, we're talking about Hugo Schmitt, right? The director?

SAM: (*After a cold drop of sweat rolls down his spine*) I never . . . I never said that.

O: That's okay, Sam, you didn't have to. I've heard his voice on enough TV interviews to recognize it, now that I can put a name to the voice . . . God, he is a *genius!* What a master at pacing! I swear to you, I saw *Beyond Heavenly* at least four times.

SAM: Yeah, unfortunately, you and only six others. Thank God for overseas box office.

O: Yeah, I hear that in France they think he's a deity!

SAM: Right. *Viva la France.*

O: *Mais oui* . . .

SAM: So, um, how much do I owe you for this call?

O: We're at seventy even. Tell me, Sam, was it as good for you as it was for me?

Within the next twenty-four hours, Sam had accomplished the following:

First, he got Hugo to take Lucinda on a ten-day vacation to Las Ventanas al Paraíso, a secluded resort in Cabo San Lucas. Waiting there for them was a roaring fire, an open bottle of Veuve Clicquot La Grande Dame, a lovers' massage, a box of assorted sex toys (remnants from the not-so-dearly but definitely departed Chastity), a family-size tube of an orgasm cream sold only in Europe, and a ten-day supply of Viagra.

Sam's directive to Hugo was simple: "Don't come up for air."

Upon hearing this, Hugo got that strangled look on his face, as if he'd just been given a life sentence. Too bad. If Archie's accountants got hold of Hugo, he'd find out the hard way that Cabo was nothing like Pelican Bay State Prison.

Next, Sam met with Archie at the mogul's usual banquette in his favorite hangout, Dan Tana's, to get him onboard with the Hugo/Kat/Nathan project, which he sold to Archie as "*Sideways* meets *Before Sunset* . . . with the dark humor and the youthful *joi de vie* of *Garden State*."

At first Archie didn't get it. "*After the Sunset?* Wasn't that some lousy Pierce Brosnan crap?"

"No, no," answered Sam. "It was that French girl and Uma's ex talking each other to death, for six hours or something."

Now Archie remembered it. "That kid looked anorexic, or something. Hugo's not planning on hiring him, is he?"

"No. As a matter of fact, we've got some great new talent in mind. His name is Nathan Harte. We're putting him opposite Katerina McPherson."

"Works for me. She's got a great set of knockers. Not like that French girl."

"So, you're in?"

Archie paused, then shrugged. "Hugo's never been good business. But he's family."

Sam breathed a silent sigh of relief. *So Lucinda hasn't filled Archie in about the credit card charge. Praise the lord.*

"And who knows?" Archie continued, despite a mouthful of medium-rare prime rib. "Maybe this one will actually make money . . . Speaking of which, do you think you can talk her into doing a nude scene?"

"Nope, not even for a fifteen-million-dollar paycheck. She's a real *artiste*, that one."

"Thought not. Hey, no harm in asking."

Of course Sam picked up the tab.

And at five-thirty on the dot, Nathan showed up at ICA. With Nina.

Watching them together—her obvious love and pride in her husband, coupled with his transparent sense of ownership in her—made Sam's heart break just a little. She gave a deep laugh as Nathan, with a cocky flourish, signed his ICA contract. Looking up at Sam, she said as reverently as if she were in church, "*Thank you.*"

He smiled broadly and nodded, wondering if she'd feel that way in a month, when production on the project had started.

And Kat had begun her seduction of Nathan.

Nope, it dawned on Sam as Nathan shook his hand vigorously, *that's when she'll realize that she actually hates my guts.*

And for the first time in his life, he hated himself; particularly when Nina, before following Nathan out the door, impulsively kissed Sam on the cheek.

He did not look forward to going home alone that night.

In Hollywood, there is no such thing as an overnight success. Heck, the last five years of Nathan and Nina's lives were proof of that.

However, once a Hollywood hopeful (such as Nathan) got even an *inkling* that he was finally on his way to being made, naturally he presumed that success would make its move *fast*. *Very fast*.

Say, as fast as an industry player in the Skybar's rooftop pool lounge during last call on a Saturday night.

In their own ways, both Nina and Sam tried to warn Nathan that this might not be the case. Sam had a couple of auditions in mind, and of course things would come up periodically, but in the meantime Nathan should peruse the casting notices religiously for roles that he felt were right for him . . . so that he could go up against two hundred other guys who all felt exactly the same way.

The name of the game was to get out there and audition, audition, audition—for movies, TV, commercials, whatever.

"Hey, do you have a commercial agent?" asked Sam. "No? We have a division here in the agency that handles that. I'll line you up with Suzette over there . . . And maybe Kevin in the TV division, too . . . You know, for some immediate pocket change, like a movie of the week, or a guest shot on a *Law &*

Order or *CSI* or something, until this movie you're up for gets greenlighted. But that should happen any day now, so don't worry. And you're a shoo-in, believe me. I don't have to tell you, guy, but your future is in features all the way . . ."

Even if the film was greenlighted, and Nathan got cast in it, the paycheck wouldn't necessarily be more than a little above SAG scale, Sam warned him, but he'd negotiate a gross point or two, on the back end. After all, appearing in a Hugo Schmitt film was mostly about the prestige.

He also pointed out to Nathan that the average movie took at the minimum a year, maybe even two, from the first day of shooting until it hit the theaters. Even longer than that, if it was a dog that no one wanted to distribute. That said, Nathan's paycheck would be doled out piecemeal as well—that is, once his contract had been hashed out, renegotiated, double-checked, then approved by legal, yada, yada . . .

In other words, Nathan and Nina could be dining on mac-and-cheese for a *very* long time yet.

In the meantime, there was a lot the actor could do in preparation for when success inevitably found him—which, Sam assured him, was only a matter of time.

For Nathan, the prep work was the *easy* part. Already he was spending at least an hour or so a couple of times a week at the 24 Hour Fitness at the Arclight, where he could work on his pecs and at the same time make some much sought after industry contacts, albeit with more B- and C- than A-listers. Now he'd work out every day.

And he'd been taking lessons with his acting guru, the esteemed Euphegenia Du Barry, since he and Nina had landed Hollywood. But now that he had Sam Godwin, "Don of the

Dealmakers," (à la *Hollywood Reporter*) as his agent, he could ramp up those key activities to an almost-daily basis, too. In fact, he told Nina seriously, he should hire a private physical trainer, and work with Euphegenia in private, too: real proof that he'd arrived.

Sweet.

Of course, all of this would mean quitting his job at Disneyland.

Immediately he tossed out that concept to Nina. "What other client of Sam's works there?" Nathan pointed out. "*None.* You won't find real actors there. Besides, I have to keep myself available for any auditions Sam and his people set me up on, right?"

Nina saw his point. Then again, they still needed to come up with the money for all those extra acting lessons and gym workouts . . .

And for the upkeep on that cute little '61 Corvette roadster that Nathan bought on a whim the day after he'd signed his ICA contract, because, he insisted, it was one of the few used cars "hot enough to fit my new edgy image . . ." (That is, on the few occasions it wasn't sitting on a tow truck on its way to a mechanic's bay in San Dimas.)

All of this was exciting . . . and certainly *scary*.

Particularly the money part.

To make this gamble work, O would have to take on an extra shift or two.

Sensing her concern, Nathan added, "Don't worry honey. Sam thinks that the audition for that movie will happen sometime toward the end of next week, and the role is supposed to be big. *Really* big."

His eyes opened wide, as if to will Sam's declaration into fact, if only for her benefit. "He also says I'm exactly what the director is looking for. *To a Tee.* I'll ace it, too, since I've been preparing for it with Euphegenia. What's taking so long is that director is still locking in the final financing."

"After the audition, when will you know for sure that the role is yours?" she asked cautiously.

"Soon, hon. real soon. And once I get my fee, it's your turn up to bat. No more Tommaso's, on your feet all day. It'll be my turn to support *you.*" He pulled her down into his lap and gave her a long, loving kiss.

"That's good. I'm retiring O, too . . . just as soon as that check of yours clears the bank. *Yes!* I can't wait to quit! I've already checked into voice-over lessons, so that I can start auditioning for radio spots or cartoons. It's the perfect kind of freelance to do while Jake's at school." The worry left her eyes. She was all smiles again.

"Sure, whatever makes you happy, babe. We're Team Harte, remember? *All for one and one for all.*"

That was all she needed to hear.

And so Nina worked around the clock, for Nathan's extra acting lessons, his gym membership, his car's maintenance, and his new headshots.

Then again, she wasn't working just for him, but for *them.*

For Team Harte.

O: Hello, handsome. Boy have I missed *you.* So, how's my favorite guy?

WILBUR: O, darling . . . Jeez, I've missed you, too! I've been . . . well, out of the country.

O: Well, sweetheart, welcome home.

WILBUR: (*After a guilty silence*) Uh, well, you see, that's just it . . . I'm not home yet . . .

O: Oh . . . You're at work?

WILBUR: Sort of . . . I'm with my wife . . . in Cabo.

O: (*Laughing*) Gee, Wilbur, you lead a hard life . . . Speaking of *hard*, how's *that* going?

WILBUR: (*Frantically*) It's not! That's just the point! I . . . *I need your help.* Or else my life will go up in smoke. Didn't Sam explain?

O: Yep, he did. By the way, speaking of Sam, sorry but I've got to ask: Does this call have the Sam Good Housekeeping Seal of Approval?

WILBUR: Fucking A, this call has been preapproved and pre-billed on my very private preprogrammed "only to O" Platinum Moto, at that. In other words, the sky's the limit.

O: Good. Because I'd never want to get you in trouble, Wilbur, you *know* that, right?

WILBUR: I feel the same way about you, doll. Really, I do.

O: So, um, you say you're with your wife?

WILBUR: Yeah. And . . . truthfully? *It just ain't happening.* Get my meaning?

O: You're coming in loud and clear, Wilbur. So listen, I think I have an idea as to how we can be together . . . down there.

WILBUR: You're coming down? *Here?*

O: In a way. Try to follow me, Wilbur: If I were with you, right now, you'd be hard as a rock, right? You'd be running your hands gently all over my soft sweet body . . .

WILBUR: (*Blissfully*) Yeah . . . I see you now . . . I—I can feel you beside me.

O: Well, Wilbur, there's something I want you to do. Better yet, what I mean is that there's something I *don't* want you to do.

WILBUR: (*Confused*) What's that?

O: *Come* . . . that is, until you get back to your room . . . and your *wife.*

WILBUR: But that's just it! I can come with you. I just can't with *her.*

O: *Yes you can,* Wilbur. If you just do as I tell you. And here's what I want you to do: I want you to buy a couple of silk scarves at the hotel gift shop and take them back to your room with you. Then I want you to ask your wife to allow you to blindfold her—and make love to her. Ask her to blindfold you, too.

WILBUR: That sounds . . . sort of kinky.

O: (*Giggles devilishly*) I know, Wilbur. Isn't it? And it makes it perfect for me . . . *to be with you.*

WILBUR: How do you mean?

O: Well, while you're both blindfolded, you can *imagine that I'm there*, beside you. You can kiss her, gently . . . on the lips, then down her neck, softly moving to her right nipple and taking it in your mouth . . . and sucking, sucking *hard . . . harder . . .* until it *explodes* at the touch of your tongue. Then you'll move to her left nipple, licking it voraciously, awakening it, too . . . while your hands gently explore every square inch of her soft, supple skin. Prodding every nook and cranny of her with your fingers, until she is wet, and *throbbing* and *hot*, and moaning *for you to come inside of her* . . .

WILBUR: She'll . . . be moaning?

O: Oh, Wilbur, yes! *YES!* She—she'll *come!* Again . . . and again . . . *and again* . . . with you! With you thrusting into her, harder, never stopping . . . never . . .

WILBUR: I . . . I have to go back! To the hotel, right now!

O: (*Softly, joyously*) You do that, Wilbur. You do that. Oh, and Wilbur?

WILBUR: (*A bit distractedly*) Yeah, O?

O: Listen, Wilbur, from now on, do me a favor. I'd like you to call her O, too, okay?

WILBUR: Sure, O . . . I . . . I guess. If that will make you happy.

O: It does. Oh, and Hugo, ask *her* to call you Wilbur. Tell her that those are your new secret nicknames for each other, which you're to use only when you're making love. Get it?

WILBUR: (*In awe*) That is *truly inspired.*

O: I knew you'd think so. Now go have *fun,* you naughty boy.

That very afternoon, Archie called Sam to say that he was doubling the budget for the Katerina Project.

Oh, and that Lucinda and Hugo were extending their vacation another ten days.

Maybe I didn't need to give O my card in the first place, thought Sam. *Maybe all Hugo needed was a few odds and ends from the International Love Boutique.*

Go figure.

He called Nathan and Nina's house to let them know that the audition was finally set for eleven days from then.

On the day of Nathan's audition, Nina was calm and peaceful. She *knew* how good Nathan was. And she knew he was prepared to give a very electrifying read of a very moving scene, as requested by the director, from the movie's script, because they'd rehearsed it for hours on end, every day for at least a week prior to when the audition was finally scheduled.

They had spent the morning having über-fabulous sex, if she did say so herself. The sex they shared always burned white hot, as if they provided each other with the fuel they both needed to keep going—to keep *believing*—in themselves.

She was right. Nathan was primed, pumped, and chomping at the bit to prove himself as an actor of incredible potential.

And if the lovemaking hadn't done the trick, perhaps the Rescue Heroes Mission Car Jake put in his daddy's jacket pocket as a good luck talisman would.

"Go get 'em, tiger," she purred out to him as he left her tangled in the bedsheets while he showered off.

Of course Nina wouldn't be there to cue him during the audition, and that sort of bothered her.

"I guess they'll just have some assistant reading the other part," she fretted.

"Yeah, probably," said Nathan breezily. He approached every nerve-wracking challenge as if he'd already won it. That arrogance was part of his charm. "Hell, it can be a stuntman for all I care. Sam didn't say, but I'm guessing that it'll probably be an assistant casting person."

The reason Sam didn't say was that Katerina was going to read with Nathan herself.

Sam had thought about that one long and hard: Should he suggest that Nina be there, just so that Nathan wouldn't be put in a very uncomfortable position right off the bat?

What, *was he kidding himself?* From what he saw of Nathan, the kid would enjoy whatever Kat threw his way.

The only one who would be uncomfortable would be Nina. He could never do that to her.

No, if the kid was going to have his fall from grace, there was nothing Sam could do about it now.

Or ever, for that matter.

TRANSCRIPT OF NATHAN HARTE AUDITION TAPE
[1/30/2XXX]

(INT. FLAGRANT STUDIOS—DAY)
(FADE IN ON: TWO EMPTY STOOLS, sitting in the center of the room.)
SFX a COUGH from the cameraman, FRED, who is fiddling with the camera).

Voice Over of NATHAN: Hi, um, I'm Nathan Harte . . . Gee, Mr. Schmitt, I have to tell you that it's an HONOR—

V/O HUGO: Yeah, hi, Nathan. Looking forward to seeing if you can live up to Sam's assessment.

V/O NATHAN: *(Gives a nervous cough)* I'll, uh, do my best . . . So where would you like me to—

V/O HUGO: Take a seat on the stool there . . .

NATHAN HARTE *(Comes into the frame, holding his script. He sits gingerly on the stool.)*

V/O HUGO: Hey, uh, Frank, can you move in some? Edie, can you adjust that backlight?

(CLOSE-UP on Nathan. The camera goes in and out of focus as it adjusts for clarity, and the room seems to go a bit lighter as a halo envelopes Nathan, who looks right into the camera's eye, smiles broadly and winks at it before running his hand through his hair and giving his head a toss.)

NATHAN: *(Clears his throat)* Um . . . There was that scene that Sam mentioned . . . Unless you'd prefer for me to do a cold reading—

V/O HUGO: Nah . . . we wouldn't do that to you . . . We'll stick with the scene we discussed with Sam. Speaking of which, uh, you wouldn't mind reading with the film's female lead, would you?

NATHAN: (*Sitting up a little straighter now*) Heck, no. I think I can do that, no prob.

V/O HUGO: (*Chuckling*) Yeah sure, okay . . . Edie, darling, can you let Ms. McPherson know that we're ready anytime she is? Thanks.

(*At first, it seems that Nathan is drawing a blank. Then, as the name registers, his mouth drops open a bit. He smiles to himself, and he nods his head in wonder. It's obvious that he thinks he's won the jackpot.*)

(*WIDER ANGLE as KATERINA McPHERSON leisurely saunters into view. Nathan jumps off the stool to shake her hand. She smiles up at him before taking his hand in hers, then pulls him in close to her as she gives a soft approving laugh. This makes him blush.*)

KATERINA: Nathan . . . *well* . . . I've been looking forward to meeting you. You know, I saw your reel—

NATHAN: (*In shock and awe*) Ms. McPherson, *wow* . . . Gee! I'm— I'm *speechless* . . .

KATERINA: (*Feigning modesty*) What? Did Sam not tell you I was going to read with you? (*She gives another knowing chuckle*) He's . . . he's such a *naughty boy*, that Sam. I, uh, hope that won't throw you . . . or anything?

NATHAN: What? *NO!* No, not at all . . . I'm just so . . . *honored.* (*He now looks off camera, at Hugo*) Um, Mr. Schmitt, just . . . whenever you say go . . .

V/O HUGO: Great . . . uh, how about picking it up on page 43? Nathan, feel free to build the kind of tension you think is necessary for this scene, and Katerina will follow your lead, okay? . . . Great. Frank, can you cue the scene?

V/O FRANK: (*FX of a series of BEEPS and there is a flash of LIGHT, indicating that the scene is starting.*) Nathan Harte audition, take one.

KATERINA: (*Looking off-camera, at Hugo*) Um . . . Sorry, Hugo, darling, I . . . I was just wondering . . . Before we start, would you mind if . . . if Nathan and I could just take a moment and . . . well, I know this sounds *odd*, but . . . can we *kiss* first?

V/O HUGO: (*Confused*) *Kiss?* Hmmm . . . Well . . . uh . . . That's not in the *scene* . . .

KATERINA: I know, my darling Hugo . . . It's just that—well, I'm going on my gut here— (*She takes a single finger, and lays it on her bosom, then lets it travel slowly, achingly down her well-defined abdomen, to just above her exposed belly button. Nathan seems somewhat fixated by this.*) —But I think that our doing so might . . . you know, take the edge off of Nathan's audition. I mean, I want Nathan to see that—(*With a sweet giggle*)—that I'm only human . . . Just like the girl next door, right? Is—is that okay? *You* wouldn't mind, would you, Nathan?

NATHAN: (*Still in shock*) Um . . . *no!* Not at *all.*

V/O HUGO: Uh . . . (*Hesitantly*) Sure, yeah, okay . . . I mean, heck, the script has a couple of sex scenes in it anyway. Might as well see if there's, um, any chemistry, right?

KATERINA: (*Looking Nathan right in the eye*) *Ummm.* Yeah. Chemistry. I'm guessing we'll have no problem there. Right, Nathan?

(*Nathan blushes, nods slowly. The look on his face says, "What, is this a dream or something?"*)

V/O HUGO: Okay . . . well, the camera *is* rolling . . . *So—*

(*Katerina puts a hand on Nathan's face. He turns his head to kiss it, gently. With just the slightest hesitation, he pulls her closer to kiss her face, too. She melts into him, her hands playing him as if she was Lara St. John and he was a brand-new Stradivarius. At first he freezes. But then, slowly, he reciprocates, his hands roaming her body as if he were a blind man reading Braille.*)

(*TIGHTER ANGLE as the kiss lingers on . . . and on . . .*)

V/O HUGO: Well . . . *that* certainly seems to work . . . Gee. Okay, now . . . Cut.

(*There is no response to his direction. The camera lingers . . . and lingers . . .*)

V/O HUGO: I said, *cut!* . . . Frank, you can turn off the goddamn camera now . . . *Frank!*

(*CAMERA OUT*)

*   *   *

Here is what Nathan told Nina about the audition:

Yes, Sam was right, the part was his for the asking. Go figure!

And that he couldn't believe his very first movie would be directed by the esteemed Hugo Schmitt, a director whose technique she'd been raving about even back when they were in high school. When he heard Nina's gasp, he just presumed she was as amazed as he was over this unexpected twist of fate.

Oh, and by the way, guess who he'd be starring opposite? Could she believe *Katerina McPherson?* "She stopped by during the audition . . . and read with me." He threw it out there cautiously.

He didn't mention the kiss. *Hell, no. No way.*

Because he knew how she'd react: first with surprise, then shock, and finally hurt.

And then she'd ask him if he had liked it.

And even if he said, "No! Of course not," Nina would know he was lying.

So he kept it to himself.

"Omigod! That must have been—awesome!" murmured Nina. "Wow, I can *totally* see her in that role . . ."

Nathan watched her face for any signs of concern, or jealousy . . . but only saw her joy for him. Which only made him feel guiltier than ever.

And which was why he took her in his arms and kissed her . . . hard . . . then he took her in the bedroom and made love to her . . . longingly . . .

. . . and all the while, he hated himself for imagining that he was making love to Katerina McPherson.

Afterward, as they lay in each other's arms, Nina mused out loud, "So is she nice? Gee, I can't *wait* to meet her!"

!!!ADORABLE ALERT!!!

It's not every day I sound an Adorable Alert, my righteous readers, which is why this little tidbit gets CAPPED AND BOLDED,
so pay attention! Rumor has it that a new hunka burnin' love is
roaming the halls of this adult high school we call Hollywood.
Apparently he's not only handsome, but has the chops to "go the
distance" . . . Ummm, don'tcha just love the sound of that? So
look for this New Man on Campus on a big screen near you . . .
and the bigger the better, ladies, in order to see what (er) "assets"
he has that have got everyone going gaga . . .

Baxter Quinn's Hollywood Exxxposé, 1/30

6

The Seduction

"Wow, what a stud. Too bad his headshots suck."

Because the criticism came from Fiona Truman—the head partner of Truman, Lyle, & Callahan Public Relations, which now could proudly claim Nathan Harte, the stud in question, as a new client—Sam fully anticipated that this minor issue would be resolved in a matter of days.

Sam knew better than to argue with her. Instead he stared down at the black and white photos of Nathan that Fiona was perusing with a photographer's loupe and sighed. Of course, Nathan would be disappointed that the photos wouldn't be used, particularly since they were brand new. Well, too bad. Fiona's recommendations were golden: no ifs, ands, or buts. And although Fiona ostensibly answered to Nathan (and not the other way around), in reality, her marching orders were set by Sam in a weekly meeting Sam had with Fiona every Tuesday morning to run down the publicity agenda of all his clients who were handled by TLC.

And Sam's orders for Fiona were, quite simply, to do everything in her power to make Nathan a star, now that *Forever and Again* had been greenlighted. Filming had begun over a week ago, to accommodate a six-week window in Katerina's jam-packed schedule. If they had waited any longer, her next available shooting date would have been years off, and by then, Katerina would have been too old for the lead role, anyway: that of an innocent albeit nubile college freshman.

Not that she'd ever admit to *that*.

"Yeah, well, I'm not surprised you think they're crap. Nathan told me—quite proudly, I might add—that he got them done for only fifty bucks."

"Yikes! Well then, if that's the case, then frankly, I think the poor guy got ripped off." She crumpled them up, one by one, and tossed them into the conference room trash can.

Sam got the message. "Right. Okay, so, let's get them re-done. Whom would you suggest?"

"Let me see if Jack Guy can squeeze him in sometime this week. If not, I'll get James White to do it. Either way, I'll have some stock cover poses shot at the same time. You know, for the second-tier mags, general editorial purposes, fan club blogs, and so on. Already the tom-toms are beating about him. Did you see Baxter's column this morning?" She tossed her auburn curls, a habit Sam had come to recognize as her way of making mental notes.

"Sure did. Great work, Fiona. So, what's your take on Nathan's overall look?"

"Well, we've certainly got a lot here to work with. He's got fab cheekbones. Those soulful eyes should definitely melt a few hearts. Um . . . a little shaggy in the brow area, but we can work on that . . . although it hasn't hurt Gyllenhaal, right?"

"True. At the same time, we don't want the tabs comparing the two, because Nathan will come off as the clone, since he's the newbie."

"Gotcha. When I set him up with Burton Machen at Pickford for a cut, I'll also get his opinion on shaping Nathan's brows. We'll do it just prior to the photo shoot. And I'll go in with him on both appointments."

She did the head toss again. He assumed she was rearranging her own agenda in her mind, to accommodate the client who would make her year for her when the fanzines started touting him as the rising star to watch. "I'll schedule a manicure and a facial, too, while we're at the salon. Hey, he's not one of those fly-over state types who will balk and call it 'too girly,' is he?" Fiona asked.

"So what if he does? Set him straight. Just tell him Tom and Russell do it. That should shut him up," said Sam.

Fiona nodded knowingly. "Yep, works every time. Within a year he'll be hooked on the thought of being the newest poster boy for metrosexual manhood." They both chuckled. She then clicked off the other things she felt they had to discuss.

First on the agenda was his wardrobe. Because of Nathan's height, broad shoulders, and washboard abs, certainly Armani and Sean John were a good start. "I'll go shopping with him, and make sure that he throws in some Hugo Boss. Prada's got some new stuff out that looks like it was just made for him." She smiled knowingly. "And certainly, we've got to put that cute ass of his in some DIESEL denim. Gay vague, you know?"

"Sure, go for it," murmured Sam. "But don't try to explain that to Nathan. He may not grasp the concept."

"Gotcha. All he-man, eh? Well, we'll keep it our little secret." When Fiona was through with him, the kid wouldn't have much of a first paycheck, but this was what was called "investing in one's career," so too bad; he'd have to bite the bullet.

As for his social agenda, Fiona felt that, currently, Nathan's left a lot to be desired. "His outside interests are his gym and his acting classes. Mostly he stays home with his wife. Apparently he doesn't do much clubbing. Hell, he told me he's never even seen the inside of Chi. Go figure." Fiona was puzzled. "I mean, how could you claim to be an actor in Hollywood and have *not* been there, for god's sake?"

"Yeah, well, I don't get the feeling that Donald Ducks have a heck of a lot of discretionary income to play with, anyway."

"You've got a point there. Not only that, but I could hear some whiny brat—sounded like a boy—in the background—"

"She—he has a *kid*?" This was news to Sam. Nina hadn't mentioned it, and because she looked like such a baby herself, he would have never dreamed she'd had a kid. He blushed just thinking about her and her small, taut stomach.

Did knowing that she had a kid make him feel differently about her? *Hell yeah.* Suddenly he realized that any man who was willing to get involved with her couldn't jerk her around, not ever.

Not that he planned on doing that: *getting involved . . .*

Or, if it just so happened that they *did* get involved, he certainly wouldn't jerk her around.

She's just too good for that . . .

Damn! Damn! Stay on track! Focus . . . Focus . . .

"Where do you want to start?" He threw the issue of Nathan's social agenda back in her court.

"Well . . . he should certainly get out at least a couple of nights a week. Do the red carpet for a premiere, or a well-covered party. And definitely he should hit some of the hot spots, you know: Concorde, LAX, Mood, Privilege, and of course the Grill. I'll have my assistant, Dominique, get him on the appropriate VIP lists. I don't suppose he has a Sidekick or something, so that we can update his schedule as events are added?"

"Here's his cell number." He wrote it down on a business card and slid it across the desk to her. "Call him there until you can get him a Sidekick. You can bill it here."

"Will do. I'll ask him to come around to my office to pick it up, and I'll teach him how to work with it. I don't suppose he'll have an assistant anytime soon, eh?"

"Not yet. I'd suggest keeping Nina—his wife—in the loop. She strikes me as . . . quite efficient."

Fiona nodded, but he could tell she was not convinced. "We'll keep planting juicy tidbits with Serenity and Baxter, and Liz, of course. Rush & Molloy, Page Six, Jeanette. Certainly Ted at E! Network. I'll hit the phones the minute we finish."

"With what kind of hook?" he asked.

"Well, we've got the Hugo/Kat project. A second angle is that he's another adorable dude from Brad's home state of Missouri. That alone begs the question, 'Is he the next Brad?' And from what I hear from Kat, Nathan just may be that . . . particularly if she can convince him to dump his wife for her." Fiona gave Sam a knowing look.

"What exactly have you heard?" Already the word was out on Nathan's audition tape, eh?

"Heard? Heck, I *saw* it. That tape is *priceless*. If the Academy had seen it, she would have that Oscar already, hands down. To hell with having to bulk up thirty pounds, or wearing some damn prosthesis. Gee, it's too bad they don't give an Oscar for soft porn."

Not good, thought Sam.

"Where did *you* see it?"

"Kat requested a DVD of it . . . for her own personal viewing pleasure. I was at her place, going over her media calendar for the coming week, when it arrived by messenger, from Hugo's studio. She couldn't wait to show me. She is really smitten with this kid."

"Great. Just great. *Damn!* If Nathan dumps Nina for Kat before he's even launched, that might kill his career, not make it." Sam turned to his speakerphone. "Riley?"

"Yeah, boss?" Sam's assistant always listened in to his conferences and took notes. Even disemboweled through the intercom, Riley's voice had a Zen quality to it. Just hearing it made the tension go out of Sam's shoulders.

"Get Hugo on the phone."

"Will do."

A few moments later, Sam heard Hugo's greeting: "I know why you're calling, Sam. Believe me I do, and—"

"Oh yeah?" Sam took a deep breath. "What the *hell* happened over there, Hugo?"

"Things got—well, they got a little out of hand. But I'm way ahead of you, guy. Trust me, I personally burned the film. I *swear.*"

"That's good. Otherwise, this project goes *up in smoke*."

"Got it. Hey, by the way, Lucinda and I are celebrating my birthday Wednesday night, over at Ago. Care to join us?"

"Sure, I'll be there. But I'm warning you, Hugo, if some of that X-rated footage you shot of my boy ends up on *Entertainment Tonight*, I will personally wring your neck. You won't live to *see* another birthday."

Sam hung up before Hugo could say anything else. He was pissed at Hugo, who, of all people, should have known better than to let Kat have her way with Nathan. On DVD no less.

Damn, maybe I should see this clip . . .

"So, just what *is* the situation with the wife?" Fiona's question brought him back down to planet Earth.

"She's a saint. Pure as driven snow. Definitely an asset to him."

"Then again, if he dumps her—St. Nina becomes a liability that needs damage control."

"Which is why you've got to make sure that this little fall from grace stays under wraps."

Fiona hesitated for a moment. "Look, Sam, if it *does* get out—well, personally, I'm not all that sure that it's necessarily a . . . a *bad* thing."

"You're kidding me, right?"

"No, now just hear me out: If Nathan and Kat do become an item, it might just *help* his career. I mean, Federline was unknown before Britney, and he dumped the mother of his child, and *she* had another kid on the way. Hooking up with Brit put him in the limelight, am I right? And when Marc Anthony dumped Dayanara for Jennifer, not even a year after *their* second kid was born, no one batted an eyelash."

"Yeah, well, Anthony already had an established fan base. *And* a prior divorce. And at the time, Federline didn't have a career to speak of. Then again, Nathan won't, either, if his gets killed from the get-go, just because he's viewed only as Kat's new boy toy. He's got to be able to stand on his own rep. Otherwise—"

Otherwise, what?

Otherwise Kat gets her wish earlier than she anticipated, and Nathan's marriage breaks up earlier than expected?

Otherwise the release of the audition video boosts interest in the movie?

Otherwise Nina, heartbroken, is dumped . . . and Sam can pick up the pieces?

But I don't want it to happen that way.

Well then, how is it supposed to happen?

That was a very good question. But at that moment, Fiona's question took precedence: ". . . until then. Whattaya think of that?"

Focus . . . Focus . . . "Huh? Sorry, I missed what you said."

"I was suggesting that we play down the family angle for now, and play up his talent. I know that Kat was instrumental in choosing Nathan to play opposite her, but despite that, the script calls for a strong male lead, and I got the distinct impression that Hugo has no doubts that Nathan will be brilliant in it. Why don't we just lead with that, and feed the press periodic snippets of footage that bears this out?"

She was right.

Nathan Harte was a film publicist's wet dream come true.

And by the time Fiona got through with Nathan, he'd be granted his own digit on the cell phone speed dials of every important director in town.

* * *

SAM: (*Clearing his throat, then very businesslike*) Hi, O. Sam here. Just, um, checking in on—you know, Wilbur.

O: (*With a sultry purr*) My goodness, Sam, is that really you? Great to hear your voice! I've *truly* missed you, handsome.

SAM: Yeah? I bet you say that to all the boys.

O: (*With a husky chuckle*) You're right, I do. I don't always *mean* it, though.

SAM: I'm happy to hear that I'm the exception to the rule.

O: Without a doubt, lover. As for an update, I can honestly report that Wilbur hasn't exactly been burning up my phone line lately. I guess he's . . . *preoccupied*, as they say.

SAM: Yeah, I sort of figured that. As you can imagine, I'm relieved to some extent . . . Oh, of course, I plan on honoring our deal for as long as Hu— *Wilbur* wants to keep in touch.

O: That's because you're an honorable man, Sam. I'm sure your . . . *girlfriend* . . . appreciates that.

SAM: At the moment, O, I'm footloose and fancy-free.

O: You don't say? In a total state of bachelor bliss, as it were?

SAM: (*He pauses before speaking*) Well . . . I wouldn't say that . . . I guess you could say that I'm admiring my ladylove from afar.

O: Oh? And why is that?

SAM: Well, if you must know . . . the woman of my dreams . . . she just so happens to be married.

O: (*With that tinkling laugh of hers*) Isn't *that* convenient . . . choosing some unattainable object of desire means no strings attached, doesn't it?

SAM: (*Somewhat huffy*) Believe me, I'd marry her in a second if she were available!

O: *Really?* What, did you skip Psychology 101 that day? Come

on, Sam, admit it: If she weren't married, you'd run like hell
in the opposite direction.

SAM: I don't know when I've ever given you that impression
of me—that I'm some kind of confirmed bachelor, or
something. I *do* want to get married . . . to the *right* woman.
And I want to have kids, too. In fact, my . . . my ladylove already has a child . . . So, what do you say to *that?*

O: (*After a pause*) Hmmm. I stand corrected. I guess I've thoroughly misjudged you. I'm impressed . . . In fact, if I were
there with you, right now, *I'd suck your toes.*

SAM: (Laughing heartily) And I'd let you, you nut! Damn, this
is the first time I've laughed all day.

O: That bad, huh?

SAM: Yeah, boy. Everything's going to hell in a hand basket.
I've just signed this new client, and . . . and, uh, *"she"* lucked
out, just like that. A big feature film . . .

O: Way to go, girl!

SAM: Yeah, good for her . . . except for one thing. The leading—
the leading, uh, "man" is all over her.

O: What, he wants her fired already?

SAM: No, worse. He wants her to sleep with him.

O: Bastard.

SAM: Yeah, it's—it's making things rough for—for "her." You
see, she's married—

O: *Not* good.

SAM: Exactly. And . . . they have . . . a kid . . . a . . . a "daughter."

O: (*Sighs*) Gee. It's a shame this jerk is leaning on her so hard.
Still, if she loves her husband, she'll find a tactful way to say
no . . .

SAM: (*With a harsh laugh*) Babe, when you've got stars in

your eyes, and the hottest star on the planet wants to jump your bones, somehow you seem to forget that little "I do" . . . Maybe that's why I'm so cynical about finding true love in this crazy town.

O: Have some faith, Sam. Besides, it always takes two to tango. She's got to want it, too.

SAM: That's the problem. I think she *does*.

O: Well, then, there's nothing *you* can do about it, agreed? When it comes right down to it, we all choose what we are willing to lose. Or, as George Eliot once said, 'Our deeds still travel with us from afar, and what we have been makes us what we are.'

SAM: (*Softly*) Aptly put. You've got a quote for every situation, don't you, O?

O: (*Laughs heartily*) Believe it or not, Sam, there's more to this job than moaning and dirty talk. As for your ladylove, hey, look at the bright side: If what you say is right about love in LaLa Land, odds are you'll end up with her after all. And *then* you'd have to put your heart where your mouth is, big boy.

SAM: That's what I love about you the most, O: You're always ready to put me in my place.

O: It's what most men pay me for . . . Now next time, don't be such a stranger.

SAM: Gotcha. You'll be hearing from me soon.

"He's baaaaack . . ." hissed Tori, doing a super-bad imitation of the *Poltergeist* girl.

Damn! thought Nina. *Why him? Why now?*

Because it was Wednesday, that was why. And like clockwork, there he was: Mr. Baxter, Tommaso's most ardent pescatarian.

And worst yet, Mr. Baxter was a very picky, very finicky pescatarian, who thought nothing of tossing about adjectives such as "smelly," "rancid," and (heaven forefend!) "farmed" when perusing whatever catch of the day was proffered to him.

"I know your tricks," he'd sniff at the "fish consultant" on duty. "You put out all the best fish in the morning, for all the Guatemalan cooks and the Brentwood trophy wives to fight over, and leave this—this bacteria-ridden *dreck* for the rest of us!"

Usually such proclamations left the guy behind the counter in tears. After the store had run through three fish consultants, Nina had asked Tori if she could handle the matter.

After that, whenever Mr. Baxter showed up, Nina was there to greet him, smiling beatifically like the badge-winning Girl Scout cookie seller she once was as she accompanied him to the fish counter. Once there, in minute detail she gave him a play-by-play on the fish she insisted she had personally seen being filleted, including its vitamin and mineral content. Then, after he'd made his selection (the halibut steak today), she even went so far as to suggest side dishes and ingenious recipes (in this case, pineapple and mango salsa, couscous, and a Waldorf salad).

This was why he adored her.

And Mr. Baxter didn't adore just *anyone*.

In fact, he despised most everyone.

Which was why he just loved his job as a syndicated Hollywood gossip columnist more than anything: It allowed him to play favorites, and to punish those who thought that their secrets were none of his business.

"Mr. Baxter" was, after all, *Baxter* Quinn.

Right now, his *absolute* favorite subject was Katerina McPherson, but only because she'd recently gotten herself on the wrong side of his rival and archenemy, Serenity Lancaster, for dropping Baxter a few very juicy and totally exclusive tips.

Well, that was just too bad.

In fact, right now he was onto some truly choice Kat clues, about some new boy toy: an up-and-coming actor by the name of Nathan Somebody-or-Other. But because the dude was married, Baxter's lead on the story would have to be delicate. As always, he'd give his readers *just so much*—

—then yank it away from them.

In other words, he would keep them wondering about who, what, where . . . and most definitely *how many times*.

In this case, four. *Thus far.*

Thank *gawd* for lovers in high places with Machiavellian agendas, right?

Like the executive suite at ICA.

Like Riley McNaught.

Or, "Naughty," as Baxter so fondly called him.

And tonight he was having Riley over for dinner, to pump him for more on this Kat/Nathan—Nat?—thing. Surely with these recipes this sweet gal at Tommaso's had suggested, Riley was just going to *love* the halibut . . .

. . . among some of the other things Baxter had in store for him.

And by that, Baxter *wasn't* referring to the couscous.

Nina was getting headaches every night.

Well, every night that Nathan informed her he'd be coming home late from the set.

Ironically, that was turning out to be almost every night since the film had gone into production. Almost two full weeks now, to be exact.

It wasn't as if she could afford these headaches, either. Nighttime was when O had to put on her game face—or, in this case, game voice. She had hoped to quit PSO'ing by now, since Nathan's career was on the launch pad. And while he was due to get his very first check from Hugo's production company any day now, he'd only get part of his movie fee up front. The rest wouldn't come in until the movie was completed and released, so she had to keep them afloat, at least until then.

Besides, a lot of expenses had to come out of that first check. Like Sam's 10 percent, and the publicist's retainer, too. And all the new things Nathan needed to look the part of an up-and-coming Hollywood star. Not to mention his union dues, now that he qualified for his SAG card.

And they couldn't get SAG insurance without a SAG card, which meant that she couldn't quit Tommaso's yet, either until they were sure that Jake's asthma was covered.

Which was why her head was throbbing now.

Not that she could say that to Potty Mouth.

Mrs. McGillicutty had begged her to take the call. "I have to warn you, hon, he's a total asshole. Heck, he's already run through half my girls. Most of them end up in tears within the first five minutes. But he only calls once in a blue moon. And since you say you need the money . . ."

Nina braced herself, then murmured, "I do, so go ahead and put him through."

All Potty Mouth wanted from her was a few choice words: truly raw profanities, to be exact. He'd order her to start off with things that best described him; or, to be more specific, his penis (*tube steak, lust muscle, skin flute, throbber, pork sword, sex pistol, blue-veined junket pumper*, whatever). Then he demanded that she move on to more colorful names for her own intimate place of pleasure. (For the life of her, she could never comprehend why nicknames like *kitty, coochie, hole, trim, beaver, snatch*, and *muff* were considered mood elevators for women . . . although *cake* might work . . .)

The last fifteen minutes of their tête-à-tête was a command performance in which she was instructed to describe what she *just knew* would happen should these two body parts ever meet. In her mind, it would be something similar to the Bobbitt incident of '93. But for a buck a minute, she sucked it up and kept in character, cooing acts of disgrace and degradation in a stimulating stream of (un)consciousness until Potty Mouth finally wrangled his purple-headed trouser snake and grunted in satisfaction, "Fair enough. So, uh, what's your name, anyway? For the next time I call?"

She winced, wondering what she could say to avoid any more calls from him, then muttered, "What say you take a guess, big boy?"

The jerk guffawed at that. "Hell yeah, I got one for you: How about Cunt?"

"Yeah, that works," she muttered. His lack of originality was priceless. "But how about some tit for tat? Can I call you Potty Mouth?"

"Sure, if you want to show me your titties, you can call me anything you want—Aw, damn! My wife is calling, gotta go." He slammed down the phone.

So much for the magic.

The conversation (if you could call it that) left her exhausted, angry, nauseous, and ready to call it quits *for good.*

But she couldn't.

At least not until the last half of Nathan's film fee was safely in the bank.

Instead, she called Mrs. McGillicutty and told her never to put Potty Mouth through to her again.

Then she cursed the fact that the only aspirin in the house was Baby Tylenol.

And *that* bottle's contents had expired.

It was sometime after four in the morning that Nathan stumbled back home. Relieved that Nina was fast asleep, he headed for the shower.

Otherwise, Nina would know that he'd been making love.

To Kat.

He hadn't planned on that happening . . . or, for that matter, having *real feelings* for the film star, either.

In fact, he never assumed he'd feel that way about any woman for the rest of his life . . . other than Nina, of course.

That was not to say that he hadn't been with other women. Of course he had, but before Nina. And in the six years since then, he had sorely been tempted many times over. Heck, he was just like any other hot-blooded twenty-four-year-old American male, right?

Besides that, he had the kind of bedroom eyes and bad-boy smile that drove women crazy. And if L.A. city proper was anything, it was 1,430 square miles of unadulterated temptation, the most tantalizing of which could be found on that infamous mile and a half strip of Sunset on any given night, when no less than a thousand (about a third of the population of Joyous, mind you!) stiletto-heeled, Miracle-Bra'd, O-ringed, and V-stringed babes traipsed saucily between the House of Blues, Skybar, the Viper Room, the Lounge at the Standard, the Comedy Club, Whisky A Go Go . . . and back again.

Oh yeah, *for sure*, he'd been sorely tempted.

And to his dismay, he had slipped up, too . . . *once*.

With Helene, his scene partner from Euphegenia's master acting class.

Helene had come over one night to rehearse her scenes for the next day's class. Nina was working the evening shift at Tommaso's, and wasn't due home until ten o'clock that night. After Jake had finally nodded off to sleep and they could then get serious about their scene study, Helene got *very* serious about something else altogether:

How far *she* was willing to go beyond their usual innocent flirtations.

The kiss she gave him was one thing. The blowjob was something else altogether.

He'd almost caught his dick in his zipper when he jumped up suddenly, antsy because he heard what he thought was Nina's Civic pulling up to the curb.

It wasn't. It was, however, enough to get him stammering that "Things are getting—out of hand . . . Maybe we shouldn't ever again—*you* know . . ."

That was all he needed to say.

Thank God.

Not that he hadn't liked Helene's surprise. Because he had. *Too much, in fact.*

Of course, Helene was disappointed. Still, she resigned herself to worship him from afar, because she knew if she made things too uncomfortable for Nathan, she'd lose him as a scene partner altogether, and she was fully aware of the fact that there was a line of other budding actresses in Euphegenia's class ready, willing, and able to take her place.

Then again, there was only one Katerina McPherson, and *she* wasn't taking no for an answer.

Nathan had tried, *he really had*, to keep things just friendly with her, too. But how do you brush aside the fawning attentions of the victor of *FHM*'s "I'm Made If I've Laid . . ." online contest three years straight?

How do you shake off the urge to pull her close to you, after she's brushed up against you time and time again—*on purpose?* Particularly when you know what that purpose *is . . .* and you want it badly, too?

How do you avoid a boner when you're spending hour-after-hour, day-after-day (*for two weeks straight already!*) trading heart-wrenching dialogue, staring deep into those limpid, lust-laden eyes, and kissing that tantalizingly moist mouth . . .

. . . in front of an all-seeing camera, while an all-knowing crew hovers around, just waiting for the inevitable: *your fall from grace.*

It had finally happened today, just before their lunch break on the set.

All morning long, Kat had been arguing with Hugo over his direction of a scene she claimed was the one nearest and dearest to her heart. In fact, she insisted tearfully, it was *the very scene* that had sold her on the script in the first place, because in it, she was supposed to be yearning—forlornly, *longingly*—for the unattainable: *Nathan.*

That is, Nathan's character, Artemus.

To help her "reach transcendence" (as she put it), she asked for Hugo's approval to do the scene in the nude. (This request was a first for any A-list actress, and didn't Hugo just know it!)

Certainly, Kat insisted, if that were the case, it would just *have* to take place on a closed set. And of course, Nathan, even though he wasn't supposed to be in the scene, should be on hand—"for inspiration" was how Kat put it.

"*Hmmm* . . . Yeah, okay, Kat, but you realize that I had planned on shooting it as a close-up, right?" asked Hugo, who was now at the end of his rope. He certainly didn't need *this* shit, and on his birthday, of all days! Nope, what he needed was a very dry Grey Goose martini, along with one of Ago's mouthwatering burratas, a hunk of barely charred rib eye . . . and afterward, to hit the sack with Lucinda, some Liquid Silk, and that Wavy G dildo she'd grown fond of since their little getaway in Cabo . . .

. . . And to forget about this on-the-set diva and her newest obsession.

Hugo knew that Kat's demand to close the set for this little indulgence of hers was just one more way in which she could be a pain in his ass. Why should everyone except Hugo, his cameraman, and her makeup and hair slaves be told to take a coffee break while she put on a private show for her new boyfriend? What was this, some tawdry back alley Hollyporn production over in Chatsworth? *Come on* already!

"That's not the point." Kat pouted. "I need all my emotional facets in primo form, and Nathan is my—well, he's my *muse.* Aren't you, my dearest?" She looked over at the object of her desire with the tenderest of glances.

Having been put on the spot, Nathan turned beet red. Certainly he didn't want this laid at *his* feet, no sirree. But there it sat, like a turd on the tips of his brand-new suede Bruno Magli loafers.

"Really, Hugo. If it will help—well, I . . . I don't mind."

Yeah, thought Hugo, *I'll just bet you don't.*

Fuck it. They were already behind schedule by two days, due to Kat's insistence that the first thing they shoot be the script's three love scenes—*ad nauseam*, as it turned out, since she found something to complain about after each take. He had indulged her in this, but enough was enough already! For sure, this was one Hugo Schmitt production that would *never* garner an Academy nomination. However, it was a slam-dunk for an *Adult Video News* award for, say, "Best All-Sex Release." Or, more likely, "Best Sex Comedy."

Well, now at least Archie Hardaway would have that nude scene of Kat he coveted, and without having to lay out a plug nickel of bonus money for her to do it, either!

Hugo didn't know why, but that pissed him off. And he didn't like being pissed off on his birthday, considering that it didn't look as if Kat's crap would end anytime soon. At least, not until she finally got her way . . .

. . . With Nathan.

So why not?

Resigned to all their fates, he turned to the object of his star's affection. "Look, Nathan, can I talk to you for a moment? Just the two of us."

Puzzled, Nathan nodded and followed Hugo off the set, into the postproduction office. He didn't know why, but he was uncomfortable with Hugo's silence and the way in which the director was sizing him up.

Finally, Hugo came out with it. "You know, Nathan, Kat is ... *quite fond* of you."

No shit, thought Nathan, but he kept silent to hear where Hugo was going with this.

"I'll be honest with you: I've never asked an actor this before. Heaven knows it's none of my business, but if you level with me, it might go a long way to—well, in saving this production. And, for that matter, my ass."

A crease of concern crossed Nathan's noble brow as the thought of his first feature film going up in smoke entered his mind. At this point, he was willing to do anything to keep from fucking this up. *Anything.*

"Sure, ask away."

"Are you boffing her?"

Nathan turned white. "No! Of—of course not!"

Hugo paused, then stared him right in the eye as he asked, "Well, *would you like to?*"

The kaleidoscope of emotions that crossed Nathan's face said it all:

Hell, yeah, I'd love *to jump her bones!*

But she'll eat me up alive—and don't I know it!

Not to mention that I'd hate myself in the morning for doing it . . .

But if you, Hugo Schmitt, are giving me permission to go for it— and, of course, it will save all our asses . . .

Then shouldn't I be able to live with this decision—for the sake of our art, I mean?

Of course I should . . . Damn right, I should . . .
THEN HELL, BRING IT ON!
. . . As long as it stays our little secret.

Right, thought Hugo, sure, our little secret. Yours, mine, and Kat's . . . not to mention the hundred or so others in Hugo's tight-knit merry crew.

"Look, guy, no harm, no foul." Hugo put his hand on Nathan's shoulder for moral support. "Hey, think of it as a little birthday present, from you to me. Or if you prefer, an early one from me to you. We'll break for lunch now, I think. You and Kat can, er, 'rehearse' in her trailer. We'll be ready to shoot again at, say, one-thirty. Just tell Kat that the scene gets played *as written, as previously discussed, no bullshit.*"

Sure, Nathan understood. All of a sudden he was excited . . . *and scared.*

In a matter of minutes—more like an hour or so, considering his staying power—*Nathan's life would be changed forever.*

And so would his marriage.

Then another thought hit him: "Uh, Hugo, what about Kat? Won't she—be mad that we aren't doing it her way?"

Hugo shot him a look that said it all: *Are you a sucker, or what?*

"Trust me, she *is* getting her way. Eventually it was going to happen. At least, this way, I'll get the picture I want, too."

And you'll get your first piece of A-list ass. So enjoy it, kid.

Despite the guilt, the initial performance anxiety, and an old football injury, Nathan did enjoy it.

Again. And again. And a fourth time, too. In the sack, Katerina McPherson was everything he had fantasized she would be: innocent yet sultry, playful *and* knowledgeable . . . and best of all, *insatiable*.

That is, he enjoyed it until he got home and hit the shower, where he could curse himself for betraying Nina without being heard.

When Nina awoke the next morning, he had already taken off for the set. But he had also left her a note that read, simply, "I will always love you with all my heart. Nathan."

After that, her headaches went away.

DOES KAT KISS AND TELL???

YOUCH!!! I just got an earful from the publicity peon for our fave golden girl, who is trying to deny what my spies (with their very own little eyes) saw occurring off the set of our Milady's latest flick: a scintillating lip-lock with her very married costar! Granted, onscreen, their N-U-D-E scenes (yes, you heard it here first, folks!), the brunt and grunt of which supposedly take place on a hot sweaty college dorm bed, are sizzling, to say the least. Is Our Miss Kat keeping this cinematic newbie after school for some, er, extracurricular activity, in order to ensure that he's sufficiently hot and bothered when the cameras roll? We'll play nice-nice (for now, anyway) and presume this is not the case. (Yeah, right, sure . . .) For his sake, here's hoping this New Man on Campus is getting an A++ for effort.

Serenity's Scandal Sheet, 2/8

7

The Affair

The men's room in Ago wasn't the most convenient place to take a meeting, but it was the best that Sam and Hugo could do, considering that Hugo and Lucinda were perpetually in lust these days, and therefore joined at the hip whenever they were together. So whenever this noted regular or that celebrity patron came in to relieve himself of too much great food and good wine, Sam and Hugo's fervid discussion about the shenanigans happening on the set came to an abrupt halt. This was met with more than a few raised eyebrows, but Sam couldn't care less. Between the interruptions, he garnered from Hugo that Nathan had, on that very day, finally succumbed to the onslaught of Katerina's ardent advances.

Not only that, but apparently the kid was quite a cocksman, or at least, from initial indications anyway, he was living up to her ravenous expectations: After their inaugural tryst at lunch, at every subsequent break the two of them had stolen off to Kat's dressing room to continue their lovemaking marathon.

They'd also been the last to leave after the shoot wrapped that evening, and Hugo fully expected a formal complaint from studio security any moment now. Surely the night watchman had quit making his rounds in order to park himself outside Kat's trailer for the duration of his shift, having discovered that their ecstatic moans were the perfect accompaniment to whatever issue of *Hustler* or *Playboy* he had to keep his hands busy.

"How did I know they'd go at it like a couple of horny tomcats?" Hugo whispered frantically, over the grunts and flushes of two Hollywood heavy hitters, who had obviously overindulged themselves on the ziti special. "It makes me wish I hadn't encouraged the kid to—"

"*You encouraged him*! Hell, Hugo, why did you go and do that for? Nathan's got a wife and kid!"

"He does? Shit! I just assumed . . . he's so young and all . . . and, to be honest, it's not like he put up much of a fuss . . . Well it's spilled milk now. Or *something*."

They both shut up quickly as the door opened again. Sometime later, when a guy they both recognized as a Lakers guard finally did his business and left them alone again (*who knew that the dude would need a full five minutes to drain that lizard of his!*) Sam said, "Okay, okay. I guess I'll have to get in both their faces and set the record straight, before this whole situation ruins the project."

"I'd appreciate that, Sam. I've talked with Kat until I'm blue in the face, and Nathan seems to melt like Jell-O whenever she's around. Of course, who can blame the guy?" He smiled wickedly.

"Well, *you* seem to be able to keep it together. So, I gather things are tout sweet between you and Lucinda, huh?"

"Couldn't be finer. I have O to thank for that."

"Yeah, I guess I misjudged her to some extent. She is quite a peach."

"And quite a fluffer." Hugo sighed his contentment. "I guess I should just call and check in . . . not that I need a 're-fresher' or anything . . . you know, *strictly* as a buddy. We haven't talked in so long. How about you?"

"Me?" Sam was a bit startled by the question. "I—well, um, to tell you the truth, I talked to her just yesterday, you know, only to say hi. That's all." He was embarrassed that anyone, even Hugo, knew he was talking to a phone sex operator.

As if Sam Godwin needed to talk to a PSO. Heck, not him!

"See? *See?* What'd I tell you? You know, she's a really sweet gal—"

"Big deal. Lots of women are 'sweet.' So what?"

"Well, you've got to admit it, phone sex is a lot less of a—I dunno, *hassle* than dating."

"Thanks, but no thanks. It's still a cheap thrill, and you still have to pay for it. I prefer a warm body," Sam retorted. "But unfortunately, the one I prefer most already has a permanent bed partner." Although, from what Hugo was telling him, not for long.

"That's too bad. . . . Jeez, I never had you figured for 'the other man' type, you know, wait your turn until some little Malibu matron crooks her finger in your direction so that you'll come running—"

Just then there was a bang on the door. The two of them heard Lucinda hiss, "Hey, I'm concerned about you two! And so is half of Hollywood, so you better get out here and let everyone know that I've got nothing to worry about!"

Hugo's kiss confirmed this to her. However, feeling that he

owed Sam something, Hugo made the decision to call O later that night.

But it would have to be *really, really* late that night. After all, it was his birthday, and Lucinda had promised him a *very* special surprise when they got home . . .

HUGO: Hi, darling. How ya been?

O: Hugo, my man! How's it hanging? (*She gives a sly chuckle*) You know I meant that rhetorically, right?

HUGO: I feel honored that you even asked. Things are . . . they're wonderful! Really. Lucinda and I couldn't be happier right now.

O: Wow. Awesome. True love makes my heart sing, you know?

HUGO: You said it . . . (*Sigh*) Wish I could say that was true for our old friend Sam.

O: Sam? Why? What's up with lover boy?

HUGO: That's just it . . . He's . . . well, he's got this tendency to choose women who are . . . well, shall we say, he picks them for *all* the wrong reasons.

O: (*Laughing*) That doesn't surprise me. Then again, I'd say that's true of about ninety percent of all guys. And believe me, women aren't immune to that fate, either.

HUGO: Keep that in mind, the next time he calls. Frankly, I think you two would make a cute couple.

O: Oh? What makes you say that?

HUGO: Just something he said. About how you're the most interesting woman he's met in a long, long time. Coming from him, that's a high compliment. Besides, I have a hunch about you two, and I'm usually right about these kinds of things, so don't write it off.

O: Hugo, if I didn't know better, I'd think you were trying to set us up. The next thing I know, you'll be encouraging me to flirt with him, or something.

HUGO: (*Now he was the one laughing uproariously*) O, darling, the last thing I'd ever tell *you* is how to get a man to sit up and take notice of you. You've got that down pat.

O: Let's hope so, hon. Otherwise I'd have to close up shop.

HUGO: No worries there. Gotta run, sweetheart. But remember, if he calls—

O: I know, I know. Keep an open mind. It will be interesting to see if Sam can do the same. Have a good morning, handsome.

The following week, in Jake's Sage Oak "Parent Pack" was a small envelope, addressed to both Nathan and Nina. In it was a handwritten invitation, which read:

Dear Mr. and Mrs. Harte,

I would be honored if you'd join me for tea and conviviality on any afternoons that suit your very busy schedules.

Your very humble servant,
Brad Pickering

Finally, thought Nina. *We're in!*

So in, in fact, that on Friday, Mr. Pickering himself was waiting for her when she drove up to collect Jake and Plum so that he might personally escort her into his inner sanctum that very afternoon.

As with all children whose parents were "taking tea with the headmaster," Plum and Jake had already been plucked from the curbside cattle call and lovingly relocated to "The Kinder Garden"—a lush, well-appointed, and well-supervised playground, that, as described in the SOA Handbook, was "conducive to enviable hands-on learning experiences, both stimulating and calming, that pique our students' curiosity and seemingly insatiable desire to know 'why.' "

This wonderland had been strategically placed right outside the two-story atrium window in Mr. Pickering's library, where, each afternoon, the parents attending the afternoon tea could point out, boast about, and coo over their precious progeny.

Because Becca had, on at least a few occasions, actually graced the school with her presence, Plum was no stranger to the after-school protocol of the Kinder Garden. However, Jake was only allowed to step foot into it during the prescribed forty-eight-minute "activity hour," wedged in between his "Junior Ethicist" and "Stock Market Mini Math" lessons on Mondays, Wednesdays, and Fridays, and, on Tuesdays and Thursdays, between violin lessons and the "Maid en Español" super-intense language course (which was chock full of easy-to-learn terms deemed helpful for ordering about Latino help staff, such as "*Haga por favor mi desayuno*"—"Please make my breakfast"—and "*Quisiera que usted ahora dibujara mi baño*" —"I'd like you to draw my bath now") so of course the little boy was thrilled to pieces for this extra time on the Gazebo Play Loft, the faux rock-climbing wall, the Turbo Toob Slide, and the sandbox filled with authentic sugary white sand, imported from Destin, Florida.

Jake demonstrated this by throwing a bucketful of the sand in the face of Tre Hanover (a.k.a. Lawrence Walter Wrigley Hanover III), to Mrs. Hanover's horror.

And Nina's too, for that matter.

As she ran to the window to motion Jake to stop his rampage, an arm reached out to stop her.

"Don't worry. Time-outs are short in the Kinder Garden. Otherwise the parents would take their kids home immediately, and Pickering wouldn't have time to pump us for gossip. Besides, Tre started it when he stole Jake's dump truck." This reassurance came from the freckle-faced redheaded woman whom Nina knew only as "Ben's mommy," from the school's last Earth Day extravaganza and fund-raiser.

At that function, Ben and Jake had played emperor penguins who had been separated from the birds' breeding ground when the ice shelf it nested on had cracked due to global warming. The two boys had been directed to stay "stranded" in the back of the tableau while the other penguins told this sad tale. Instead, Jake and Ben stole the show by acting, however inappropriately, like seals, which got them big laughs and a whopping two thousand dollars in donations for that cause. ("A ham, just like his pa," proclaimed Nathan proudly between yelling "Encore! Encore!")

"I'm so relieved it wasn't all Jake's fault." Nina laughed nervously. "Otherwise I'd feel guilty about being inside while he's being incarcerated." She made sure to take just a dainty nibble of her German chocolate cake. It wasn't until after she picked up the gooey concoction that she noticed that none of the other mommies was likewise indulging, but had opted to sip tea instead. Their sacrifices were obviously paying off: not one of them was any less buff than Uma Thurman mid-*Kill Bill II*. And although Nina was a size 4, she felt pudgy next to this pack of Pilates princesses.

As if reading her mind, Ben's mommy stuck her finger in the icing of Nina's cake, put it in her mouth, and gave a blissful sigh.

"Sorry. Just couldn't help myself. Glad *someone* finally broke down after all these months and took a piece." She wiped her finger on her low-riding Hard Tail yoga pants and stuck out her hand. "We haven't been properly introduced. My name is Casey Cattrall."

Nina stuttered back, "Nice to meet you. I'm Nina, uh, Harte."

Of course Nina knew the name Casey Cattrall! To put Ben's mommy's face with it, though, was something she hadn't done before now. Casey was *the* Casey Cattrall, as in wife of Jarred Cattrall, Oscar and Golden Globe winner twice over. As in Casey Cattrall, producer in her own right, of the third-largest grossing box office film of last year, which had been based on a truly inspiring story of female empowerment.

Casey and Jarred were also perennial contenders in *People* magazine's "Hollywood Hottest Couples" list. Their marriage was considered "one of the happiest in tumultuous Tinseltown" by practically every celebrity magazine's standards.

"Hey," said Casey. "Have you met some of the other people here?" She herded Nina over to Susannah Myers, a very pretty, very skinny brunette with a husky voice and infectious smile, whose husband was an independent producer; and Jill

O'Keefe, a willowy blond who had retired from a highly rated sitcom to be a full-time mom.

"I think it's time to blow this pop stand," murmured Susannah. "We're taking the kids over to my place, in Brentwood. Tea is okay, but I'd like something with more of a bite to it, like an appletini. Would you and Jake like to join us?"

Nina wouldn't pass it up. Besides, she told the others, Nathan had already left a voice mail that he'd be home late from the set. "He's playing opposite Katerina McPherson," she said proudly albeit a bit shyly. She didn't want to come off as if she were boasting.

Upon hearing this, the women exchanged glances.

"Kat McPherson, eh?" Casey wrinkled her brow. *No Botox there, thank God.* "Have you visited the set yet?"

"Uh, no," Nina replied sheepishly. "I didn't know I was allowed to."

"Don't wait too long," counseled Casey firmly. "It's *always* a good idea to meet the leading lady. And the sooner the better."

Seeing the four of them head for the door, Brad Pickering made a beeline for Nina. He was just about to ask her if she had enjoyed his generosity (in the hopes that she would say she had—when she spoke next to Mr. Cahill, that is) when suddenly the sound of little voices chanting, *"We want cake TOO! We want cake TOO!"* was heard emanating from the Kinder Garden. Having noted his mommy's chocolate bounty through the window, Jake had decided it was time that he and the other students lobby Headmaster Pickering to bend one of the cardinal laws at SOA: *no sugar-laden foods for the children.*

Needless to say, Pickering would never fold on this demand. He did, however, concede defeat in getting gossip out of Nina, as she and all the other parents dispersed to appease their children's cries for something substantially tastier than the tofu panna cotta provided by the Kinder Garden staff.

The trill of the telephone sang out to Nina and Jake long before they opened their apartment door. She fumbled for her house key in her pocketbook, juggling Jake's backpack, his half-finished juice box, his asthma aspirator, and her appeltini to-go cup all at the same time. The search was that much harder because she was more than just a *wee* bit tipsy from her poolside initiation into what Susannah called the "Mothers Without Fear" Club. When she finally found it, she wrenched open the door, stumbled through the living room and on into her bedroom, where she grabbed the phone, only to spill the remainder of the fruity concoction on the carpet.

"Damn—" she declared before she realized that the receiver had been knocked off the phone, then: "Hello? Um . . . *Hello?*"

First there was a telling silence before she heard a woman's haughty murmur, "Yes. *Hello.* And to whom am I speaking?"

"Nina. Harte." Taking a second to collect her breath and her patience, Nina added, "And *you* are?"

"Serenity Lancaster, *Mrs.* Harte. So *very, very happy* to have this opportunity to talk to you—*personally.* I've been *so eagerly* following Nathan's career . . . *So* exciting, isn't it? And so deserved, considering the personal struggle you two have had . . ."

Serenity Lancaster? As in the syndicated columnist and renowned "chronicler of the stars" Serenity Lancaster?

Calling Nina? To compliment Nathan?

This was just too much!

"Um, yes, it is!" Flushed from both the appeltini and Serenity's kind words (and because she had yelled a profanity in this very powerful woman's ear just now), Nina added, "Gee, Ms. Lancaster, coming from you, that is quite an . . . an accolade!"

"Ah, my dear, get used to it. You'll be hearing a lot in regard to that handsome hunky hubby of yours," Serenity's words were pure silk. "In fact, darling, I can just imagine how your ears must be *burning* right about now, what with all those *annoying* little whispers about Nathan and Katerina McPherson—"

"Nathan . . . and Kat? Oh . . . I'm sure that's just—you know, mindless gossip." Nina tried to shake off her vodka buzz. Jake, having found the remote control under the pillow where Nina had hid it in the hopes of coercing him to do his "junior stockbroker" homework first, had already flicked on Nickelodeon, and was now shouting a warning to Jimmy Neutron as he flew into peril.

Nina's nagging suspicion that she was doing the same was confirmed with Serenity's sugary sweet response: "Well, you know what they say: Where there's smoke, there's fire . . . Then again, maybe you're right. Maybe there's nothing to it . . . By the way, Nathan's shoot wrapped early last Wednesday evening because it was Hugo Schmitt's birthday. Did you enjoy the party afterward, at Ago?"

The set closed early last Wednesday? There was a party later, at Ago?

But—but hadn't Nathan been working late on the set that night?

And if not, then why hadn't he asked her to go with him? Or at least come home?

Because of Katerina?

Ashamed to admit that she hadn't been invited, Nina mumbled some inane excuse as to why she had to hang up now, and gently laid down the phone. She then picked up the note Nathan left for her Wednesday night, and reread it, again and again.

No way, she thought. *No damn way he is falling for Kat.*

Then again, there was only one way to find out.

After calling Casey to take her up on her offer of an impromptu play date for the boys ("They're inseparable anyway, so why not? Sure, drop him on by . . .") Nina scooped up Jake and headed out the door.

8

The Betrayal

KAT'S QUOTE OF THE DAY

Sure, there are things I'll regret having done, but that's why I look at each day as a gift: No matter whom I've hurt, or what cruel thing I may have said to someone else, give it twenty-four hours and they'll have already forgotten it. Now, *that's* true friendship!

Posted on Katerina McPherson's official website, WeLoveKat.com

All the interior shots for *Forever and Again* were being filmed at Flagrant Studios, which rented space on the Fox lot on West Pico. It was studio protocol to check in with the guard in the security kiosk before be-bopping on over to stage twelve to see movie magic being created.

Or, in this case, not.

If the visitor was not on the day's guest manifest, a call was made to the director's assistant, who then checked with the director as to whether the guest should be allowed on the set. Since the guest in question was one Nina Harte, who claimed to be the wife of the film's male lead, Nathan Harte, and as it was the tail end of the crew's dinner break, that answer should have been a cursory "Sure, send her on over."

Instead, Hugo's production assistant told the guard to have Nina sit tight while she rustled Hugo from his inner sanctum, where he was viewing that morning's rushes, fully oblivious that the best melodrama of the day was about to be played out off the set, right then and there.

Heck, too bad there weren't cameras in the actors' trailers, thought the PA, making a mental note to mention to Hugo that he should consider doing so.

If cameras had already been in place, the money shot was in Kat's candlelit sanctuary, where, courtesy of the reverse cowgirl that she'd opted for, the actress was enjoying the final throes of orgasmic ecstasy . . . for the third time.

Climbing down off her very studly stallion with a sigh, Kat murmured, "So, handsome, how about being my date for the Oscars?"

Nathan was confused. "You mean—you, me, and *Nina*?"

"What are you *crazy*? No, you dolt!" Miffed, Kat roused herself out of his arms and, without any warning at all, slapped his face.

Hard.

"*Ow!* Shit, Kat! Why'd you do *that?*" His eyes flashed angrily as he rubbed his sore cheek. Reflexively he started toward her . . . but then thought better of it.

Damn! She knows how to get my juices flowing, he thought.

Suddenly he was aroused again.

As if sensing this, Kat's mouth puffed up into a pout. During these little boink breaks, she'd discovered that Nathan *loved* a little physical abuse now and then, guessing (and rightly so) that he craved penance for the guilt he was feeling over their affair.

"Because you can be such a—a *pussy*, sometimes, Nathan! Jeez, just make something up, okay? Hell, tell her that costars of films in production always escort each other to these shindigs, you know, in order to publicize their new movie before it comes out. That it's just par for the course. Believe me, she'll never figure us out."

"Sure. Okay." He didn't sound too convinced, though. Not that he was going to call Kat a liar to her face. Heck, *that* would only assure him another slap. And if that happened, he promised himself he'd haul off and slap her back.

Or make love to her for a fourth time.

Besides, he knew Nina would be hurt if he went to the Oscars without her.

Maybe even *pissed*.

Or worse yet, she might figure out what was going on behind her back.

As if the fates had read his mind, just then Hugo's PA banged frantically on Kat's door, imploring Nathan to come out and greet his wife, who was making her way through security in the front lot of the studio *at that very moment*.

Jumping into his Jockey boxer briefs and jeans as if a fire bell had gone off, Nathan bounded out of bed and out the door.

Kat's slap still hurt like hell. He hoped he could find a makeup artist who could cover up the bruise before Nina saw it.

"I am *so* excited to meet you . . . *finally*."

Nina was trying very hard to be cordial. She was *really, really* trying.

And really, how much kinder could she be?

Katerina McPherson, that is.

Sitting there, naked—except for that very flimsy robe, which wasn't tied very tightly at all (this Nina realized because it kept opening up, exposing Kat's fully inflated breasts—all 37CC of them), Kat put out a limp hand for Nina to shake.

Of course Nina shook it, quickly though, then she tried hard not to glance down to compare Kat's most obvious assets to her own meager 34Bs.

Not that Kat would have noticed. She was too busy running that oval horsehair bristle brush through her hair while yammering on and on about how Nathan sang Nina's praises constantly ("He was *so* right! You are *so gorgeous!* You're an actress, too, right?"), that is, when he wasn't relaying stories about their cute little boy ("What's his name again? Jake? Why, how *sweet!* So—*boyish!*") or reverently studying his script.

As he was now. *By himself*. In his own trailer, Kat readily assured her.

What finally did catch Nina's awed attention was when Kat tossed out the words *Oscars* and *gowns* in the same sentence.

"I never seem to have a date for these things. Gosh, I'm beginning to feel like a spinster! Well, at least I've got some *great* choices. Both Valentino and Versace want me to wear them, but I've sort of got my eye on this *gorgeous* Elie Saab sheath . . ."

Suddenly she stopped brushing and turned excitedly to face Nina. "Hey, I have a *super* idea! Why don't you come over to my place when my stylist brings them over, and help me make my decision?"

To think, Katerina McPherson wants me to give her my advice on her OSCAR gown! Me, Nina Sue Wilder, of Joyous Missouri!

Nina was confused. And concerned and, well, *torn*.

She'd been duly warned. And since she was a firm believer that, as Serenity had said, where there was smoke, there was fire, she knew that she had better be damn well certain flames weren't licking at the love nest she'd built with Nathan.

Then again, Kat was being *so* nice. She was just *a normal girl* . . .

And wouldn't it be fun to at least *touch* a couturier gown?

"—kind of disappointed that Nathan blew me off when I asked him to escort me—"

"I'm sorry," murmured Nina, half comprehending what she was hearing, "did you say that you invited Nathan to go to the Oscars . . . with *you?*"

"Oh, yeah, sure . . . but that was a while back. Ha! That silly goofball turned me down, flat. Said he'd feel *really* bad going without *you*. What a gentleman, huh?"

She looked up at Nina with wide-eyed innocence. "*Of course*, I said I understood. But sometimes these guys just don't understand women, do they? I mean, how would *he* know that the *last* thing you'd *ever* do is keep him from going to the Academy Awards. My God, am I *right?*"

She paused from brushing her long, satiny curls to catch Nina's reflection in the mirror. "Just think of the exposure that would have given our little movie . . . not to mention Nathan's career . . ."

Kat leaned forward conspiratorially, which forced her robe to fall open. *Ooops, there was that boob again! Yep, it was certainly more than a handful* . . .

"Can I let you in on a little secret? And puh-*leeez*, don't tell anyone, *especially* not Nathan . . . I have to tell you that, personally, I'm just a wee bit worried that this film may . . . well, that it might get overlooked. By the public. *And* the reviewers." She sighed sadly. "Don't get me wrong, Hugo's a *great* director. I feel so honored to have been chosen to work with him, believe me . . . And just *think* of the opportunity this gives Nathan . . . that is, if it *doesn't bomb*. Still, it *is* very small budget, you know. And Nathan—well, he's not exactly a known name who can carry a film—at *this* point in his career, anyway. That's why any promotion we can do will be *so* important. You know, for *all* of our careers."

She went back to brushing her hair slowly, methodically, but kept on chattering. "Hey, and don't think I'll be upset if you say no to the idea of Nathan going as my escort. I just thought it would be a nice gesture, you know, since he's such a newbie and all. If he passes, I'll just have the Owen brothers escort me. They'd *jump* at the exposure . . . Or maybe George. He's always a blast at those things. Hey, have you met him yet?"

Suddenly she stopped brushing. "Aw, gee, wouldn't it be just awful though, if—" Kat thought better of whatever it was she was thinking and shrugged instead.

This prompted Nina to say, "Uh, I'm sorry, if what were awful?"

"Oh . . . well . . . *hmmm*. I guess I'm putting my foot in my own mouth, but I'd *hate* myself if it *did* come true and I could have stopped it . . . What I mean is, wouldn't it be just awful if Nathan never even *got* another chance to go to the Oscars?"

Never got another chance? Because of me?

Nina could never live with herself if that were the case.

Of course I have to let him go.

Without me.

With her.

With her smile frozen in place, Nina murmured something about how great it was to meet Kat, too, finally, and then she headed out the door.

To find Nathan.

And tell him the good news: He was going to the Oscars.

With Kat.

Hauling ass from Wilshire and Rodeo to West Pico in the middle of the afternoon rush hour is no joy ride, and certainly something Sam avoided unless it was an emergency.

Well, being there when Nina discovered Nathan in Kat's sinewy Pilates-pumped arms was certainly *that*.

Hugo met Sam as his Ferrari squealed to a halt next to the sound stage where *Forever and Again* was shooting.

"So?" growled Sam.

Hugo jerked his head in the direction of Kat's trailer. "She's in there. With Kat. *Just the two of them.*"

Sam strained to hear any yelling, cursing, or shooting.

Dead silence.

He gave Hugo a puzzled look. Hugo nodded wide-eyed, then pointed to Nathan's trailer. "And he's in there. But he may have passed out by now, he was hyperventilating so hard."

"Did she talk to him first?" If so, Sam reasoned, the fear in Nathan's eyes might have given the game away. Then again, Nathan was such a good actor that she might have believed whatever lie he'd come up with to cover his ass.

"Nope. Just politely asked to meet Kat." Hugo shrugged. "Sweet enough kid, but you know, nothing special. My God, with Kat around, *she's toast.*"

Any other time Sam would have argued the point. Instead he said, "Just stay here and keep watch. When Nina comes out, escort her over to Nathan's trailer, but talk loud enough that we know you're coming."

He bounded into Nathan's trailer, where he found his newest client sitting down, his head bent low between his knees. Nathan looked up when Sam entered. Seeing his agent, his protector, his confidant brought a glimmer of hope back into his heart—until Sam hit him right between the eyes with: "So, Nathan, tell me, was it worth it?"

Nathan slumped down again, as if to brace himself from the wrath he knew was due him.

"Because if it wasn't, then you better prepare yourself to lose Nina."

The sound that came out of Nathan was like that of a man being strangled. He gulped, then started again. "I thought I could . . . I thought I could handle it. You know, keep the lid on it. But things are just happening—too fast!" He began pacing the room. "It's—it's been like some surreal dream, both wonderful and at the same time, terrible! You understand, don't you, Sam?"

Sam stood there, poker-faced. For a moment there, he actually felt sorry for the sap.

That is, until Nathan added: "Nah, I guess *you* wouldn't."

As he turned away from Sam, Nathan caught his own reflection in the mirror. His eye lingered there, if for only a nanosecond.

Still, that was one nanosecond too long for Sam.

Goddamn arrogant bastard!

"What, you think that you're the only guy who Kat's allowed into that funhouse she keeps between her thighs?"

Sam's lip curled into a cruel grin. "Sure, maybe *this* week, but trust me, Nathan, we're not talking VIP status at the Grill here. You're just the latest in a long line of clueless dudes! Or haven't you figured that out yet?"

"Don't talk that way about Kat!"

Sam stared at him. "Oh, so that's it, huh? You'd take Kat—over *Nina*?"

"*What?* No! I mean—I mean, why . . . *why does this have to be so hard?*"

Nathan was breathing so heavy that Sam thought he was going to pass out. He felt sorry for him, really he did. To be that young, and that naïve . . .

He put his hand on Nathan's shoulder. This seemed to calm the kid down to some extent. At least enough for him to whisper, "Sam, please . . . what do I do now?"

"You tell Nina that all the bullshit she's been hearing is nothing more than that, a load of crap." Now sure that he had Nathan's full and complete attention, he took a deep breath and added: "And you break it off with Kat. *Cold turkey.* Put it behind you, once and for all. Just focus on your role, your career, and your family . . . and savor the memory."

Hell, who wouldn't? At least Kat was sure to have made it memorable.

"I'll—I'll do my best."

"Fuck that! You'll do it, *period*—"

Just then, they heard Hugo's booming laugh. "Yeah, well, thanks for the compliment! It was nominated for a Palm d'Or, did you know that? Oh, you *did*. What a labor of love. Literally. Heck, it didn't make a dime, but at least I got to enjoy the French Riviera for a couple of weeks—"

The door to the trailer opened and Nina stepped inside. Hugo, on the other hand, hung back. Within seconds, he was hightailing it back to the postproduction trailer.

Sam wished he could go with him. He was sure Nathan felt the same way.

Well, too bad. It was time to face the music.

Nina looked from Nathan to Sam, then back again.

"I—I hope I'm not interrupting anything," she murmured softly.

Nathan jumped up and gave her a kiss. "No . . . no, hon. Not at all . . . Just discussing—a little business, that's all."

Sam nodded in agreement. "I was leaving anyway."

As he said that, both Nathan and Nina shot him looks of desperation, and said in unison, "No!" Because both were surprised at the other's outburst, they stared back at each other.

Great, thought Sam. *Now I've got to play Dr. Phil for these two?*

Nina's look said it all: *Please. Help us.*

Sam put his happy face back on, the one embellished with his patented "We're all winners here" smile.

"Well, Nina, all I can say is that it's—about time you showed up. Nathan was getting worried that you'd never—well, that you'd never have a moment to . . . to stop in and see what he's been up to these past few weeks and all . . ."

They both stared at him as if he'd lost his mind.

Help me out, folks, I'm dying here.

After what seemed like a decade of silence, Nina said softly, "Well, Sam, I'm glad I came here, too. And I'm glad I had a chance to—to meet Katerina."

Prepared for the worst, Nathan sucked in his breath while Sam closed his eyes. Train wrecks weren't his thing.

"She's such a sweetheart. Yeah, *really*. I—I'd heard some—some rumors . . . about her . . . and I have to admit it, Nathan, some of them involved *you*."

She turned to face him. Taking in the shocked look on his face, she added, "Oh, please sweetie, don't be mad at me! I—I know it must seem as if I'm some kind of jealous fool, coming here like this, without calling first"—she put her arms around his waist—"but in a way, I'm glad I did." A tiny frown creased her forehead for just a moment. "It put to rest my worst fears. So please don't be angry for me, for even thinking—"

Relief drained into Nathan's face. "Angry? Me? At—at *you?* Why—why *no*, doll! I—"

Instinctively he drew her close into a hug, then gently tilted her face up to his own for her lips to meet his.

It was a long and satisfying kiss . . . for everyone . . . except Sam.

When they finally parted, they were both smiling jubilantly.

Her smile said, *How could I have ever doubted this wonderful guy?*

His said, *Jeez, did I ever dodge a fucking bullet, or what! That was* way *too close!*

Sam smiled, too. His said, *You lucky son-of-a-bitch.*

He turned to leave. But before he could make it out the door, he heard Nina say, "Honey, I know just how to make it up to you: How would you like to go to the Oscars—with Kat? She's got an extra ticket, and she told me she'd be happy to have you escort her. Think what a break *that* will be for your career . . . and Hugo's movie!"

Sam closed his eyes in disgust.

It was too early to cry on O's shoulder.

But it wasn't too early to go out and get shit-faced.

Because he got to the Standard Downtown's rooftop bar early enough, Sam was able to take possession of one of the poolside candy apple red space pod–like cabanas all by himself, where he gave the waitress a fifty-dollar bill and told her to keep the Dewar's coming.

Then he loosened his tie, lay down spread-eagled on the pod's vibrating waterbed, and stared up at the sky.

The appearance of each twinkling star overhead seemed to be accompanied by another noisy hipster making the scene there on the roof. In a half hour's time, the crowd was at overflow. Any sounds from the street below that were not drowned out by the DJ's expert hotmixing were finally obliterated by the drone of gossip and big talk emanating from those who considered themselves L.A.'s finest, this claim validated by their physical presence on the coveted side of the Standard's velvet rope, on a Friday night, no less.

None of this, however, made Sam invisible, which allowed Katerina McPherson—entourage in tow—to find him.

"Well, well, well. Look who we have here," she snarled. Her minions, who included her gay hair stylist, her not-yet-out-of-the-closet trainer, her could-easily-be-a-tranny clothing stylist, her anorexic nutritionist, two of her BFs from her former " 'hood" (as if lily white Newport Beach, California, could be described as such), and her worshipful albeit hetero personal assistant, Rain Jennings, giggled on cue.

Sam sighed but kept his eyes closed.

"TGIF to you, too, Kat. However, office hours are now closed."

"That's no way to treat your number one client, now is it, Sam?"

He sighed again, silently counted to five, then opened his eyes to find her balloonlike breasts hovering over him, barely restrained by her flimsy spaghetti-strapped crop top. Because she was so close, he noticed for the first time that the planes of her face were buffed to a smooth porcelain finish. Although the frown lines had been plumped and lasered away, with her eyes narrowed into dark slits and her lips turned down cruelly that way, all her renowned beauty faded instantly.

No doubt about it: Kat was pissed at him.

She snapped her fingers, signaling her minions that she wanted a few minutes alone with the object of her disaffection. They dispersed like the chlorine in the bar's shimmering, lighted pool.

Sam sat up to make room for her on the water mattress. As she leaned back onto it, she set in motion a series of gentle waves that he found somewhat arousing. She smiled knowingly, and placed her hand over his.

That sent a cold shiver up his spine. *There went that lovin' feeling.*

"You're a control freak, you know that, Sam?"

Her tone was light, but he knew better. "Whattaya mean?" He was trying hard not to slur his words, but already he was three Scotches to the wind.

"I think you know what I mean." She flopped over on her toned abdomen and stared out at the pool. "I think you feel that you can control Nathan. And by doing that, you control me, too."

"I'm not trying to control you, Kat."

"That's smart of you, Sam. Because you never will." She leaned back on one arm and looked him squarely in the eye. "Or Nathan, for that matter. So *leave us alone.*"

He yanked her foot by its Manolo-encased stiletto until she was at his side. The water mattress undulated wildly, practically tossing her into his lap. She tried to jerk her foot away, but he held tight to it.

"Is this your idea of foreplay?" she snapped at him. "Because if it is, I can see why you're such a lonely guy. Your technique stinks."

"I'm not playing games, Kat. And you shouldn't be, either, with Nathan's life. He's just starting out, so why don't you give him a break?"

"Anyone who's seen with me *is* getting a break. You know that." She smiled. "Under any other circumstance, you'd be sending me roses for taking him 'under my wing.' What's it to you anyway, Sam?"

"He's got a wife. *And* a kid. You've got to have some kind of conscience about that, Kat."

"If he doesn't, why should I?" She had a point there.

"Look, Kat, this isn't up for debate. Cool your jets, and everyone will be happy."

"You mean *you'll* be happy."

She stood up and stretched, an action that caused her crop top to rise high enough that the gawking crowd got what it was waiting for: *peek-a-boo* . . . "Although I can't figure out why . . . yet. Well, Sam, your butting out would make *me* happy. And if that's something you can't do—or *won't*—then I'll find another agent who will."

She left him floating in his pod.

The version of their discussion that Riley heard from Rain the next morning, over macchiatos and biscottis at the Sunset Plaza Coffee Bean, included a few more profanities and the inference that Kat had also gotten in a well-targeted kick to Sam's groin. However, Rain was so smitten with him that she was bound to invent a few juicy details to make it worth his while to forgo their usual form of communication—text messaging— and actually meet her in person instead.

Riley could forgive her for that. Rain had done good, and he rewarded her with what she lived for: a very public, very sloppy kiss, and a teasing squeeze on the thigh that promised more was yet to come—*if* she kept delivering the goods.

As he walked away, he wondered what her reaction would be when she finally found out that he played for the other team, as it were. His guess was that she'd probably be so mortified she'd move back home to Ketchum, Idaho.

Good riddance.

When Nathan told Nina that Fiona had gotten them invited to the Playboy Mansion Valentine's Day's bash, she couldn't believe her ears. In fact, it wasn't until the limousine pulled up to their apartment building that it actually registered in her mind that, yessirree, *the Hartes would be hot tubbing with Hef in the infamous Grotto!*

As well as several dozen naked nubile Playboy bunnies, each one equipped with her own built-in flotation device.

Nina's euphoria over partaking in the quintessential L.A. celebrity experience subsided somewhat at that realization, coupled with another: that for the first time in six years, she and Nathan would not be sharing a romantic, intimate Valentine's Day, just the two of them.

Nina wondered if it bothered Nathan as much as it bothered her.

Obviously not. He'd already downed almost a full complimentary bottle of Taittinger on the ride over. The sloppy smile on his kisser and the way in which he was staring out the window—like a kid on the way to Disneyland—was proof positive that Nathan thought he was living the American Dream—

—Or at least, the *Entourage* version of it.

After having been given their security clearance by the infamous talking rock, their limo made its way through the massive wrought-iron gates and up the expansive driveway, passing an aviary, a redwood forest, monkey cages, a Japanese koi pond, roaming peacocks, flamingos—and of course rabbits—on their way toward the twenty-one-thousand-square-foot Gothic home of Hef and his human menagerie.

Nina, on the other hand, suddenly felt as if she had been dropped into her worst nightmare. As far as the eye could see was primo grade-A T-and-A clad in barely-there babydoll lingerie or too-tight cut-down-to-there tank tops paired with too-short miniskirts or belly-bared skin-tight jeans, or perhaps the ubiquitous Playboy bunny corset, tail, and semi-erect ears—possibly the only things at half-staff on the five and a half acres that made up the estate's grounds.

Sure, Nina was dressed up too, all cute and sexy: She'd paired a classic colorful Cavalli silk miniskirt she'd found at a secondhand shop on Melrose with a white chiffon halter top that Casey had lent her. Could such classic elegance compete with overt wall-to-wall come-and-get it voluptuousness?

Hardly. Which was why she, too, grabbed a bottle of Taittinger before exiting the limo and, in the course of a half hour, chased it down with a cosmopolitan proffered to her by one of the many human bunnies holding trays of sloshing martini glasses.

The drinks did little to help her keep up with Nathan, who in no time was surrounded by a bevy of long-legged, big-breasted Amazons, all of them salivating over the newest star on Hollywood's ever-changing horizon—according to *Us*, *People*, *In Touch*, and *Life & Style*.

"Well, he certainly seems to be enjoying himself, doesn't he?"

At the sound of Sam's voice, Nina turned around. She smiled first, then blushed a bit as the memory of Hugo's very broad hint to O—that Sam had a crush on the PSO—came back to her.

Her sudden shyness did nothing at all to alleviate Sam's crush—with Nina. In fact, it only drove home to him the reason she was such a special commodity in their town: She was fresh, wholesome, and solely without an agenda.

So what was she doing here, in L.A.'s most celebrated lair of lasciviousness?

For that matter, what was she doing in L.A. to begin with?

"Yes, I can honestly say that Nathan seems to be taking to this like a fish to water." She looked around at all the celebrities—both men and women—who obviously felt at home in the festivities. "I guess I should get used to it. Although, I've got to admit, it's not easy." She found it hard to take her eyes off Paris and Lindsay as they strolled by, toned arm-in-arm, with their posses keeping a respectful distance from them, and from each other.

"Yeah, it's like being in some sort of celebrity side show, isn't it?"

"Except that *I'm* the only freak here," she murmured as a Bunny with size 38DD chest came into sight, anchored on each side by a Wilson brother.

"Trust me, it's not you who's the freak. Although you *are* somewhat of an anomaly in a town where most twenty-four-year-olds have already had cosmetic surgery. The trick is finding the ones like you, who haven't."

"Maybe I should reconsider my stance on that," she said as she watched the tide of women ebb and flow around Nathan. For a second there, she thought she might have seen a familiar face—Katerina's? But it disappeared into the crowd.

As did Nathan, who was suddenly nowhere to be found.

Watching her look off after him in that direction, Sam declared, "Hell, don't do that! You're absolutely perfect."

"Well, thank you for the compliment. It's very kind."

"It's more than that. It's the truth." Once again, her cheeks pinked up. He really had been telling the truth, but the last thing he wanted to do was to make her feel uncomfortable in any way, so he changed the subject. "Hey, have you seen the Grotto yet?"

"Nope, not yet." She tried to steady herself by laying a hand on his sleeve. Suddenly she was too dizzy even to care where Nathan might have gone. Thank God Sam was there so that she wasn't totally alone. Catching her breath, she added, "And since I'm here, I guess I should take in that infamous site. Lead the way."

Elbowing their way through a thicket of off-season professional athletes, rock stars, sitcom kings, and Ocean's Thirteen wannabes, Nina caught a glimpse of the midget whom she thought had played Mini-Me. He was dressed as Cupid, and he had his hand up the red velvet miniskirt of a pantyless Playmate, who was squealing with delight.

That sight, combined with Nina's champagne and vodka chaser, made her queasy again. She reached out to grab Sam's hand so that she didn't lose him, too, in the crowd headed for the Grotto.

The steam that enveloped the man-made cave was stifling. Bare flesh was everywhere. She tried hard not to stare, opting instead to look through the water, but the shimmering lights, reflecting on the cave walls and back into the undulating pool, were making her dizzier by the minute.

Finally she spotted Nathan—although she thought: *That can't be him, because he's kissing that woman . . .*

. . . That woman who looks just like . . . Kat.

It was Kat.

And yes, that was Nathan with her.

Kissing her.

Sam, noticing the look on her face, scanned the crowd to see what had shocked her.

Just then, Nathan looked up and saw them staring. He waved uncertainly, then headed over. Kat stayed at his side.

"Hi!" she said brightly, as if being in a lip-lock with Nina's husband was an everyday occurrence.

It was, but Nina didn't know that.

Until now.

Nathan stood by warily, waiting for Nina's reaction.

He didn't have to wait long.

She threw up—*on Kat.*

*   *   *

"Jeez, Nina! What the hell did you go and do that for?" He
hadn't said a word to her the whole way back from the Grotto,
or even as they stood curbside, waiting for their limo to pull
around. But once they were safely ensconced inside the leather-
clad tomb, he scolded her as if she were . . . well, a child.

A child with an active imagination.

One who only *imagined* that another woman had been kissing her husband.

"I—I couldn't help it! It just came . . . up!"

The words came out between sobs. She turned to the window, then came right out with it: *"Why the hell were you kissing
her, anyway?"*

"What?" He acted distracted, as if her question was not
worth the breath to answer it. "That? It—it was *nothing!* A—a
friendly little peck. She's . . . a little down. About being alone
on Valentine's Day, and all. That's—well, you know how hard
that can be for women."

"Yeah, sure, I feel for her, really I do. But let me tell you
something, Nathan Harris Harte, it's not *nearly* as bad as
spending Valentine's Day with your husband and oh, *by the
way*, a hundred beautiful women!"

He felt the heat in her words and turned to face her.

"It's my job, remember? Fiona says that it's important that I
get out there. You know I have to make the scene, get my name
in the columns." He frowned angrily. "How many times are
we going to have this discussion? Look, if it bothers you so
much, then next time don't tag along!"

"Tag along? *Tag along?*" She fairly spit out the words. "Have
you forgotten that today is—*Valentine's Day?*"

Until he saw the haunted look on her face, yes, he had forgotten that it was any day other than one on which he'd finally been allowed to play with the big boys.

And the very big girls. *And Katerina*, who didn't feel that any woman was her competition, let alone Nina.

He felt like a heel for forgetting.

And for lying about the kiss.

He reached over to her. Even though she shrugged him away, he held her tighter, pulled her closer, and nuzzled her until she quit fighting him.

By the time they'd reached the apartment and he'd tipped the limo driver, they'd kissed and made up.

When they got upstairs, they made love.

Tenderly at first, then tempestuously.

It was make-up sex at its best.

Afterward, spent and sweaty, they cuddled until Nina fell asleep.

When she woke an hour later and reached over for him, she saw that he was standing beside the bed, dressed again in his new Sean John jeans, a black T-shirt, and an Armani jacket.

"You're going back there?"

Of course he was.

"Why don't you just say it: *You just don't trust me.*" Whenever he was annoyed, Nathan's Greek god–like profile seemed etched in impenetrable granite.

If I don't answer, she thought, *he'll know he's right and he'll leave angry.*

I can't take that, again. Not on Valentine's Day.

So she lied. "Of course I trust you. It's just that—that I

would . . . miss you too much if we were apart . . . tonight especially."

Still, he knew he'd gotten what he wanted: her uneasy agreement to let him go.

He bent down and gave her kiss. "I won't be long."

Then he went out the door.

Happy Valentine's Day.

She got up, made herself some coffee, and went to work.

In reality, she was too angry to be on the phone with men who were seeking the kindness of strange women. Too bad. Her kid was at a sleepover, her husband was at the Playboy Mansion, and she was on the war path.

Bring it on.

Poor King Kong. He had the misfortune of dialing her number in anticipation of fifty-eight minutes of erotic empathy.

As if there is such a thing.

What he got instead was O's dissertation on the sensual advantages of being a hairy man, which included the wherewithal to stay warm in colder climes, not to mention being able to keep his buxom buck-naked partner warm during chilly nights. By the time she asked this supposedly big hairy brute if he might like to take a razor to her nether regions and sculpt it into some work of art, then allow her to do the same to his back, King Kong, flushed and cocky (in both the physical and literal senses), admitted that he was as hairless as a chihuahua . . .

And oh, by the way, was she into dwarfs?

Nina vomited for the second time that night.

Leave it to a guy nicknamed King Kong to present her with yet another reason to get out of the business.

9

The Beginning of the End

Normalcy. That was what Nina and Nathan needed.

And what could be more normal than a cookout with some of their loving friends around them?

Nina got that bright idea after a week in which the two of them lived like strangers: passing in the same hallway, sharing the same rooms—even the same bed—but strangers nonetheless.

Albeit very polite strangers.

Neither of them wanted to rock the tiny sailboat that was their marriage, particularly in what were already turbulent waters.

Nathan jumped at the idea. Put him in front of their portable Weber with a bag of Kingsford charcoal briquets and he was king of the world! Nina would wheedle some perfectly marbled New York strips from Tommaso's butcher at a fire sale price, grab a couple of six-packs of some of the store's chichi microbrewed beer, and they were in business.

"So, who would you like to invite?" Nina asked warily.

Was he foolish enough to say Kat? Of course not. The last thing in the world Nathan needed was to have the two women he loved within spitting (or barfing) distance of each other.

Besides, ever since Nina had caught them kissing at the mansion, she'd become suspicious and anxious. And as for Kat—well, Kat was acting less covert about their affair, and more possessive: throwing tantrums when they were called back to the set before she was done "cuing him" (her little euphemism for their daily love trysts), pouting if Hugo called for additional takes when she was ready to call it quits for the evening, sulking or crying whenever Nathan couldn't get away to meet her, or if he tried to end their rendezvous before she was through with him first.

And that was the problem: *She was wearing him out.*

By the time he got home, he was too tired to even consider sex with Nina. It didn't matter that she had stayed up all night waiting for him just so that they could make love.

At first when he begged off, she was surprised, but understanding. "I'm sure it must be exhausting on that set all day," she murmured, concerned and perturbed at the same time. After a week or so, though, she took matters into her own hands—*literally*—with scented oils and some expert finger manipulation, while wearing her sheerest babydoll camisoles.

Nina realized instinctively that she was in a battle of the sexiest.

What she didn't know at the time was that she'd already been outmaneuvered and outflanked on every front.

Not to mention the backside, too.

It was only when Nathan began faking being asleep that she realized how close she was to losing the war for his affections. Upset and disillusioned, she pulled back to reassess the situation. She was willing to concede that he was tired. And, from what she had witnessed when she saw him with Katerina, maybe—*just maybe*—he had a little crush on the star, and was reveling in the attention she was showing him.

And obviously Katerina must have been somewhat flattered. She certainly admired his "tenacity and stamina on the set," as she so eloquently put it once, when she had called the apartment looking for him to remind him of "a little business" they had discussed for the next day . . . something that had to do with his bringing his old varsity jacket to the set.

When Nina questioned Nathan as to why he needed it, he muttered, "It's for a little role playing—I mean, a Method acting technique Kat wants to show me."

Oh, really?

Nina found that hard to believe. Still, it was easier to buy into than the thought that Kat might be reciprocating Nathan's crush. Just the fact that Kat was being so open with her was reason enough that Nina couldn't, in a million years, believe that Nathan and Kat were anything other than a tabloid pipe dream, or gossip used by the publicist to fuel the public's interest in the film.

Besides, if he ever had an affair with Kat, or *anyone*, that would be the end of their marriage—no ifs, ands, or buts about it—as well as everything they'd spent six long years building together.

Not to mention their tiny, happy family.

And didn't Nathan just know that.

Which was why he was tense and irritable at home, but afraid to do anything other than what he was told on the set, whether it was Hugo or Kat calling the shots. But unfortunately, from one day to the next, it was hard for him to tell who was running the show.

He jumped at the chance to do something normal, like a cookout on Santa Monica Beach, where he could escape the tension with a little Frisbee, some volleyball, and a couple of rides with Jake on the pier's Ferris wheel.

"I was thinking we could invite Jamie," he answered almost too cheerfully.

Nina winced. The few times Nathan had connected with his pal since he had signed with Sam, Jamie had been a bit of a wise guy, accusing Nathan of having "graduated to the big leagues" now that he no longer came to class with the rest of them but instead took private lessons from Euphegenia.

"I guess he's too good for us now, huh?" Jamie once muttered at Nina, when he called to ask why Nathan had skipped class.

"No, it's nothing like that! He's just . . . well, he can't break away from the set so Euphegenia is coaching him privately a couple of times a week. But he's only doing that because the production is running behind schedule. They're working him *really* hard, and he's always tired."

She didn't have the heart to tell Jamie the truth: that he was right, that Nathan now felt that going to class with other less successful actors was beneath him. Besides, now that he could afford to have Euphegenia all to himself, why shouldn't he indulge himself? It was only, what, a couple of hours of additional phone time for O, no big deal.

To him.

"Yeah, I can just *imagine* what's making him so tired." She could almost feel Jamie's leer through the telephone.

Granted, Jamie made her cringe, but still, just the fact that Nathan even suggested inviting Jamie meant that he, too, was looking for things to go back to the way they were.

"What do you think about me inviting Casey and Jarred, or Susannah and Rolf? You like them, right? And that way Jake will have someone to play with, too."

Nathan shrugged. He'd finally met both couples at the school fund-raising auction, but they were more Nina's pals than his own. This was obvious by the way both women had scrutinized him closely, a clear indication to him that they'd been reading the tabloid headlines that were popping up recently about him and Kat. As for their husbands, Rolf immediately started pitching him some cockeyed indie projects that needed a "name" to attract any real financing, and that rubbed Nathan the wrong way. *Hell, where was that offer when he was a nobody, huh?*

On the other hand, Jarred's nonchalance toward him hurt Nathan's ego.

Not that he could say any of this to Nina, who finally felt a part of the SOA family, now that she'd found a few kindred souls to hang with.

So instead he said, "I dunno. I'd be afraid that Jamie might—you know, glom onto Jarred. Also, he may come on to Susannah."

Nina could easily envision both of those scenarios occurring, and would feel ashamed if they did, so she didn't push the idea of having her new friends join them.

"What about Helene?"

The question was innocent enough. Nathan smiled benignly and nodded. "Yeah sure, why not?" In truth, he would prefer to let sleeping girlfriends lie. But since he was going for anything that resembled their old lives, he'd just have to hope that Helene would demonstrate her appreciation for this invitation from the rising star and his wife by keeping her yap shut.

That was too much to ask for.

As the men stood sentry over the Weber, Helene and Nina laid out the rest of the picnic spread on a nearby table downwind from the billowing smoke. Sometime between setting out the Hungarian sour cream potato salad and slicing up the bruised or overripe ortaniques, pomelos, satsumas, and tangelos Nina had pilfered from Tommaso's fruit bins, Helene nervously grilled Nina about Nathan's new life: the role he was playing, the hours he was putting in, the thrill of working with Hugo, and of course, what it was like to costar opposite Kat McPherson.

"She's been very sweet to him," Nina said cautiously.

"So you've met her?" Helene, still cutting up the pomelos, looked up sharply to gauge Nina's reaction.

"Yes, of course." Nina's tone was belligerent, but she couldn't help it. She knew what Helene was referring to, and she hated the thought that their friends would even *think* that about Nathan.

She took a deep breath, then scanned the beach for Jake. He was chasing sandpipers in and out of the surf. "I've seen those stories too. About Nathan and Kat. They're garbage. Why do you ask?"

"No reason," Helene responded quickly. *Too quickly.*

"No, that's not true." Nina walked over to where Helene was standing, picked up the thick pomelo skins the lanky blond had peeled off the fruit, and fairly threw them at the trash can. A couple of scavenging pigeons scattered, then reconvened greedily. "You wouldn't have said anything if that were really the case."

Helene put down her knife and looked over at Nathan. "I really don't think you want to know."

"Try me."

Helene hesitated. "Okay, you asked for it. The bottom line is that Nathan isn't as innocent as you think." She picked up a satsuma and, with meticulous precision, focused on peeling it.

"Oh." Nina felt as if the wind had been knocked out of her. "Tell me: Have you ever seen him come onto anyone?"

"No . . . nothing like that."

Nina put her hand on top of Helene's so that her friend would stop peeling and look at her. Whatever Helene had to say, Nina wanted to be sure to read the truth in her eyes. "How about you, Helene?"

Helene froze, but she didn't glance away. "No. No, I can honestly say that he hasn't. Not that I didn't want him to." The smile that came onto her lips involuntarily was a sad one. "Let's just say that he's . . . susceptible."

"If that's the case, then why are you warning me now?"

"Because—well, if it were me, I'd want to know, so I thought you might, too."

"Thanks. But if and when it happens, I think I'll know."

"Know what?"

Helene and Nina looked up to find Nathan standing there. Helene turned beet red and suddenly took an interest in rearranging the fruit on the platter. Nina went up to him and put her arm in his.

"I was just telling Helene that I think I'll know when your fame gets the better of you."

"According to Jamie, it already happened."

Nina looked around for Jamie. He was stalking off angrily toward the street, where he'd parked his Harley, the one status symbol he shared with his idol, George Clooney. Hopping on, he kick-started it and revved off noisily, toward Coronado Avenue. "What, now he's upset?"

"Yeah, you could say that." Nathan laughed caustically. "He's pissed because I won't introduce him to Hugo. I mean, the movie's already been cast! What, does he think he can just talk his way into a part of something? He's such a loser sometimes."

The women stared at him blankly. Sure, both of them thought Jamie's bluster left a lot to be desired. Still, they'd all started out at Euphegenia's together. Just because Nathan was the first to move on to bigger and better things didn't mean that Jamie—or by that definition, Helene and Nina—were losers.

Or did it?

Either way, Helene didn't like the implication. Slowly she wiped her hands on a paper towel. "Well, um, maybe I should be going, too. I've got class tonight, and if Jamie blows it off now that he's angry, I'll need to prepare a monologue to take the place of the scene we were supposed to do together. You know how it is with us losers. We keep plodding along, no matter what."

"Hey, look, Helene, that's not what I meant to say. You know that," Nathan walked up to her and put his arm around her, but she wriggled out from under it.

"Okay sure, whatever. But if I were you, Nathan, I'd remember the old saying: 'Be nice to the people you meet on the way up, because they're the same people who'll be stepping over you when your new friends kick you to the curb.' " She turned to Nina. "You've got my number, right? Keep in touch, okay? You never know how things may work out."

As she sauntered off, Nathan looked anxiously at Nina. "What did she mean by that?"

"Nothing," she answered, but Nathan could tell that she was upset at him, too. Suddenly Nina had no appetite, which meant lots of leftovers for the boys. She went off to call Jake to come and eat.

Damn, thought Nathan, *can't I say or do anything right? So much for going back to the way things were before.*

Maybe that's for the best.

Needless to say, because it considered itself the epicenter of its clients' world, Tommaso's had an exceptional newsstand. There, its discriminating clientele (never customers, always clientele) could find every specialty magazine imaginable (*Spa*, say, or *Daruma*, even *Outre* and *Raw Vision*, and always *Placebo Journal*), major newspapers from every state capital *and* twenty-two foreign nations, and eighteen or so financial publications, not to mention a handful of existential manifestos filled with erudite social commentary.

And of course Tommaso's newsstand also had every gaudy, glossy celebrity magazine imaginable, many of which featured the most renowned of its clientele.

When Nathan's beefcake photos began appearing in the gossip rags that stared up at Nina from the shelves lining the checkout counters, she tried to ignore them, pretending that her husband wasn't the guy *Cosmopolitan* had placed as number three on its list of "Hollywood's Ten Hottest Hunks," or that *Life & Style* hadn't proclaimed him the "Naughty Hottie of the Month."

But then *Us Weekly* questioned whether he was "Kat's New Mystery Man?" and did a follow-up article putting Nathan and Nina's marriage in its "Danger Zone" column.

That was something Nina couldn't ignore.

When she showed the magazine to Nathan, he threw it against the wall and swore. She was glad Jake was already in bed sound asleep.

"I don't know where they get that crap," he fairly shouted. "They—they are *so* off base! Kat's just—you know, a friend . . ."

Seeing that Nina's look of concern barely wavered, he shrugged and muttered something about publicity being the part of the job he hated most.

Well, guess what, she thought, *I hate it, too!*

She said as much to Sam one evening. It was on a Tuesday, which was the only night she worked until seven. By happenstance (or so she assumed), Sam had gotten into the habit of coming to the store to do his shopping every Tuesday evening about that time (to his maid Margarita's dismay, since invariably he'd forget half the items on her meticulous grocery list). Usually he meandered in about a half hour or so before the end of Nina's shift. The first couple of times he'd shown up, she watched him as he helplessly roamed the aisles, as if on a scavenger hunt. Soon, though, the moment she saw him enter, she'd gently take him and his list in hand, and escort him around the store until the items he sought were in his cart.

True, his helplessness was endearing. Still she felt obligated to tell him, "You know, Sam, you can always have Margarita call or fax or even e-mail the order to the store, and we can have it waiting for you when you get here. That way, you don't waste any time."

"If I didn't know better, Nina, I'd say that you don't cherish these few precious moments we spend together."

She smiled wryly. "I'm almost embarrassed to tell you that these little visits have become the highlight of my week. It certainly beats going home to an empty house."

"Thanks . . . I think. Even if that wasn't a compliment, I'm going to imagine that it is."

He picked up a jar of gourmet hot sauce, pretended to be impressed with its ingredients, then put it down again. "If you must know, I find grocery shopping to be a great stress reliever. Much more calming than Tai Chi, don't you think?"

"You're asking the wrong girl. Having never taken Tai Chi, I couldn't tell you. Then again, you've never shopped with a four-year-old, either. That might change your mind about the whole experience."

"I'm sure it would." They had reached her checkout

counter, so he began unloading daikons, Asian turnips, salsify, and raw milk cheeses (all foods he felt would make her think he was a really healthy eater) onto the conveyor belt. Not that he knew what the heck to do with the stuff. Soon it would be joining the other foods he'd purchased on other Tuesday nights, which were now rotting in his refrigerator, to Margarita's mortification.

"An empty house, huh? Where's the little guy?"

"At play rehearsal, until nine. He's been cast as Henry Higgins in a school production."

"What, *My Fair Lady*? But—I thought he was only, like, four."

"He is. But we're talking Sage Oak Academy, an educational institution catering to the stars and starlets of tomorrow—at least, according to their gifted parents. Sorry, I guess that sounded sarcastic. Sometimes I get tired of the über-parent game."

She then explained that the play's controversial casting had caused a furor at the school: Plum, who had been taking private singing and acting lessons since the age of two, had won the role of Eliza hands down, albeit over the tearful objections of at least ten other mothers, all of whom were used to getting their way with Mr. Pickering. This put Pickering in a tizzy because, as he pointed out to Deborah Marcom, the school's theater teacher, he had originally felt the musical *Chicago* would be "more accommodating to our bevy of talented little tykes."

Too bad, exclaimed Ms. Marcom, a perfectionist whose productions were Broadway-worthy spectacles in miniature. She overruled him, proclaiming that she had an exquisite Eliza and a perfect Higgins. Pickering knew better than to rock the boat. After all, Ms. Marcom was already being wooed by several competing preschools. However, to placate the upset mommies, he had secured the services of Badgley Mischka to custom-design their daughters' costumes for the Ascot race scene.

Another backstage negotiation concerned the male roles. While Ms. Marcom had reassured Nina that Jake outshone every other boy who had tried out for the role of Higgins, at the same time she'd had a hard time casting the second male lead, that of Colonel Pickering, because none of the other boys wanted to play a character who shared the same name as their pompous headmaster. Finally Casey was able to convince a very wary Ben to take it—but only after eliciting a promise from Ms. Marcom that the school would secure the rights to *Star Wars, the Musical* for next year's production, and that Ben would be guaranteed the role of Luke Skywalker.

"From what you're describing, I certainly wouldn't want to find myself across the negotiation table from some of those women."

That remark brought a smile to her face. "I know what you mean. I'm sure that Jeff and Scott are dreams compared to a few of those SOA mothers." She grimaced, then smacked the register's keys as if they were on fire. "And, of course Nathan's still 'at the studio.' "

Sam shifted his feet uncomfortably. With as much sincerity as he could muster, he countered, "Of course he is. Don't go believing the tabloids."

"Yeah, okay. If you say so. They can't all be right, now can they?" She pointed to the *People* beside the counter. Scarlett Johansson, pouting her patented Mona Lisa smile, was on the cover, but the inset photo of Nathan and Kat, set above the masthead under the heading, "Love Match?" stood out like a neon light to both of them.

"Anything's possible. But I have no doubt that Nathan loves you." He glanced away for a second. It was hard for him to lie to her. He wondered if Nathan was finding it any easier to do nowadays.

"It's nice that one of us does."

She waited for him to hand over the American Express Black he'd pulled from his wallet. He lived for this moment, when his hand slowly brushed her delicate fingers. His only regret was that he couldn't allow it to linger there, or to interweave his own fingers with hers.

Or, better yet, draw them up to his lips and kiss them gently.

Not that he could say any of this to her. Then again, did he have to? He searched her wide brown eyes in the hope that she could read his thoughts. For a moment there, as they locked gazes, he felt she could.

"Say, since you're flying solo tonight, how about joining me for a drink when you get off work?" There, he'd finally asked! To hide his anticipation, he fiddled with his wallet while she ran his card through and considered his offer.

"Sure. Why not? It's seven now, so I can clock out. Although we aren't supposed to leave with, you know, Tommaso's clientele. Can I meet you somewhere?"

He was in shock. She had said yes! She'd agreed to meet him somewhere!

How he'd love to take her back to his place, to sit out on his

deck and listen to the waves lapping up against the sand, just
the two of them . . . holding her hand . . . kissing her fingers . . .

Among other things.

He roused himself. "Yeah . . . let's see . . . um . . . how about
the Veranda Bar, at the Casa del Mar? That's near your place,
isn't it?" He hoped she hadn't noticed the tightness in his
throat.

"Yep, that works. I'll probably be ten minutes or so behind
you. Order me an appletini, will you?"

"Yes ma'am. I'll count the minutes."

Little did she know that he'd meant that literally.

Eleven minutes and twenty-one seconds after Sam ordered
their drinks, Nina strolled into the lobby lounge of the Hotel
Casa del Mar. The bar was set up like a large, plush living
room, with many sofas, settees, and cushy chairs bunched into
a multitude of intimate groupings. It overlooked a lighted pool
that was set down in an intimate terrace garden. Beyond it was
the ocean, an inky indigo in hue, for already the sun had set
deep into the evening fog that hugged the coastline.

Nina was still wearing her Tommaso's khakis, but her pale
green button-down Oxford shirt was now rolled up at the
sleeves and three buttons were undone, exposing a locket on a
thin gold chain and a lacy white camisole underneath.

How he'd give anything to be that locket, lying there above
the soft swells of her breasts, listening to the gentle beating of
her heart.

As she walked up to him, Sam rose up instinctively from the
sofa he'd been holding for them. He resisted the urge to give

her a kiss, although her fragrance, an intoxicating musky scent, made him want to bury his head in her neck and breathe deeply.

If only he could.

Instead he made small talk, answering her questions about this director and that production in progress, and bringing her up to speed on the town's biggest deals (a *Lords* prequel, another biopic—this one about Churchill, and rumored to star Russell, who'd have no issue with packing on the pounds). He also asked her questions about herself: how she liked working at Tommaso's (hated it), what she planned to do when she left it (voice-over work, maybe some live theater), and whether she'd turn into a stage mother, now that her son had a starring role. ("What, are you kidding me? Not in a million years! I know better.")

All safe subjects.

In other words, they talked about anything and everything but Nathan.

She was on her second appletini when she asked, "So, what's a nice boy like you doing in a dirty town like this?"

He laughed. "Same old story. I grew up in the town. My dad was a scriptwriter, and my mom was an actress before they married. She gave up fame and fortune to raise my brothers and me. I went to Malibu High, then UCLA to study film, then to law school there. I always knew I wanted to be in the business, but I didn't have the creative chops." He downed his Scotch. "That's why I became an agent. I like to consider myself a guardian to those who have the talent that eluded me."

"If you ask me, I think you would have made a pretty good actor yourself." Turning to face him, Nina placed one elbow on the back of the couch and leaned in, grazing his thigh with her knee as she did so. He didn't move away. But then again, neither did she.

Sweet.

"Really? What makes you think so?"

"Well, you're a smooth liar, for one thing."

He felt his ears turning red. Suddenly he appreciated the low, romantic lighting in the lounge, if only for the fact that it kept her from seeing the evidence of her summation firsthand. Other than that, he found the lighting a nuisance in that it aggravated his uncontrollable urge to walk over to the front desk and reserve an upstairs suite, then attempt to sweet-talk her into joining him in a bubble bath for two.

"A liar, huh? Gee, and to think I thought you only found me witty, forthright, and charming. I have to tell you that I'm crushed, Nina."

"Okay, I'll say it: You're charming, too. Does that make you feel any better?" Her dimples deepened at first, but then that dazzling smile disappeared from her face. "Maybe even a bit too charming. You've almost made me forget about Nathan tonight. But that was the game plan, wasn't it?"

Of course, she was right, but for all the wrong reasons. Hell yeah, he didn't want her thinking about Nathan! But only because he wanted her only thinking of *him*.

"Not that I blame you," she continued. The smile was back, but it was sad now, reflecting the haunted look in her eyes. "It's your job to do whatever you have to do to protect your clients. I understand that. Even if it means babysitting their wives."

"Is that what you think I'm doing, babysitting you?" He patted her hand, but he let it linger on top of hers. She didn't move hers away, either. "Well, you're wrong. I'll have you know that I've dreamed of this moment since . . . well, quite frankly, since I first met you. This is exactly where I want to be, and you're exactly who I want to be here with."

He couldn't believe he was saying this, now, out loud to her. And from the skeptical grin on her face, she couldn't believe it, either. "What, now you're laughing at me? My God, woman, you're crushing me! You're breaking my heart."

She was silent for a moment. Then she murmured, "For a moment there, I really thought you were serious."

"I am. Not that it matters, to you, anyway. Somewhere you've gotten the idea that I'm some sort of party animal, or depraved womanizer. But I'm not. I'm just a nice guy who likes the company of a nice woman."

"Oh, I believe you. In fact, I know you better than you think." She was looking at him strangely, although he didn't know why. Then she shrugged. "I only hope that I can live up to your expectations. In this town, people slip off pedestals pretty easily."

He guessed her thoughts were no longer with him, but with Nathan.

Well, so much for that bubble bath.

"Nina, take my word for it: Very few people deserve to be up on that pedestal in the first place. And the ones that do— well, they should be allowed one slip-up now and then, shouldn't they? After all, nobody's perfect."

Dammit, why am I pleading that asshole's case for him? Right this very second, he's out there breaking her heart, when he should be here with her, holding her, kissing her . . . making love to her . . .

As if reading his mind, she leaned into him, laying her head gently on his shoulder with a sigh. "I sound like an ungrateful fool, don't I? I'm not, really. For whatever the reason is that you're here with me, I appreciate it. Tonight you're my Prince Charming. And I needed one, badly. So put any thoughts of any other women out of your mind. At least for a few moments. Otherwise, I'll be jealous. I mean it."

He murmured, "Believe me when I tell you that you are the only woman who's crossed my mind this evening." *Or any other evening since we met, for that matter.*

It was her turn to laugh. "I know better than that, Sam. You've got some unattainable object of desire sitting up on some pedestal deep in the recesses of your heart, don't you? Don't pretend you don't! Go ahead, admit it."

If only she knew, he thought.

Instead he shrugged. "Is it that obvious? Okay, you got me. You're a mind reader, Nina."

"She probably doesn't even know it yet, does she?"

He looked at her sharply. "That's right. How do you know?"

Nina murmured, "Well, let's just call it woman's intuition. Nothing more."

She looked away, as if he'd put her on the spot. Only when he patted her arm gently to let her know that wasn't the case did she relax again, leaning back against him. With a trembling voice, she whispered, "Whoever she is, she's a very lucky girl. Do her a favor, Sam: Don't let her get away. You both deserve a lifetime of happiness."

Don't worry, sweet Nina. I won't let you go. I'll always be there for you.

Softly, he rested his chin on the top of her head, taking in her scent again.

Heavenly.

They sat there silently for at least a half hour, listening to the murmurs of the other couples and quartets grouped around them, the soft jazz emanating from the piano, and the waves lapping the beach. After a while, though, she rose, swaying just a little. He reached out and caught her arm to steady her.

"It's the witching hour. Well, Prince Charming, before I turn into a pumpkin, I'd better head on home."

Tossing down enough cash to cover their tab, Sam stood up, too, but he didn't let go of her arm.

She didn't seem to mind.

Together, they headed down the lobby's grand staircase and out the front door. She hadn't valet-parked, but had found a spot two blocks up, almost next to Ocean Avenue. He offered to escort her to her car, and she nodded. There was a brisk ocean breeze, and she leaned into him as they walked.

When they got there, she fumbled for her keys, apologizing profusely for being such a klutz. She could not have known that he was dreading the inevitable: when she would say good night, then drive off, and he'd have to wait a whole week to see her once again behind that counter at Tommaso's, in order to touch her fingers again ever so lightly.

But it didn't happen that way.

Of course, she said good night. And yes, she did drive off.

But before doing so, she gave him the tenderest of kisses.

It made the next seven days just that much harder to endure.

Damn! If only he could see her—or at least *talk* to her, before then.

But he knew he couldn't.

Then again, he could always call O . . .

But no, that would spoil it. His relationship with Nina was pristine.

That was something O could never understand.

Entertainment Tonight Segment from 2/25

*(CLOSE-UP of Katerina McPherson at Golden Globes,
V/O by Mary Hart.)*
Some of the world's top fashion designers are biting their nails waiting for word as to what that sultriest of Oscar contenders, Katerina McPherson, will be wearing to this year's Academy Awards ceremony!

*(CUT TO medium shot of KATERINA McPherson,
modeling HERRERA gown.)*
Will it be this passionately pink Carolina Herrera backless body-skimming mesh-over-chiffon halter dress?

*(CUT TO another shot of MCPHERSON,
this time in a SAAB gown.)*
Or perhaps this electric blue Elie Saab strapless organza gown with trumpet skirt . . .

(CUT TO MCPHERSON in VERSACE.)
Then again, she might choose this hand-beaded crystal and embroidered corseted gown, with its crisscross straps and a high asymmetrical side slit, courtesy of Donatella Versace . . .

(CUT TO MARY, IN STUDIO)
What she chooses to put on her back may be a toss-up, but who will be at her side as she walks down that red carpet is almost a sure bet: the odds-on favorite is the costar of her new movie, the up-and-coming Hollywood heartthrob, Nathan Harte . . . so stay tuned!

(FADE OUT to Entertainment Tonight theme song)

10

The Oscars

Kat never called Nina to come over and see the dresses she was considering for the Oscars.

For some reason, that didn't surprise Nina in the least. In fact, she was somewhat relieved. She would have been too envious of the woman who would be on the arm of her husband during the town's biggest event of the year.

Damn! Damn! What was I thinking? How could I have been so stupid to even consider letting him go with her! Well, it's too late now, thought Nina. If she asked him to drop out now, he would know she didn't trust him with Kat, and that would become another bone of contention between them.

Besides, would forbidding him to go really stop an affair, if it were in fact happening? Of course not, she reasoned—although it might assuage her hurt ego.

Which was why she would have to let him go anyway.

Theo, the stylist sent over by Fiona, had five tuxedos for Nathan to choose from: a Perry Ellis, a Sean John, two Armanis, and a Versace. As he tried them on, Nina pointed out that she liked one of the Armanis the best. He nodded noncommittally, but told Theo he wanted to hang on to all of them for at least another day.

"I don't get it," said Nina. "What was wrong with the Armani?"

"Oh, uh, nothing." Nathan hesitated, then added, "I just— well, I wanted to give Kat an opportunity to look these over before I make a final decision. You know, since she's done this kind of thing before and knows the drill." He watched her closely. "You don't mind, do you?"

Of course I mind, she wanted to scream. *I'm your wife!*

But she didn't. Instead she walked out of the room.

He came home from the studio after three that next morning. Nina could only assume that he had been doing more with Kat than modeling tuxedos.

By Oscar weekend Nina was a nervous wreck. Since the nominations had been announced, the whole town had been whipped up into a frenzy. It wasn't enough that, on practically every other week of the year, there was some movie premiere, gala, über-VIP party, or awards ceremony to celebrate; the Oscars were the town's biggest soiree of the year, the equivalent of homecoming court, debutante cotillion, bar mitzvah, couturier runway show, and the senior prom all rolled into one.

Because both Kat and Hugo were up for awards, as were several of Hugo's crewmembers, filming was put on hiatus from the Friday before the Sunday event until the following Tuesday. Nina had assumed that the break would give Nathan and her some time together, just the two of them. *Wrong.* Nathan explained his absence from home—and proximity to Kat—as part and parcel of the publicity needed for the film.

For example, on Friday morning Nathan informed Nina that Hugo expected him to attend some "industry function" that night, since buzz on the movie was crucial, and his job was to get out there and create the buzz.

"Then I should go, too, shouldn't I?" Nina had asked. "I wished you would have said something beforehand. I'd like to buy a new dress—"

"Oh, uh, sure. But you really don't have to go." His response was so halfhearted that it hurt her feelings. The truest cutting remark, though, was what he said next: "I mean, I doubt you'll be able to find a babysitter this late."

Of course he was right. In this town, particularly on Oscar weekend, sitters were as elusive as that coveted statuette.

"You mean 'we.' You doubt that *we* will find a babysitter. Jake is your child, too."

"Yes, I know that." There was an edge to his voice that rivaled her own. "But this job is mine—not *yours*—which is why *I* need to be there. But you don't necessarily have to, particularly if Jake needs you here."

She pushed him away when he attempted a good-bye peck on the cheek.

That night, he came home just before dawn.

Later, Nina found out from Casey that the industry function had been Ed Limato's renowned annual pre-Oscar bash. Certainly she and Jarred had seen Nathan there.

And, yes, he and Kat had been joined at the hip the whole night.

Nathan finally stirred sometime around ten on Saturday

morning, but immediately slipped out again without her: this time, supposedly to the Diller–von Furstenberg brunch.

At least, that was what he claimed when he finally stumbled home that night, drunk as a skunk.

"You mean to tell me you've been there all this time?" She stared at him suspiciously.

"Well, yeah . . . Hey look, it's only two o'clock now!" To make his point, he pointed over to the clock on the wall.

"In the *morning*, Nathan. You left here *fourteen hours ago!*" He was still staring at the clock when she slammed the bedroom door behind her.

He slept on the couch.

When she woke up at eight that morning, he had already dressed and fed Jake. The coffee was made, and he was flipping pancakes. Though his smile was shaky, he was doing his best to pretend that things were normal, so she decided to meet him halfway—

Until he declared that he was supposed to be at Kat's place in Bel-Air within the hour, so that he could start the process of getting ready for the big event.

"But it doesn't even start until five or five-thirty this evening, right? I thought we'd, you know, take time getting you ready, and then you'd be picked up here, at two or whatever!"

"What, are you crazy? We—*she's* got to walk the red carpet at three-thirty! Traffic to the Kodak is going to be horrendous! They've told everyone to arrive as early as possible. Believe me, it's easier for me to get ready over there. She's got a hot tub and a sauna, which should relax me, and I've already told Theo to meet me there. Besides, Kat's got a whole team—

her hair stylist and facialist, a couple of makeup people—to help me, too. You know, trim me up, work on this zit that's popped up . . ."

Hair, facial . . . I'll bet she'll talk him into having a manicure, too, thought Nina. She couldn't remember the last time she'd had a manicure; it seemed like a million years ago.

"Oh. I see."

But she didn't. All she knew was that she was being excluded from this very important day in his life.

Because of Kat.

She only realized how excluded she was when she saw them together, arm-in-arm on the red carpet. Nathan, as elegant as she had ever seen him, was wearing what must have been Kat's choice of tux: the Versace. Kat, glamazon *par excellence*, wore a iridescent turquoise silk Dior sleeveless fluted gown that was cut out on the abdomen and cut away fully in the back, showing off her buffed arms, unnaturally concave tummy, and broad, sensual back.

They looked perfect together.

Clicking around with the television remote from ABC to E! to TV Guide, Nina watched as Nathan and the omnipresent Katerina—her long, tapered fingers never far from his arm or hand or the small of his back—moved from Jann to Joan to Vanessa, where they were complimented, purred over, and called the inevitable:

Kat and Nat.

It was all Nina could do not to upchuck the leftover meat loaf she'd eaten for her coffee-table dinner with Jake.

"But that's not my daddy's name!" yelled Jake indignantly at the TV set. "He's Nathan, you dumb-dumb!"

Nina knew just how he felt. It took all her self-control to resist the urge to toss the remote at the TV screen. No need to set a bad example for Jake.

She'd just toss Nathan's latest script revisions in the trash instead.

Yeah, now, *that* would make her happy.

By the time the awards ceremony actually started, Jake was already bored with all of Hollywood's prettiest people (who wasn't? thought Nina), and he flat out refused to sit still through another three hours of stilted in-jokes, pat speeches, and endless commercials. Nina allowed him to change the channel to Nickelodeon while she went off to her bedroom, leaving the door open, but just barely, so that she could keep an eye on Jake, but he wouldn't hear her moans and sobs over the high-pitched squeals of the Rugrats.

Later, after she put him to bed, she watched the last half hour of the awards show with the sound off.

Kat lost. But that was okay. Her consolation prize was a heartfelt kiss from her ever-attentive date, Nathan. And because she was in the row behind the winner (the well-deserving Renée, as fate would have it), the television camera caught both Renée's jubilation, and Nathan's tender move.

It was the last image on Nina's television's screen before the remote control slammed into it, breaking the picture tube.

Still, the image was burned into Nina's memory.

When Sam reached the *Vanity Fair* post-Oscar party at Morton's, he found that Kat and Nat were already there, table hopping. Having first gone to the Governor's Ball, Hollywood's finest had had plenty of time to see Nathan and Katerina together, and to acknowledge them as Hollywood's hottest new couple.

Despite the fact that Nathan Harte was married to someone else.

When she saw Sam walk over their way, Kat's radiant smile shifted into a smug grimace.

Nathan's shit-eating grin melted under the guilt he suddenly felt.

Sam wasn't smiling at all, and they both knew why.

"No lectures, please, Sam. The night has already been exhausting enough." Kat tossed back her curly golden mane and looked over at Nicole's table, a clear indication that she felt she had better things to do—like schmoozing with Marty, or Steven and Kate, or *anyone*, for that matter—than to listen to him preach at her.

"Don't worry, Kat. I fully realize that there is nothing I can say to stop this train wreck you've got Nathan on."

It was only then that Sam smiled, which made Nathan turn white and Kat glower. She leaned in close to Sam and whispered, "For once you're right, so just keep your yap shut, why don't you! He can make up his own mind. He's a big boy." She grinned wickedly. "Believe me, I know firsthand just how big."

With the din of a million conversations around them and lounge jazz tooting in the background, Nathan couldn't hear a word she'd said to Sam, but by the look of disgust on Sam's face, he could certainly guess the gist of her remark.

For good measure she pulled Nathan's mouth down onto hers, then walked off. From the way Nathan's shoulders sagged, Sam could only assume that she'd sucked the life force out of the poor guy.

It was like watching a Dementor go after an innocent.

But Nathan isn't really innocent, is he, Sam reasoned, as the two men stood there for a full five minutes, not saying a word, not even looking at each other.

Finally Nathan glanced over and asked, "You think I'm a fool, don't you?"

Sam closed his eyes, thought a moment, then opened them again. He looked directly at Nathan with the hopes of making his point. "Yes, but so what if I do? You're not going to listen to me, no matter what I say to you. That's okay. You've got every right to ignore me. The only thing that matters is what you think . . . and Nina. But you already know that, don't you?"

"Yeah, I do." Nathan put his hand on Sam's shoulder and swore fervently, "Trust me, Sam. I won't hurt her. I *swear* I won't."

"I have no doubt you don't *want* to. But guy, I have to tell you, if you stay on this path, *you will*." He took a step away, causing Nathan's hand to fall at his side. "And once you do, be prepared: Things will never be the same again."

The look on Nathan's face said it all: He really believed he had nothing to lose.

Too bad, kid. I guess you'll find out the hard way.

Nathan left Sam to find the woman who now held his heart in the palm of her hand.

Sam wished he could do the same. Instead, he'd have to settle for the next best thing.

He left the party. As he pulled onto the Pacific Coast Highway, he speed-dialed O.

*   *   *

O: Speak to me, lover boy.

SAM: Hi, O . . . Uh, wow. It took you a while to answer the phone. Busy, I guess, huh?

O: (*Pauses, as if thinking of how she wants to say what's on her mind*) I'm never too busy to talk to you. I live for your calls, Sam. You know that.

SAM: Stop it, you tease. You're making me blush.

O: If only that were true. And, for the record, I'm being completely and totally honest. In fact, I'd taken the night off. I only picked up because it was you. *So there.*

SAM: Gee . . . I feel—honored . . . But now I also feel—well, like an ass.

O: Oh? Why is that?

SAM: (*Sighs deeply*) Because I called to talk to you about . . . about, you know, that woman I mentioned.

O: (*Pauses, then says sarcastically*) Oh yeah, the one you have that little crush on, right?

SAM: Well, when you put it that way . . . No, quite frankly it's *not* just 'some little crush' . . . I dunno. Maybe you're not the right person for me to be telling this to, anyway.

O: You're right Sam, I'm not. If you were smart, you'd be telling her instead.

SAM: You know I can't do that. I already told you—

O: Yeah, yeah, I know. She's married. So big deal. When did that ever matter in this town?

SAM: Gee, that's a bit sarcastic, isn't it? Look . . . uh, O, maybe tonight's not the right night for this conversation.

O: I beg to differ, Sam. Tonight is the *perfect* time for it. I don't

think I've ever been in a better mood to hear a man rhap-
sodize about true love. Or whatever.

SAM: What do you mean by that?

O: What I mean, quite simply, is that I'm going to take you in
hand now—figuratively if not literally—and allow you to
play out this little fantasy of yours once and for all. You
want to bare your soul to her, right? So, go ahead. Pretend
I'm her. Tell me all those naughty little things you'd do to
her if you got her alone—just the two of you—for a whole
night.

SAM: (*With a thoughtful murmur*) What would that accomplish?

O: A lot. It's going to be a relief to us both, big boy, believe
you me . . . Unless . . .

SAM: Unless what?

O: Unless you don't *really* want her . . . you know, that way.
Maybe you've got her on too high of a pedestal, or some
bullshit like that.

SAM: Don't be silly. Of course I want her. *In every way.*

O: (*Purring*) You don't say? So, tell me—tell *her*, Sam, what
would you do? And how? How would you make love to her,
if you ever got up the nerve?

SAM: The nerve. You know, you're turning this into some sort
of joke! To you, it's just *role playing*.

O: So, *let's play*.

SAM: Sure . . . Sure, okay, I'll play . . . I guess the first thing
I'd do is take her over to my place—

O: Describe it . . . Go on . . .

SAM: Okay, already! . . . Well, I live at the beach. My place has
a big window in the living room, overlooking the sand and
surf. That's where we're standing.

O: (*Gently*) Nice . . . I can hear the waves pounding the beach. Almost as loud as my heart.

SAM: (*Softly*) Mine, too. Because I've taken you in my arms. Or rather, you've melted into them.

O: *Hmmm*. You're more than a head taller than me. I've got my head right on your chest. In fact, my lips can graze your nipples . . . do you feel my mouth there?

SAM: Yeah. That's . . . that's nice . . . I unbutton your shirt.

O: Good . . .

SAM: And I slide my hands up, gently onto your abdomen . . . then, slowly, up to your breasts.

O: My nipples are so . . . so hard. Because there's a chill in the air . . . and because your fingers are playing with them . . .

SAM: I've lifted up your camisole. I have my lips on them now . . .

O: They grow as you put them in your mouth.

SAM: Umm, yeah . . . I've noticed. Not that they weren't healthy to begin with.

O: And pert. Don't forget pert.

SAM: How could I? I can't take my eyes off of them. At the same time, my hands are busy elsewhere: I'm now unzipping your pants.

O: I'm doing the same . . . to you . . . Wow! I'm impressed.

SAM: You haven't been the first woman to say that to me.

O: (*Laughs heartily*) Your modesty is *so* becoming . . . Do you like what I'm doing now?

SAM: Wait. . . . I'm . . . I'm sorry. I wanted some realism. I've actually moved into my living room now. (*Sound of a dog barking.*)

O: (*Seriously*) Down, boy! Oh, not you, Sam.

SAM: Hey! How did you know he's a . . . never mind.

O: Oh! Uh . . . just a lucky guess . . . You were saying?

SAM: I was saying that my lips are all over you . . . on your breasts, on your neck . . . *umm* . . . I love your scent . . . musky . . .

O: What? What did you say?

SAM: The way you smell. It's . . . glorious . . . Now, I take that locket around your neck in my teeth, and I bite it off—

O: My—my *locket?*

SAM: Yes. It's a little heart. Tiny and perfect. Just like you . . . And I whisper in your ear, "Tell me. Tell me what you want me to do, and I will do it. Anything. Anything you want." And you laugh that husky laugh of yours and whisper back to me, and I nod because it's so perfect for right here, right now. I pick you up and you wrap your legs around my waist so that we can do what you want: make love . . . standing up . . . to the sound of the waves. . . . *(He pauses, waiting for her to answer him)* O . . . O? Are you there?

O: *(Heartbroken) Umm* . . . yeah, Sam, I'm here . . . Look . . . I . . . I've got to go now.

SAM: You're . . . you're *hanging up?* Well, now, that's gotta be a first in *your* business.

O: You're . . . you're probably right . . . Sam, did you mean . . . did you mean all of that?

SAM: Hell yeah I did! Every word. If—if only we could.

O: *We?*

SAM: Uh, sorry, O. You know what I meant. I meant—I meant if I could . . . with Nina.

O: Did you say—*Nina?*

SAM: Yeah. That's her name. I've never mentioned it to you, have I? *(Laughs)* In fact, I've never told anyone about her but you . . . until last week. Believe it or not, I actually told her, finally. But she doesn't believe me.

O: (*Stunned*) Oh . . . yes she does. She knows . . . (*Click!*)

SAM: O, do you really think so? *O?* Are you there? (*Pause*) (*Click!*)

So, Sam loved her.

He loved *her*. Not O.

So much for Hugo's male intuition.

It was sweet. *Sam* was sweet. And kind. And gentle.

Except when he thought about being with her. At which point, he became a passionate lover who wanted to satisfy her every desire.

No one had ever wanted to do that for her before.

That wasn't to say that Nathan wasn't a satisfying lover. He was—as long as *he* was the one who had been satisfied first. Only then would he consider Nina's needs, too.

But since he'd met Kat, it had been a while since he'd considered Nina. *At all.*

She stayed up all night, thinking about Sam: his face, his laugh, his smell, and most of all, his large but gentle hands.

She imagined his hands on her, exploring her body. She let her own hands wander over it, pretending they were Sam's . . .

Until Nathan came in, sometime around dawn. Then she pretended to be asleep.

Even as Nathan snuggled up behind her in bed and gently clasped her locket with his hand—an indication that he would like to be forgiven, and, of course, make love—she acted as if she were dead to the world.

Because for the first time since she had known him, what Nathan wanted didn't matter to her.

What she wanted did matter, though. This she realized as she drifted off to sleep.

She wanted someone to love her unconditionally, to desire her. *Just like Sam.*

If only . . . if only Nathan *were* Sam.

11

The Breakup

The Desperate Housewife who enjoyed Sam's expert counsel wasn't too happy about the parts being offered her during her summer hiatus from the show. It was up to Sam to explain to her that she wasn't competing against Renée or Charlize or Nicole, and certainly not against Scarlett or Natalie or Kirsten, let alone Jennifer, Jennifer, or Jennifer. And while she didn't want to hear it, the truth was this: any film director who might be interested in her delectable services would also be considering Kim or Ashley or Diane. In fact, there were several roles that might fit *that* bill, if she (or, perhaps, her bank account) was open to such consideration—

Her teary lament was interrupted by Riley's subtle but still very emphatic murmur, in Sam's earpiece, that Serenity Lancaster was on the line.

To verify a scoop.

About Kat and Nat.

Sam muttered back "Code Blue," an indication to Riley that

he was to buzz him on the intercom so that Sam could pretend that he was, at that very moment, being called by Steven, who had expressed an interest in maybe, *just maybe*, considering that very same Desperate Housewife for a featured role in the blockbuster he was filming this summer . . .

Perhaps she could let Sam take the call? He'd touch base with her later—certainly before he went into his next meeting—to bring her up to speed on the who/what/when . . .

Why, of *course* she would! He could reach her on her cell, which she was sure Riley had at his fingertips . . .

In fact, the part was real. But because she was adamantly opposed to any nude scenes (alas, the role called for one) *and* she'd be playing a mom—to Kirsten, no less—Sam already knew her answer would be an adamant no anyway, so he had absolutely no qualms in telling that fib. Of course, if she had a sudden change of heart, he'd call in a favor and ask the director to let her read for the part anyway. No harm, no foul.

After she sashayed out of his office, he took a deep breath and braced himself for Serenity's interrogation.

"So Sam," heaved Serenity with no further ado, "I'm leading tomorrow's column with a tip I've received about Nathan Harte's imminent divorce filing. Would you like to confirm this?"

"Hell no, I wouldn't!" Sam fairly shouted. "Who fed you that load of crap anyway?"

"Why, Katerina, of course," she hissed triumphantly. "With or without you, doll, it's going to run. I was just giving you a chance to soften the blow."

"Thanks. *For nothing*, Serenity."

The way he slammed down the phone gave her all the confirmation she needed.

He made it over to Flagrant Films just as Hugo was wrapping the final scene for the day—or, better yet, Hugo was trying to wrap things up, but since he was in a heated debate with his leading lady over whether she should be reclining or sitting up while giving a pivotal speech in the plot, it looked like the crew was in for another stomach-gnawing hour of Kat-induced fun and games.

Sam motioned Nathan to follow him into the actor's trailer.

"Okay, tell me what I just heard wasn't for real."

"Huh? What did you hear?" Nathan stared at him blankly.

Was he really Bambi in the headlights? If so, then maybe Sam had nothing to worry about and Serenity was just shooting spitballs. Then again, maybe Kat was blowing smoke up Serenity's ass, just for the fun of it.

At this point, he'd take either option.

"Word is out that you're filing for divorce. *Tomorrow*."

The way Nathan hung his head, he knew that he'd have to settle for the truth:

Serenity wasn't lying.

"What? How—but it's . . . no one was supposed to know!" Nathan ran his hands through his hair and fell back down on the trailer's couch. "How the hell did that happen? I—I'd hoped I'd be able to do it quietly. You know, just slip in, file, and slip out, before the press got ahold of it."

Well, then, you dumb ass, if that's the case, why did you tell that bitch girlfriend of yours when you were going to do it? Sam wanted to shout at him. Instead, he just shook his head, as if he couldn't believe what he was hearing.

"Too bad. It's out, so now you've got to deal with it." He paused, then came out with what he really wanted to know: "Tell me, how did Nina take it?"

"Well, she doesn't exactly know it's coming down." Nathan suddenly got busy looking at his script.

"What exactly does *that* mean?"

"It means that . . . well, it means that Kat and I made the decision only a couple of days ago, but I haven't gotten around to mentioning it to Nina yet. Of course, Kat's pissed at me about that."

He sighed and looked out the window. Kat and Hugo were still slugging it out. He didn't know what was worse: being out there with them, or explaining to Sam why he'd procrastinated on the inevitable. "Hey, listen, it's not all my fault, either. Nina's shut me out since . . . well, really, since Oscar night."

"That was, what, almost two weeks ago?" Sam found that hard to believe. He knew how Nina hung on Nathan's every word . . .

But then again, maybe not, as of recently anyway. In fact, the two times he'd seen her since then—both times at Tommaso's, on what he jokingly referred to as "their regular date night," she hadn't mentioned Nathan at all. *Not once.* Now that he thought about it, whenever he'd brought up Nathan's name (which he didn't do very often), she winced involuntarily . . . and changed the subject to something more pleasant. As if cremini mushrooms fell into that category.

It surprised him that he hadn't picked up on it before now. Maybe if he'd taken her out again after she'd gotten off work, she would have opened up about it. But the thought of asking her out, particularly after that very arousing conversation with O, was guaranteed to put him on one very slippery slope: If she agreed to go, he'd be tempted to ask her over to his place . . . and relive the fantasy he'd played out on the phone.

Or, worse yet, he might be told by her that, sorry, she just wasn't interested.

Because she loved Nathan instead.

Nathan's troubled sigh brought him back to Earth. "Hey, and don't think I didn't try to set things right by her. Believe me, man, I tried, really I did! I even arranged for us to get away for a weekend . . . but she blew me off. She's using the excuse that she's working around the clock."

"Nights too?"

"Yeah sure, nights. Lately she's . . . *really driven*." Nathan stared out the trailer window again, to gauge how much time he'd have before he'd be called back. Kat was still ranting at Hugo. He was safe for, oh, at least ten more minutes. "I know she's doing it to get back at me. I can tell by the way she is on the phone."

"On the phone? What do you mean? I thought you said she's not talking to you."

"She's not! But that doesn't stop her from talking to—" Catching himself, Nathan paused, then started again. "To other people. It's just the tone she uses nowadays is sort of harsh. *Cruel*. You know, real cold."

Sam hadn't heard that in Nina's voice at all. Nathan's just giving himself another excuse to dump her, he reasoned. Well then, if that was the way it was going to be, then better sooner than later. It might be better for damage control anyway.

Damage to Nina's heart.

"And we haven't—well, what I mean is that she won't let me touch her. Not since that night."

Sam almost smiled. *Good*, he thought, *because you don't deserve to touch her after what you've done to her.*

"So, lately, I've been . . . I've been sleeping out. I guess the writing is on the wall, and we both know it. There really isn't anything else that we *can* do at this point, even if either of us wanted to."

So Nina wanted to end it, too? Why?

And why now?

"Well, still you've got to talk to her now! Serenity is breaking the news of your divorce filing in tomorrow's column, for God's sake. Nina shouldn't have to read about it that way. Now, *that* would be cruel."

As Sam started out the trailer door, Nathan muttered, "Sam—look, Sam, I need you to . . . to do me a big favor. Could you tell her for me? *Please?*"

That stopped Sam cold. "What, are you crazy or something?"

"No, I'm not crazy—I just—I just don't want to be the bad guy. Man, I just can't *stand* the thought of having to look into those big brown eyes of hers when she hears it!"

No shit, thought Sam.

"Please, Sam, I'm begging you. If she hears it from you—well, she respects the hell out of you, so maybe she won't be so upset." Nathan slumped down deep on the couch.

"Nathan, no matter how it's put to her, she's not going to take it well. You realize that much, right?"

"Yeah, I know." His eyes were damp, but they pleaded his case for him. "Still, like you say, it's better she hears it from . . .

from someone who cares about her, before she sees it in to-morrow's newspaper, right?"

"Yeah, okay. Whatever. I better go to her now."

It really was okay, because there was nowhere he'd rather be than beside Nina when she got the news.

Well, breaking it to her certainly meant he'd gotten his wish, as twisted as that was.

When Sam walked into Tommaso's and up to Nina's counter, her heart did a flip-flop. She could feel her face get warm, a common occurrence now whenever he appeared, at least since O and he had discussed his love for Nina.

Since then, she couldn't help but be a bit infatuated with him, too. Unfortunately, she also felt guilty about hearing his heartfelt confession, particularly since he didn't know to whom he had been confessing. When the time was right, how could she explain it to him without him hating her?

She didn't want to think about that right now. And, from the look on his face, he wasn't in the mood for her confession, either, even if she had been ready to make it.

"Can you take a break?" he asked nonchalantly.

Intrigued, excited, scared—and knowing how busy his day was, flattered that he'd even taken the time to come and find her this way—Nina motioned to Tori to take over, then fol-lowed Sam outside to Tommaso's "Garden of Delight," a lat-tice alcove that was originally designed as an alfresco gathering spot for the store's patrons willing to choke down the carbon monoxide fumes emanating from West Beverly Boulevard while chewing through their organic salads and gourmet sandwiches. But because of its unfortunate location, it now served primarily as the employees' ad hoc smoking lounge.

Sam leaned up against the store's grimy stucco wall—a brave act, considering the five-figure price tag of his custom-made Brioni suit, which comfortably hugged his jogger-trim physique. Before he spoke, he ran his hands through his dark, tousled hair. It was the only subtle indication he gave that his news wouldn't be something she'd welcome.

"So, when was the last time you heard from Nathan?"

"Well, if you must know, yesterday morning." Nina's response had an edge to it, but she didn't elaborate. "Why do you ask?"

By his grimace, she could tell that Sam was annoyed with that bit of information. "Look, I wanted you to hear it from me first: I know there's been a lot of talk about Nathan and Katerina McPherson—"

"Listen, Sam, if you're here to convince me not to worry about it, then really, don't waste your breath. I'm fully aware of what's going down."

"You are?" The crease in Sam's brow eased up a bit. "Then you've already heard?"

"Yeah . . . At least, I've heard what he wants me to believe . . . and you, too, I guess." She looked him squarely in the eye. "Sorry, Sam, but I know you've tried to help him cover up their affair. I don't know, maybe you thought you were doing me a favor or something, but I know better. Hell, I've seen the way she plays him." She stared out at the cars whizzing by on the other side of the lattice wall. "Nathan knows, too, by now, that I'm in on the lie. I know he does because he's been trying to make it up to me. He's asked that we get away together, just the two of us, for a romantic weekend." A tear trickled down her cheek and made it to her chin before she wiped it away. "I said no, but . . . well, I think I owe it to our marriage to reconsider." She smiled at him, glassy-eyed but still beautiful, as far as he was concerned. "I do owe him that much, right? In spite of everything that's happened?"

"No, you don't, Nina," Sam said bluntly. "You don't owe him a damn thing—"

"Look, Sam, I don't expect you to understand, not after how you feel about—"

"That's what I came to tell you, Nina!" He grabbed her arm to make his point. "You don't owe him anything because— well, it's going to be announced tomorrow that Nathan is asking for a—a divorce."

A divorce.

Nathan wanted to divorce her . . .

. . . *So that he can be with Kat?*

Nina couldn't believe her ears. Angrily, she turned toward Sam. "But—but how could that be? You're making that up, right? Because you—"

"Because I what?" He, too, was angry at Nathan for breaking her heart. Not that she would know that. Although, the way she was looking at him—hurt, confused, angry—at him, no less—indicated to him that she wanted to shoot the messenger.

"Because . . . I don't know why you'd do it, why you'd want to hurt me this way—" Her voice trailed off.

Because I know you love me, she thought, although she couldn't say that. Not now, anyway.

But all that mattered now was that Nathan—her husband of six years, the father of her child—didn't love her, even if Sam did.

"I wouldn't lie to you, Nina. You know that." The dark rims under his deep-set blue eyes made him look older than his thirty-three years. "The bottom line is that Nathan is leaving you. He told me so himself, just a half hour ago."

"He told *you* first? Why would he do that? Why didn't he tell *me?*"

But she already knew the answer to that:

Because Sam was Nathan's agent. On the other hand, Nina was just Nathan's wife.

There was, after all, a pecking order in Hollywood.

Nina didn't remember doing so, but she sat down. Unfortunately, the faux wrought-iron chair under her held a puddle of droplets that had fallen off the well-watered bougainvillea cradling the arbor above. Reflexively she jumped up—much too quickly for Sam, who had bent down to steady her.

They smacked heads. He reeled backward in pain.

"Omigod! Are you okay?" Nina ran over to him. The top of her head was throbbing, but she knew that his eye had taken the brunt of the collision. Tenderly, she moved his hand away and examined it carefully. He didn't flinch when she laid her fingers gently on his temple. In fact, he moved into it, as though he were craving her touch.

She noticed that a bruise was already forming.

He noticed that, when she was sad, her eyes turned the color of amber.

It suddenly dawned on her that he wasn't half as concerned about his own pain as he was about hers over Nathan.

If he thought she'd let him, he would have kissed her, right then and there.

And she would have, too, if only he'd asked.

It would be so easy for me to do it, she thought. *And afterward, to know I'd have someone I could trust, someone to run to, to help me forget what Nathan has done to me . . . to us . . .*

But that was just it: *us* was she and Nathan . . . and, of course, Jake. To take advantage of Sam's adoration now, before she even knew if she could return it, would not be fair to either of them.

She backed away from him, ashamed that she had even been tempted to take advantage of him that way.

Or, for that matter, to consider betraying Nathan.

Without thinking, she murmured the first thought that came to her mind: " *'Our deeds still travel with us from afar, and what we have been makes us what we are.'* "

"What did you say?" Saddened by the sudden look of remorse she gave him, he closed his eyes and tried to recall where he'd heard that before, but he couldn't.

"Nothing. Just . . . something I'd heard once." She shrugged. "I'd better get back inside. Got to make the dough to pay the attorney's fees, right?" She looked behind her, at the wet spot that now covered the seat of her pants. "I hope I don't have to chase down any heirloom tomatoes for some lazy Beverly Hills housewife. I hate the thought of people thinking I'm incontinent or some—"

"Look, Nina, whatever happens—"

"Don't worry Sam. I'll be okay. I'll survive." She smiled feebly. Then, with her head held high, she walked back inside.

He got back into his car and headed back to his office. He

wanted to call Fiona immediately and tell her to initiate the damage control plan they'd discussed.

By the time he hit Wilshire, it dawned on him where he'd heard that remark: *from O.*

Gee, I finally found something that the two of them have in common, he thought wryly. It was the first good laugh he'd had all day.

She needed to get out of there, and fast.

She needed to go home, to be there when Nathan came home, to confront him for doing this to her, to Jake, to the life they were making together.

Without a word to Tori, who was taking care of the business Nina should have been doing—ironically, explaining to some woman the differences between one heirloom tomato and another—Nina slipped into the employee lounge, grabbed her purse, and headed out the back door by way of the stockroom, where she swiped the most expensive bottle of wine she could find: a 2000 Chateau Haut Brion Graves.

In her opinion, misery deserved the company of a great Bordeaux.

Surprise, surprise: Nathan had already been there and gone. For good.

He did, however, leave a note for Nina:

Hi, Babe,

By the time you read this, I guess you'll know the truth: that I'm a bastard.

Yes, I'm that all right, but I'm also feeling very lost and confused at the moment. Of course I still love you, and deep in my heart I know I always will. But right now I also know that I'm just not "in love" with you. If what we have is going to last a lifetime, I should be able to say I am in love and really mean it, right? Quite frankly, can you say that you're still in love with me, too?

I'm guessing no. At least, you haven't been acting as if you are.

In the long run, you'll realize that it was better this way for both of us. And for the little guy, though it may not seem that way at first.

I'll call him later to tell him I love him. Don't hate me too much, okay?

Love always (seriously, I mean that!)
Nathan

Bullshit. All of it was bullshit.

With each gulp of the Haut Brion Graves, she dissected every word and phrase for its crap factor:

Wholeheartedly, she agreed that he was a bastard. No argument there.

Crap #1: "Lost and confused"? Try star-struck and horny!

Crap #2: She could not accept that he "wasn't in love" with her. What, and now all of a sudden he was in love with that collagen-choked bleached blond whore? No, he was *in lust* with the bitch, and that was all. End of story.

But that wasn't the end. It was only the beginning. She and Jake would have to start over again, scrounging even harder for what they wanted in life, because the life she had planned to share with Nathan, he'd now be sharing with Kat.

It just wasn't fair.

As for his contention that their marriage had failed because she, too, had fallen out of love, well now *that* was the biggest turd of them all!

Or was it?

Maybe he had noticed the change in her since O's conversation with Sam, and if so, it might have spurred his own decision to move on.

The thought that she might have unwittingly pushed Nathan into Kat's arms made her physically ill.

Then again, it could have been that half bottle of wine on an empty stomach. In either case, the result was the same: She fell onto her bed, curled up into a ball, and cried herself to sleep.

His encounter with Nina stayed on Sam's mind for the rest of the afternoon. Because he couldn't stand the thought of her sitting there alone, grieving the loss of her marriage, he canceled the dinner meeting he had scheduled with the up-and-coming teen queen who was angsting over whether she should take the featured role that was offered her in Wes Anderson's next project, or hold out for the girlfriend role in Warner's next big comic book adaptation, which was sure to be an ongoing franchise (and multimillion-dollar paycheck for years to come) but would certainly tie her up from doing the complex indie award-winning roles she lusted for.

The truth, Sam knew, was that she was going to take the advice of her Indian guru over his anyway, so why waste the time? He rescheduled her for lunch at the Ivy, then headed over to the address Riley gave him for Nathan and Nina's apartment.

He got there just in time to see Ylva, Plum's nanny, shoving Jake through the front door. The little boy ran in and out of view.

"Hi," he said cautiously, as she gave him an appraising onceover. "Is Nina home?"

The Swedish bombshell shrugged and tossed her long white mane coquettishly, then murmured, "Don't know. It vas her day for pick-up. She pulled a—how do you say?—a 'no show.' So I leave my manicure and go get the brats. See?"

She held up a hand on which three of her five fingers were painted blood red.

How apropos, Sam thought.

"I now get Ploom back to her vickett vitch mother, or she vill jell at me for making her late to Kabbalah mixer. Vorry not, the boy vill be okay. This Yake, he is a smart one."

Without further ado, she promenaded down the staircase, the click-clack of her Kate Spades counting down each sultry step she took. She didn't have to glance back to see if Sam was watching her. Why, of course he was. And, *hell ja*, that was perfectly fine with her. In her mind, men who drove Ferraris could do no wrong.

Au pairs who left kids unattended weren't appealing to Sam, however. He knocked on the open door. Jake peeked out from the hallway. "Hi, Jake, it's Sam. Remember me?"

The little boy nodded slowly. One Saturday morning, when Mommy had to work at the store, Daddy had taken him to the nice man's big office, where Daddy had to sign a bunch of papers. Afterward, he and Daddy had gone to a movie. Some skinny blond lady with fat balloony lips had sat with them—well, with Daddy, anyway. Practically in Daddy's lap, in fact.

Even with that big mouth of hers, she never really smiled at Jake, not even once. That was okay. He didn't like her, either, because she'd never once taken her hand out of Daddy's lap. *Ewwwyuck!*

"I'm looking for your mom. Do you know where she went?"

"She's asleep and she won't wake up. And *I'm hungry.*" The boy's lower lip trembled as he talked, a clear indication to Sam that Jake was scared, even if he didn't say so out loud. For that matter, Sam was suddenly worried, too. Had she been dumb enough to take a bunch of sleeping pills?

Glancing around the small apartment, Sam noticed the half-empty wine bottle sitting on the dining area table. By following the trail of clothes Nina had strewn on her way to her bedroom, Sam rightly deduced the direction he'd find her . . .

. . . *And* the condition.

She was sprawled out on the bed, naked. Beautifully and gloriously so. He stared for a moment, smiled gratefully, and then gently covered her with one of the rumpled sheets that lay at the foot of the bed. Feeling the sheet come up around her, Nina, still groggy, frowned, moaned tantalizingly—

—and kicked it off again.

Well, she may be a bit tipsy, but she's certainly alive, he thought. Happily he resigned himself to accept her subconscious desire to shed all her inhibitions along with her clothes. Still he took another long and appreciative glance before closing the door.

"She's just taking a nap. Must have worked pretty hard today." Jake nodded, visibly relieved. "Say, feel like getting a burger at Mel's Diner? We'll leave a note for your mom. We can bring a burger home for her, too."

Almost instantly, the tears vanished from Jake's round face. "Yeah, that'd be great!"

Sam grabbed a scratch pad and pen off the kitchen bar. As he began writing the note to Nina, Jake ran his Transformers G1 Smokescreen down Sam's arm as if it were a racetrack, making the task more difficult for Sam than he'd anticipated.

Suddenly Jake asked, "Hey, shouldn't we bring home a burger for Daddy?"

"At this point, I'd say that your dad prefers having his cake and eating it, too," muttered Sam.

"Yummy! Cake! If I eat all my hamburger, can I have some, too?"

"Yeah sure, kid, maybe when you're older, if that's how you want to play the game."

Hopefully, thought Sam, time would prove that the kid wasn't a chip off the old block. At least, not in that regard.

They returned with the extra burger to find Nina up and about (and modestly covered up in a chenille robe) albeit a bit shaky, and certainly in no mood to down a grease-laden hunk of choice grade A chuck.

However, she did take Sam up on his offer to scramble up a couple of eggs for her while she tucked Jake into bed.

By the time Nina came back, the eggs were on the table, along with toast and coffee . . . black.

She gave him a smile that was both grateful and teary at the same time. "You must think I'm the most awful mother in the whole world, passing out like that."

"No, no way. It's perfectly understandable. I don't know a woman in this town who wouldn't, after her idiot husband had thrown her over for the town's numero uno slut diva. He's just lucky you didn't grab a gun and shoot off his balls instead. Although, from what I've seen, the jury is still out on whether he has any in the first place."

That made her laugh and bawl at the same time.

"I—I really didn't expect to find you here. How can I ever thank you for . . . for . . . well, for everything?"

This time her eyes did not waver from his. Right then and there, she wanted to tell him everything. How hurt she was that Nathan had dumped her. How touched she was that Sam was there for her. That she knew he had feelings for her that went deeper than either of them would admit. And that, yes, she, too, was attracted to him, but knew that, in her vulnerable state, acting on them wouldn't be fair to either of them . . .

Most of all, though, she wanted to come clean with him over the fact that she was O.

But she didn't.

Because it was all too much, too soon, and happening way too fast.

Instead, she sat there tearfully, recalling every memory she had about Nathan and her in Los Angeles: their dreams, their struggles, their fears, their hopes . . .

And Sam let her babble on while he sat there silently: listening, nodding, laughing, brushing away the strands of hair that fell across her face, and lending his shoulder as she bowed her head under the weight of all those precious memories.

Afterward, when she'd fallen asleep exhausted from crying, Sam carried her into her bedroom and tucked her in.

He wished he, too, could just fall sleep, but he couldn't. There was too much he wanted to say.

When he got home, he called O.

The phone rang for what seemed like an eternity. Finally, she answered. Her voice, husky with sleep, lacked its usual playful cadence. Instead, it was sweet and tender when she said his name.

He was glad for this, because he was in no mood to play games. Instead, he ranted, mostly about all the things he should have said to Nina, right then and there, when he'd had the chance: about how he'd always loved her from the moment he first saw her, how deeply he felt her pain, and how he'd always be there to love and protect her.

By the time the sun came up, he had no more to say.

The fact that O said nothing at all during his long-winded soliloquy spoke volumes. *She's hurt that I'm in love with someone else*, he thought.

When she finally did speak, all she said was, "She's a very lucky girl . . . Good-bye, Sam."

They both knew he'd never call back again.

12

The Tabloid War

KAT 'N' NAT: IT'S OFFICIAL!!!

For all of you with insatiable appetites for Kat-nip, feast on this juicy tidbit: Our fave buxom babe has done it again! Yep, it's official! She's snagged yet another up-and-coming Hollywood hunk. Whattaya think: Does Kat 'n' Nat' have a cute ring to it? Those in the know insist this is THE REAL THING—and he'd better be, coz Kat's Nat has dumped a missus and a mini-me in order to play with this naughty kitty!

Baxter Quinn's Hollywood Exxxposé, 3/10

Nathan, Katerina, Hugo, and Fiona attended the powwow Sam had in his office the next day, concerning damage control related to the breakup. Riley was also there, since he was needed to take notes that were supposed to keep the others on task, as opposed to on top of each other—which, by the way she pawed Nathan the whole time, was all Kat seemed to want to do.

"The most important thing we have to keep in mind is that

we must, at all costs, protect the images of both Katerina and Nathan," Sam said sternly, "and the integrity of Hugo's movie as well. This can't—I repeat, *can't*—become a tabloid free-for-all. Are we all in agreement on that?"

No one said a word. Not because they agreed with him, but because they *didn't*.

Hugo kept his mouth shut because, in his mind, any publicity—good or bad—helped his picture. Besides, what did it matter if Nathan's marriage was becoming an early casualty of his own success? Hell, in this town, when a star was on an upward trajectory, it was bound to happen sooner or later anyway. The fact that it was occurring now, and with Kat, was great for everyone: him, Nathan, Kat . . . even the ever-insatiable public, which ate up Hollywood romances as if they were prime rib platters at Sizzler's.

As for Kat, public empathy for the two lovebirds assured her that Nathan was hers for keeps. He'd be too caught up in the media frenzy to contemplate any second thoughts about the divorce—which was why her game plan was to ramp up the controversy, and the sooner, the better . . .

As a publicist, Fiona agreed with Kat's logic: a very public liaison between the two stars could only increase their box office standing—and their future fees, which was why Fiona couldn't understand Sam's sudden empathy with the soon-to-be ex. And she knew Kat well enough to realize that the star would ignore Sam's directive, and order her to do the same—which meant that Fiona's ability to answer to two masters was going to be sorely tested that week . . . another reason, when all the brouhaha was over, to book that long-overdue getaway to the Bacara Resort's spa.

Riley readily anticipated all their various agendas, which complemented his own: to force-feed gossip on the lovebirds to both Baxter and Serenity. Doing so would only endear him to the columnists *and* Kat. At the same time, it would undermine Sam—particularly if Sam kept stepping on Kat's stiletto-encased toes, as he had a tendency to do lately.

Only Nathan, who had the most to lose both personally and professionally, shared Sam's opinion: "I don't want it said that I raked Nina over the coals."

"My sentiments exactly," said Sam, maybe a bit too quickly. Suddenly all eyes were on him. He put on his best poker face. "We wouldn't want Katerina coming off as a home-wrecker, now would we?"

"Home-wrecker? *Moi?*" Kat fairly spat at him. "Don't be ridiculous! The public knows what a darling I am. Besides, everyone craves a good love story, and that's the hook we have here. Right, lover?" Her long fingers closed tightly around Nathan's wrist, like a shackle.

But for once, Nathan didn't kowtow. Slowly, he disentangled his arm from her clench. "Kat, I said I'm leaving her, and I am. But that doesn't mean I want to see her crushed. And darling, neither should you."

Sam couldn't help but smile. *Finally, he's found his balls!*

From the uncomfortable coughs emitted from the others, that very thought had crossed their minds, too.

Kat zeroed in on Nathan, like a cat on a mouse. "Quit treating her as if she's your wife," she hissed. "She's now the enemy, remember?"

"No, she's *not* our enemy. And, by the way, she *is* still my wife, until the divorce is worked out. So, if we truly want this to *happen*"—she, like everyone else in the room, caught the emphasis there—"then we've got to make sure that she isn't hurt in the process."

"With that in mind"—Sam jumped in—"we should show her as much goodwill as possible. Nina looks up to me, sort of like a big brother, since I helped launched Nathan's career. Nathan, if you don't mind, I'd like to assist her in finding suitable legal counsel. That way it doesn't come off as if she's been steamrolled in this whole event."

"You'd do that, for me? For Nina? Sure, Sam, I think she'd appreciate that." A kaleidoscope of emotions crossed Nathan's face as he thought about Sam's offer: relief, gratitude, regret . . . and, for just a nanosecond, suspicion. The one that won out was relief.

None of this was lost on Sam—or Riley, for that matter.

"That's a *great* idea!" Kat simpered. Like fans watching a tennis match, all heads bobbed her way, intrigued at this latest volley. "Sure, go ahead, Sam, play Mr. Nice Guy for what it's worth. That way, we'll know exactly what her moves will be, and we can counter them."

Her smile sent chills down his spine.

"Oh, but one thing: Don't get her *too* good of a lawyer, okay? Because if she wins, *you lose*."

Sam's first call was to Lavinia Hannigan, one of the town's premiere celebrity divorce attorneys, renowned for her barracuda tactics on behalf of her star-studded clientele.

"Why the wife? Why not Nathan and Kat?" Lavinia sniffed.

Jeez, another egomaniac. Okay, let's see if this will assuage the pain . . . "Hell, Lavinia, no one doubts that you're the best in the game. And that's all the more reason Nathan feels you should be representing his wife. He's one of those do-gooder types, and he never wants it to be said that he took advantage of her. Of course, Kat's totally upset about that. Says that you should be swinging for our team. But since you *are* the best game in town for these things, Nathan insists that the soon-to-be ex should get first shot at you. Hell, with all the negative press they've drummed up over this affair, a decent settlement should be a slam-dunk for you, right?"

Lavinia grunted, still not convinced. "So, who's going to represent Kat—I mean, Nathan?" she asked warily.

"Howard Cross." He winced as he said the name. The dude was known to be a pig—albeit a pig who had a proven track record for securing the best divorce settlements for his clients—or better yet, ruining their ex's opportunities for one.

He also happened to be Lavinia's biggest courtroom nemesis.

"Humph! Well, now, isn't that just dandy. He gets to stand next to Kat when the cameras are rolling, while I huddle with the homely ex? I dunno, Sam. I've gotta think about that one. Besides, I don't think you'd be doing Mrs. Harte any favor having me on her team. I'm also representing Howard Cross's wife in her divorce proceedings against him. For that reason alone, he's sure to come out swinging. So, good luck in finding someone who won't get on his bad side—if there is such a person." She hung up abruptly.

Sam sighed. If anyone could beat Howard, it was Lavinia. But he'd have to make it worth her while, sweeten the pot. No prob. He'd call one of his network buddies at CNN and see if he could land her a regular spot as a legal expert. Everyone wanted to be a star. Okay, sure, if she'd consider taking Nina's case, he'd make her one, too.

"Face, it Bertrand, chartreuse just isn't your color. And frankly, for that matter, the thought of you stuffing that sausage of yours into a size 6 thong isn't doing it for me."

O was cranky, and it showed. Usually her weekly conversations with Bertrand the Cross-dresser were hour-long gabfests in which he minutely described his latest purchases from Victoria's Secret and some of the raunchier exotic lingerie catalogs, while she oohed and ahhed jealously. Then O was expected to describe (also in minute detail) how she would bite these satin and lace trifles off his supposedly hot bod before voraciously devouring what was underneath. Tonight, however, she was in no mood for his little fantasy, which was why she gave him a brutally honest opinion on how that touchy shade of green would fare against his sallow complexion.

The four-minute silence at the other end of the line was proof positive, at least in her mind, that most people couldn't handle the truth.

"Well, little Miss Too-Cute-for-Words, if that's how you feel, then don't let me waste another minute of your precious time!" (*Click.*)

Ouch.

The next call she got was from Mrs. McGillicutty. "Hell's bells, O! Bertrand just asked for his money back! Is it that hard to tell the guy he looks sexy in a leather bustier and fishnets?" The dispatcher's Fiersteinesque croak made Nina wince. "You know, sweetie, I've already gotten several complaints about your attitude these last couple of days. You're blowing your client retention rate to smithereens. What's happened to that sweet gal we all know and love?"

Nina gulped. She had no defense. "I'm sorry," she murmured feebly.

"Yeah, well, so am I. But I'm still going to have to dock you my cut on his call. Sorry, kiddo."

McGillicutty's reality check was the only reason she took one last call.

Just her luck: *Hugo.*

"Don't scold me, sweet thing, for staying away so long." Of course, the truth was that he wanted to be scolded.

She sucked it up as best she could, under the circumstances. "Boohoo. I cried myself to sleep each night, just waiting by the phone in hopes that it was you."

"Yeah, well, I know you better. Still, it's mighty sweet of you to say." Obviously, her sarcasm went right over his head. "Seriously, I wish I could have called earlier, but I'm having a bitch of a time on this project of mine. I've got a diva witch prima donna and a scared shitless novice I have to coddle, and they're both driving me crazy."

"Heck, how can *you* complain, with all the publicity you're getting? You know as well as I do that you're going to be laughing all the way to the bank with this one."

"I'm not in it for the money. You know that." He sighed heavily. "This is my art, and those two are quickly turning it into a piece of crap! They go at it at every break, like a couple of humping hyenas. How am I ever going to get this picture finished? They're killing me!"

"You're telling me," she muttered. She wanted to scream at him, to tell him who she really was and what he and his damn movie had done to her life so that he could put things in perspective; better yet, so he could feel sorry for her instead.

But she didn't.

Sorry? Did she *really* want him to feel sorry for her? Hell no. She was doing a great job feeling sorry for *herself.*

And that was the problem. Now, at the worst time in her life, she needed to be the strongest she'd ever been . . .

And to keep her mouth shut about her own predicament. After all, whatever info he spilled on the diva witch prima donna and the scared shitless novice might come in handy, when the time was right.

So instead, she said all syrupy sweet. "Gee, Hugo, from what you're describing, you've got a porn set on your hands. Well, you know what they say: When life serves up lemons, maybe it's time to make lemonade . . ."

"Lemon—what? . . . *Huh.*" Her answer took him by surprise. "Jeez, that . . . that may not be such a bad idea . . ." With a few small changes in the script and some cinema verité sleight of hand, maybe, just *maybe*, he actually had some pretty tasty lemonade on his hands.

It would be a new kind of cinema: intelligent and erotic, all at once.

Cinephallia, as it were.

The sex-starved film buffs who worshipped at his feet would just lap it up—no pun intended.

In fact, he'd coin the term—as if he'd thought it up right then and there, spur of the moment—in his upcoming interview with *Cineaste*. The reporter would *love* that.

"Look, gotta go. And, gee, O, *thanks!*" He hung up before she could answer him.

Crap, she thought. That was only, like, about a quarter of his usual call time!

Her candor was costing her too much money. Tomorrow she'd work on that.

An A-list actor's professional life was everything Nathan thought it would be, and more.

However, a superstar's personal life was a living hell, and that was certainly disappointing to discover.

Sure, he could very easily get used to the on-call limo and driver, the ever-underfoot personal assistant (make that plural in Kat's case, since Rain had two assistants of her own—essentially minimum wage fans with more time on their hands than brains in their heads—to whom to hand off the more mundane duties). And he had absolutely no problem with the team of pampering professionals (including a personal trainer, dietitian, stylist, hair designer, personal growth guru, and the lot) that seemed part and parcel with the life.

And certainly it was no stretch *at all* making himself right at home in Kat's palatial fourteen-million-dollar Bel-Air manse, what with its ten spacious bedroom suites, in-home gym, pool-side cabana, twelve-seat home theater, and requisite downtown view, all on five lush security-patrolled acres, no less.

Still, what was missing, at least how Nathan saw it pertained to Kat, was the *means* to this rewarding end.

The blood, sweat, and tears that came with the journey.

The fun of being part of a family—whether that be in an acting class, or one of the multitude of plays rehearsing on any given night in town, or, for that matter, on a film set—

—In none of which a superstar, like Kat, was ever included.

Most of all, what was missing was any thirst for that elusive role of a lifetime.

Because once you were a star, there was no more blood, sweat, and tears, or community.

Or elusive roles, for that matter.

At least, from watching Kat, that's what Nathan deduced.

Yep, the phones were ringing off the hook—Sam's, with directors begging to work with her; Fiona's, for this photo opp; that media interview, or another one of a million promotional events; and Rain's, who was in charge of funneling all this to Kat, who then, depending on her mood or whimsy, picked and chose the projects she wanted to do. More than likely, however, she chose the ones that fit her already-set-in-stone image. Afterward, Rain would memorialize the choice on the Official Kat Kalendar, which was scheduled down to the minute and two years out, and no less detailed than a Pentagon war room battle plan.

How different would it have been, he wondered, if Kat weren't already a star, but just another starlet grasping for the next rung on the Tinseltown ladder, a "working actor" who was still schlepping from one casting agent's office to another, or from one audition to another—or from one acting class to another, for that matter? Would she have held the same appeal for him? Would he have left Nina for her?

Would the public that now watched Kat 'n' Nat's every move still give a damn whether it was a "match made in heaven"?

No, not at all.

Her attraction—to him, and to her adoring public—was the fact that she *was* a star.

The way Katerina McPherson played the star game (or, as she explained during one of her too few prescheduled moments to luxuriate out by the Olympic-size pool, how *everyone who was anyone* played the game) was to keep to the playbook created for her unique publicly perfected persona—her *brand*, as it were.

That way, all the nail-gnashing guesswork magically disappeared.

Sure, it was okay to tweak your brand now and then, to stay fresh in the public's mind. But seriously, what was the advantage in striving—and most likely, unsuccessfully—to be some film-to-film chameleon, *à la* Meryl or Cate?

After all, very few were *that*.

Hell no, warned Kat. Messing with the formula was asking for trouble. If some of the other A-list ladies wanted to be "actors," well then, more power to them. She, on the other hand, would settle for being a mere star.

Either way, she'd get her hour of glory on *The Actor's Studio*, thank you very much. And so would he, she reassured Nathan while giving him a massage. With her at his side—or straddling his back, as she was now—it was only a matter of time.

It was remarks like that one that kept Nathan up at night long after Kat—finally sexually sated, her face slathered with the wrinkle-reducing miracle serum *du nuit*—fell into a gently snoring slumber. Frankly, he *enjoyed* the struggle inherent to his profession. He *wanted* to compete for the meaty, offbeat roles. Nathan *lived* for the subconscious nod, that thoughtful contemplation, and, finally, that phrase every director says when you've nailed the role: "That's it! I think we've got our guy . . ."

. . . Because he loved being an actor.

He just wasn't that crazy about being a star.

As Sam had warned Nina, within forty-eight hours of Nathan's divorce filing, the imminent demise of her marriage was bannered on the cover of every celebrity magazine, becoming fodder for public speculation and (in her mind, at least) pity.

"Kat Nips New Lover's Marriage in the Bud" gushed *Us Weekly*, while *People* heralded, "A Harte to Harte with Kat," and *In Touch* screamed, "Kat to Nat: No More Nina!" as *Star* asked, "Nina Who? Nat Prefers Kat!"

Page Six was a lot less coy: "Hot Hunk Kisses Kat Hello and Wife Good-bye" ran alongside a photo of Nathan's infamous Oscar kiss with Katerina, while Rush & Molloy proclaimed: "Nat to Nina: It's Kat, and That's That!" and Defamer.com mused: "Kat's Li'l Kittens? Vegas Oddsmakers Say So . . ."

" '*Kittens*'?" Kat fairly howled at that one. "Pray tell, why would Vegas bookies think that *those* odds would work?"

"Because I told them it would," retorted Fiona. "I'd rather see you come off as a madonna than a wicked stepmother to Nathan's kid."

"Madonna? Who said anything about me being like Madonna? My fans don't think Nathan is *that* much younger than me, do they?" Panic-stricken, Kat picked up a mirror and perused her face for any telltale signs of natural aging.

"No—I didn't mean Madonna, as in the star, I meant *a* madonna, as in angelic mother icon."

"Oh." Kat put down the mirror. "*Hmmm* . . . Yeah, I think

I could get into that. Kids are, like, so *in* right now. Everyone's got a cute one but me!"

She frowned. This Fiona knew, not because Kat's forehead was creased (as if it could anymore, what with all the Botox she'd had) but because the star's inflated lips had turned down somewhat at the corners. "I mean, hell, I missed out on that whole chihuahua thing, and now I'm getting passed over on the kid thing, too! I never get invited to those hip baby showers, and none of those cute baby boutiques have me on their swag lists . . . Yeah, I could totally see having a kid around. But not if I have to do that whole *childbirth* thing. I'd rather pull a Nicole. You know, avoid stretch marks, or even, God forbid, a C-section."

"Well, since, Nathan's already got a kid, you could get away with that if you just adopted his."

"Omigod! Fiona, you are a *genius!*" Kat ran up to her and gave her the one thing she assumed all of Team Kat coveted most from her: an air kiss.

Fiona pretended to be honored, then added cautiously, "Of course, his wife might not like that idea."

"Bull! Who wouldn't want their kid raised in the lap of luxury? She'll fold eventually. What's the brat's name, Jason? . . . *Jake?* Damn! It's just too bad he's not a girl! Their clothes are so much more fun to shop for . . ."

While Fiona was force-feeding the celebrity press corps, Rain was given the task of dishing the minute-by-minute scoops of Kat poop into Serenity's ear, who in turn wrote public sympathy notes to the star, something to the effect that "Despite having to deal with the trauma of all this nerve-wracking divorce brouhaha while filming what she's told those nearest and dearest to her is 'the role of my career,' she is being a real trouper on the set, to the awe of the rest of her cast and crewmembers . . ."

At the same time, Riley was smearing Nina as much as he could to Baxter, whose next column began, "How nuts is Nina, Nathan's soon-to-be-ex? Let me tell you, readers: Neighbors say she's as fruity as they come! Seems that her crying jags are what drove our man Nat into the arms of his gal Kat in the first place . . ."

Within a week's time, it was an all-out war between the two gossip gadflies. Day after day the public was barraged with late-breaking "Kat 'n' Nat News Alerts"—both in print and online—as each columnist tried to one-up the other. At the same time, both were wondering *where in the hell* the other had found the so-called exclusive dirt that had just been flung.

The biggest scoop that week came in on the night of Sage Oak Academy's sold-out production of *My Fair Lady*. Unfortunately the Hartes had reserved only two seats, and these were adjacent, as requested: a *big* mistake, considering that Nina and Nathan were now separated—*and* Kat insisted on taking one of those seats, too. Or, as she exclaimed to Nathan, she was just dying to see "our little boy." (Unbeknownst to Nathan, that was what she called Jake whenever she'd forgotten the child's name—at least it was her nickname for the kid when Nathan was in hearing distance. Otherwise, "little brat" was preferred).

After a long, hard day at work, Nina rushed into the mobbed school auditorium with her front-row-center ticket in hand—only to find Kat sitting in her reserved seat.

A hush fell over the milling crowd. Everyone pretended to look in other directions, but all ears (not to mention a few camera phones, including one that just so happened to be carried by the ubiquitous Rain) awaited Nina's reaction. Stunned and trembling, Nina purposefully ignored Kat as she growled at Nathan. "*What the hell is* she *doing here?*"

Of course, he hadn't meant to hurt Nina. He'd just forgotten the seating situation. In fact, he had hoped that he and Kat would be able to slip in and out of the play without too much fuss being made over them—

Before he could say a word, Kat smiled graciously and leaned in slightly so that her whispered response could only be heard by Nina: "I'm not leaving, so live with it—unless you want to make a scene and embarrass that brat kid of yours. Of course, if you do, *Nathan will hate you forever.*"

Later, half of those who were there—at least, those who knew Kat, aspired to know her, or believed everything they read in the fanzines—would claim that, if looks could kill, the actress would have been buried right there on the spot by the glare emanating from Nathan's half-crazed soon-to-be ex. The other half—those who knew Nina, if only to exchange a few friendly remarks at the monthly SOA PTA soiree—would insist that she looked as if her heart had snapped in two, right then and there.

Both sides were right. And both sides would have been in agreement that what Nina did next was pure class. Taking a deep breath and holding her head up high, she walked slowly to the back of the auditorium, where she stood throughout the two-hour performance, ignoring the pitying glances cast her way.

Of course, to read Baxter's column the next day, you would have assumed that Nina had threatened Kat's life before running home to slash her wrists. Then again, who wouldn't, after seeing the accompanying photo (courtesy of Rain and six other "anonymous sources") of an angry Nina standing over a sweet, smiling Kat?

13
The Slap

No doubt about it, Jake hated Balloon Lips, which was what he secretly called Daddy's new girlfriend.

He knew it was because of Balloon Lips that Daddy never came home anymore. She was also why Daddy had forgotten to pick up Jake for their last two Team Harte catch-and-throw dates. And worst of all, since his parents' separation, Jake now had to spend every other weekend at Balloon Lips's house, where he was forbidden to go into any room other than the one with the gigantic TV, or the room designated as his bedroom, which was all the way on the other side of the house from where Daddy slept.

With Balloon Lips.

Even when Jake was in the TV room, he wasn't allowed to sit on the furniture, just on the floor. And not with any food or drink, either, because, as Balloon Lips once said to him out of earshot of Daddy: "This Oriental carpet is worth more than you'll ever be, kid, so just suck it up."

One Saturday, he took her words to heart and sucked up the only thing she allowed him to drink—that horrible fizzy water she bought by the case. Then, when he couldn't hold any more liquids, Jake did what any little boy with a full bladder would do: He peed—although not in a toilet (heck, not one of the many adults floating around with those blue knobs crammed in their ears had even *bothered* to show him where the bathroom was!) but into one of the potted plants that filled the humongous TV room.

Being bad never felt so great.

So great, in fact, that the next time he had to go pee, he didn't even bother to run to the plant. He just stood up and did it right there on Balloon Lips's damn Oriental carpet.

Soon, discovering new places to pee became a game. The house had lots of nooks and crannies, so finding a nice, quiet corner wasn't a problem at all. As the weekend went on and on (without Daddy, since Balloon Lips always pouted whenever Daddy left their bedroom to check up on Jake), he got bolder, choosing spots right out in the open, like the formal dining room, or by the back door.

That night, Daddy came to tell the little boy that he had to take Balloon Lips to some party, so to go to bed when that girl Rain told him to. Oh, Jake went to bed, all right: to Daddy and Balloon Lips's bed—where he took a poo, right after peeing in some fancy shoes (named after some little boy's train, "Jimmy Choo-Choo," he thought) in her closet.

When they got home at dawn, Balloon Lips's screams could be heard even as far away as Jake's bedroom. It sent a chill through him. The four-year-old hovered in the dark under the blanket, not knowing just what to expect. But he could hear her coming, cursing and ranting each step of the way.

He prayed he was invisible, that when she flipped on the light he might vanish into thin air. At first he thought his prayers were answered when all he could hear was the sound of his own asthmatic breathing. But he was wrong. This he knew when she peeled back his covers, jerked him up by his pajama shirt, and slapped his face.

Just once, *but hard.*

His whimpers didn't stop, even when Daddy picked him up, cuddled him, and drove off with him, far away from Balloon Lips's evil castle.

Only when Jake saw Mommy's face did he stop crying, because he knew he was making her cry, too.

Daddy didn't cry, though, because he was too big of a boy for that. But Jake could tell he wanted to, because of the tears in Daddy's eyes.

And that was the only reason the little boy would finally forgive him.

Usually the Sunday crowd at the original Urth Caffé on Melrose was too hip to stare at this celeb gulping down his Old Grandpa, or that starlet sipping her Spanish latte, even when such luminaries were practically sitting in one's lap, which was most likely the case, considering how the tiny bistro tables were crammed onto the private patio.

Still, it was hard not to stare at Nina, whose old Honda Civic barely screeched to a stop curbside before she jumped out and stalked angrily through the cafe.

Spotting her prey—Kat, trying to look inconspicuous in oversize Prada shades (if that were even possible) as she and Nathan leisurely perused the Sunday *Los Angeles Times*—Nina strolled over to their table, picked up the actress's very large mug of Manhattan Mudd, and tossed it onto Kat's ostrich feather–trimmed Betsey Johnson cropped cardigan.

The actress's earth-shattering screech was hard to ignore, as were the large, dark wet spots on her sweater, which was now clinging damply to her, giving her adoring public two more reasons to further contemplate her upper anatomy.

It was later reported by Serenity that Nina's parting words were: "If you ever touch my son again, I'll punch you so hard you'll need at least three plastic surgeries to fix your ugly puss . . ." or something to that effect. Then she casually purchased a cappuccino on the way out while the actress very loudly berated her boyfriend for his choice in exes.

Kat's payback was devious: She sent Nathan to pick up Jake under the pretense that she wanted to apologize to the little boy. Hoping that such a big move on Kat's part would assuage some of Nina's anger, he did as he was told.

As Kat suspected, just being in proximity to his father's girlfriend brought the little boy to tears. That was exactly the look she wanted from him. After the so-called apology, Rain took Jake to the kitchen under the pretext of getting him some ice cream, when in truth her mission, as ordered by her devious mistress, was to take a close-up picture of the bruise Kat's slap had created on Jake's face—which she was then immediately to hand deliver to Riley, who would then promptly pass it on to Baxter, who led with it in the next morning's column.

Because Nina's new philosophy on the tabloids was based on that old adage "ignorance is bliss," she wasn't even aware that, once again, mud had been slung her way.

Besides, she was much too busy breaking up a fight between Mr. Baxter and Ms. Hannigan, the imperious attorney whose standing order of Beluga caviar was one of Nina's many responsibilities, as both laid claim to the last of the sea bass.

So, when Tori whispered fervently into Nina's ear that Sage Oak Academy was calling to inform her that Ylva had pointedly abandoned Jake at the school, which, now that it was six o'clock, was closing for the evening, Nina was thrown for a loop.

"If you'll excuse me," she murmured to the bickering customers before racing up the aisle to grab the phone. Frantically, she punched in Ylva's cell number.

"Ja?" The Swedish au pair's boredom was obvious, even with *Elmo's Happy Tapping* playing in the background.

"Ylva! The school just called," Nina hissed into the phone. "They say you've left Jake there. Why didn't you take him home with you and Plum?"

"Because Vecca say you are child veeter. No more carpool, she say."

"What? She called me a—a *what?*" Between Ylva's accent and all the tap dancing in the background, Nina couldn't grasp what words the au pair had mangled.

"I say 'child *veeter*'! You hurt Yake, ja? So now Vecca feel Ploom is not safe. Now *I* must drive *every day*." Her tone clearly indicated that Nina was at fault for that unpleasant change in her circumstances.

Tears rose in Nina's eyes. "How dare she say—why, I've never hit Jake!"

"The papers, they have the pictures. Brat Ploom calling. Bye-bye now!" Plum's petulant appeal was silenced with a click from Ylva's handset.

Pictures? In the newspapers? Nina grabbed a *Daily Times-News* from the newsstand. Scanning the lifestyle articles, she came across *Baxter Quinn's Hollywood Exxxposé* column.

There it was, under the headline: "Battered Up: Nat's Nina Is Slap-Happy with Son!" Alongside the photo of the bruised and tearful Jake was Quinn's exclusive interview with Kat in which she tearfully recounted the two incidents in which her life was "threatened" by Nina—at the school play, at Urth Caffe—and then claimed that she now feared for the lives of "the two guys she loved most." And herself, of course. "That woman is dangerous, and I have the photos to prove it!"

A smaller inset photo showed a close-up of Kat's low-cut, coffee-stained cardigan. Her pose did little to call readers' attention to anything other than her breasts.

Obviously, that was the point.

Omigod, thought Nina. *So now everyone in the world thinks that I beat Jake?*

Of course they did. There it was in black and white. It was all the proof they needed.

Heck, it had even persuaded the starstruck Becca (whose role as the Hartes' carpool partner had finally paid off by allowing her to bask in Nathan's newfound fame, too, albeit vicariously) to dump Jake in SOA's after-school day care, without even a courtesy call to Nina.

The bitch.

She had to get out of there! She had to go, *now*, to Jake, so that he wouldn't feel as if he'd been abandoned.

By a mommy whom the whole world thought beat him.

Tears streamed down her face. She looked around for Tori so that she could tell her she was clocking out. Then she remembered where Tori was:

Refereeing the brawl between Mr. Baxter and Ms. Hannigan, who now could be heard throughout the store threatening to sue Tommaso's for breach of sea bass.

Nina ran back down to the fish department. "Stop it!" she shouted. "Please—please, stop it!"

They ignored her, as did Tori, whose high-pitched screeches weren't helping the situation.

I have to get out of here . . . I have to get out of here . . .

Nina grabbed a cleaver from the fish counter, raised it, and hacked the bass in two. Picking up both pieces, she slapped one into Mr. Baxter's open hand, and the other in Ms. Hannigan's.

"There! Are you satisfied?" she roared at them. "Now . . . now *you can both have the damn thing!*"

All three of them stared at her, as if they'd seen a ghost. One thing was for sure: Whoever this person was, standing in front of them with a fish cleaver in her hand, she certainly wasn't the sweet, quiet Tommaso's concierge they'd come to know all these years.

No, I'm not that woman anymore, thought Nina. *I'm a bitch who supposedly beats my son.*

It was that thought, coupled with the realization that Nathan hadn't cared enough to stop Kat, that took her breath away.

She fainted.

When she came to, Mr. Baxter was fanning her face with a

fish recipe card, while Ms. Hannigan was yelling at the 911 operator to "get an ambulance here *tout sweet*, or baby, I'll have you tied up in court until it's time to meet your Maker . . ." while Tori was repeating the store's address to her, over and over again, like a mantra—

It felt nice to know that a few people actually cared about her.

Nina tried to sit up. "Mr. Baxter, I didn't mean to—" She couldn't help it. The tears started streaming down her face again.

"Hush!" He whispered. "It's okay, doll face. Just a little too much excitement." He grinned down at her. "That Escada-wearing battle-ax didn't know what a hissy fit was until *you* showed her how it's done right—"

I've never seen him smile like that before, ever, she thought. The notion that Mr. Baxter *could* smile made her laugh tearfully.

Seeing her reaction, he chuckled, too. "Now that's *much* better, babycakes." He helped her to her feet. "So, give, sweet thing: What took your breath away? Surely not *this* little tiff."

By now the others had realized that Nina had come to, and were anxious to hear the same.

"Oh . . . no! God, no . . . I—I just found out that—that people are saying I beat my son!"

"What, little Jake?" Tori was horrified. "Why, that's the most ridiculous thing I've ever heard!"

"Yes, I know!" Nina picked up the paper she'd tossed down on the fish counter when she grabbed the cleaver, and handed it to Tori. "But there it is, in *Hollywood Exxxposé*. They're calling me an—an abuser!"

Mr. Baxter glanced down at Nina's nametag.

Suddenly he put two and two together. Unconsciously he dropped his precious sea bass on the floor.

"You . . . you're *that* Nina?" Both Mr. Baxter and Ms. Hannigan exclaimed at the same time. For some reason, they both looked uncomfortable.

"I'm Nina Harte, yes," she said proudly. She didn't flinch at all under their sudden scrutiny. "My husband left me for—for Katerina McPherson." Nina couldn't help it. She started sobbing again. "Now she wants my child, too . . . even after she *hit him*!"

"There, there," Ms. Hannigan patted her hand helplessly. "We can't let that happen. We *won't* let that happen! I will personally—I'll sue that bastard who wrote that crap—"

"Nina, I'm sorry," said Mr. Baxter sadly. "Please forgive me. *I'm* the one who—who wrote that awful crap . . . about you."

"*You?* But how . . ." She didn't get it.

"Nina, what I'm trying to tell you is that *I'm Baxter Quinn.*"

"Omigod," murmured Nina, "You're *that* Baxter? Baxter *Quinn?* But . . . I thought . . . Why are you saying all those awful things about me?"

The tears were streaming down her face again, but she looked him straight in the eye as she declared, "I would never hit my child. *Ever.*"

Why of course she wouldn't. He could see that in her eyes.

Suddenly he realized what a fool he'd been. Both Riley and Katerina had been playing him like a fiddle!

Well, from now on, he'd be singing a different tune.

"I've made a horrible mistake! Just horrible! But I'll make it up to you, I swear."

"I'll say you will," growled Lavinia Hannigan. "Or else we'll bury you, along with that Kat." She handed Nina a business card. "Call me in the morning Nina. Oh, and don't forget my beluga on Friday, okay?"

As she strolled off, Baxter Quinn murmured, "Something tells me Kat's going to have her hands full with that one. But that's nothing compared to what I'm going to do to her." He smiled wickedly at Nina.

"I certainly appreciate the fact that you're going to give a retraction. But the damage has been done, hasn't it? I'm already being ostracized. Even people who know me would rather not be seen with me."

"Nina, honey, the one thing I've learned in this town is that everyone loves you when you're a star, and no one loves you when you're down and out. Just watch how quickly Kat falls off that high horse she's on now, when her star loses some of its luster. And I'm just the guy to throw a little mud on it." He winked knowingly. "Speaking of which, I think this sea bass is now officially inedible. How about some tiger prawns instead?"

As she scooped the prawns out of the seafood case, Baxter plotted his revenge. For Kat, a choice item in tomorrow's column would be only the beginning. For Riley, who broke out in hives followed by diarrhea whenever he ate shellfish, it would start tonight:

Baxter made one hell of a shrimp soufflé that came out of Riley almost as fast as the truth about Kat's little game.

Saints Preserve Us:
And Nat's Nina is All That, and More . . .

YIKES! Sorry, readers, I owe you—and Nina Harte—a big fat apology, so I'm coming clean, right here and now.

Nina, darling, I hope you'll be able to forgive me for
yesterday's column, which was filled with a very big boo-
boo, based on a lie told to me by a flaccid (in every way,
believe me) flack of Kat McPherson.

Yep, you heard it here, folks, Baxter is self-flagellating.
Usually that feels *mmm* good, but not today, coz it's no fun
being duped, and boy, was I ever!

Apparently that petulant screen queen has unsheathed
her claws in an all-out publicity war with her latest
himbo's sweet soul of a wife, going so far as to blame this
devoted mom for that horrendous slap mark—a TOTALLY
unconscionable act—*which this nasty kitty administered
to Nina's little boy herself.* Talk about adding slanderous
insult to bullying injury!

Yep, you heard it first here, folks: It was Kat who
slapped little Jake Harte. So hard, in fact, that it left her
paw mark on the poor kid's face! Wake up, Nat: You'd be
a fool to trade in Nina, the perfect mom, for *that* Mommy
Dearest.

Some celebs can be just positively pissy, particularly
when we gossipy gadflies spill the beans about their illicit
hook-ups and all the nasty consequences that follow suit.
Kat, if you're mad that I'm telling it like it is, well then,
that's just too bad. Your public deserves the straight
scoop—and, in regard to your double dealings, that's exactly what they're going to get from me, from now on.

Baxter Quinn's Hollywood Exxxposé, 4/2

Everyone was laughing at her.

She could tell from the moment she walked onto the set.

And Hugo, *that fucking bastard*, refused to close the set for her.

So Kat endured their snickers. She just put on a big, happy smile and pretended she couldn't hear them, or, if she caught them pointing at her, she looked them straight in the eye, as if daring them to do the same.

Of course, they wouldn't.

Then again, Nathan wouldn't look at her, either.

And that hurt the most.

He, too, had read Baxter's column. Then he cursed at her and slammed out of the house.

Kat stayed up all night, wondering if he'd gone home to Nina, but when she got to the studio, she found out that he'd slept in his dressing room instead, thank God.

She went to him, totally contrite: the perfect geisha, ready to do his bidding.

Not that he wanted her to bide anything for him at all, anytime soon. Or, as he put it: "I'm just not in the mood."

So she broke down, right then and there. She sobbed endlessly over how sorry she was, how she'd do anything to make it up to him, to Jake, to Nina. She'd even fire Rain— who, she claimed falsely, had fed that perfectly *awful* lie to Baxter in the first place, thinking that she was doing them a favor, that imbecile! Why, Kat was just as upset about it as he was. Just *look* what it had done to her credibility with her public!

Not to mention her relationship with Nathan.

No, they could not have any loose cannons in their lives, like that awful Rain.

Crawling on her knees to him, as the tears flowed down her

professionally sculpted cheekbones, she asked in a the softest baby-sweet whisper she could manage, "Darling, please, say you forgive me. *Please*?"

He fell for it, hook, line, and sinker.

They made love (well, *she* made love to him; he was still so upset that he barely made the effort; in fact, he could barely get it up), then she made her way back to her trailer——and fired Rain, right there on the spot.

The poor kid didn't know what hit her.

After Rain left—totally in shock—Kat put in two phone calls. The first was to the security company that guarded her home: she wanted to be sure that someone took all of Rain's things and put them outside the house. *No way, no how*, was that weirdo allowed to go back inside!

Kat's second call was to Fiona. "Get me some do-gooder cause to front, pronto, before Baxter blows my brand to hell!" she screamed into the phone. Fiona said she'd see what she could do.

Later that week, Kat found herself on some major corporation's private jet on her way to Davos, Switzerland, for the World Economic Summit, which was convening that week.

As the press put it:

Kat Puts Out for Pooches

4/8 LOS ANGELES (Reuters)—Katerina McPherson has shot a 60-minute documentary for the Animal Planet Network, in a bid to end the illegal trade of puppies for their pelts.

The star, who recently received an Academy Award

nomination for her role in the historic saga *Destiny*, narrated the film *Pups of the Slaughter*.

As the actress explained in that celebrated breathy voice that infatuates millions of ardent fans the world over, "I am so proud to be a part of this noble humanitarian—I mean, *canine*—endeavor. Hopefully, it will put an end to the exploitation and trafficking of cute little furry puppies, which are used for all sorts of horrendous—not to mention *tasteless*—fashions!"

In the film's most controversial footage, young furry canines are slaughtered. Later their pelts show up on the backs of socialites in cities like Bangkok, Thailand, Munich, Germany, and Houston, Texas.

The documentary premiered later that afternoon at the World Economic Forum. British prime minister Tony Blair, French president Jacques Chirac, and former president Bill Clinton were among the leaders taking center stage at the event, an annual meeting of the rich, powerful, and famous. Other cause-concerned celebrities, from rock stars Bono and Paul McCartney to actors Robert Redford and Leonardo DiCaprio, are also attending the five days of meetings that are taking place in the Swiss resort of Davos.

Says McPherson: "These are beautiful dogs—flat-coated retrievers and Dalmatians—whose lives are being taken. And it's not like we're talking couturiere here. We're talking *off-the-rack!* If ever there was a need for fashion police, well, this is it!"

The day Kat landed back in Los Angeles, Baxter's column ran the headline "The Bitch Is Back" and caustically derided

Kat's "sudden concern for canine couture" as a publicity stunt, to which he added, "And you thought only dogs could be bitches?"

Kat was reading the paper while hanging from her Pilates trapeze table when she came across Baxter's column. Tossing the paper on the floor to Nathan, who had just completed his 437th sit-up, she shrieked, "That bastard! Who the hell does he think he is? I froze my ass off shilling for those mutts! So Fiona picked the wrong relief charity. Hell, nobody's perfect! Not even that mealymouthed little Miss Goody-Two-Shoes you were married to!"

Kat's teary promise to make it up to him—or, for that matter, Jake and Nina—had come to naught, unless you could call a never-before-attempted tantric position and a couple of blowjobs fair compensation.

"Technically, hon, I'm *still* married to her," Nathan growled. Then realizing her proximity to the barbells, he ducked, just in case. "And the fact of the matter is that Nina truly is a saint. Heck, she held down two jobs the whole time we were struggling."

"Big effin' deal. She's a grocery clerk! What, does she moonlight at Walgreen's, too?"

"Hell, no, there's no money in that. She's also a phone sex operator."

"A—a *what? Are you kidding?*"

It suddenly dawned on Nathan that, with a simple slip of the tongue, he had just ruined Nina's life.

A cold chill of shame ran through him. If there had been any way he could have taken it all back, he would, but it was too late. In no time at all, Kat unstrapped herself, dismounted with a perfect back tuck, and speed-dialed Riley so that he could give Serenity the scoop of the year.

Naughty Nina! Nat's Ex Is Obviously Not Tongue-tied

You've heard the old saying "Those who live in glass houses shouldn't throw stones," right? Well, here's one helluva boulder, and it's fallen right smack dab in the middle of the House of Harte.

Seems that Nathan Harte's soon-to-be ex-wife has more than a few skeletons in that walk-in closet of hers. That's where she keeps one very private phone line, which this gutter-mouthed gal answers whenever anyone who's willing to pay by the minute calls for some hot-and-heavy XXX-rated dirty talk *par excellence*.

Turns out that Naughty Nina's quite a fluffer to many of our town's heavy hitters, if that little black book she keeps is any indication. Poor Nat! Who can blame him for seeking solace and refuge in Kat's arms!

Another gossipy gadfly (who shall stay nameless in *this* column) has fallen hard for her sweet-as-sugar line. He (Oops! Sorry, hope that wasn't *too* big of a hint) even went so far as to write her up as the next Mommy Teresa. *Don't make me laugh!* If what I hear is correct, she is *quite* the strict disciplinarian—at least, she is to all those big bad boys who have her not-so-private number on their speed dials.

Want to hear Naughty Nina's seductively salacious spin? For sure, there are a lot of "call" girls out there, but you'll recognize Nina by the sex phone operator nickname she uses: O, as in "O boy, is *she* a wrong number." A second hint: Nina's Red-Hot Hotline is also listed with the rest of those XXX phone sex numbers in the grungier tabloids . . . No, I didn't say it was in *Exxxpose.* (*Hmmm* . . . Then again, considering all the plugs the X Man has given her lately, maybe they have worked out a trade of some sort . . .)

Serenity's Scandal Sheet, 4/13

14

The Truth Comes Out

Those who were taking lunch meetings at their usual tables at the Ivy would always remember the ominous
hush that came over that revered establishment on the day
Nina was outed in Serenity's column.

Sam, who had not yet perused the gossip columns (the only
papers he could stomach before lunch were *Variety* and *Hollywood Reporter*), knew something was amiss, but he hadn't yet
heard what.

He was sitting at his usual table on the Ivy's back patio listening to a pitch by an up-and-coming screenwriter (who was
enjoying his first lunch at the revered watering hole, and just
assumed that everyone was speaking in fervent whispers because they were as awed as he was for being there), when his
cell buzzed silently. Noting from the phone's caller ID that it
was Hugo ringing him, Sam politely excused himself, stood
up, and walked toward the restaurant's lobby.

He hadn't even made it out of the patio before Hugo's

outraged expletives could be heard pouring out of Sam's Motorola Q.

"Hugo, what—what is it? What's happened?" Sam had to calm the director down, not just because he was ruining everyone's lunch in the unusually morguelike Ivy, but because he was worried that Hugo might actually have a heart attack.

"What a little sneak! What a liar! Can you *believe* it?"

"Who, Kat?" Sam sighed wearily. "What did she do now?"

"No. *Not* Kat." Hugo hissed. "*Nina.*"

Hearing his beloved's name, Sam went on full alert. "Did something happen to Nina? Is she hurt? Did Kat hurt her?"

"Hurt? *FUCK NO!*" Hugo's retort was so loud that Sam actually had to move the phone away from his ear. "She's been playing us, Sam. Do you get it? It's her! *She's O!*"

Sam walked out of the restaurant to see if his cell reception cleared up. If he wasn't mistaken, Hugo had said that Nina was O . . .

And heck, there was no way . . .

"What? *What did you say?*"

"You heard me. I said, NINA IS O. It's in Serenity's column! What a joke, huh? I feel—I feel so . . . *violated.* Shit, I feel like a *girl* . . . Hey, are you there? . . . Sam, can you hear me? . . . *HELLO?*"

It was easy to see why Hugo assumed the line was dead, what with Sam having quit breathing for two or three minutes. At least.

Although it seemed like a lifetime.

The part of his life that Nina had entered flashed before his eyes, as if his mind was doing an instant replay while it searched for the clues he'd missed: the first time he saw her, there behind the counter at Tommaso's; the look in her eyes when he promised to look at Nathan's DVD; her joy at Nathan's signing ceremony, and the gentle kiss she gave him afterward; all those stolen moments on those Tuesday evenings, when he was pretending to do his own shopping; that wonderful scent of hers, as she laid her head on his chest at the Casa del Mar; Nina, passed out and naked, stripped bare by Nathan's defection, both physically and emotionally . . .

And all those flirting, teasing, taunting conversations with O . . .

. . . In which he had told her how much he loved Nina.

Loved *her*.

Why, she knew she was talking to him all along.

Hell, she had certainly known who he was when she handed him Nathan's reel. That she had admitted, right then and there.

She had done it all for Nathan: sucked up to Sam, played him like a fiddle, then crushed him like a bug under that delicately arched foot of hers.

That bitch. *That cunt.*

Once again he had trusted a woman, only to have his heart ripped out of his chest and pounded into the ground.

He tossed a twenty at the valet along with his parking chit. The dude had his car there in no time flat.

The screenwriter had anticipated he'd have to pick up the check, but he hadn't anticipated that Sam would leave without hearing his pitch. Of course he'd be pissed when he found out. *Well, too bad,* thought Sam. *I'll catch the guy later.* Right now, it was payback time.

*   *   *

Because Jake was complaining of stomach cramps, Nina had kept him home from school that morning. She had no doubt that his tummy ache and the way he was sucking on his inhaler as if it were a pacifier were symptoms of his anxiety over the divorce, coupled with all the whispering that was now going around the little boy's school. With her cell phone turned off and far away from the tabloid headlines that stared out at her from Tommaso's newsstand (not to mention the stares from the store's clientele, who could not help but recognize her from her pictures in those same tabloids), she was blissfully ignorant of the latest tempest brewing around her.

It was only after Jake went down for his afternoon nap that Nina decided to flip on O's phone line. She rarely worked during the day, and she didn't expect any of her regulars to anticipate her availability, so she was pleasantly surprised to see Sam's telephone number pop up on her phone's caller ID. He had not called O since he'd confessed he loved Nina, and she was glad about that, because she would have felt horrible keeping up the charade, but now she longed to talk to him.

In fact, she knew that it was time to come clean with him. Just the thought of doing so gave her a sense of elation. She'd played the conversation over and over in her head so that she'd have the right words ready. It was important that he understand the serendipity of it all: how he and Nina met, his connection to Hugo, Hugo's connection to O, and the final, most fateful link of all:

O and Nina.

And in knowing how he felt about her, she could now tell him how she felt about him, too.

That she wanted to love him as much as she loved Nathan.

But that was the problem: *She did still love Nathan.*

If Sam could accept that—and accept her mandate that they take things slowly, learn about each other, and most importantly, never lie anymore to each other—*then it just might work.*

"Hi, handsome," O said breathlessly.

"Hi, yourself . . . O."

Something was wrong. She could tell immediately, just in the way he'd spoken O's name.

O knew how to bring him back to her. "I'm so glad you called. I've missed you. *Terribly.*"

"I'll just bet. Hey, O, tell me: Is there anyone in that little black book of yours who *doesn't* get that line from you?"

She laughed uncertainly. "You've always been special to me, handsome. You know that."

Silence.

She didn't know what he was fishing for. *Maybe he's having a bad day*, she thought. *Well, when I tell him, he'll feel better. Of course he would . . .*

She started with: "So, I've got a surprise for you—"

"*Really?* A surprise? Well, well."

Why was he mocking her?

"Let me guess: Is it some new trick you've learned to do with your tongue? Will it make me hard? Will you promise we'll come together?"

"What?" She was surprised. He had never taunted her like that. "No, nothing like that . . . What's with you, Sam? Is everything okay?"

Silence again. Then: "I'll say, O. Everything's just fine and dandy. Now that I've gotten over *that bitch Nina.*"

It was as if she'd been hit hard in the chest. It took her a few long moments to catch her breath, to be able to answer him without gasping. "What do you mean, Sam?"

"Well, O, I have to tell you. There I was at lunch, enjoying the peace and quiet of the day, when it suddenly dawned on me: *That Nina is a lying bitch.* She's just a piece of ass— albeit a very cute piece of ass—but nonetheless, she's just like every other woman who's ever stomped on my heart. Ever had that happen to you, O? You know, when someone just tears you up inside with their lies, one right on top of the other—"

"Sam, what are you saying—"

"I thought I was making myself very clear." He spit the words into the phone. "I'm saying that she's just a piece of ass . . . just like you. You like it when I call you that, don't you?"

She didn't know what to say. Not that she could say anything while she choked back her tears.

"Talk dirty to me, O," he dared her. "Make me come. For once, give me my money's worth. That's what this is about, anyway, isn't it? The money? Hey, that's okay, I get it . . . at least, I will on this call. You'll get me off this time, right? Because I'm getting tired of your little head games. If you can't get me off, then you're just like Nina: *a fake.*"

She was stung by his hurtful jibes. Moreover, she was angry. At him, for being cruel. At Nathan, to whom she'd been so loyal, and for whom she became O in the first place.

And at herself, thinking any man deserved her love.

Certainly Sam didn't deserve it.

Not after what he was saying about her. Not after what he'd just asked her to do.

So instead, she gave him what he wanted. In a steady voice devoid of any sensuality, she recited every lusty come-on, every sad sexual cliché, every raw put-down she could think of: not just words that defiled the human anatomy, but unadulterated triple X–rated blather in which every orifice was described minutely, then objectified obscenely.

When she was done, she couldn't tell if he was still on the line.

I have to make him speak to me, she thought, *to tell me what I've done to deserve his hatred. Damn it, I've already lost Nathan! I can't lose Sam, too.*

All of a sudden, she couldn't stop crying.

She didn't know how long she wept, only that she had never hung up the phone.

Apparently, neither had he.

When he finally spoke, she learned why he hated her:

"You need to look at a newspaper, Nina."

Then he hung up.

So he knows.

And he hates me for it.

She ran to her computer and went online to see what he was talking about, scanning Ted's column in *E! Online,* then *Page Six,* Liz's column, Cindy's, Jeanette's, Baxter's, Lloyd's . . . and finally Serenity's . . .

There it was, in Serenity's column:

That Nina was O.

Serenity went on to call her two-faced, and shameless for the way she was apparently fluffing up half of Hollywood with her gutter mouth . . .

. . . To the horror of poor Nathan, who, Serenity declared, should now be forgiven for seeking solace in Kat's arm.

No wonder Sam hated her.

From reading this, it was natural to assume that every word she'd ever said to him had been a conniving lie. But this *wasn't* her. She had to tell him that, to let him know what his friendship meant to her. *No way could she lose his friendship.* She needed Sam, now more than ever. She would go to him, and explain everything.

With a feeling of dread, she dialed Casey's cell. Had she read Serenity's column, too? And if so, was she still Nina's friend?

"Hell, girl, it's about time you called! Hey, uh, this one's on the house, right?"

Casey's teasing jibe almost made Nina laugh. "You've got quite a sense of humor this afternoon. Wish I could say the same."

"All in good time. Is Serenity's crap why you kept Jake home today?"

"No! I didn't even know this was coming down . . . which is why I'm calling. Jake's got a stomachache, but he's not contagious, and I really need to go out and—and straighten out this mess—"

"Say no more. Bring him on by. He can go with me to pick up Ben." Then Casey's voice got serious. "But Nina, I have to warn you: Not everyone is taking this in the right way. As Susannah so eloquently put it, you're a hot potato right now, particularly since Rolf is in discussions with Nathan about that indie he's trying to get off the ground."

A tear fell down Nina's cheek. Not that she hadn't expected this. In a town where your success was predicated on which stars you'd hitched your own career to, in her so-called friends' minds, Nathan was definitely a better bet for the long run.

"And Jill—well, Jill asked that I tell you not to call her anymore. She's also telling the school that Jamie isn't allowed to play with Jake."

"She's taking it out *on Jake*? That's so unfair! I mean, I understand if she thinks what I did was—"

"I've already told her that I think so, too . . . only I don't think I put it as politely as you did just now. Look, it's how this town plays the game. A year from now she'll be hitting up some producer to play you in the biopic they'll be making on your life. And she'll use her friendship with you as the reason why she'd be perfect for the role."

Ironically, Nina realized how right Casey was. "That's so disgusting. I'd just puke if that ever happened."

"It won't. You know as well as I do that the role will go to someone like Natalie or Claire. If it's any consolation, even if Jill did get it, just imagine how washed out she'll look as a brunette."

"When I said it was disgusting, that's not what I meant—"

"Duh. I *know* what you meant. Hey, see you in a few minutes."

By the time Nina got to Sam's place, the late afternoon sun had already moved out to sea, and the long shadows emanating from the house only emphasized how feebly its warmth held up against the strong breezes blowing in from the beach.

She couldn't tell if Sam's car was in the garage, so she didn't know if he was home or not. Of course, all she had to do was ring the bell.

But she didn't. Instead, she stood outside the gate for what seemed like the longest time.

And prayed.

She prayed that he'd have had time to cool down; and that, if and when she got up the nerve to ring the bell, he would actually let her in and give her an opportunity to tell her side of the story before demanding that she leave and to never bother him again, ever.

She was still praying when he came up behind her. Well, when Towser came up behind her, and put his wet, sandy snout in her hand.

She flinched and opened her eyes. Just then a wayward ray from the setting sun found its way onto her face, illuminating it softly.

Lovely, Sam couldn't help thinking, and doing so made him even angrier.

At her, for being *so damn beautiful.*

At himself, because he couldn't help but be aroused.

"Can we talk?" she whispered.

He paused a moment, then opened the gate, nodding slightly his permission that she should follow him in.

For the longest time, neither of them said anything. She walked toward the big picture window that overlooked the beach and stared out onto the setting sun, almost as if she was afraid to face him, face his anger. Finally, he couldn't stand it anymore.

"I don't have all day," he muttered. "Just tell me one thing:

Did you do it for the money? Or do you truly enjoy turning on dirty old men who can't get it up any other way?"

The color rose in her cheeks. Good, he thought, she's angry. *God, she is so beautiful when she's mad.*

"Would you say that describes you?" she asked. "Because you know, Sam, you were a pretty regular john yourself!"

A john. *Him?*

He found himself right next to her, so close to her, in fact, that he could feel her warm breath on his face. He raised his hand, trying hard to resist the urge to slap her.

She stared at it at first, then she took it lovingly, raising it to her lips, kissing his fingers ever so gently.

But he didn't want to be gentle with her. Roughly, he yanked her close to him. She gasped, not in fear, though, but anticipation. Her open mouth was all the invitation he needed.

Their lips met, finally—

Finally.

They never even made it to the bedroom.

What she remembered afterward was the way he ran his hands over her naked body, softly, worshipfully, as if he'd discovered some precious treasure that would surely dissolve under his touch; and how he paused when he reached her breasts, as if mesmerized. Then, light as a feather, he kissed them, gently, until they hardened. As his tongue circled them hungrily, she let out a moan that stopped him for a moment . . . but only until she indicated that she longed for him to continue, which she did by grasping his swelling penis firmly in her hand, then guiding it between her legs before wrapping herself around his waist . . .

. . . Just like it happened in his fantasy, his thrusts moving in tandem with the lapping waves . . .

Their orgasm was explosive. They erupted in unison. This he knew because she arched up and moaned ecstatically before convulsing against him, their hearts racing, then, eventually, beating in tempo.

At least, until she whispered in his ear how badly she needed to feel him inside her again.

That time, though, there was no need to rush. Leisurely, he traced every curve, every inch of her, with his tongue, his fingertips . . . until she groaned with desire.

It was long after the sun had fallen below the horizon before they stood up again, shaky, limp, and aching from the pleasure they'd made.

"Are you hungry?" he asked, kissing her gently on the forehead.

"That depends." Her answer, so playful, reminded him of O.

O.

She's still standing between us, he thought.

As if she read his mind, the smile melted from her face.

"I think I owe you an explanation," she said.

He sighed and nodded. Yes, he was all ears.

She started at the beginning: her puppy love for Nathan, and how their immature passion and desire to team their god-given talents took root in what they'd hoped would be a life-long love.

Then they got to Hollywood, where nothing was permanent.

The daily rejections they faced, coupled with their almost-penniless existence and Jake's imminent birth—those were the reasons she took on the phone sex job. It was the one way they could survive and buy time until Nathan's big break came along.

"The end justifies the means. Isn't that what they say? It was only when you came into our lives and got Nathan on Hugo's project that I could finally quit! As soon as Nathan's fee was paid and our SAG insurance kicked in, O was going to disappear, just like that." She snapped her fingers.

He nodded slowly. It wasn't that he didn't believe her; he just couldn't help the fact that his ego was still bruised.

And whether he wanted to admit it or not, there was a part of him that missed O.

Not that he could say that to her.

Sensing his ambivalence, she added, "Remember, you were the one who said that few people deserve to be up on that pedestal in the first place, that no one is perfect, and that everyone should be allowed one slip-up now and then. Well, Sam, my slip-up was in taking that job in the first place."

She reached up and cradled his face with both her hands, as if willing him to see her point. "Look, I'm not proud of what I did. But I can live with *why* I did it, because it kept us going when we might have called it quits. Then I met you . . . and he met Kat."

Sam winced at the mention of Kat's name. It was his time to come clean about his role in Kat's infatuation with Nathan, and he knew it.

"Nina, I didn't arrange for Hugo to audition Nathan solely based on his reel. The truth is that Kat requested it."

"*Kat?* So, she knew Nathan even *before* the audition?" Nina's face crumpled.

Sam knew what she was thinking: that Nathan's deception had begun prior to the day of Hugo's birthday.

He couldn't let her believe that. No matter what he thought of Nathan, he wasn't going to strip Nina of the last vestige of fondness she had for him.

"No, believe me, he never met her until the audition. She walked into my office while I was watching Nathan's reel and fell in lust with him at first sight."

"Wow." She steadied herself onto his couch. Towser laid his head on her knee, and she stroked it absently. "And to think, if I hadn't handed you his reel . . . well, I guess I promoted Nathan right out of my life."

"Don't blame yourself. Hell, I've been kicking myself since she sank her claws into him. I should have stopped it somehow, told her anything to keep her away."

"Yeah, dammit, why *didn't* you?" Nina was suddenly angry. "You could have made something up, said he'd had a shotgun accident—or that—"

"Hey I know—Jeez, why hadn't I thought about it before? *I could have told her that he's gay!*"

Even as he said it, Sam couldn't help but laugh, and neither could Nina. In fact, she was laughing so hard that tears were running down her face.

"Nathan *gay*? Why, he's so homophobic that he thinks giving a baby boy the wrong name will have him playing for the other team!"

Upon hearing that, Sam doubled over with laughter again. He fell over on her, gasping for air.

She held him close. In fact, she wouldn't let him go. That

was okay. If he could, he'd stay at her side forever. There was nowhere else he wanted to be.

"Hey, Sam, be proud of yourself. You kept your mouth shut, for your clients' sake. You didn't even tell O, remember?"

That was true. "If I had told O, how would you have taken it?"

She thought for a moment. "I would have fought for him, of course. But look, Sam, I'm no fool. If it hadn't been Kat, it would have been someone else, right?"

She drew his face toward hers and kissed him fervently. "Then again, if he had stayed, I wouldn't have you."

That night, she had him as often as she wanted.

The next morning, as they opened the front door to go out for a walk on the beach with Towser, they found a battalion of cameras waiting for them.

"Nina, look this way—"

"Nina, is he one of your johns? So you make house calls, too?"

"Hey, Nina, do Nat and Kat know you're screwing their agent?"

That very thought struck Nina and Sam at the same time: Well, they sure would by the time the photos were uplinked to that afternoon's newswires.

15

The Backlash

The weekly partners' meetings at ICA could be described as part accounting seminar/part pep rally. After going over the dull-as-paste business of monthly fee projections, number crunching, budget allotments, and expense reports, everyone was then given an opportunity to show and tell: to boast about done deals, crow over the successful signing of an established star who had jumped ship from another agency, or beat one's chest about some new fresh-faced talent who had the potential to make it really big.

In other words, lots of tickles, and maybe a couple of farts.

The calling of a special partners' meeting meant that something had gone terribly wrong.

Certainly it could be categorized as a major fart.

Sam's affair with Nina fell in this category.

That was not to say that it was the first time in the town's history that an agent was caught in bed with a client's wife.

Hell, in Hollywood, naughty little affairs were so common, they often went unnoticed.

What did get noticed, and what was frowned upon, was any behavior that might cost the firm business, and Katerina McPherson and Nathan Harte were *big business* to ICA; business that, if pissed off enough at Sam's disloyalty, could justifiably jump ship to another shop.

Already the tom-toms were beating: the very desirable duo had been seen at L'Orangerie with two partners from CAA, dining and (justifiably) whining about their current representation over the *amuse bouche*. So of course Sam's partners felt justified in calling a special partners' meeting to discuss this potential loss of income.

"To boink a client's wife—then to have it plastered all over the gossip rags? Jeez, Sam! Do you know what this has done to the firm's reputation?" His inquisitioner, Randy Zimmerman, was a partner whom Sam was not particularly fond of. Perhaps it had something to do with Randy's poaching come-on, which resembled that of a desperate Sunset Strip tranny hooker's worst line on a rainy Sunday night: "If you need someone to whip, hey, guy, I'm your man . . ."

Was it any wonder that both Toms had put out a restraining order on him?

"Not a good move, huh, Randy? Tell me, how does it compare to the time that soap actor you represent caught you massaging his wife's breasts? Look, just because you got him on that *CSI* spinoff as a series regular and he was kind enough to forgive and forget doesn't give you the right to be such a sanctimonious pig."

At that less-than-fond memory, Randy turned the same

burgundy color as his Prada loafers. "They don't compare at all, and you know it! Even if he had jumped ship, what would it have cost the firm? Ten, maybe twenty thou, over the course of three years? Hell, that little piece of ass of yours could cost us several hundred thousand over the same period of time! You know that."

No one else in the room said a word. *Fucking two-faced cowards*, Sam thought.

Randy, fully aware he had his partners' backing, threw out his trump. "Look, Sam, if it comes down to losing you or Kat, everyone here is in agreement that you don't make the cut. Having another Oscar nominee on the roster means added prestige for this agency, not to mention that she's one of the top three actresses at the box office. And with the press he's getting, Nathan is nothing but potential, too." Randy leaned in for the kill. "Hey, you still have a chance to pull one out. Believe it or not, Kat and Nat are both willing to stay put—*with you*—under one condition."

"Oh yeah? What's that?"

"You've got to dump Nina. If you're willing to do so, they feel that we can all put this behind us and move on."

Dump Nina, for more fun and games with Kat and Nat? *Not in a million years.*

"Fuck that. Sorry. I'm sticking by Nina," was Sam's response. "I can make up the billing with other clients."

"Not at this agency, you can't. We're siding with them. In fact, we guessed you might feel that way, and we offered them an alternative: If Katerina and Nathan are agreeable, they can transfer their representation to any other ICA agent they prefer."

"How convenient. If you're asking my permission, you've got it. The three of you deserve each other. The subject is closed." Sam started out the door.

"Thanks for the vote of confidence, Sam, but quite frankly, I wasn't asking your opinion. Not that I didn't put that very same suggestion out there to Kat. I don't know why, but for some reason, she said she'd pass. Go figure."

It was on the tip of Sam's tongue to say that the thought of Randy's hands on Kat's breasts was possibly the deal breaker, but then he remembered that they were talking about Katerina McPherson, queen of the A-list mactresses, so that wouldn't have been the case. Kat loved knowing she was a turn-on, to anyone and everyone.

Hell, she'd even come on to Sam on more than one occasion.

Not that he'd ever let Randy know that. It would only give the agency's resident manwhore more ammo to use against him.

"Wow, you mean she turned down the opportunity to have you handle her? Gee, now that's a surprise. Well, I guess CAA bags another one."

"Not necessarily. Now that you've officially tendered your resignation, it's made room for one of our junior associates to make the leap to partnership—that is, if he's able to keep the loving couple happy. The partners all feel that Riley Mc-Naught just might be the person to do that."

"*Riley?*" Sam couldn't believe his ears. Suddenly, it all made sense. So it was Riley who had provided Baxter and Serenity their scoops! He'd probably given the stalkarazzi the heads-up to watch Nina's apartment, too.

And unknowingly, she had led them right to Sam's doorstep.

Sam started laughing. "Sure, Riley will be perfect for the job."

"Huh. We're glad you agree." It was obvious in Randy's tone that he was disappointed at Sam's positive reaction. Still, he couldn't resist getting in one more jibe. "Well, anyway, Katerina certainly thought he'd fit the bill. In fact, she implied that he might have been doing the job all along."

Randy's condescension was too much for Sam. This time, when he reached the door, he didn't look back. If Riley had indeed been doing her bidding all along, he'd now have the corner office to prove it.

That morning, when Nina got to the employees' lounge at Tommaso's, she noticed that there was a padlock on her locker. A Post-it note slapped on it instructed her to see Tori *immediately*.

She found Tori blessing out the produce manager for the lackluster condition of his fruit, a daily ritual that accomplished nothing other than to make the poor, hardworking sap's life a living hell, which was why the other store employees likened his gig to that of the boatman Charon on the River Styx. Upon seeing her, Tori motioned for Nina to follow her into her office, where the Person-Formerly-Known-As-Tony then proceeded to avoid eye contact, choosing to fidget instead with the French tips on her long, tapered nails.

Finally, Nina couldn't stand the suspense any longer. "Tori, what's the deal? Why can't I get into my locker?"

"Because you don't work here anymore." A couple of tears formed in Tori's heavily mascaraed eyes. Reaching up to wipe them away, she accidentally stuck a nail in her eye. "Damn hormone pills! Damn fake nails! This fucking acrylic polish *stings*!"

"Fired? Why? Has a client complained about something—"

"No, are you kidding? Everyone loves you." The tears started falling again. This time Tori knew better than to put her talons anywhere near her face. She wiped her tears with a monogrammed hanky instead. "It's management, hon. They've heard about your little, um, 'side job,' and they're now worried that you were using our client list to solicit your—do you call them johns?"

"No. In fact, I don't call them at all. They call *me*." Nina wanted to cry, but held her head up high. "You know I'd never, in a million years—"

"I know, Nina. Believe me, I personally think they're making a *huge* mistake—but I can certainly understand why they feel they have to do it. They don't want this place to become a carny sideshow." Coming from the first ever six-foot-three-inch transsexual store manager the chain ever had, that was quite a statement. "You're the best employee this store has. And you know I don't pass out compliments to just anyone."

In fact, they both knew that she'd never complimented anyone.

"But—but I need the insurance! What about Jake's asthma?"

"If they yank it, you might have to file a grievance. But they feel they have a pretty strong case against anything beyond a couple of weeks' severance."

That was it? For five years of loyalty, she'd be walking out of there with less than half a month's rent!

Numbly, Nina stumbled toward the door. Tori followed her out to her car, then asked Nina not to drive off until she cut her severance check. Fifteen minutes later Tori was back beside the car. Not only did she have a check, but she had a cartful of groceries with her, too.

"Here," she said, shoving bag after bag into the backseat of Nina's Civic. "Consider it a going-away present."

"Tori, I can't take this! They'll accuse me of stealing it! Or you may get fired!" Nina reached across the backseat and gave her ex-manager a kiss.

"Hey, watch the lipstick!" Tori muttered, but Nina knew she was touched. "I chipped in for the wine, but the groceries were a gift. You've got an admirer in the company."

"Huh? Who?" At Tommaso's? She had never even been introduced to any of the brusque, dark-suited men who showed up periodically for the unscheduled walkthroughs that always terrorized the store employees and usually put Tori in a dither for the following twenty-four hours.

"Some bigwig on Tommaso's board. Seems he shops here often and has always been impressed with your customer service skills. Anyway, he owns a large amount of Tommaso's stock, but apparently it wasn't a big enough chunk to get the majority of the board to go along with his suggestion that you be given a reprieve. Do you remember that really old guy, Herbert Cahill?"

Herbie! What a doll. The next time he called, she'd have to do something extra special to thank him. Better yet, Fraulein Von Berens would give that "bad boy" a tongue-lashing in German that he'd remember for some time to come.

According to Mrs. McGillicutty, Nina wouldn't be speaking to any of her clients in German, or English either, for that matter, until things cooled down a bit: Most of her regulars were now scared to call O.

"Face it, doll, you're just too hot to handle right now, particularly for those Hollywood studio executive types who like to come off pure as driven snow."

Well, there goes the other half of the rent money, thought Nina. "Maybe I could change my phone name. If I do, will you still send calls my way?"

"To be honest with you, hon, even if you did, I wouldn't be able to keep you on right now. Or any of my girls, for that matter. A friend in high places tipped me off that my phone lines are hot right now with the Feds."

"Omigod! Mrs. McGillicutty, I certainly didn't mean to ruin your business for you!"

"Well, it was fun while it lasted. In the past twenty-four hours, the number of calls to the service have increased by four hundred percent! Your regulars may be hiding out, but everyone else is looking for you, kiddo. Although I suspect that half of those guys are reporters."

Nina sighed. She had no doubt that the dispatcher was right. That was another reason to stay off the phone until things cooled down.

Mrs. McGillicutty continued, "Look, kid, don't worry about me. Hell, as soon as I find the right guy to pay off, I'll be back in business, so be thinking of another nickname you can use when this crap gets straightened out."

"I don't know. I may just find another line of work altogether. If I don't starve in the meantime."

The dispatcher gave one of her foghorn guffaws. "You

won't, not with that voice of yours. Keep in touch, O . . . or whomever. I'd hate to lose you to another service."

When Nina went to pick up Jake at school, Mr. Pickering was waiting curbside with him. It was obvious that the little boy had been crying.

"Jake, what's wrong?" cried Nina as she jumped out of the car and knelt down to give her son a hug.

"I was just explaining to Jake that, just because he has to leave the school, it doesn't mean he'll never see any of his little friends. That is, if their parents don't mind."

"Leave? But, of course, he'll be back tomorrow—"

"No, he won't be coming back, *Nina*—you don't mind if I call you Nina, do you? Seems that everyone else is being so—*informal*—with you these days." Nina looked up at him, surprised. On school grounds, parents and staff weren't allowed to call one another by anything other than their surnames, preceded by Mr. or Ms. The last person she expected to lift the sacred veil was Pickering—until he added, with a dirty smirk: "Or would you prefer if I call you *O*?"

Nina stood up. Blowing her bangs out of her eyes, she patted Jake on the head and nudged him toward the car. "Go ahead and buckle up, Jake."

The little boy knew that tone in his mother's voice, and rushed to do as he was told. He was so glad it was directed at the headmaster, and not at him. Perhaps Plum was right, and Mommy was going to give Mean Mr. Prick Ring that spanking after all!

"Are you telling me that my son is no longer welcome at Sage Oak Academy?"

"Well, since you put it so bluntly, yes." He leaned in toward her—too close for comfort, for sure. "Bluntness is a specialty of yours, I've heard."

Nina fumed silently. She wasn't going to give him the pleasure of watching her explode in fury in front of her child.

Prick Ring's just lucky I don't have him alone in a dark alley.

Ignoring her silence, he continued. "In any event, due to your, er, 'change in profession,' the *majority* of the board"—his emphasis on the word majority was his way of saying that he had triumphed in having Herbie overruled—"felt that Jake would be better off in a more *accommodating* academic environment. If you'd taken the time to read the SOA handbook, you'd recall that this sort of behavior is grounds for dismissal from our strongly ethical community."

"Well, then there goes half your parent body"—Nina smiled up at him sweetly—"because I know several fathers in this school on, shall we say, something a little more intimate than a first-name basis. Tell me, *Brad*, can you say the same?" She gave him a naughty smile. "You don't mind if I call you Brad, do you? Although if you prefer 'Prick Ring,' I think I can say it without gagging."

He turned blue—not just because of the taunting nickname (by now he was resigned to it, and even suspected that some of the other parents used it when referencing him as well) but because she was right:

He had no real allies—let alone friends—within the parent body.

Among the daddies at the school, he had never been considered "just one of the guys." But then again, how easy could that be when most of those guys just so happened to be the town's biggest movers and shakers? In their world, he was merely another fawning sycophant.

Suddenly a cold dread crept through him: In a community that so highly coveted notoriety, infamy, and celebrity, had his insistence on the Hartes' ejection—over the strenuous objection of the board's president, no less—been sheer folly on his part? Instead of the anticipated outrage at the Hartes' continued inclusion, would the expulsion instigate a mad exodus from the school?

Perhaps he'd unknowingly opened up a political can of worms! Pickering sighed out loud. Before he found this out the hard way, he'd better come up with an exit strategy, and quick!

He made a mental note to start looking for another headmastership immediately—in a town *definitely* more chaste than Hollywood.

As if there really was such a place . . .

One of the items that Tori had put in the Tommaso's care package was a pint of Ben & Jerry's Cherry Garcia: manna for a little boy whose world was caving in around him. Nina didn't even bother to dish out a premeasured tummy ache–proof scoop of the chewy, gooey concoction into one of his baby cups. Instead, she just handed him the pint with a spoon and the remote control. Hell, the kid deserved to binge, just like everyone else caught up in this mess their lives had become. She'd deal with the sugar high sometime later.

O's phone might be silent, but Nina's was still ringing off the hook—from what she could tell through caller ID, most of the callers had numbers she didn't recognize. Naturally, she assumed they were reporters.

Her voice mail verified that. The people she was most desperate to hear from—like Sam, and of course Lavinia Hannigan, whom she had phoned twice already that morning—had yet to return her calls. However, *Star, Globe, National Enquirer, Insider, Entertainment Tonight, Extra*—even Diane and Barbara!—were clamoring to give Nina an opportunity to tell her side of the story, to cry on their shoulders about Nathan's departure, to come clean about her phone sex work—not to mention her affair with Sam.

As if her life was anyone else's business.

She could only imagine how news of her tryst with Sam had gone over with Nathan and Katerina. She had no doubt that Katerina had hit the roof and was calling for Sam's head on a platter for daring to be disloyal to her. And as for Nathan, well, Nina could only imagine the jealousy he must be feeling right about now, knowing that his agent had been comforting his wife (that was, his soon-to-be ex-wife) with the kind of intimacy that she'd experienced with only one other man her whole life:

Nathan.

Well, that's too bad, she thought.

Lost in the heady fantasy of Nathan choking on some of his own bitter medicine, Nina absently picked up the insistently ringing phone.

"Nina, hi, it's Susannah."

Susannah.

As in I-dumped-you-as-a-friend-because-you're-too-hot-right-now Susannah.

"What do you need, Susannah?" Of course she wanted something. Why else would she be calling?

"Look, Nina, I—I have to apologize for—for dropping you the way I did. It was a cowardly thing to do. Please forgive me."

Whoa. Talk about out of left field!

Funny what little is left of your heart when you've been burned by a friend, thought Nina. It certainly seems to grow a thicker skin.

"You still haven't told me why you're calling, Susannah, and I really don't have all day. Gotta field calls from the press, know what I mean?"

There was a silence on the other line. Finally Susannah spoke: "I—I was wondering if you could put in a word for me with—with that company you work for."

"Tommaso's? Just go on in and pick up an application. Hell, I know they've got an opening, because *I* just got fired." Of course, Nina knew Susannah wasn't talking about Tommaso's. It was fun to hear her squirm, though—for McGillicutty's number, of all things!

"Uh, no. Not the grocery store. I mean . . . you know, that call center."

"Oh, I see. You want to do phone sex! Gee, I don't know, Susannah. Has this request been cleared by Mr. Pickering?"

"*Pickering?* What does he have to do with it? He doesn't— omigod! *Does he call you, too?*"

"No, you don't have to worry about Pickering. At least, not at my service. Oh, and by the way, I haven't heard from your husband, either."

"Oh. Well, that's good." Susannah sounded almost surprised.

Considering what a prick the guy is, I guess that is somewhat surprising, thought Nina.

"Look, Nina, it's hard for me to ask this, but I have to. You see, Rolf's hit a—a bad patch, financially, that is. He's thoroughly in over his head, what with this film he's producing. And now he owes money to some people. Some *really bad* people. I've got to do something, you know? I just hate the thought of losing the house, but if we don't come up with some money fast—"

Despite Susannah's desertion, Nina couldn't help but feel sorry for her. She knew that Susannah's stately Brentwood mansion was her pride and joy. "Look, uh, Susannah, I'll give you my dispatcher's number, but I have to warn you, she's not putting on anyone new right now. Truth is, she's having to close up shop for a while, over this whole O thing."

Susannah said nothing, but Nina could hear her sniffling on the other end of the line.

"Susannah, I'm really sorry. I wish that there was something I could do!"

"I know, Nina. You're a sweetie. You always were. Well, I guess I'll just have to call around to some of the other services. Or go back to . . . to what I did before."

"Modeling? That pays fairly well, right?"

Susannah snorted. "Oh yeah, right. I forgot that's what I've been telling all the other mommies. Well, since I know your dirty little secret, I'll let you in on mine: I never modeled. I did porn."

Nina was stunned. Having anticipated that reaction, Susannah laughed harshly. "Yeah, yeah, I can just imagine what you're thinking: that I'm a two-faced bitch." A sob caught in her throat. "Hey look, I've got nothing to apologize for what I did. It got us out of the Valley and into Brentwood, right? And trust me, honey, SOA's PTA is full of ladies who've gone down on their knees—literally—to stay in their beloved Blahniks and Botox."

"But, Susannah, there's got to be another way than doing that again!"

What a scandal that would be if it got out around SOA! Heck, Nina's activities would be considered child's play in comparison. "Even if you earn enough to pay off Rolf's debt, how will you explain to him where all that money came from?"

"What, *are you kidding me?*" Susannah was laughing so hard that Nina thought she was having a nervous breakdown. "Honey, he produced my last three porn films!"

Then, bitterly, she added, "If only he hadn't been so adamant about going legit, we wouldn't be in this mess now . . . Oh, shit! Little Rolfy's tennis coach is here, and I don't know what the kid did with his racket. Sorry, sweetheart, gotta run!"

Nina hadn't heard the door open because Jake's sugar high had finally crashed and she had been putting him to bed.

But as she walked back out into the living room, she saw him there, silhouetted in the streetlight filtering through the closed window blinds, looking as handsome as he had when she last saw him.

Nathan.

He had on a hooded sweatshirt. He'd come in through the back door, not chancing that some of the stalkarazzi out front would even assume that a star of his caliber would shimmy up a three-story fire escape, then hike himself over the lattice screen that divided their apartment's back terrace from their next door neighbor's patio.

He stood there for the longest time, not saying anything. She, too, was afraid to speak, as if doing so would break the spell that had him standing there before her.

Besides, if he was real, then maybe the past two months had just been a bad dream.

She knew that wasn't the case when he turned to her, stone-faced, and growled in a low, hoarse whisper, "*How could you?*"

She couldn't believe her ears. *He* was blaming *her?*

Without realizing it, she'd come up beside him. Although she kept her hands clenched at her side, she really wanted to hit him, to hurt him somehow, *some way*, so that he could feel at least a little of the pain she'd been feeling these past few weeks.

"You've got some nerve!" Heartache seethed from every word she uttered. "It wasn't me who was screwing around, remember? *I'm* not the one who left to live with that—that woman!"

"How do I know you weren't seeing Sam all this time?" Nathan leaned in, as if daring her to slap him. "It seems awfully funny how he wanted to stay close to you, even after we separated. And now I know why. Hell, the whole world knows it!"

"That's what's really got you upset, isn't it, the thought that others will think that I was running around on you first? My God, Nathan, how selfish can you be?"

The way he flinched told her she'd hit her mark.

Realizing this only made her madder. All of a sudden the

memories—of all the hard work, the financial struggles, the emotional and professional sacrifices she'd made over the past six years, *for him!*—flooded her consciousness, suffocating her in a tidal wave of pain.

"Just when was I supposed to be carrying on this so-called affair? While I was on my feet all day, at Tommaso's? Or was it happening when I was home with Jake, while you were spending nights with that bitch?"

"Oh, you weren't that lonely, Nina." He smiled cruelly. "Don't forget your evening job, sitting there flirting with all those guys, fluffing them up, hearing them while they . . . while they—"

She slapped him. *Hard.*

That shut him up.

Oddly, though, he seemed to like pain. She could tell by the way he smiled down seductively at her, his eyes half closed but alert with passion, assessing her anger against the desire so apparent in her face.

"Tell me the truth: Did *he* ever call O?"

From the beginning she had made it a point never to discuss her many gentleman callers with Nathan—and he never once asked. He knew that the only reason she had done it in the first place was to support him while he'd struggled for bit acting gigs. Besides, he was jealous whenever another man merely glanced her way! Then again, Nina didn't have to tell him that Sam had called O. He knew by the look on her face.

"That son of a bitch! I'll—I'll *kill* him!"

"You've got it all wrong! We didn't meet that way at all! We met at the store, when I gave him your audition reel—"

"My—reel? What? . . . When?"

"Remember that night you met him? It happened then, that same day!"

This stopped Nathan cold—for a moment. "Then why didn't you tell me about it?"

"Because—because you were so excited about having made the contact on your own that—that I thought I'd let you take the credit."

"Well, that certainly played right into his hands."

"If you're saying that Sam planned all this, you're crazy!"

Nathan grabbed her by the arm. "Nina, just think about it for a moment: The only reason Sam took the reel from you in the first place was because he was trying to get into your pants. Yeah, okay, he takes a few minutes with my reel so that the next time he sees you he'll be able to say he did it, and that he'll keep me in mind—particularly if *you* play ball with him."

Of course, he was right. Sam had even admitted to Nina that he had agreed to look at Nathan's tape only because he was infatuated with her.

Nathan continued: "But then Kat walks in while he's watching it, and she insists that I audition for Hugo. She told me so herself, told me that was when she fell in love with me."

Nina frowned. Well, that little revelation of Kat's certainly scored major points with Nathan.

"Sam only sent me up for it because Kat asked him to. She also said that Sam put me down to her, that he insisted I was too green for the role. Yeah, sure, he's *really* looking out for my best interests!" Nathan grimaced. "But Kat insisted he set it up anyway. In fact, she told him that was the only way she'd do the film."

"You're proud of that, aren't you?" Nina retorted. "Gee,

you don't have much confidence in yourself. I mean, do you really think that Sam would have put you up for Hugo's movie if he didn't feel you had the chops for the role in the first place? Frankly, the way I see it, this proves that Sam wasn't trying to break us up. *He was trying to keep us together*."

"Bullshit! He tried to talk her out of it because he—he's always had a thing for her."

His words fell on her like hard blows. She could tell that he drew some satisfaction hurting her, in pointing out to her that she was not so desirable.

Either to him, or to Sam.

Not like Kat, who was desired by everyone.

Apparently even Sam.

"She told me that they were once hot and heavy. But she wanted to cool it with him because he was way too possessive of her—"

"In her dreams! Trust me, Nathan, you don't know what you're talking about. She's just playing you with that lie."

"And he's playing *you*!"

She had to admit it: In Nathan's scenario, things would have worked out somewhat conveniently for Sam.

Throwing Nathan within Kat's suffocating grasp would accomplish two things: First, it would allow Sam to be in the right place at the right time to comfort Nina after Nathan's defection.

Most certainly, it would pique Kat's jealousy and interest in Sam once again.

And all this would occur at whose expense? Why, hers and Nathan's, of course.

Interesting.

Watching the emotions play out in her face, he knew he had her. Triumphantly, he slammed his hand against the wall. "So I'm right, huh? Now do you get that this was all a setup?"

"No! Of course not! I mean—well, I don't exactly know what I mean!" Suddenly she was confused.

How much of what had happened was fate, and how much of it was some grand scheme by one of Hollywood's savviest players?

Things were moving too fast for her to think. Still, if she told Nathan that she, too, suspected Sam, he'd feel justified in thinking that he'd been set up for a fall.

For that matter, maybe he was. Then again, he certainly seemed to have enjoyed the arms into which he'd fallen.

"Let me ask you a question, Nathan. Was it Sam who forced you to have sex with Kat?"

He had no excuse for his cruel desertion, this they both knew.

His shoulders sagged under both her logic and his guilt. Without thinking, he leaned into her, seeking both the physical and the emotional support he so desperately needed. Her first inclination was to shake him off, to throw him out with all her might . . .

But she didn't.

She didn't move at all.

It was all so familiar, her lying there on his chest, their hearts beating in unison. He brushed her forehead with his lips. Then lovingly, with one hand, he raised her face to his and slowly, gently, lowered his lips to her own.

She didn't stop him.

Of course she ached to kiss him; to have him again, inside her, mind, body, and soul. To know that he wanted her, too, just as before . . .

. . . and not just because someone else now wanted her.

But that's the only reason he's here, she thought sadly.

She pushed him away. Then, with her head held high, she walked to the back door and opened it. "I think you need to go back to Kat now."

Reluctantly, he nodded. As he reached the door, he turned back. "The last thing I ever wanted to do was hurt you. And I'd hate to think that will happen to you again, Nina. *With Sam.*"

Then he was gone.

Would Sam hurt her?

She could hear Jake's asthmatic wheeze from his bedroom. She hesitated for a moment to give herself time to place a serene smile on her face before going in to comfort him.

When she got there, he was already sitting up and he had his inhaler on his mouth. Rubbing the sleep and tears from his eyes, he muttered groggily, "Mommy, I had a dream that Daddy came home . . ."

She held him in her arms until he fell back asleep.

16

The Doubts

Lavinia Hannigan was avoiding Sam's call.

He knew this, because he'd already put in three to her within a twenty-four-hour period. Each time she had conveniently been "in meetings."

In fact, everyone he'd called since the news broke that he was "pursuing other opportunities outside ICA" had been "in meetings." Or at least they'd instructed their assistants to use that excuse if Sam called. Or they just let their cell phones roll over to voice mail after noting his number on their caller IDs.

He knew the game. Hell, he'd played it enough.

It had been quite some time, however, since it had been played on *him*.

Which was why, the fourth time he called, he did so from Hugo's offices, and had Hugo's receptionist call and say that it was Hugo who was on the line.

That certainly got Lavinia to the phone, and fast. "Hugo, darling! What can I do for you?"

"Oh, hi, Lavinia. It's Sam. Remember me?"

"How could I forget you, Sam?" Ice gripped every syllable. "You're plastered all over the tabloid news. Along with your *girlfriend*, Nina, the soon-to-be-former Mrs. Nathan Harte."

"Well, Lavinia, you said you'd prefer to represent the biggest celebrity in the case. I'd say that we've delivered as promised, right? Now, are you in, or are you out?"

"You also said you'd deliver a slam dunk. I think that Nina's little side gig is going to make that harder to do now, don't you?" She paused and then added more gently, "Look, Sam, personally I like Nina. Hell, she was the best thing Tommaso's had going for it. But let's get real. Howard Cross is going to crucify her! In the public's mind, she's already positioned as an unfit mother. Nathan and Kat will win custody of the child hands down."

"So you won't even give it a shot? You owe her that much, Lavinia."

By her silence, Sam could tell he'd gotten his point across.

"I don't do pro bono, Sam, and she can't afford me without a settlement. You know that. And I'm assuming you can't exactly be her knight in shining armor, since, from what I read in this morning's *Hollywood Reporter*, you'll be doing some belt-tightening, too."

"Don't worry about me, Lavinia. It's Nina and her son, Jake, who are at stake here. Look, whatever it takes, I'll cover it. And if you do your job the way we all know you can, Nina can pay me back with some of the proceeds from the movie rights."

Lavinia laughed. "You certainly know how to cover all the angles, don't you Sam?"

"It's what I get paid to do, Lavinia. I'll have her in your office first thing in the morning."

The Superior Court of California for the County of Los Angeles wasn't exactly as friendly as Disneyland by any means. However, as the sweet, pert receptionist assured Nina as she and Lavinia filed her Petition for Custody and Support of Minor Children, it was certainly the court's aim to make the tearing asunder of any union first blessed with good intentions but then inevitably cursed by irreconcilable differences (not to mention an affair or two) as painless as possible.

With that in mind, the receptionist handed Nina the court's version of a VIP swag bag and strongly encouraged her to peruse it at her leisure. In it was:

1. A pamphlet explaining all the court's definitions, terms, and procedures as they pertained to legal separation, the nullity of marriage, filing a Summary Dissolution of Marriage, custody and visitation rights, how to petition for child support as well as spousal support, how to attain a restraining order, and what to do about civil harassment. (To Nina's disappointment, it had nothing in it pertaining to harassment by the press.)
2. A phone listing of the area's mental health counselors. (As of that moment, Nina wasn't contemplating suicide or murder, but with the way the media was chasing her down, she wasn't ruling it out either.)
3. *The Manual of Procedure for Processing Default and Uncontested Judgments Submitted by Declaration Pursuant to Family*

Code Section 2336, certainly light reading by any neurotic divorcee's standards.

4. A directory of "child custody evaluators" or, as the directory so diplomatically put it, "professionals trained to assess the concerns that either parent may have about the care of the children in the home of the other parent . . ."

Nina suddenly realized, right then and there, that Jake could be taken away from her.

Forever.

Her stomach did a flip-flop at the thought of losing her sweet little guy to Nathan and Kat. Choking down the bile that crept into her throat, she turned to Lavinia and whispered frantically, "No way, no how, am I going to let someone 'evaluate' me! Not with all the bad press they're sure to have heard!"

"Sorry, Nina, you have no choice in the matter. It's part and parcel of how custody will be decided." Lavinia put her hand on Nina's shoulder. "Look, I have no doubt that once the evaluator actually meets you and sees how much Jake loves and needs you, she'll realize that you're not the monster the press has made you out to be."

"What about Kat? If she gets a hold of that woman, she'll suck up to her and at the same time shoot me full of poison darts!"

Lavinia smiled wryly. "Tell you what: I'll make sure that we're the last ones to see the evaluator. That way, whatever harm Kat and Nathan do, we'll have a better chance of countering it."

Nina nodded, but she knew it would be an uphill battle.

Last but in no way least, the receptionist added enthusiastically, if Nina *really* wanted to see the process from a lawyer's perspective, then she was certainly welcome to attend the court's annual "Family Law Walk-Through Program," a two-and-a-half-hour informational (if less than fun-filled) tour of the court and all its proceedings, which was due to start in half an hour.

In the politest way possible, Nina passed on this eye-opening opportunity. Instead, she headed back to Casey's cabana house—her new hideout from the paparazzi—where she could drink appletinis and cry on her best friend's shoulder while their sons doused each other with the arsenal of Super Soakers kept poolside.

Marjean Higginbotham was perfectly suited for the job of child custody evaluator. A good girl who had been raised to respect her elders, never question authority, and (most importantly) pass judgment on others in anticipation that they, too, were passing judgment on her, Marjean prided herself on her ability to tell, within the first five minutes of observing a child with his parent, whether he was happily and properly situated.

Or so she thought.

More to the point, Marjean was perfectly suited to evaluate Howard Cross's celebrity clientele. This the lawyer knew from having observed firsthand the timidity and awe that overcame the mousy, star-struck Marjean while in the presence of his luminous clients. These interviews invariably ended with the court-appointed evaluator shyly requesting their autograph over a most flattering picture culled from her very impressive collection of *People* back issues.

Needless to say, no one dared not oblige.

So the minute Howard heard from one of his courthouse spies—family court's very friendly receptionist, in this case—that Nina Harte had taken the necessary steps to file for custody, he put in a call to Kat and suggested that she call the family court *immediately* to request Marjean as the Hartes' evaluator.

Kat was only too happy to make the request. Hell, she'd do anything to break Nina's heart, and sucking up to some star-struck fan would be a piece of cake. In a voice sugar-sweet and dripping with kindness, she asked Marjean if she would be her guest, that very afternoon, for petit fours and lotus blossom tea.

For someone who devoured celebrity magazines by the carton-full each week, this was a dream come true for Marjean! She canceled the three appointments she already had scheduled, then dove through her stash of magazines for the perfect picture of Kat 'n' Nat (their Oscar red carpet promenade in *People*, of course) in the hopes that she could impose on Katerina and Nathan to autograph it for her.

Not that anyone *ever* turned her down . . .

From the Diary of Mary Frances McLaughlin
April 17th, 2—

Dear Diary,

Today, I wrote up the most difficult child custody evaluation I've ever done in twenty-two years!

It concerns the case of the sweetest, cutest little boy: Jake Harte, whose father, the actor Nathan Harte, is divorcing a woman who is a phone sex operator. Pretty disgusting, huh? Of course, I consider myself a crack professional who is rarely swayed by surface evidence, and I'm proud to say that this case was no exception.

As requested, my first stop was the father's home. I thought I'd broach the topic of joint custody. Nathan Harte was totally open to the concept. In fact, he had nothing but kind things to say about the mother of his child . . .

But then THANK GOD I'd also met with Nathan's fiancée, that GORGEOUS and KIND Katerina McPherson. (Lucky man! What an ADORABLE couple they make!) As much as she wanted to support Nathan's wishes, on the sly— he'd gone off to play catch with little Jakey—she filled me in as to what that Nina Harte person is REALLY like! How, after a hard day on the set, Nathan would come home to find the woman either drunk out of her gourd, or worse yet, "entertaining" men in her bedroom—while little Jakey slept in the next room! Nathan was always worried that Jake would wake up and find his mother . . . well, you can just imagine the rest!

Poor Katerina begged me not to put any of this in the formal report. She said that Nathan would never forgive her for telling me the truth about Nina, but that, if she had kept her mouth shut, she would not have been able to live with herself, particularly if that woman had gotten custody—even partial custody—of little Jakey. Besides, if it was written up, it could become public knowledge, and that would mean more bad publicity for Nathan and poor little Jakey . . . although, I agree with her, that there can be no such thing as bad publicity for the likes of a Nina Harte!

Not that I'd ever tell a soul . . . not even Serenity Lancaster, whom Kat talks very highly of. She asked me if I knew Serenity. (Ha! If only!) When I said no, she readily added that Serenity was such a nice person! In fact, she even intimated that I reminded her of Serenity, and perhaps we should all have tea together sometime . . . Now, wouldn't that be unbelievable!!!

Kat encouraged me to make a surprise visit to Jake's mother as soon as possible. I promised her that I would go right after I left her house—unannounced, of course.

Not that Nina Harte actually has a home. (Strike one!) For the time being, she is living in the cabana house of the star Jarred Cattrall. (It was on the tip of my tongue to ask her if he was one of her—ahem—"johns," but then I thought better of that; I don't want to come off as predisposed, as it were).

Although Katerina had warned me, I was still shocked to find Nina drinking appletinis with a girlfriend in the middle of the day, while their little boys were playing in the pool! Nina Harte was so surprised to see me that, unbelievably, she asked me if I'd like a drink, too! Of course, I declined. I couldn't get close enough to detect any alcohol on her breath, although I could only imagine it was there. By the look on the other woman's face, I guess my disapproval was pretty obvious . . . at least, to someone who was sober!

Still, I was determined to keep an open mind throughout the evaluation. Granted, this Nina person was very polite, and certainly very sweet throughout the interview, and I must admit, that little boy seemed so happy there with her, hugging and kissing her, and patting her hand constantly . . .

But then again, as Kat so eloquently put it, "Things aren't always as they seem . . ."

In any event, the meeting has reinforced my decision to keep

*my promise to Kat. I won't recommend unsupervised custody
for Nina Harte. I'm justified in this decision because the facts
bear this out: She is, after all, homeless. A second strike against
her is her obvious drinking habit. And of course, strike three is
her "occupation." All of this certainly takes Nina Harte out of
the parenting game!*

*On a good note: That sweet Kat and Nat gave me their au-
tographs! If only she'd won that Oscar! Wouldn't that have
been something?!? Well, there's always next year . . .*

"If I didn't know better, I'd think you're avoiding me."

Sam's mumbled accusation was something that Nina
couldn't deny. But she didn't have the heart—or perhaps the
guts—to tell him why:

She didn't know if she could trust him.

They were sitting together in the conference room of
Lavinia Hannigan's law firm, where the attorney had been
grilling Nina with the kind of questions she knew Howard
Cross would be throwing Nina's way. While Nina and Sam
had talked on the phone two or three times a day since that
night in his beach house, they'd both agreed that it was best
not to see each other publicly until the custody hearing was
over.

Well, the custody hearing was tomorrow. After that, Nina
knew she'd have to level with him about her distrust. She also
planned on asking him to level with her about his role in the
breakup of her marriage.

To buy some time until then, Nina put her finger to her lips
to indicate that she was too caught up with the task at hand to
answer him. He raised an eyebrow in consternation. Still, he

took the cue—for now. But she knew he'd expect an answer as soon as the mock deposition was over.

Nina sighed. She hoped she'd be able to dodge his pointed questions as adeptly as she had been evading Lavinia's. Then again, the accusations Lavinia was tossing her way were ones she could answer in her sleep:

Had she become a phone sex operator because she loved the power she had over men? Of course not, Nina answered emphatically. I only did it to pay our bills—both mine *and* Nathan's.

Didn't it disgust her to rant out all that filth, with her child playing in the next room?

"My child never heard me talk that way," Nina answered calmly. "I only took calls when he was asleep. I did so in a closed room. And if Nathan wasn't home to look after him, I'd put on the BabyCam, so that I could monitor him while I worked."

" 'Work,' huh? What a *quaint* euphemism for talking dirty at a buck a minute. Admit it," Lavinia insisted, "You were turned on, too, dishing out all that verbal masturbation!"

"No, never," Nina countered in a firm, clear voice. "If you say those phrases enough times, soon they mean nothing to you. They're just vacuous words. In fact, most times my mind was elsewhere. Usually I'd be making up a bed, or straightening a room while I was on the phone."

"Vacuous words?" Lavinia thundered. "Come now, Nina, admit it! You *enjoy* knowing that you are getting men off by saying all those disgusting, naughty things to them, knowing that with a well-chosen phrase, you can physically incapacitate them!"

"Incapacitate them? Gee, Mr. Cross, I'm not a special ops navy SEAL, you know! Just a pretty good listener to a few lonely guys," Nina replied with wide-eyed innocence.

"It just goes to prove that you're one helluva good actress," Sam murmured appreciatively to Nina. "Jeez, I'm beginning to feel sorry for the poor saps who really fell for your lines—"

Suddenly he remembered how turned on he'd been the first time he'd heard the CD Lucinda had made of O—*Nina*—and Hugo. At the time she was fluffing up his pal, she was probably folding laundry, or something else just as mundane! He blushed, thinking about how he'd almost driven off the road just listening to her voice!

Lavinia agreed. "You'll certainly hold your own against Howard, and that's good, Nina, because he's going to do every thing he can to break you down, tear you up, and spit you out in front of that judge—and, unfortunately, a peanut gallery of press and gawkers."

"You're joking, right? You mean it isn't going to be a private hearing?" Sam couldn't believe his ears.

"What, are you kidding? It's an election year, remember? Judge Jessup is running for the State Supreme Court, and Nina—along with every other 'unfit mother'—is going to be his election issue."

"So what you're saying is that I don't have a snowball's chance in hell of keeping Jake." Tears welled up in Nina's eyes.

"Not necessarily. That depends on how well you can answer this question: Have you ever met any of your phone johns in person?"

Nina hesitated just a moment, but it was enough to make Lavinia frown.

"Yes," Nina murmured. What she didn't add was that it had been *Sam*. "But it was only after—"

"Just answer the question, please, Ms. Harte! *Did you have sex with him?*"

Nina glanced over at Sam. Slowly she nodded.

"You just lost custody of Jake." Lavinia took off her glasses and rubbed the bridge of her nose, a habit she had when things weren't going well.

Like now.

Nina closed her eyes for a moment. When she reopened them, she smiled and said brightly, "Heavens, no! My client is eighty-seven if he's a day! Even when we talked on the phone, it was only to commiserate about how poorly the Dodgers were doing. He thought of me as the Dodger-loving grand-daughter he never had. In fact, he was upset when Jeff Weaver hit that pitching slump—"

"Good save, as long as you make it clear that the client is old and *not* wealthy. Just lonely," Lavinia said dryly. "So be careful. If Cross catches you off guard, you're cooked, Nina." She leaned across the table to make her point. "You've got to think of everything coming out of his mouth as mud. Remember, he wants to throw as much of it as possible on you, with the hopes that it sticks in the mind of the judge, and for that matter, everyone in the courtroom."

"Don't worry, Lavinia. I'll remember," Nina promised her meekly. "I can't afford to forget."

The lawyer nodded. "Well, it's already after nine. I guess we should call it a night. We've certainly got a big day in front of us."

Nina was silent as she and Sam rode the elevator the forty-two stories down to the parking garage in the bottom of Lavinia's building. He, on the other hand, chattered away, about the difficulty he was having in rebuilding his client list (thirty-first floor), how good it felt to discover that his most valued clients were also his most loyal (nineteenth floor), and how relieved he would be when they both could put this behind them and get on with their lives . . . together . . . (eighth floor).

And that's when he leaned over to kiss her.

His mouth fell on hers hungrily, greedy for the pleasures it had enjoyed once, and now so sorely missed.

She didn't have the heart to struggle. Nor did she participate, however.

Realizing this, he pulled away.

The elevator did a little jump before coming to a halt on the underground parking garage level. "Ah! Here we are!" Nina said brightly. She started out the door. She hadn't taken three steps before he grabbed her by the hand, forcing her to face him.

"Okay, out with it."

"What? I don't know what you—"

"Nina, tell me the truth: Why the cold shoulder?"

"It's—it's just, you know, this hearing. That's all—"

"No, it's not. It's something else." His eyes searched hers for any telltale sign. Not seeing anything, he glanced away, disappointed. "Have it your way. I'd hoped we were beyond all the game playing, but if we're not, it's good to know that now. You're too good of a liar, I guess. Okay, well, I'll see you tomorrow in court. Good night." He headed off in the direction of his car.

"What?" Suddenly Nina was angry. Her head was pounding from the anxiety she was feeling: over Lavinia's interrogation, the obvious bias she'd felt the other day from the family court evaluator, her fear of losing Jake, and Nathan's suspicions of Sam.

And now, to have Sam accuse *her* of lying to him—

Well, that was just too much!

He'd already gotten into his car and started the engine. She ran up to the driver's side window and tapped on it angrily. Surprised to see her standing there, he rolled it down.

"Don't—don't walk away from me like that!" She could barely contain her hurt. "Okay, you really want to know what's bothering me? I'll tell you: *I think you planned all of this!*"

"What? Are you crazy?" He couldn't believe what he was hearing. Whatever it was, though, he didn't want to hear it in a parking lot. "Get in the car."

"No, I won't!" Nina retorted. "I'm tired of being at everyone's beck and call. If you want to talk to me, you can do so out—"

"Nina, I'm not going to stand there while you yell at me in front of a bunch of security cameras, only to watch it on *Extra* tomorrow night. I said GET IN!"

He had a point. Meekly, she did as ordered.

He turned to face her. "Okay, now, in the calmest voice you have—and believe me, I know you have one, because I've heard it firsthand in many a phone conversation—tell me about this conspiracy theory of yours."

"It's not my theory. It's Nathan's. He thinks that you planned—"

"Whoa, whoa! Back up! How did Nathan get into this?"

"He . . . he came over to the apartment."

"Oh. I see." Sam closed his eyes, and shook his head.

"No, you *don't* see. Nothing happened between us." The color rose in her cheeks. *Nothing except the fact that we kissed. And I almost let him take me in the kitchen . . .*

"I take back what I said in the conference room. You're *not* that good of a liar. At least you aren't too convincing right now." He slammed his hand on the steering wheel. The sound of his horn made them both jump.

"Okay, let me get this straight: what you're saying is that Nathan—brainiac that he is, and with not the least bit of a conscience for his role in any of this fiasco—has convinced you that none of this is his fault, and better yet, that it's all mine. That I devised some evil master plot to break up Donald Duck's marriage by introducing him to the horniest nympho in Hollywood. You know, someone who he'd be unable to resist, no matter how much he loved and cherished the wife who would do anything to help him, including stay up all night working as a phone sex operator, after working on her feet all day as a supermarket clerk."

Angrily, he turned back to look at her. His eyes were damp. "And I did this all because I fell in love with . . . I fell in love with the sweetest person I've ever run across in this town, whom I happened to meet, by sheer fate, at the checkout counter of a store *I normally never go into.* Yeah, okay, I'll buy that. Maybe I can even sell it to Touchstone because it sure as hell would make a great chick flick. Hey, maybe we could get Scarlett, or Kate, or Clare to sign on to play you! Of course, they'd have to be open to going brunette—"

She'd been a fool.

He did love her. And while he might have been the catalyst

for the series of events that wrecked her marriage, it wasn't he who had walked out on her.

That had been Nathan.

In fact, Sam was doing everything to save her life, so that, eventually, they could share a life together. She could see that clearly now.

To even think that Sam had anything to do with Kat's desire for Nathan, or Nathan's desire for Kat, or for that matter, that he'd done it to get back into Kat's good graces was so ridiculous, so *stupid*—

Gently, she placed a finger on his lips to silence him. Then she stroked his cheek. If she could have climbed over the gearshift, she would have done so, right then and there. Instead, she leaned in so that her lips could find his once again, hungrily, greedy for the pleasures it had enjoyed once, and now so sorely missed . . .

But he didn't kiss her back.

Instead he muttered, "Frankly, I think your gut instinct is right. We should cool it some, until we've both had a chance to sort out our feelings."

She nodded mutely. She'd now given him reason to doubt *her.*

All because she had listened to Nathan.

"Nina, I do love you." By the look in his eye, she had no doubt that was true. "But until you feel the same way about me, until you can say in your heart that Nathan means nothing to you anymore, I think we should let fate take its course."

He was right, of course.

And they both knew that, at that very moment, Nathan was still entrenched deeply in her heart.

Then again, after tomorrow, that might not be the case.

Certainly they could wait one more day.

Once more, with heavy hearts, they went their separate ways.

Earlier that day, the very sexy, very tanned mailman whose route was the Century Park Plaza dropped two similar packages—both without return addresses—in East Building.

The first one went to *Exxxpose*'s office, on the thirteenth floor. As always, Baxter was there to personally collect the mail himself. To hell with coffee breaks! He'd gladly forgo caffeine in favor of some of that sweet eye candy in U.S. Postal Service regulation shorts!

While most of Baxter Quinn's really hot tips on stars doing lots of naughty things came in via fervently whispered voice messages or quickly typed (and therefore typo-ridden) e-mails, every now and then Himbo the Mailman took Baxter's fantasy one step further by playing Santa, too. Well, today was one of those days, and *thank gawd* for that, considering the *horrible* funk Baxter was in over Serenity Lancaster's recent scoop on Nina's lascivious night gig.

After giving Himbo a come-hither wink and breathless thank you, Baxter went back to his office, closed the door, and opened the anonymous package.

It was postmarked Ketchum, Idaho. *Hmmm*.

It contained an unmarked DVD.

Popping it into his computer, Baxter watched, fascinated, as the audition tape of Nathan Harte being flirtatiously teased, soulfully kissed, and seductively fluffed by that darned Kat played before his eyes.

So that's how the seduction began, thought Baxter. It certainly made the concept of Nat and his precious Kat as Jake's legal custodians less palatable.

"I'm only human . . . Just like the girl next door, right?" she breathily implored Nathan.

As the DVD played on, Baxter wondered how many other girls next door knew some of *those* moves. At least one, it seemed. From Ketchum, Idaho.

He'd be sure to describe the video, in detail, in tomorrow's column. And, of course, uplink it on his website.

The second package from Ketchum, which had been delivered to the palatial offices of Hannigan, Weiss, & Young on the Twenty-second floor, was opened very late that night, after Sam and Nina had gone, and Lavinia was left pulling out her hair over their lousy case. After reviewing the DVD, however, her whole take on their situation changed. Jubilantly she opened a jar of Tommaso's Premium Beluga Caviar in celebration of what might have to be her trump card in Nina's case—even if using it would mean breaking Nina's heart.

17

The Trial

HOO-HAH! Howard Cross was totally pumped.

From the vibe he was channeling as he gazed on the jam-packed courtroom, he could just feel it: Victory was imminent.

Extra was there, as were *Entertainment Tonight, Celebrity Justice, Access Hollywood,* and *Inside Edition.* And Nancy, Greta, and Catherine had sent correspondents, as had all the tabloids, which were sporting such headlines as "Sex Operatrix Has Hollywood's Number" and "Hollywood Dials O for Orgasm" . . .

Right on!

Most of Hollywood was represented, too, albeit surreptitiously. (That is, any player who suspected he was in O's little black book had sent a lowly assistant to take copious notes, because no one who was anyone dared to show his face in that courtroom unless he wanted his presence there to be "misconstrued" as proof positive he was listed.)

The rest of the seats were filled by the just plain curious who lived to be front row center at the biggest courtroom carnival since Wacko Jacko made pajama chic the attire of choice for that elite group known as the Infamous on Trial. Hell, the "Harte-to-Harte Custody Battle" (that nickname was courtesy of Page Six) was drawing even more gawkers than the Tobey Maguire Poker Game Slander Trial taking place across the hall, in which Ben had been accused of having one too many aces up his sleeve by Leo.

Now, *who's ya daddy?*

And all because everyone wanted to know what muckety-mucks' names were in that bitch Nina Harte's little black book.

Big fucking deal. So some little silver-tongued coochie had been chatting up a few of L.A.'s finest. What was the crime in that? Hell, even Howard liked a little telephone foreplay every now and then. Considering the sweetness and light emanating from the tart Little Miss Harte, he couldn't even fathom the kind of phone sex she'd be able to dole out. Certainly not the kind of hardcore filth he liked to get off on. Just thinking about tearing her up on the stand (which would be made even easier, considering the parent evaluation he'd heard she had received, through his spies in family court) was giving him a hard-on.

Which reminded him: Later tonight he should sweet-talk his phone sex service into hooking him up again with that one girl that he'd liked so much . . . what had he called her, Cunt? Yeah, boy, now *she* was certainly a sassy one! She'd even come up with a nickname for him . . . what was it again?

Oh yeah, Potty Mouth.

He chuckled to himself. What he'd give to hear Cunt's

breathy litany of twatalicious tongue-twisters in his ear *right that very second* . . .

HOO-HAH! Bring it *on!*

So, that's the infamous barracuda, Howard Cross? He doesn't look so scary, thought Nina, glancing across at her soon-to-be ex-husband's attorney as she took her place beside Lavinia at the defendant's table.

The man—mid-fifties, balding, and portly, with glasses—was so nondescript that he could have easily passed for an H&R Block accountant, albeit he was wearing a much better suit than the typical number cruncher. Howard Cross caught her eye and gave her a friendly wink. She smiled back at him sweetly.

Maybe this wouldn't be so bad. Maybe shared custody could be worked out in a reasonable fashion after all. Nina breathed easier, leaning back into her seat.

Then Nathan walked in on the sinewy arms of that BITCH DIVA WHORE Katerina.

They looked picture perfect, both golden-haired with big dimpled smiles and shining blue eyes . . .

Yep, they were the perfect couple.

Of course, it helped that they dressed the part: for Katerina, that meant a pencil-thin pale yellow silk skirt, with which she wore a high-collared yellow and white polka dot organza blouse. Conservative, yes, and certainly not what you'd expect to find on the back of the victor of *Maxim's* recent online poll, in which panting male participants were asked to name "the woman you'd want to lose your virginity to—that is, if you could do it all over again." Score points there.

Nathan was in Armani: elegant enough to infer "star," but casual enough not to intimidate those lowly minions around him, who were swathed in Van Heusen.

Hand-in-hand, the lovebirds, trailed by Riley and Fiona, made their way toward the front of the courtroom as casually as if they were taking a Sunday morning stroll on Santa Monica's Main Street. Waving to well-wishers, Katerina took it up a notch by blowing kisses to the VIP reporters in the gallery, many of whom she knew by name—Dominick, Ted, Jeannette, Michael, Richard, and most certainly Serenity: all celebrities in their own right, whose pens were poised to document, speculate, or pontificate from an already chosen point of view. The loving couple pointedly ignored Baxter Quinn, but he didn't seem to mind at all, giving Nina a raised eyebrow and a thumbs-up that put a shaky smile on her face.

Upon reaching the first row of spectator seats, Nathan situated Katerina right behind the chair that he was to occupy, then leaned in to give her a kiss. It was tentative, hopeful, and heartbreaking, and he lingered into it just long enough that any cell phone camera pointed in their direction would get the money shot.

Nina wondered how many times they'd rehearsed that move. She had to admit, though, that Katerina's choreography was spot on.

At Lavinia's insistence, Jake was waiting with Casey in an empty office next to the courtroom where the hearing was to take place, and Sam was sitting in the back of the courtroom somewhere, so that his presence wouldn't call any more attention than was necessary to Nina's own state of affairs. Already every man who entered the courtroom was being scrutinized severely as a possible "client" of the infamous O.

That was exactly what Howard Cross had hoped would happen. In fact, unbeknownst to his opponents, Howard had planned to introduce into evidence O's phone records, which he had obtained through a subpoena of the phone company.

Hoo-hah! Now, *that* should release a few bladders!

But first things first. When Judge Jessup queried both parties as to whether the temporary arrangement of joint custody was agreeable, Lavinia put forth that her client found it acceptable.

However, Howard, in a dark, ominous voice reminiscent of James Earl Jones channeling God, said his client *did not*. No sirree, not under any circumstances whatsoever.

Oh . . . *kay*. Moving on, Judge Jessup asked for a counter proposal from Howard.

"We are proposing *sole legal custody* for my client, Your Honor. It is the only situation that would be acceptable—"

Lavinia objected, loudly and haughtily. To Nina's chagrin, Nathan sat in stone-faced silence. He understood only too well that any move he made that was empathetic to Nina would incur Katerina's wrath. Realizing this, Nina teared up.

"—and, I might add, Your Honor, my client's uncompromising position is due to the immoral activities conducted by Mrs. Harte, which have put Jake Harte's welfare in jeopardy, and most certainly make her an unsuitable custodian for the child."

A murmur hummed through the courthouse. Judge Jessup banged his gavel severely. It was obvious to him that Howard was bound and determined to turn these proceedings into a celebrity courtroom Cirque de Soleil. Normally the judge would have curbed the pompous attorney's grandstanding, but hey, it was an election year, and he knew that the notoriety could work in his favor if he played his cards right. He just didn't want Howard trumping this nicely dealt hand with a courtroom free-for-all.

"Well, well, that was a very pretty speech, Mr. Cross. However, if you haven't noticed, I'm a judge, not a preacher. Therefore, my ruling will be predicated solely on any evidence presented here that may substantiate your client's claim that even partial custody by the defendant will do harm to the child. By the way, am I to assume that your client is asking for sole physical custody as well?"

Howard growled back: "Leaving that poor child in the hands of that woman would be an egregious oversight of this court, Your Honor, as we will prove today . . ."

Judge Jessup sighed. "Proceed, then."

Lavinia patted Nina's hand gently and winked consolingly at her. Still, that didn't stop the bead of sweat that rolled slowly down Nina's back.

She closed her eyes and prayed for a miracle.

Wrong, wrong, wrong. That McLaughlin woman's report was *so damn wrong.*

First off, she was not homeless, Nina wanted to shout, just temporarily relocated, thanks to the paparazzi climbing up her back patio and rummaging through her garbage for disparaging evidence.

And second, a couple of appletinis in the middle of the day with a sympathetic friend did not make her a drunk.

Okay, well, *maybe* a pathetic loser temporarily down on her luck, but *certainly* not a drunk.

And finally, yeah, okay, so she didn't have a job that very second, but how could she be blamed for that? For five long years she'd held down *two* gigs—and did such a great job with both that she was always getting commendations from her bosses . . .

Granted, one was a hormonal transsexual, and the other was a phone sex operator dispatcher . . . but that was beside the point.

Nina couldn't wait to get up on the stand and set that creep, Howard Cross, straight on all of it!

Howard Cross's first few questions were innocent enough. "Tell me, Ms. Harte, how long were you and Mr. Harte married?"

"Just over six years."

"In fact, you met in high school, did you not?"

"Yes. I guess you could say that we were high school sweethearts."

"How *touching*. That's quite a quaint term. In your line of work, you must know a lot of 'quaint' terms."

"What do you mean? I was at Tommaso's for over five of those years. Not too many fruits and vegetables are what you'd call quaint."

A chuckle ran through the courtroom.

"Ah, you're a comedienne as well. I'm sure that such a sprightly sense of humor comes in handy, too . . . for a *phone sex operator*."

Unconsciously, Nina flinched.

"And, how long did you hold down *that* job . . . as a phone sex operator, I mean?"

"Not quite five years."

"I see. *Half a decade.* In other words, you were *a phone sex operator* even *before* your little boy Jake was born."

"Yes. You see—"

"Just answer the questions, Ms. Harte. That's a lot of dirty talk, isn't it?"

This time Nina said nothing.

"How many days a week did you work your job as a sex phone operator?"

"Three. Sometimes maybe four," she muttered.

"I'm sorry, I didn't hear you. I think you said *four* nights a week?"

"Yes, sometimes," Nina growled louder.

"And you'd do this for how many hours a night?"

"Five. Maybe six."

"Humph! That's a lot of talking . . . I'm surprised you weren't. . . . hoarse afterward."

Several people in the courtroom let out with raucous chuckles. Nina peered at Judge Jessup in the hope that he would reel in the attorney, but the judge didn't seem to care that she was being skewered in public.

Well, he just lost *her* vote.

"How many—I don't know what do you call them, clients, customers, *johns*—did you talk to?"

"I called them only by whatever they asked of me," Nina retorted.

"I can imagine that whatever those names were, they weren't their real names. After all, any man who would masturbate while some strange woman on the phone filled his ear with dirty, filthy, disgusting sex talk must be *very imaginative* in his own right, wouldn't you say?"

It was on the tip of her tongue to say that, yes, some were, when it hit her: The way he said "very imaginative" sounded familiar . . .

She knew that voice from somewhere . . .

"You didn't answer my question, Ms. Harte. How many customers would you talk to, on any given night?"

"I'm sorry, I—that varied. It could be as few as five, or as many as twenty—"

"Twenty men, four nights a week, for fifty-two weeks out of the year . . . That's, let's see, four thousand, one hundred and sixty dirty conversations a year . . . twenty thousand, eighty hundred filthy dialogues over the past five years . . . with horny, lascivious men to whom you—"

"Your Honor!" Lavinia stood up angrily. "I object to this line of questioning!"

"—open your mouth wide in order to—"

"Your Honor! *Puh-leez!*" Lavinia's thunderous cry seemed to wake Judge Jessup from his catatonic state. The judge frowned—more at Lavinia than at Howard.

Dammit, he thought, what is Howard doing, going for an Academy Award?

"Mr. Cross, you don't have to paint us a picture here."

"Yes, Your Honor." Howard smiled at Nina with his tiny feral teeth. "So, tell me, Ms. Harte, while you were on the phone, what was Nathan doing?"

"He was usually in the living room, listening out for our son, who was asleep. Of course, some nights Nathan was at rehearsals, or at his acting class. Or working. He would bartend at parties."

At that point, Howard turned back toward Nathan, in order to lift his hand in tribute to his client, as if to imply *What a great guy you are!*

"And I assume your little boy heard *none* of these conversations."

"No . . . not at all." She turned red as she thought of the one time Jake had climbed out of bed for a cup of water and walked in on her as she was cooing naughtily into the phone. He had heeded her silent plea to say nothing, but that had not stopped him from climbing into her lap and scrutinizing her intently until she could jump off the call and put him back to bed. "If you let me stay up and watch Nick at Nite, I won't tell Daddy you said all those bad words," Jake promised. She broke down and let him, just that once, and she stayed off the phone for the rest of the evening. As she watched him giggle through *Full House*, she wondered if what he'd heard had, subconsciously of course, made him hot to trot for little Michelle Tanner.

"I'm glad you're so certain about that. Of course, I'll be calling up little Jake later on, to see what *he* has to say on the matter."

Jake, testifying? Nina tried to keep the fear out of her eyes. From the cruel smile on Cross's face, she knew she was doing a lousy job at that.

"Now, when you told your husband you wanted to take on that profession, what was his reaction?"

Nina paused. "He . . . he wasn't too happy, I guess."

"*You guess*. You mean you didn't know how disgusted he was at the suggestion? Or how it tore out his heart and broke it in two each and every time you got on the phone to pump up the egos—not to mention the . . . *libidos* . . . of these other men?"

Nina dropped her head. Tears fell into her lap. She would feel like a fool if she lied blithely, if she pretended that Nathan hadn't cared.

Because she'd known all along that he had hated it.

And after her last conversation with him, she knew exactly how much.

That's why she'd never mentioned any of her callers to him. She'd never told him about the men who had begged her to be their ultimate fantasy, or the little boys who called her with their parents' credit cards to hear her talk dirty to them, or the many guys who asked her to coo filth at them in her patented little girl voice.

But hey, it paid the rent, right? It allowed them to stay in Los Angeles, so he could keep acting, didn't it?

At that time, that was all that mattered to Nathan.

And now he was taking her son away from her because of it.

"Your honor, I can answer that."

Upon hearing Nathan's voice Nina looked up. The courtroom froze. So did Howard, who was shocked that his client was opening his mouth—against his attorney's wishes, and for that matter, Katerina's, too.

"No sir, honestly it didn't bother me in the least. In fact, the only reason Nina did it in the first place was because I asked her to."

Baxter Quinn's Nat 'n' Nina Custody Battle Blog
4/25 1:32 P.M.

Libidinous lawyers! Election year grandstanding! Public confessions!

Don'tcha just LOVE L.A. law?

If I'm moving too fast and furious for you, readers, you'll have to forgive me, but the atmosphere is SO hot and heavy in this courtroom that I may NEVER need another perm as long as I live! (Sigh! Too bad it doesn't have the same effect on highlights. Although, if things keep going the way they are, Kat McPherson's hair may turn gray overnight. More on that later . . .)

First things first: I never thought I would say this, but I tip my hat (that is, if I wore a hat—and my darlings, if that were the case, it would definitely be something a little less Kangol and a little more Borsalino) to that studly hunk, Nathan Harte, for standing up for his li'l woman, Nina (and, unfortunately for him, soon-to-be ex–li'l woman) while she was being persecuted by his very own attorney!

Nathan-Doll actually INSISTED on taking the stand so that he could confess—listen closely here, gang, 'cause it's hotter than Boston Legal during a ratings sweep (LOVE that Danny Crane!)—to coercing sweet, innocent Nina into taking the phone sex operator job that has put her in the hot seat in the first place!

"She really didn't want to do it," he admitted. "But she was pregnant. So I asked if she'd consider that horrible job, just to make me happy. Otherwise we couldn't afford to stay in Los Angeles so that I could follow my dream to act. Believe me, she

cried about it, but she did it anyway, for me. She did make me promise, though, that she could quit once my career got off the ground. She would have, too—but then I met Kat."

To shut him up, the noble lug's attorney asked for a recess. I'd give anything to be a fly on that wall when Kat gets ahold of him! She was hoping to avoid any (ahem!) unseemly bumps in her future by absconding with Nina's little guy. Hey, if she doesn't want to get preggers or adopt another kid, she could adopt one of those abused pups she's always moaning about, right?

My next posting of sizzling pixels will be up soon, so stay tuned . . .

"Lavinia, something's not right." Nina's heart was beating too fast. She felt a bit woozy, as if she was going to faint.

"Sweetheart, should we call a doctor?" Sam put his arm around her to steady her. Suddenly he realized how difficult Howard's inquisition had been on her, not to mention the toll that everything that had happened in the past month—the discovery of Nathan's affair, the divorce filing, and now the custody battle—was taking on the woman he loved.

And then I go and put pressure on her about our future, he thought wryly. *Her first priority is saving the life she's made with Jake. I'll just have to wait, with no strings attached, until she indicates that she's ready . . .*

"No, I—I don't think I'll need a doctor." Nina sat down and took a deep breath. "I just need to get that man off my back. Yuck! Now, that's an awful thought!" She shuddered.

"Right now, I have a feeling Howard is climbing up one side of Nathan, and Kat is crawling up the other, poor guy." Sam smiled at the thought.

"Yeah, I can just imagine! I have to say, though, it was sweet of him to come to my rescue! I'll always be grateful to him for that."

Already she's forgiven him for putting her through all this, Sam thought sadly.

A grimace pierced Nina's face. "I guess they'll make him retract everything he just said, won't they?"

Lavinia laughed. "Look, when we go back in, I'll get my chance to cross-examine Nathan. Believe me, if he changes his story between now and then, I'll pull out the heavy guns." Lavinia rummaged in her briefcase and pulled out the DVD of Nathan's audition.

"What's that?" asked Nina.

Lavinia popped it into her laptop so that Nina could witness Kat in action with her husband—and, after his initial shock, his enthusiastic response.

Nina blinked away her tears. Seeing her reaction, Lavinia murmured, "Nina, I'm sorry you had to see this, but I think we need to be prepared to present this as evidence if we're going to have any chance of getting the judge on your side. Believe me, no woman in that courtroom will side with Kat after we play this. And Jessup isn't going to want to side with her, either."

"I don't know, Lavinia. I don't see how Nathan and I slinging mud at each other is helping Jake. For all we know, the judge may decide that neither of us is fit to have custody and put Jake in a foster home." Just saying that out loud brought terror to Nina's eyes. "Oh my God, Lavinia, could he do that?"

"No, he won't. Because pulling Jake away from both of you will mean more court time, and that guy wants this over just as fast as the rest of us." Sam's soothing summation was seconded by the look on Lavinia's face. "The only one who seems to want this to drag out is that sadistic creep, Cross. Speaking of which, I've got to check in with my office. You know, I'm representing Howard's wife in their divorce, too, and she's been calling every hour for updates on how this hearing is going. She's worried that he's going to really play dirty if I beat him up too badly today. Unfortunately for you, Nina, the way things are going now I don't think Mrs. Cross has anything to worry about. And considering the amount of alimony she's asking for, that should be a relief to her." That said, Lavinia hurried out the door.

Sam put his hand on Nina's shoulder. "The ball game's not over yet. Listen, kiddo, if Cross puts you back on the stand, try to do whatever you can to neutralize your fear of him." He snapped his fingers. "Hey, I know: Try to think of him as a kid around Jake's age, or something." He laughed. "Better yet, just think of him as one of your johns."

That put a smile on her face. "Yeah, you're right. That always makes it easy." She thought about Bertrand and King Kong and Herbie and the sadistic Potty Mouth—

Potty Mouth.

Nina bolted upright. Omigod, she thought, Cross is that gross cretin, Potty Mouth!

"Wait, Sam, wait! You won't believe this but—I think that Howard Cross is actually *one of my johns*!"

This stopped Sam cold. "Wow! If you're right—listen, Nina, do you just think that he is, or do you *know*?"

She nodded her head with certainty. "It's him, all right. I nicknamed him Potty Mouth because he made me recite every name I knew for penis; you know, skin flute, trouser trout, pork sword . . . disgusting, isn't it? Then, of course, I'd have to go through all those horrid nicknames for a woman's—well, you get the picture. In fact, he came up with a sweet name for me, too. Starts with a C. I'm sure you can use your imagination." She shivered. "Is it fair that Potty Mouth can represent Nathan?"

"No. He's certainly got a conflict of interest. Then again, if we let Lavinia know that now, she'll have to call for a new hearing, and you—and Jake—will be put through this all over again."

"I can't have that! I'd just—we'll just run away—"

"Don't say that, Nina! If you did, and they caught you, then you would lose Jake for good. Let me think for a moment . . . I've got it!"

"What? What should we do?"

"*We* are doing nothing. I, on the other hand, have got to take a meeting. Just leave it to me. And whatever you do, don't mention what you know to anyone—particularly not to Lavinia."

He leaned down and gave her a kiss; not just any kiss, but a kiss that had her believing that he was going to save her little world for her.

Then he sprinted out. His destination: the second floor men's room in the Los Angeles Superior Courthouse.

Everyone was pissed at Nathan, and boy, didn't he just know it.

Kat especially. "What are you, crazy or something?" she shrieked. "Taking the fall for that little bitch—how could you do that to me?"

"I didn't do anything to *you*, Kat," he said in the calmest voice he could muster. "I did something *for* Nina. I don't like Howard making her out to be an unfit mom to the whole world, because she isn't! She's a *great* mom."

He glared over at Howard, who smirked and shook his head. "You're a fucking pinhead, kid, do you know that? Next time, stay on script. Or didn't they teach you anything in that acting class of yours?"

Nathan leaped in his direction, only to be held back by Riley. "Whoa, cowboy, he's on our side, remember?" Riley snapped his fingers in front of Nathan's eyes. "Look, he was only doing his job. You want the kid, right? Well, you just came off as if you care more about yourself. That's pretty much blown your chances. Right, Howard?"

"Not necessarily." Everyone looked at Fiona in disbelief. "Well, to tell you the truth, *I* certainly didn't believe him, so maybe no one else did, either. Better yet, I'm guessing that every woman in the courtroom fell in love with Nathan right then and there, for trying to take the rap for Nina. I sure as heck did."

"She's right," Howard growled tersely. "Pinhead here came off looking like a saint. Either that was sheer genius on his part, or it's proof that he should go for a refund on those acting classes."

Riley tensed for Nathan to break loose for another shot at Howard, but Nathan just shrugged off the taunt. Heck, the way he'd just been treated at ShoWest, he was beginning to suspect Howard was right.

It was Fiona's idea that he go to the annual Las Vegas theater owner/filmmaker/movie star schmoozfest with Hugo, in order to screen some of the footage of *Forever and Again* for theater owners interested in upcoming indie releases. Besides, Nathan thought, putting a little distance between himself and Kat might not be a bad thing after all. She was so self-centered that she was getting on his nerves!

But the press conference proved to be a big mistake. Instead of tossing Nathan softballs about the movie, the reporters laid into him: Was he a serious actor, or a pretty boy stud? Was his relationship merely a stunt, a way for him to bask in the glow of someone who had already made it in Hollywood? Why would he be so careless to allow his career—which had barely begun—flame out in a tabloid fury? In other words, was he pulling a Kutcher?

"All those assholes cared about is my relationship with you!" Nathan groused to Kat when he'd gotten back to L.A. "They didn't ask one question regarding *Forever and Again*, or my upcoming projects . . . Jeez, not that I have any. Riley's been lousy at locking anything down for me, other than that crappy *Scream* knockoff!"

"Well, what did you expect, lover? *I'm* the best thing that ever happened to you. Why, everyone knows that." Kat looked up from her lighted mirror, where she had been scrutinizing the effects of her latest Botox injection. "Hey, now, don't knock Riley. He's doing okay . . . for me at least. He swears that I'm a shoo-in for Scorsese's new film . . . Damn, but I hate ensembles! Although, if Leo's involved . . . Hey, if nothing comes up in a month or two, maybe Marty can fit you in somewhere. It's a cast of thousands. There's got to be some little part . . ." Having tracked down a tiny new wrinkle below her left eye, Kat missed Nathan's shudder.

Jeez, he thought, *if I don't get out from under her—literally and figuratively—no one will ever know what I'm capable of doing . . .*

As soon as this whole custody thing blows over, he decided, *I'm dumping this high-priced skank! Hell, I might as well, since she doesn't do it for me anymore, anyway.*

He laughed out loud at the thought of how Kat would react if she knew that, the last few times they'd made love, the only way he could even get it up was to imagine he was with Nina instead.

"What's so funny?" Kat looked up suspiciously. Had he noticed the wrinkle, too?

Sam had figured Howard Cross for a tiny bladder, and he was right. Within sixty seconds of dismissing his client, the rotund attorney headed for one of the men's room stalls.

Noting this, Sam casually followed his prey into the men's room, but not before hanging the "Out of Order" sign he'd found in the janitor's closet on the outside knob of the door. Once inside, he locked the door to ensure that the two of them would not be interrupted, biding his time at one of the two sinks in the restroom.

It took only a minute before Potty Mouth's stream gave out. He grunted, zipped up, and started toward the door. Realizing that someone else was in the restroom, he paused, ran some cold water over his hands, then ransacked the paper towel rack with a vengeance, just for show.

Sam was disgusted. Instead of shuddering, though, he murmured, "Germs. Disgusting, aren't they? Particularly the ones on the old pork sword, huh?"

That stopped Potty Mouth cold. Warily, he turned to Sam. "I—I beg your pardon?"

"You know: the dipstick. Schlong. Skin flute. What, do I have to paint a picture for you?"

Howard's eyes got small. "No, I get you." He shrugged. Then, with as much dignity as he could muster, he headed for the door.

"Oops. Sorry! Didn't mean to be such a, you know, *Potty Mouth*."

Yep, that got Howard's attention. He whipped back around. "Who the hell are you?"

Sam leaned against the wall. "A friend. Whose, I can't say yet. I might be your friend, Howard . . . I can call you Howard, right? Or do you prefer Potty Mouth—when you're not on the phone, I mean?"

Howard went for the door, only to find it locked. Panicking, he kicked it a couple of times and rattled the handle.

"Then again, maybe I'm Mrs. Cross's friend. Does she know about Potty Mouth? If not, maybe she'll want to find out before your divorce goes to settlement discussions."

Sam walked over to the door and unlocked it. He was just about to walk out when he heard Howard's strangled gasp, "Wait! Wait—*no!* That bitch—that bitch hasn't been able to find anything—before now . . . *What the hell do you want, anyway?*"

Slowly Sam turned around. He smiled at Howard. "You strike me as a very fair-minded and moral man, Howard. In fact, I'm sure you're fair enough to see that this custody battle between the Hartes is nothing more than some little misunderstanding. That's why I'm counting on you to get your client to agree that joint legal custody would be the best thing for little Jake, with primary physical custody going to Mrs. Harte. After all, Nathan keeps a *very* busy schedule and all . . . What do you think? Does that sound fair to you?"

"I'll have to think about it," the attorney said stiffly. "I'll get back—"

"Aw, now, Potty, that's just your meat whistle talking again. I think you can work *something* out. And the sooner the better. Because if you don't, then I'm sure that the soon-to-be-ex Mrs. Potty Mouth might have a better idea of what's fair and equitable—particularly when she gets an earful of some of those *imaginative* phrases you love so much."

From the anatomically specific expletives that followed him halfway down the hall from the men's room door, Sam figured that Potty Mouth had come to see things his way.

When the hearing was called back into session, the first thing Howard Cross did was inform Judge Jessup that his client had reconsidered his stance on sole legal and physical custody, and was willing to cede legal custody to Mrs. Harte if an arrangement for partial physical custody could be worked out as well, say, for every other weekend, alternate major holidays, and perhaps a month each summer.

Because Lavinia Hannigan murmured her client's assent to that proposal, Judge Jessup was content to do nothing more than shrug and put his blessing on the deal. Besides, in his mind he'd done enough courtroom harrumphing on the topic of phone sex operators. Time to go back to what he did best: campaigning.

He wondered how many votes from L.A.'s phone sex operators Howard's antics had cost him. He hoped it didn't include that of his own favorite PSO.

Joy. Sheer joy.

Sam could see it in Nina's face, but just for the few seconds he could see her at all, before she was swallowed up by the sea of humanity that flowed around her, dogging her every footstep, shouting questions at her about how she felt now, and why she thought Nathan had changed his mind about sole custody for Jake.

Hearing her son's name, Sam saw her turn around expectantly, in search of the one person whom she knew she loved with all her heart.

Her son.

Someday, she will love me that way, too, Sam thought.

In a blink of an eye, she was gone. Sam assumed she'd somehow made her way into the hall in search of the little boy, who was now cradled in the arms of his father.

They looked picture perfect, both with golden hair, big dimpled smiles, and shining blue eyes . . .

Nina's boys.

Did she see them? Yes, of course. How could she miss them? Like Nina, they, too, were the center of attention, even as they waited, in happy anticipation, for her arrival at their sides. And when she reached them, she would hug them both, this Sam realized because he knew her so well.

She had sincerely appreciated Nathan coming to her rescue, proving to be her knight in shining armor.

Once again.

But that shouldn't change anything between us, thought Sam. *Could it?*

As Nina pushed her way through the crowd, Katerina reached them first, shoving Nathan so hard that he almost dropped Jake.

"Hey, what—"

He didn't even finish the sentence before Kat pushed him again. "You are *such* an ass! How could you just—just cave in like that? Why, even I've got bigger balls than you do!" She glared down at Jake, who cowered and ducked his head in his father's shoulder.

Nathan set his son down on the floor, then turned back around to confront Kat. "That's what I've always suspected," he retorted. "And let me tell you, sweetheart, it ain't a pretty trait in a girl."

Angrily, she slapped him hard, in full view of the ever-hungry paparazzi.

Nathan was too much of a gentleman to hit back, but not Jake. He'd had it with Balloon Lips. If he could pop her some-how, would she shrivel up and go away? He was certainly will-ing to try.

He took a bite of her thigh, and didn't let go.

Later, her yelp would be described by *Us Weekly* as "more piercing than that of the wounded animals she so fiercely protects . . ." The footage caught by Court TV would bear this out.

And just like a wounded animal, she lashed out at her at-tacker. Grabbing Jake by the collar, she was just about to slap him when Nina cold-cocked her, right on those renowned lips.

Was "Meow! Kat Fight" too obvious a headline to use, Baxter wondered, as he blogged furiously, hoping to get a jump on the competing columnists who were gawking, shocked, at the comatose Katerina. Nah, I'll go with it, he reasoned, because if I don't, someone else will.

He was right. Later, six other columns sported the same phrase. Still, he was the first.

To sidestep the pandemonium, Nathan grabbed both Nina and Jake and pulled them away from the teeming, screaming throng. Sam couldn't make out what Jake was trying to say to Nina, but whatever it was, it took her completely by surprise. She smiled and blushed deeply. Nathan, seeing their grins, wrapped his arms around both of them, enveloping them with his love before nodding in agreement, and leaning in to ask Nina something himself.

What had Jake said to make her so happy? Sam needed to know. He shoved to get closer, but he never got near enough to hear what Jake said next. Not that it mattered because he could easily make out the words Nathan was mouthing to Nina as he looked down to her lovingly, soulfully:

Nina, please, will you marry me again?

What? her shocked look seemed to say. *You—you love me?*

Of course he does, thought Sam. Who wouldn't love you?

He could tell that she was about to reply, but then Jake began jumping up and down, vying for her attention. His shrill cries could be heard above the din. "Say yes! Say yes! Please, Mommy! Say yes!"

Soon the whole crowd was shouting: "Say yes! Say yes! Say yes!" But Nina just stood there: shocked, confused, laughing, crying—

Sam couldn't take it anymore. He turned and made his way down the opposite end of the hall.

A naughty-but-nice girl next door. A repentant husband. An adorable kid.

He knew a Hollywood ending when he saw one.

18

The Wedding

Nina knew she should have been ecstatically happy that Nathan so desperately wanted her back, but she wasn't.

She knew, too, that she'd have to make it clear to him, up front, that there was so much still standing between them. Yep, a *hell of a lot*.

And yet there was no way she could say any of that in front of Jake. It would break his heart.

He hadn't liked it when Daddy "moved away." And when Daddy saved him from Balloon Lips and Mommy smacked that mean old witch—well, he just knew that Daddy would come home again with them . . .

Right?

Her little boy put it to Nina just like that, while Nathan and the whole world looked on. So, what could she do? She smiled and started on some patented noncommittal mommyspeak, something to the effect of "Well, we'll just have to see . . ." or

"Let's talk about that when we get home . . ." when Nathan pulled her close to his side, looked her in the eye, and asked flat-out:

"Nina, please, will you marry me again?"

She could have killed him for that.

How dare Nathan do such a thing? And right there in front of Jake, in front of everyone!

Oh no. Had Sam seen it, too?

She looked around, but she didn't see him anywhere. Not only that, but she could barely hear herself think, what with Jake yelling, "Say yes! Say yes!" In no time at all, the crowd around them had picked up the maddening chant. It was like some sort of crazy dream! She couldn't help but smile at the audacity of the whole event . . .

Then she saw Sam. And yes, from the look on his face, he had seen the whole thing.

She knew that was why he turned and walked away.

Where was he going? And why doesn't he want to take me with him?

She tried to call out his name, but he certainly couldn't hear her over the mob's chatter, and she was helpless to follow, what with it blocking her way. She closed her eyes in anger.

Nathan, on the other hand, just smiled. So that jerk, Sam, is pissed. What of it? As far as Nathan was concerned, good riddance. He wanted his family back. He wanted his life back! And he'd do anything to get it.

Even if it meant putting Nina on the spot.

* * *

Life & Style predicted an elopement.

Us Weekly claimed that Nina had cried when Nathan had gotten down on his knees to propose.

By Jove!, a British magazine, offered the biggest fee for an exclusive on the wedding.

That was the first thing the Realtor mentioned as she showed them the cute little Outpost Estates bungalow, toward the top of Mulholland, which afforded it to-die-for views of downtown Los Angeles.

"This large, flat lawn really sells this place, doesn't it? And it's just perfect for a garden wedding! You could have it, right there out by the pool!" Having given her pitch, the Realtor walked into the kitchen to give them a few moments alone together while she checked her voice mail.

"What wedding?" Nina hissed at Nathan. "There isn't going to be a wedding! We're getting divorced, not married! Remember? You need to tell that to your publicist and your new agent, so that they quit spreading these lies."

These awful lies that have Sam so pissed off at me that he refuses to take my call, she wanted to add, but she didn't. Bringing up Sam would only make Nathan more stubborn about this nutty marriage idea of his.

Not that he was going to change his mind anytime soon, in any regard.

"Listen, Nina, can't you just forgive me? I admit I've been a total ass these past few months. But now I want to make it up to you. Please, honey, I'll do anything to get you back! And this is just the start, believe me!"

He opened his arms toward the house. "Nina, just look

around. Isn't this what we'd always dreamed of? A house like this, for the three of us? Just look at that backyard! Wouldn't Jake have a blast back there?"

"When? Before or after the so-called wedding ceremony?" she said sarcastically. She glanced out into the yard and sighed. Just put a climbing gym and a swing set out there, and it would be pure heaven for a little boy, no doubt about that.

No, any doubts she had were about Nathan.

"Tell me the truth, Nathan: Why, all of a sudden, do you want me back?"

"Because I still love you, dammit!" He walked over to her and took her hand. She tried to pull it away, but he wouldn't let go. "And you love me, too! Go ahead, tell me you don't and—and I'll leave you alone."

Did she love him?

She hesitated to answer because, in truth, she didn't know what to say. Yes, of course she still had feelings for him. Feelings that were deep but also bittersweet for what once was . . .

Not for what might still be.

But she could honestly say, once and for all, that she was no longer *in love* with him.

He'd lost her.

His eyes teared up at the realization. "It's Sam, isn't it?" He waited for her to answer.

Yes, she loved Sam instead. That she now knew with all her heart. But if Sam's silence over the past week was any indication, then he obviously didn't feel the same way about her.

But Nathan did.

Nathan, whom she had loved for the past six years of her life, as the two of them had struggled to survive while they followed the dream they shared.

Nathan, whose wit and charm and boyish good looks had set her heart on fire from the very first moment she'd seen him onstage.

Nathan, the father of her child, who would do anything he could for them.

Nathan, who'd had a fall from grace, but was now asking her forgiveness.

Now it was up to her: Could she forgive him for having broken her heart, so that the three of them could live happily together again?

What other choice did she have?

She turned back to look at the garden, a riot of English lavender, Mexican peonies, and bougainvillea.

"Okay, Nathan, we'll try again."

He smothered her in a kiss. "Yes! Awesome! Gee, wait until I get Riley on the phone and tell him that the wedding's a go!"

Albertha Hubert, the wedding planner Fiona found for them, had the kind of people skills Nina assumed would have made her a rising star in the Gestapo.

In Nina's opinion, the woman thrived on telling her how off base she was on her notions of what the recommitment ceremony (Nina hated calling it a marriage since, technically, their marriage had not been legally ended) should take place; that is, if they were to (as Albertha put it) "capitalize on this very unique public opportunity."

"That's just the problem," Nina groused. "This ceremony should be simple and totally private."

Albertha laughed in her face, then ran down "the criteria in which the wedding will achieve ultimate media impact." These included:

—*Minimally, a six-carat (preferably more like a ten-carat) engagement ring.*

—*Wedding bands in white gold, created by Neil Lane, from Nathan's "original design."*

—*A champagne-hued Vera Wang couture gown, adorned with borrowed jewelry from either Harry Winston, Neil Lane, Tiffany, or Fred Leighton.*

—*At least 250 guests, all of whom should be chosen from the A-list. ("Drop family if you need more space," sniffed Albertha.)*

—*A-list Billboard-worthy entertainment. ("Preferably performers who know you personally. What, you don't know any? Humph! Well, let me snoop around to see who's out of rehab and would love the publicity . . .")*

—*A dress theme for the guests, floating candles in the pool, live parrots in cages, doves released after the "I do's," and fireworks during the evening reception.*

—*A sit-down banquet requiring over two hundred attendants serving a meal made up of the bride and groom's favorite foods—as well as some exotic curry dish, and the requisite caviar and lobster.*

—*Rose champagne by Laurent Perrier.*

—*And an exotic honeymoon getaway, perhaps the Seychelles Islands, or maybe Jaipur, India. ("I'll get back with you on your honeymoon schedule," Albertha promised.)*

Nina told her not to bother because from all she'd heard so far, the only way this reunion was going to happen was if they eloped to Vegas again. *So there.*

Albertha literally threw a hissy fit. *"Excuse me?* Get real! You're marrying a star! Or have you forgotten that?" She sniffed. "Look, if you're worried about the cost, don't sweat it. Fiona's already negotiating with the tabloids, so it's a free ride. And she told me just this morning that Riley got a nibble from the E! Network to televise it live, perhaps even use it as a pilot for a reality series." She smiled cruelly. "Don't blow it, sweetheart, like you did the first time he asked you. Let's learn from our mistakes, shall we?"

As a consolation, Albertha told Nina that she might allow her to choose the flowers for her own bouquet.

Nina told her to go to hell.

That was when Nathan suggested that they get the input of some cooler heads. He immediately put in a call to Fiona, and Riley, too.

"Why Riley?" Nina asked. Knowing what he'd done to Sam, she could barely stomach being in the same room with the man.

"He's got a knack for this kind of froufrou stuff," Nathan replied. "If I didn't know better, I'd think he was, you know . . ."

"No, I don't. What are you trying to say?" Of course, Nina knew that Nathan was fretting over the notion that Riley was gay. Still, egging him on to confront his own prejudice gave her some degree of payback pleasure.

And lately she certainly hadn't had enough of that.

"Oh . . . nothing." Nathan shrugged it off. That was to be

expected. If this event Nathan was planning had proved anything, it was that he thrived on denial.

The vote went the way Nina suspected it would: three to one—*her*—in favor of a media circus.

She told Albertha to order gallons of champagne. She planned on downing a lot of it on her own.

Every chance he got, Nathan monitored Nina's cell phone messages just in case Sam came to his senses and tried to contact her. It was Nathan's intention to intercept that call, if and when it ever came.

When Sam had the misfortune to call while Nina was bathing Jake before bedtime, Nathan got his chance.

That was why she never got to hear Sam tell her what a fool he had been for walking out without first hearing from her, eye to eye, that she preferred to work things out with Nathan as opposed to starting fresh with Sam. She also never got to listen to him ask her to reconsider that stance, because he knew he would make her happier than Nathan ever could. She also missed hearing him choke up as he asked her to "meet with me once more, no strings attached, I swear! I just want to say good-bye to you in person."

Yeah, right. I know what's best for Nina and it's not you, asshole, it's me! The last thing I want is for you to rock my boat, so get lost, guy. Besides, if you had been a better agent, none of this would have happened in the first place!

If hanging around Kat had taught Nathan anything, it was that your agent (or better yet, your former agent) always made a great fall guy.

*   *   *

They'd been back together only a week, and already Nina's jealousy was driving them both crazy.

The affair's ghostly presence could still be felt by both of them—particularly when they went out together to industry events. Just the other night, at some celebrity "Bowl for the Cure" (one of the many publicity-worthy functions Fiona had Nathan attending to capitalize on his recent notoriety), Nina had watched him like a hawk, ready to pounce whenever another woman came even within sniffing distance of him.

And boy, was that often! In fact, every time Nathan took his turn on the lanes, in unison the comely heads of every starlet, pop star, and celebutante bowler turned to admire the butt—swathed in a distressed pair of D&G jeans—that had launched a thousand orgasms from the infamous Kat.

A particularly persistent admirer of Nathan's backside was Jillian Wharton, one of his costars in his newest film, *Thriller*, which had just started preproduction.

"Is that woman following us, or something? She seems to show up every place we go," fretted Nina to Nathan.

"Who? Oh, uh, her? Jillian?" He tried to laugh off her paranoia. "I'm guessing that Fiona's got her on the same publicity circuit. You know, she's one of ICA's clients, too. This picture is a package deal, remember?"

"Yeah, okay, whatever." Nina still wasn't convinced. "And why does she giggle that way, every time you open your mouth? She even giggles when you sneeze."

"She's just being, you know, friendly." Subconsciously, he waved over at the starlet, who waved back as she giggled again. "I've been helping her with her lines on the set. This is a big break for her, and she doesn't want to blow it."

"As long as that's all she doesn't want to blow." Nina retorted. She was up next. With no effort at all, she threw a strike. Turning back around, she expected a big thumbs-up from Nathan. Instead she caught him winking at Jillian.

She refused to talk to him the rest of the night.

He pretended not to notice, but then he attacked her when they got home. "What, now I can't even smile at another woman? Nina, it's part of my job to turn on the charm! Do you know how hard that is to do when every time I turn around, the paparazzi is waiting to catch me doing something to piss you off? Okay, I get the fact that you don't trust me! But at least when we're in public, let everyone see that we're just one big happy family, all right?"

But the truth was that they weren't happy. At least, she wasn't.

And the remarriage—wedding, affirmation of their vows, or whatever the hell they were calling it now—was less than a week off.

She desperately needed to talk to Sam.

"I just don't trust him anymore."

There. She'd said it.

Casey looked up at Nina, who was standing in a three-way mirror, trying to the come up with an excuse to why this, the sixteenth and the last of the many frothy champagne-tinted silk gowns Albertha had left for her to try on, just wasn't right to wear to what she now euphemistically called "the circus."

It wasn't that the cut was wrong, or the material. For sure, that price tag would give anyone palpitations. But the real reason was, simply, that she didn't trust Nathan any further than she could throw him.

Casey sighed. "So then why are you going through with it?"

"That's just it! I don't know! I guess because . . . because I was hoping I could forgive him, and we could pick up where we left off. And besides, Jake seems happy that we're back together."

"Does he, really?" Casey looked at her closely. " You know, two days ago I overheard him say to Ben that he wished he were a clown so that he could make you smile again." She straightened a strap on Nina's dress. "If you think that you're doing this for him, you're wrong. Nina, he knows something isn't right. He just wants you both to be happy."

Nina brushed a tear away from her eye. "I would be happy—well, happier, if I knew . . ."

"It's Sam, isn't it?"

Nina nodded. Self-consciously she fiddled with a tangled fold in the dress. "I'd hoped that Sam would have called by now, but—well, he hasn't. I guess I need to hear from him that—that he's really out of the picture."

"Yeah, I guess that would be nice." Casey plumped Nina's petticoat, then looked it over for the full effect. "But don't you think you know what he's feeling by now? I mean, actions speak louder than words, right?"

"Yeah, right. I guess if anyone knows that, it's me." Still unsure of the effect, Nina frowned. With a shrug, she hopped down from her perch so that Casey could help her unbutton the dress.

"Of course, one thing has nothing to do with the other anyway. If Sam comes to his senses, good, you'll deal with that when it happens. The first thing you have to address, though, is whether you can trust Nathan ever again." Casey's voice wavered a bit. "You know, Nina, everyone slips up. Even Jarred did, once."

Seeing the shock on Nina's face, she nodded sadly. "It's true. You see, no one's marriage is perfect—no matter what the magazines would have you think." Casey wiped away a tear. "When I found out, I weighed what we had together, and what he was willing to do to keep me, and came to the decision that I loved him too much to throw it all away on—on one slip of judgment." She patted Nina's shoulder to indicate she was done, and that Nina could now slip out of the dress.

"I'm sorry, Casey. I never knew—"

"No one does. I guess we were lucky in that regard." She sighed deeply. "And I've never regretted sticking it out."

"Then he's—he's held to his promise?"

Casey paused, then nodded. "Yeah. Well, anyway, as far as I know. Let's put it this way: I've yet to stop giving him the benefit of the doubt." She smiled again. "Don't ask, don't tell, right? Besides, I love him too much."

But I would need to know that he was worthy of my love, thought Nina as she slipped on her jeans. And that was another problem: She wasn't in love with Nathan.

She loved Sam.

Mexico. That's where he was headed.

Screw L.A., was Sam's way of thinking. At least, screw it for the next four days, while the town—for that matter, the whole world—went ape shit over the nuptials of those media darlings, Nat 'n' Nina.

His Nina.

He buried his head in his hands.

His aching head. Aching because of the large quantities of spirits he'd been guzzling.

No wonder his breath stank. Almost as much as his life did right now.

Not only that, but Katerina was on the war path about the way Hugo had quote-unquote "mutilated our movie," as she so grandly put it.

He'd seen what Hugo had done. From Sam's perspective, Hugo had saved her too-often-lipo'd ass, and she should kiss his hairy one for doing so, too.

Not that she ever would. Instead, she'd started screaming bloody murder to everyone. Specifically to Archie Hardaway, who had then decided to yank any additional financing of the project and to sever any further connections with Hugo, despite the silent treatment he was getting from Lucinda for deserting her genius husband.

Yep, Hugo was a genius. His final cut was proof of that, despite what that idiot Kat thought.

Well, Sam knew how to shut her up. He invited her over to his place to make nice-nice and talk things out. Then he made her a proposition he just knew she couldn't refuse:

Money.

Or, in this town, the next best thing: a bigger cut of the gross.

She bought it, hook, line, and sinker.

Along with his beach house, because she'd always wanted a Malibu love shack. Would five mill cover it?

Hell yeah. He'd use most of it to buy the distribution rights to Hugo's film—not that he'd tell *her* that.

Besides, if he couldn't live there with Nina, he didn't want to live there *at all*. Now every time he watched the sun set from his living room window, all he could think about was the two of them making love on that very spot, and man did that hurt!

He told her he'd have his attorney, Jasper Carlton, send over the paperwork, and he tossed her the keys.

Then he headed out.

To Tijuana. *Alone.*

No clients, no cell phones, and certainly no women. Nothing except a fifth of Jack. And Towser, of course.

Voice message on Sam Godwin's cell phone, Wednesday, 8:42 P.M.: *Oh, uh, hi, Sam. It's me, Nina. I . . . we haven't talked in a while, so I just wanted to see . . . if you're okay. Gee, I hate doing this on voice mail. Hey, can you call me when you have a minute? You know, just to check in? We don't have to meet or anything . . . Unless you want to. Frankly, I wouldn't mind . . . I . . . I miss you. (Click)*

Voice message on Sam Godwin's cell phone, Thursday, 10:15 P.M.: *Hi, Sam. It's me again. I wish you'd call me back. Look, I know that you're pissed, but please, Sam, if I ever meant anything to you . . . if you can find a moment to just . . . What I'm trying to say is that I really need to talk to you! I— I'm afraid that I'm making . . . Sam, do me a favor and don't hate me, okay? Just—just call! Please? I love you. (Click)*

Voice message on Sam Godwin's cell phone, Friday, 4:30 P.M.: *Sam . . . It's Nina . . . (sob) Listen, I . . . I'm*

scared! I shouldn't be doing this . . . this wedding crap! At the
time, I thought it was the right thing, you know, for Jake,
but—but now I know that it's just all a big mistake, and . . .
Sam, look, I perfectly understand that you—you've moved on
in your heart, and I accept that. Really, I do. Before we were
lovers, we were friends, right? We were, weren't we, Sam?
Well, I'm hoping you can be my friend now. If you don't mind,
can we meet, and just talk? I won't—I won't say I love you
anymore, because I now know that makes you uncomfortable.
(Sob) Sam, I hope someday, you can forgive me . . . I love
you . . . Damn! Scratch that! I—oh, never mind! (Click)

The estate Albertha booked for the circus sat up on the
Malibu ridge, affording them a perfect view of the ocean.

It also afforded the helicopters buzzing overhead excellent
visibility of the event. In fact, there were so many helicopters
hovering noisily over the humongous tent that had been set on
the cliff-hugging lawn that you'd have thought a mass mur-
derer had been spotted in the area.

Jake and Ben and Plum (who was there with parents and
nanny in tow because her father's studio gig deemed him
invitation-worthy, according to Riley) were so excited about
the whirlybirds that Nina was afraid they might distract Jake
from his duties as best man, which was a shame because, quite
literally, from what she could tell by the crowd that had been
invited—any industry bigwig or star Riley deemed worthy
enough to invite, even if they didn't know either Nat or Nina
personally—he really *was* the best man there.

Unless Sam had somehow crashed the event. She asked
Casey, her one and only bridesmaid, to go out and see if she

could spot him. No Sam anywhere, Casey reported back, but she did find Hugo and had asked if he knew if Sam were coming. The answer she got back was, "Hell, no! He's probably at the bottom of some bottle!"

Upon hearing that, mascaraed tears ran down Nina's cheeks. Albertha commanded the makeup artist to fix the damage before any tears fell on the dress Nina had chosen: a stunning, slim, strapless sheath embroidered with a spray of Swarovski crystals.

She had never looked so beautiful. She had never been so sad.

That was Baxter's declaration, anyway. "Those don't look like tears of happiness," he admonished her after he'd gotten a desperate hug. "But I've got just the thing to cheer you up: pre-nup gifts! One for you, and one for Jake!"

"How sweet, Baxter! Really, you shouldn't have," she cried. The box he handed her was tiny and sky blue. "Tiffany's! Wow! I'm awestruck."

"Don't be." He laughed. "The box is recycled. In fact, so is the gift inside."

It was the key to a car.

"It's the only baby blue Beetle here. Something borrowed, right?" He murmured that just loud enough for her to hear. "Nondescript. With tinted windows. I made the valet park it right out front. It's unlocked, in case you need to, you know, make a quick getaway."

She laughed weakly. "Thanks for the thought, but—but I have to go through with this. Nathan is really trying hard and . . . well, this is for Jake's sake."

"Of course, darling. Still, it's the thought that counts,

right?" He smiled devilishly. "Speaking of the little man, here he is now! This is for you, dude."

He handed Jake the other box. In no time flat the little boy had torn it open and was playing with the tiny digital camera he'd found inside.

Nina couldn't help but laugh. "Is this your way of saying you need an assistant? Very sneaky, Baxter."

"*Moi*, sneaky? Hardly, dearest! All children need to learn how to cherish memories, and the sooner, the better. But first off, they need to know how to *make* them."

He bent down to show Jake how to look through the viewfinder and push the button. "Now, kid, go out there and take some great pictures, so that Mommy can remember this day forever."

The day she made the biggest mistake of her life.

"Say cheese, Mommy!" Nina put her arms around Baxter and Casey, and pretended to smile.

In no time at all, Jake got the hang of it. When he got through taking pictures of Ben and Plum making funny faces, and after clicking off a few shots of the helicopters, he secretly shot the wedding guests doing goofy things.

Like scratching themselves, or picking their noses.

Or crying like babies, just because they were lucky enough to be at Hollywood's wedding of the year.

Or hissing bad words to each other through clenched teeth.

Or hiding in one of the many bedrooms throughout the big wedding house, so that they could make out in private.

Like Daddy. *With Ylva.*

Oh well, at least he wasn't kissing that mean old Balloon Lips.

Jake had a hard time finding his way back to his mommy's room. Still, he got there just in time to give her a nice big hug.

Poor Mommy is still crying, Jake thought sadly. *Hey, maybe if she sees how good I take pictures, she'll cheer up!*

"We need to talk." Though Nina's eyes were angry, her voice was ice-cold.

Nathan shivered. He didn't like the sound of *that*.

"Hey, I'm not even supposed to be in here, remember?" He laughed feebly. "Jeez, Albertha warned me it was bad luck to see the bride before the wedding."

"Yeah, well, I guess she also forgot to tell you that it's a *real* no-no to feel up the wedding guests, too."

Nina tossed him Jake's camera. Right there on the camera's LCD viewing screen, in full-color high resolution, Nathan saw himself sucking face with Plum's au pair. One of his hands was buried in her blouse, while the other was climbing up her very short skirt.

"I can explain! Ylva's feeling a little down because Becca—"

"No you can't explain anything, Nathan! *Not this time.*" Nina yanked the camera out of his hand, then tore off her veil and threw it on the floor.

"Look, let's just face facts: You need to be single at this stage of your life. Hey, I totally understand! You're going through a lot of wonderful changes, and you're being presented with a lot of great opportunities, and that's the way it should be. Heck, you're only twenty-four, right? But I no longer fit into your life. You know what, Nathan? That's okay, too. Because you no longer fit into mine. So let's just call it a day." She grabbed her tiny white purse and headed for the door.

"Nina, no. Don't do this." He blocked the door before she reached it. "Listen, if you walk out now, I'll be the laughing-stock of this town—again! I can't let that happen! My—my career—that will be the end of my career! Is that what you want? Is it?" He put his hands on her shoulders, as if to hold her down.

She wasn't going to let him do that. *Not again.*

"Do you really know what I want, Nathan? Well, I'll tell you. I want us both to be *happy*." She searched his face for the comprehension she sought. "And that's not going to happen as long as we're together just to save your career. Nathan, face it! We're over!"

"Nina, you can't walk away from me!" He pulled her to him again. "Right now, the media loves us. *All of us.* You, me, Jake—don't you get that?"

He ignored the look she gave him, which seemed to imply that he was crazy. "Okay, look Nina, if that's what you really want, I'll go along with another separation . . . *but later*, okay? After Hugo's movie comes out, and people see what I'm really capable of doing without all this bad-boy media crap hanging over my head. I swear I'll keep a very low profile until then. I'll be—you know, *discreet*."

He brushed her forehead with his lips, moving slowly down for a kiss. "And you can do the same, too, if you want . . ."

She couldn't believe her ears.

He wanted her to play along, live a sham, for the sake of his career.

To hell with *that.*

She shoved him off her. "I'm out of here. Don't try to stop me."

This time, he knew better.

Just as Baxter had promised, the Beetle was right out front. Jake hopped in the backseat so that he could wave good-bye to his daddy.

"Daddy's crying," he said forlornly.

"That's okay, sweetie. Ylva will know how to make it better."

When Baxter picked up the car at Casey's later that afternoon, he found the camera in the glove compartment, with a note: "Happy scoop. Love, Nina."

By the time Nina reached Sam's place, it was sunset.

Everything was just as she remembered it those few weeks past, although it was as if a million years had passed since then.

She walked through the front gate, which had been left open. The front door was unlocked, too. She took this as a good sign: that he was ready to forgive her, to hear her admit that she'd made a horrible, horrible mistake about Nathan.

About herself.

About the two of them.

Then she saw them: *Sam and Kat.*

Making love, right there in front of the picture window, just the way Sam loved it: Standing up, with Kat's legs wrapped around him, both of them moaning in rapture as he pounded away at her to the beat of the surf as it hit the sand . . .

So, Nathan had been right about one thing after all.

Numbed and emotionally drained, she walked back out to the car.

After picking up Jake at Casey's house, she headed straight

up Highway One. She didn't know yet where she'd end up, except that it was going to be as far away from Los Angeles as she could possibly go.

Kat just knew she'd seen someone peeking in on them from the doorway.

Frightened, she slapped her grunting young lover, a former soap actor who had just signed on to a *CSI* spinoff, on his very high, very rounded bum, to get his attention.

Because he'd do anything to please the woman he'd fantasized about since he was, like, twelve or something, he took that as a sign to take it up a notch and slammed into her even harder.

She sighed, then pinched his ass hard, in order to get him to look up.

"What! What is it?" he moaned exhaustedly. They'd been at it, standing up like this, for what, two hours? Hell, didn't she ever get tired?

"Someone's snooping around! Out there!" she hissed, and pointed to the door. "Go find out who it is. *Now!*"

He nodded and bolted for the front door, naked. She sighed again, and shook her head in wonder. *It's the price I pay for picking them so stupid, barely past jailbait, and testosterone-driven*, she reasoned. Well, he'll learn quick enough, maybe after his first *People* cover.

Hopefully, not naked. And with her at his side, of course.

Besides, a shot of Barely-Past-Jailbait outside Katerina McPherson's new Malibu bungalow, and bare-assed at that, would go a long way toward erasing the public's memory of Nathan's brat biting Kat's thigh while his wife was knocking her silly.

She prayed the photographer snooping around outside had a telephoto lens. Ha! As if the kid's cock wasn't big enough! *Mmmm* . . .

By the time he sauntered back in, she was primed and ready to go again.

"It was nobody. Just some girl in a wedding dress. Funny, huh?"

"Yeah, a real hoot." He could tell that he'd disappointed Kat. That was okay. He certainly knew how to make it up to her . . .

It was only on Sunday night, after he'd fought his way up through San Diego, past Irvine, and onto the Four-o-Five, that Sam reluctantly turned on his cell phone.

That was when he learned that Nina loved him after all.

No, not just loved him, but wanted him, and in fact desperately needed him . . . *Now.*

Of course, he needed her, too.

As fast as his fingers would let him, Sam punched in Nina's cell phone number and heard:

"We're sorry, the number you have dialed has been disconnected . . ."

One year later . . .

19

The Second Proposition

GENTLEMAN CALLER: Hello, my ladylove. So, have you missed me?

NINA: Of course I have, handsome. (*She gives him a deep, husky laugh.*) *My God.* As I live and breathe! I never thought in a million years I'd ever hear your voice again, Sam Godwin.

SAM: You would have heard it a lot sooner if you had given me a clue as to where you were headed . . . So how do you like living across the border?

NINA: It's fantastic, really. Stunningly beautiful, wonderful folk, great schools for Jake. And a heck of a lot of voice-over work for me, so I can't complain. Great theater community, too . . . How did you find me, anyway?

SAM: (*With a coy laugh*) I have my sources, too, you know. Hey, don't be too disappointed. Just think, it took me this long to find you, and that was with my looking every day since you left town.

NINA: Every day, huh? (*She pauses thoughtfully*) So bring me up to speed with the latest. Not that we're so much of an outback that I'm totally out of the loop. Hey, we even get *Hollywood Reporter* up here. And every now and then I look at Baxter's column on the Internet. Of course, if that fails us, there are always the tom-toms . . .

SAM: Oh, that's cute. Considering how many movies are made in Vancouver, I'd say you're almost back in the thick of it . . . In fact, Hugo's in Vancouver making a movie as we speak.

NINA: Oh, he is, is he? (*She laughs*) I have to give him credit for how he salvaged *Forever and Again*. That was sheer genius, his concept of putting hidden cameras all around the set to capture all the angst and double-dealings of Nathan and Katerina! And I loved the way he let the other actors and the crew in on it, so that they could give commentary, and improv without those two lovebirds knowing about it. Then intercutting their shenanigans into the scripted footage—I never laughed so hard! Considering all the press the movie got even before it was distributed, audiences couldn't help but love watching it unfold. Gee, I'll just bet Archie Hardaway wishes he'd hung in there instead of yanking his money.

SAM: Well if he had, I wouldn't have gotten my opportunity to produce it myself. But you're right. Hugo is a genius. Or, as he puts it, "If what you're stuck with is a bunch of goddam rotting lemons, then pulp the shit out of them and make some juice." Always the master of the paraphrase, right? Of course, when Kat saw the final cut, she went ballistic over it. Nothing she could do about it, though. Still, she threatened to sue us into the Stone Age.

NINA: Surprise, surprise. How did you finally get her off your back? I meant that euphemistically, of course.

SAM: Why, of course you did . . . What else? We cut her in for a larger percentage of the gross. Believe me, she was a very happy camper. It's been her biggest box office take to date.

NINA: Somehow that gal always comes out on top, doesn't she?

SAM: Well, she does like that position best . . . euphemistically speaking, of course. Not that I would know from personal experience . . .

NINA: Oh? Look, Sam, let's not go there, okay?

SAM: What's that supposed to mean?

NINA: I'm not blind, Sam. I know what you like . . . I've experienced it firsthand, remember? At the beach house.

SAM: (*Sadly*) Damn, the beach house! You had to mention it, huh? Boy, I miss that place.

NINA: What do you mean, you miss it?

SAM: Sold it. Hey, you'll never believe who bought it, either. *Kat.*

NINA: Wait—*Kat* bought your place? But—when did you—? How—

SAM: Over a year ago . . . I used the money to finance Hugo's distribution. I guess even selling Malibu worked out for the best . . . since I—I couldn't live there anymore.

NINA: (*Somewhat shocked*) Why not, Sam?

SAM: (*After a long pause*) Because I didn't want to live there . . . without you and Jake.

NINA: *Oh . . . my . . . God . . .*

SAM: You're telling me. Yep, in fact, I saw the face of God

several times that weekend, during a four-day binge down in Tijuana . . . Well, the good news is that, when I came out of it, I found out you hadn't married Nathan after all.

NINA: Yeah, my eyes were opened that weekend, too, and just in time . . . Well, almost, I guess. Frankly, I owe Baxter for that one. (*She sighs, and gives a sad laugh*) Gee, I guess *Forever and Again* will be the best thing Nathan will have ever done, what with that lousy agent he signed with after he dumped Riley . . . what was that creep's name? Randy Zimmerman, right?

SAM: Yeah, well, Randy has a knack for taking raw talent and pummeling it into primo B-movie fodder. Then again, from what I hear, Nathan has been taking whatever he can get these days . . . you know with the new baby and all. I think it's a girl.

NINA: Yeah, Jake told me. Or, to put it in his terms, "Ew yuck! What happened to that baby brother Daddy promised me?" Oh, well, maybe the next one.

SAM: I don't think there will be another one. Baxter's column predicts trouble in paradise.

NINA: That's a shame. I always suspected that Ylva was only in it for the green card. Too bad for Nathan. Both his personal *and* his professional life are going into the crapper at the same time. He would have been smarter keeping you as his agent. Although it certainly worked out better for you. Speaking of your recent successes, congratulations on *Mendocino*. I fell in love with it when I saw it. It certainly deserves a few Oscar nominations. I'm proud of you Sam, I knew you could pull it off . . . producing, I mean.

SAM: Thanks, Nina. You don't know how much that means,

hearing that from you. Hey, but don't write off Nathan so quickly. In fact, Hugo is considering casting him in his next film—which, by the way, he plans on shooting in Vancouver, too. So if it all works out, Nathan will get to see Jake while he's there.

NINA: Wow, now that would be wonderful! Jake misses his daddy so much, and he's growing up so fast . . . Hmmm, I'd like to seal *that* deal. Maybe I should stop by and see my old buddy "Wilbur." Do you think he'd remember me?

SAM: (*He pauses before answering*) Frankly, I don't think he'll ever forget you. I know I won't.

NINA: (*Softly*) I feel the same way about you. (*She sniffs*) Jeez, Sam, you sure know how to make a girl cry.

SAM: I'd prefer to make you happy. Would it help if I talked dirty to you?

NINA: (*Laughing uproariously*) Just the thought of that is enough to keep me in chuckles for some time to come.

SAM: Hey, come on, now! I don't think I'd be *that* bad at it. In fact, I remember that one time you encouraged me to do so, I actually had you all hot and bothered and rarin' to go.

NINA: *Mmmm.* How could I forget? Still, I'm sure that was just beginner's luck.

SAM: Maybe. But we'll never know for sure if you don't give me another shot at it.

NINA: (*Laughing seductively*) Believe me, it's tempting . . . Okay, sure, go for it. So, what would you say?

SAM: Well . . . I'd start off by telling you that not a day goes by that I don't think about you . . . that I don't imagine you lying beside me. Just the mere touch of your sweet, soft skin arouses me. I can't control the urge to run my hands over your body, to kiss the nape of your neck, to let my lips meander down between your sweet, plump breasts, taking my time with one first, gently flicking my tongue over it, until it gets hard, then allowing my tongue to roam over to the other breast, so that it, too, can enjoy the way my tongue makes it stand at attention—

NINA: (*Laughs softly*) I just love the way you treat them both so fairly.

SAM: Well, thank you, Nina. I pride myself on never playing favorites with any of your body parts . . . As I was saying, as my hands roam gently over your body, I tempt you with sweet whispers of all the ways in which I'd make love to you . . . all the ways in which *I love you* . . .

NINA: Sweet . . . I—I'm impressed, Sam. I think you've been practicing, haven't you?

SAM: No, Nina. I'm rusty in that department. I guess I'm a one-man woman. The only person I'd ever want to share my dirty little secrets with is you. To tell you the truth, there's a lot I want to share with you.

NINA: (*Wistfully*) Me, too, Sam. But we're both leading different lives now, in different places.

SAM: So, move back home.

NINA: (*Laughs*) Los Angeles isn't my home anymore.

SAM: I didn't mean L.A. I meant me. *I'm* your home, Nina.

NINA: There was a time I truly believed that was the case, Sam. When I felt that wherever you were, that was where I should be, too . . . But I just can't do L.A. again. I'm too notorious there. It will be awful, both for me *and* for Jake.

SAM: That's all in the past. You know that the town has a very short memory. Heck, you may be a pariah one moment, but have your own reality show the next.

NINA: (*Laughing*) I don't think so . . . Besides, I made a promise to myself never to go back. Believe me, a reality show would certainly be a deal buster.

SAM: Good, we'll nix the reality show then. Which means the rest is doable, right? Hey, this is a once-in-a-lifetime offer that will be withdrawn at the end of this call, so, if I were you, I'd jump at it . . . I can't live without you. I love you, Nina. And I want you to—

NINA: Sam, will you excuse me? (*She covers the phone partially with her hand, muffling her words*) Jake, honey, will you get the door? Someone is ringing . . . I'm sorry, Sam, you were saying?

SAM: Only that I can't live without you. Will you ma—

NINA Oh! I—I'm sorry, Sam, but Jake needs me. Can you hold on a minute . . . He's—he's got . . . *a dog!* (*She puts down the phone*) Jake? Jake, sweetie, where did that dog come from? Yes, I see that he's friendly, but that doesn't mean . . . *What* man says he's yours? Omigod—*SAM!*

SAM: As I was saying, Nina Harte, will you marry me?

Unlike the rest of Hollywood, in Sam and Nina's household, there was no pecking order. Everyone got to vote on everything. Believe it or not, even Jake.

For example, Nina was outvoted on her stance that she would never, ever again step foot in Los Angeles. In making his case, Jake pointed out that he missed Ben too much. In fact, he even missed Plum. And he ached to be close enough in proximity to Nathan that they could resurrect Team Harte again.

So Nina compromised: As long as they could spend summers in Vancouver, she was open to winters in Los Angeles.

Being the great negotiator that he was, Sam called it a done deal.

Another mandate in the Godwin-Harte household: No one was to keep any secrets from anyone else. However, if a secret did need keeping (as invariably was the case), there was an ironclad rule: Don't come running to Sam with it, because he was no longer the keeper of the realm. From now on, that was Towser's responsibility.

Besides, Sam had a more important job: to keep Nina happy—something he did to her complete satisfaction, both on and off the telephone.

George Stratigos

JOSIE BROWN is a feature writer whose relationship articles and celebrity interviews appear in numerous publications. She is also the editor of the internationally syndicated "John Gray's Mars Venus Advice" newspaper column.

Other books by Josie include the novel *True Hollywood Lies* (HarperCollins/Avon Trade) and the humorous fictionista chick lit dictionary, *Last Night I Dreamt of Cosmopolitans* (St. Martin's Press).

She is also the coauthor, along with her husband, Martin, of *Marriage Confidential: 102 Honest Answers to the Questions Every Husband Wants to Ask, and Every Wife Needs to Know* and the coeditor of the *Relationship NewsWire*.

Josie lives in Marin County, California, with Martin and their two children.

Check out her website at www.josiebrown.com. You can also communicate with Josie via JosieBrownAuthor@yahoo.com.